PRAISE FOR Justifiable Homicide: A Political Thriller

"McGee's writing upgrades ... fiction from coach to first class, complete with plot twists and hot towels. Return your seat to its upright position and get ready for a wild ride."

—Miami Herald

"McGee's political thriller does an excellent job of highlighting the dangers America faces as it travels down the slippery slope toward totalitarianism. Ayn Rand's *Atlas Shrugged* gave the same warning more than 50 years ago. McGee uses current examples that make the blood boil, much like Thomas Paine did in *Common Sense.* A highly recommended read for anyone who is concerned with the direction America is taking."

—Nathaniel Branden

JUSTIFIABLE HOMICIDE

A Robert Paige Thriller

ROBERT W. MCGEE

JUSTIFIABLE HOMICIDE: A Political Thriller
Robert W. McGee

ISBN 978-1-502862-13-6 (print)
ISBN 978-1-892736-03-1 (eBook)

CONTENTS

1

1:17 a.m.
Kendall (Miami)

"Ay, Raul, you're so much bigger than my brother!" squealed Gabriella Acosta as she mounted Raul Rodriguez and ground her pelvis into him. She didn't mind that he was seventeen years older. Raul's power was intoxicating. His influence extended throughout Miami's Cuban community. Most women thought he was sexy, and tonight he belonged to her.

"What!? You did it with your brother?"

She laughed. "Of course not, silly. But when we were children I caught him masturbating once. I still tease him about it."

He smirked and they resumed their activities. Gabriella moved with the grace and strength of an untamed mare in the wild. She bent forward and started kissing Raul while Celia Cruz's *Guantanamera* played softly in the background. A beautiful young woman, Gabriella's light brown skin glistened with perspiration as she straddled Raul. A breeze through the window tickled her body with the sweet breath of the night air.

"I can taste the Cuba Libre on your breath, papi. I like it."

He smiled, squeezed her ass and reached to the nightstand for his Bacardi and Coke. He took a sip, then passed it to her. Gabriella returned to a vertical position, put the glass to her lips and drank. She dipped her index and middle fingers into the tumbler and retrieved the last drops. She glazed her right nipple with the liquid, and sucked the residue from her digits. Raul's expression was exactly what she was looking for. As she allowed the glass to roll off her fingers, he thrust his hips upward and rose to indulge in the mixture.

Gabriella inhaled deeply and confirmed her pleasure while the ecstasy electrified her body. "Ah! YES!"

***

Santos could hear voices trickling down from the second floor as he edged toward the foot of the stairway, a few feet ahead of his fellow assassin. Midnight shrouded the house, except for a shaft of light emanating from inside the bedroom.

Soft soled shoes made their ascent along the tiled steps undetectable. Halfway up, the conversation grew clearer. They expected Raul to be alone, but his guest was no deterrent. Now would be their best opportunity. By the time they reached the last few steps, each word became distinct. It was time to proceed with the plan. The partners exchanged a nod and stepped into the room.

Gabriella noticed them first as the two men, dressed in black from head to toe, appeared stealthily from the shadows of the upstairs hall. She screamed in absolute terror, jumped off her lover and sank to the floor. She hugged her knees, rocked back and forth and prayed. Each gripped a Sig Sauer SP2022 9mm pistol with suppressor. It was considerably louder than the .22 caliber Ruger

Mark 3 Target pistol people in their profession preferred, but this undertaking was engineered to resemble the work of amateurs, so the 9mm was a more appropriate choice.

Rodriguez turned to see what caused Gabriella's sudden panic. The executioners had a clear shot. They steadied their pistols and fired. Santos splattered Raul's brains on the wall with two shots to the head while his partner pumped three rounds into his torso. Such a scene was much too sloppy to be anything but the work of novices. That's exactly how they wanted it to appear.

Santos's accomplice turned toward him and nodded in the direction of Gabriella. "What should we do with her? She can identify us."

"Yeah, you're right." Santos pointed his gun at her head, set his finger on the trigger, then hesitated.

Smeared mascara highlighted her swollen, red eyes. She stared downward except for a few fluttering glances up at her attacker. Crawling to her knees, backing away, she begged, "Please, don't kill me. I won't call the police. I won't tell anybody. I have a son. Please. Who will raise him?"

Santos released the pressure from the trigger but continued to point the gun at her. He thought, "She looks a lot like my sister, about five-foot four. Same long, chestnut brown hair and dark eyes." Gabriella was clearly from the same gene pool as his Cuban ancestors.

The women he'd dispatched in the past wore burqas. He usually shot them from a distance, sometimes just for fun. He justified his actions by convincing himself he'd prevent the birth of 10 or more future enemy combatants for each woman slain. This time it was up close and personal. He didn't feel good about it, but knew what he had to do.

Santos lowered his aim from her head to her heart and pulled the trigger. One well-placed shot did it, but he fired another round to complete the scene. The force of the hollow points thrust her body back a few feet, and then dropped her to the floor. She died instantly.

He heard his partner's voice from behind him. "Have you forgotten our training? Why didn't you keep to protocol and shoot her in the head?"

"She's a civilian. And she's Cuban. Her family's entitled to an open-casket funeral. Her son should be able to look at her face one last time and say 'good-bye'."

"Yeah. All right, all right. Let's get outta here."

The colleague placed a note on the bed. It read, in English and Spanish, "Those who criticize the Cuban embargo will be silenced."

The men both had FBI files, but it wouldn't matter because there wouldn't be a shred of evidence left at the scene. They wore gloves. No fingerprints. No DNA. Santos picked up the shell casings.

As they exited the bedroom, Santos turned around for one last look at Gabriella. She lay on her back. Arms limp as a rag doll, head tilted toward the door. Even in death she was beautiful. Her eyes appeared fixed on him. Her open mouth looked like she'd whispered to him, "Why? Why me?" She was the first Cuban woman he'd ever executed. He'd been living by the sword, on and off, for nearly ten years, first with the military, then as a part-time assassin who had just one client. As he walked toward the stairs, he wondered when it would be his turn to die… and how it would come to pass.

2

Saint Frances University

Robert Paige strode into his accounting classroom and was met with a cacophony of his students jabbering in Spanish. He taught at Saint Frances University, a small Catholic university in Miami.

"Professor Paige, did you hear about Raul Rodriguez?" It was Rosita Sanchez, one of the few Mexican students in his class. His classes were usually 80 percent or more Hispanic, mostly Cubans with a smattering of Colombians, Venezuelans, Puerto Ricans, and a half dozen other Latin American countries represented.

"No, I didn't listen to the news this morning. What happened?"

Several of his students started to tell him the story simultaneously.

"He got assassinated in his home, with his girlfriend. Somebody killed him because he wanted the government to lift the embargo against Cuba."

Paige carefully lowered himself into his chair, stunned by what he had just heard. Raul had been a friend of his, of sorts. Sometimes, when Raul wanted to complain about tax policy on his radio program or in his *Miami Herald* column, he would call Paige to make sure he understood the issue properly. Paige had been a tax attorney and CPA before becoming a college professor.

"Here." Rosita handed him the morning edition of the *Miami Herald*. "The story's on the first page."

He took it from her and started reading.

> MIAMI – Raul Rodriguez, 51, a local media personality, and Gabriella Acosta, 34, a female companion, were found dead this morning in Rodriguez's home in Kendall. The apparent cause of death was multiple gunshot wounds. A note left at the scene indicated the execution was due to his outspoken opposition to the Cuban embargo that was imposed in 1960. He used his platform as a Spanish language radio talk show host and weekly *Miami Herald* columnist to criticize a number of other government policies as well.
>
> Law enforcement officials declined to comment when asked whether more killings could be expected, since Rodriguez was not alone in his criticism of the Cuban embargo.
>
> Rodriguez was born in Cárdenas, Cuba, about 110 miles east of Havana, and moved to Miami with his parents as a child. He is survived by two daughters and an ex-wife. Gabriella Acosta is survived by her parents, who came to the United States from Cuba shortly before she was born, a brother, and an eight-year-old son.

He put the paper down and tried to start class, but his students were more interested in talking about Rodriguez, the Cuban embargo, and the chilling effect his assassination had on free speech. Whenever he tried to proceed with his lecture, the students would interrupt him and start discussing the assassination. He decided to dismiss the class early.

His lecture wouldn't have been very good anyway. He kept thinking about his friend, Raul, instead of concentrating on the material. He got on the elevator and pushed the button to his floor.

He viewed his reflection in the elevator mirror – dark blue suit, red tie, white shirt, rimless glasses. Most professors in Miami didn't wear ties to class. Fewer wore suits. Paige wore suits because he wanted to project a strong business image to his students.

He checked his cell phone, which he'd turned off before class. He had four missed calls from Svetlana Gregorevna Ivanova, his girlfriend. When he got to his office, he called her.

"Hi. Sveta? What's up? You called four times."

"Robert, did you hear what happened to Raul Rodriguez? He was a friend of yours, wasn't he?"

"Yes. We were scheduled to have lunch on Friday."

"I can't chat now because I'm at work. I just wanted to call to let you know about Raul. Let's talk tonight at my place. We can have dinner. Can you stop by around seven?"

"Sure. See you then."

***

"When the people fear the government there is tyranny. When the government fears the people there is liberty."
Thomas Jefferson

"History is made by minorities."
Ayn Rand

Paige stepped into the lobby at the appointed time. Sveta lived in a condo in the Winston Towers complex on 174th Street, just off Collins Avenue in Sunny Isles Beach. It used to be part of Miami Beach before it seceded, in the noble southern tradition. He lived just down the street in another condo.

She started to talk as soon as she opened the door, her green eyes opened wide. "I was shocked when I heard about Rodriguez. They don't assassinate journalists in America. And his girlfriend. She was pretty. They showed her photo in the newspaper. She had an eight-year-old son, and now he doesn't have a mother. Oh, Robert, who do you think did it?"

"The killer's note said they executed him because he wanted to lift the embargo against Cuba. There may be more killings, since he wasn't the only person who has been criticizing the embargo recently."

"I don't like it when they assassinate journalists. They do that in Russia, but they don't leave notes, and in Russia you know it's the government that's doing the killing. Everyone there is afraid to say anything, and not only on television."

Paige caressed her shoulder as they walked into the kitchen. "He criticized a lot of other policies too. TSA frisks at airports, NSA monitoring phone calls and emails, jailing people without due process or access to an attorney, assassinating American citizens. That's what made his radio show so popular."

Sveta took two plates from the cabinet and placed them on the table. "A week ago his article questioned federal budget deficits and the latest bailouts. The week before that it was about giving foreign aid to China, Pakistan, Egypt and just about every other country on Earth, including some of our enemies."

Paige picked up the silverware and placed the forks on the left side of the plates and the knives and spoons on the right side.

"Yeah, I think it's insane that we're supplying Al-Qaeda with arms in one country while trying to kill them in another country."

"Didn't Raul do charity work, too? I think you told me something about that."

He leaned against the counter, watching Sveta pour the iced tea. "Yeah, he did a lot of charity work, but he kept a low profile. He started an organization to help people who escaped from Cuba get on their feet when they arrived in Miami. Sometimes, when he couldn't raise enough money from the Cuban community, he dipped into his own pocket. I remember one time seeing him pull a wad of cash out of his pocket and giving it to some Cuban guy so he could buy a turkey for his family to celebrate their first Thanksgiving in America. I got the feeling he did a lot of things like that. It was the kind of guy he was."

They walked out to the veranda, which overlooked the Atlantic Ocean on one side and the mainland on the other. Sveta carried a tray with two tall glasses of iced tea and a pitcher. Paige inhaled the ocean air as he felt the breeze on his face. The sun set low in the sky. It shown through her medium-length blonde hair and reflected off her long, curvy red nails as they sat down. She was approaching forty, but she didn't look it.

He could feel the coldness of the glass on his palms as he rolled it back and forth in his hands. Sveta handed him the sugar. He poured it into the glass and watched as the stream of granules slowly sank to the bottom, but his head was in a different place. He had a mental image of Raul and Gabriella getting shot and wondered whether they experienced any pain when the assassins executed them.

He snapped out of his reverie and looked up at Sveta. "If it weren't for the note they left, it would be very easy to suspect either the government or someone who supports the current federal government policies killed Raul. After 9/11, Vice President Dick Cheney said that anyone who criticized the government was guilty of treason for giving aid and comfort to the enemy. Maybe the people who did this thought Raul was guilty of treason and decided to be his judge, jury, and executioner."

Sveta looked him in the eyes. She reached across the table and caressed his left hand with her right.

"I came to America to get away from that kind of government. The people in Russia want free pensions, free health care, free birth control, and free everything else, and the Russian politicians are promising to give it to them. They don't care if their phones are tapped or their emails are monitored. They're used to it. I'm scared that Americans are getting used to it too. American politicians are making the same promises Russian politicians make, and American voters are falling for it. They don't realize that nothing is free. They don't understand that a government that can give you everything can also take it all away."

"Not all American politicians are making those promises." He stirred the sugar into his tea, making a tinkling sound.

"Yes, I know. Some voters understand. But most of them don't, and it's easier to get elected if you promise to give people things. Politicians who don't act like Santa Claus can't get elected. I'm afraid that America is turning socialist, like Russia and Europe. Where will I go if that happens? I don't want to leave America."

"You don't have to start packing yet. A lot of people are waking up to what's going on. Even some of the liberal professors at my university are starting to get concerned about the direction America is taking."

"Yes, but I'm afraid it's not enough. I'm worried."

"Well, maybe things will get better soon, as more people start to wake up and see what's happening in America. You don't need to have a majority to be successful in changing the direction of a country. During the Russian Revolution of 1917, only a small minority supported the communist cause. During the first American Revolution, only about one-third of the population supported the cause for independence. What's important is that you have an organized minority who are willing to die for their cause. History is made by minorities."

3

Miami Police Department, Kendall

Paige went to the Miami Police Department's office in Kendall the next morning to see if he could learn anything that hadn't been reported in the newspaper. A pudgy Hispanic man in a dark blue police uniform sat behind the front desk. He looked up as Paige approached.

"Hello. I was a friend of Raul Rodriguez. I'd like to speak to the person who's in charge of his murder investigation."

"That would be Detective Norman Fedorovitch." He pointed a thumb to Paige's left. "He's down the hall in 114."

A long line of people waited to go through security. He always felt sad when he lined up to take his turn at those machines. Americans had become too accustomed to being subjected to routine warrantless searches as a condition of exercising their right to travel. Would that loss of freedom ever be restored? Maybe Americans would wake up and do something about it, but he wasn't optimistic. Americans were becoming sheep, or perhaps lemmings, prepared to jump over a cliff if their leaders said they had to do it for national security.

After being processed, he marched down the hall to room 114. The door was open, so he walked in. He saw a large room with a series of desks in the center. Partitioned offices lined the walls. He noticed a brass nameplate saying Norman Fedorovitch in the center of a slightly ajar door. He walked over and knocked. The man crouched at the desk appeared to be close to retirement, with thin gray hair and a ruddy complexion. The room smelled of Lysol disinfectant.

"Good morning. My name's Robert Paige. I was a friend of Raul Rodriguez. I'd like to help with the investigation any way I can."

"Thanks for the offer, but the FBI took over the investigation. We're no longer involved."

Hmmm. I wonder why the FBI's so interested in this case. "Can you tell me who to contact at the FBI?"

"No. Sorry. We were instructed not to talk to anyone about the case."

"You can't even give me a name?"

"No. Can't do it, buddy."

"Why is the FBI getting involved? Isn't this just a local murder case?"

"Look, I can't talk about it."

Great. First he had to battle Miami rush hour traffic to get across town. Then he had to put up with federal stonewalling that prevented a public servant from answering simple questions.

"OK. Sorry to bother you."

"No problem."

On the way out, he decided to call Priscilla, Raul's ex-wife. He didn't have her cell number, but she worked at the Century 21 real estate office in Kendall, or at least she did when he met her a few years ago. He found her number on the Internet and called.

"Hello, this is Priscilla Rodriguez."

"Hi, Priscilla. This is Bob Paige. We met a few years ago. I was a friend of Raul's."

"Hi, Bob. I remember. You've heard about Raul?"

"Yes. Could I stop by your office for a few minutes? I'm in Kendall. It won't take long."

"Sure. I have an appointment at 12, but I'm free now."

"Thanks, I'll be right over."

He wasn't too familiar with Kendall. He lived in northeastern Dade County and Kendall was in the southwest quadrant, bordering Biscayne Bay, so he made a few wrong turns before locating her office with the help of his GPS.

He found a place to park a few feet from the front door, which was a stroke of good luck. Parking in some Miami neighborhoods was like trying to find a room in Fort Lauderdale during spring break.

As he walked into the office, Priscilla spotted him.

"Bob, it's good to see you." She walked toward him and extended her right hand, which he shook.

The outer office consisted of a waiting area and a few desks, like many real estate offices. Two other agents hovered by the coffee machine, like hawks eyeing potential prey.

She wore a red and black jumpsuit, businesslike but also attractive. She looked good, at least for someone in the 40-50 age range. The problem was that a lot of men liked younger women. That's why she lost Raul.

It was tough being a woman in Miami. The competition was fierce. Cosmetic surgeons promoted their services on billboards and late-night television. Affordable prices with financing available.

"Would you like some coffee?"

"No thanks. I'm fine."

"Let's go into my office where we can talk."

They walked in and she closed the door. A sad expression came over her face. She lifted her chin and looked him in the eyes.

"Raul was a philandering bastard but I still loved him."

Her eyes started watering and her lower lip quivered. She grabbed a tissue and wiped away tears, working to compose herself as they sat down.

Paige nodded. "Yeah, he was quite a guy. He had his thumb on the pulse of the community."

"He also had it in other places. He was a chick magnet. Young women couldn't get enough of him. The older ones too. After a while I'd had enough. But he remained a good provider. He always paid his child support on time and put Mariela and Susana through college. They were proud to be his daughters."

"Priscilla, I need to ask you, did he receive any threats?"

"Sure. He didn't tell me about all of them. Raul didn't want me and our daughters to worry, but I found out about them. He had been receiving threats for years, on and off, usually after talking about the Cuban embargo on his radio show, but sometimes for other things as well."

"Like what?"

She gazed out the window in silence. The fronds on the palm tree across the street swayed in the breeze.

She turned toward Paige. "Sometimes, when he criticized the government, someone would call him a traitor and tell him to go back to Cuba. He got phone calls or nasty notes threatening to kill him if he didn't shut up."

"Did he report those threats to the police?"

"Once in a while he did, but usually not. He would always say that no one was going to intimidate him or silence him."

"That sounds like Raul. He really liked exercising his right of free speech."

"That reminds me. Yesterday I got a surprise visit from a pair of FBI guys. They weren't very nice. In fact, they were nasty. They told me I couldn't talk to anyone about Raul for national security reasons. If I talked to anyone, they would throw me in jail. And I wouldn't be able to get out because they wouldn't allow me to have an attorney."

Paige shifted in his chair. "Unfortunately, the Patriot Act allows them to do things like that. How did you respond?"

"I was shocked. They didn't give me their condolences or anything. They just threatened me. I couldn't wait for them to leave."

"But you're talking to me now. Should you be talking to me?"

She stood, placed her hands on the desk and leaned forward. "They can go to hell. Nobody's going to silence me. My family didn't escape from Cuba so that some new government could tell us what to do. We should be telling the government what to do." The tears were gone, replaced by a look of defiance and determination.

After Paige determined she had nothing more of consequence to share, they engaged in a few minutes of more pleasant conversation about her kids. Then Paige thanked her and left. As he walked out the front door, he couldn't help wonder. Why was the FBI so interested in this case? Not only did they swipe it out of the hands of the police, they ordered them not to talk about it, and now they threatened Raul's ex-wife to ensure her quiet obedience.

Why did they take the case in the first place?

Raul hadn't been involved in drugs or human trafficking, which were two of the main reasons the FBI got involved in local murder cases. There had to be some other reason. What could it be?

As he walked toward the car, he took out his cell phone and called Sveta.

"Hi. Are you free for lunch?"

"No, Robert. I'm too busy today. How about tomorrow?"

He liked her accent. It was cute, and just what he needed at the moment. She trilled her r's, and his name—Robert—had two of them. When she said "busy" it sounded more like "bee-zee."

"What did the police say? Could they give you any information?"

He related the conversations he had with the police and Priscilla.

She paused before responding. "I wonder what they're trying to hide. Why is the FBI taking such an interest in this case. And why are they being so mean?"

"I don't know. Yet. But I'm going to find out. I'm going to the *Miami Herald.* Maybe the reporter who's covering the case can tell me something."

"Be careful, Robert. You don't want to get in trouble with the FBI."

"Don't worry about it. I won't get in trouble. But if I don't come home for a few days, notify the media and tell them the story."

"Robert, tell me you're kidding."

"Okay, I'm kidding. But if I don't come home...."

4

Lunch in Kendall

Paige looked at his watch. Lunchtime. The alarm bells in his stomach went off. Two restaurants sat across the street. The one on the left had more palm trees, and outside tables. It was a pleasant, warm Miami day. He wanted to eat outside and watch the people go by.

He strolled across the street and sat at one of the tables closest to the sidewalk. After viewing the traffic and pedestrians for about a minute, he looked up to see a waitress walking toward him. She handed him a menu.

"Good afternoon. What would you like to drink?"

"Ice tea, please."

"Sweetened?"

"Yes, thank you."

As she turned around, he enjoyed watching her try to walk in shoes with heels that increased her height by about six inches. The tight skirt was a nice touch too, cinching her knees together. It helped make her waddle more noticeable. Her presence in the restaurant probably increased male attendance by at least 20 percent.

The Jennifer Lopez version of *Quién Será* played on the sound system. It seemed appropriate for the restaurant, and for Miami in general, although he preferred the *Pussycat Doll* version, which, in English, was called *Sway*, but a much different version than the one Dean Martin used to sing. Paige sometimes used the *Pussycat Doll* version for accompaniment when he competed in forms competitions in Taekwondo tournaments.

A few minutes later, the waitress delivered his tea and took his order.

As he ate, he glanced across the street. Priscilla walked out of the Century 21 office with two men in suits flanking her. One of them held her by the arm. She didn't look happy, but she accompanied them without resistance or looking around for help. They walked to a car parked illegally in front of the building. The other man opened the door for her and she got in. The car had government license plates.

Paige looked at his watch. Eleven fifty-three. He remembered she had a twelve o'clock appointment. She would be missing it, unless those were the guys she had the appointment with, which he doubted.

He decided he would call her on her cell phone, but not for a few hours. Something felt wrong. Calling now might get her in trouble. He would wait.

After enjoying the view and his fried pork and cheese sandwich he was ready to go. He liked Cuban cuisine. His sandwich had been very tasty, in a salty and greasy sort of way. It was a wonder Cubans could live past the age of fifty without having a heart attack.

5

A Visit to the Radio Station

He needed to visit the *Miami Herald* and the radio station where Raul had worked. Since the radio station was closer, he headed there first.

In the car, he turned to WTFM, a mostly Spanish-speaking station, although it did have a few English-language programs. Most of the radio personalities and ads bounced back and forth between Spanish and English, sometimes within the same sentence. Paige listened to it occasionally to practice his Spanish.

It took about twenty minutes to drive there in the light pre-rush-hour traffic.

The station occupied a freestanding building in one of the low rent parts of Miami. Not in a seedy neighborhood exactly, but not a safe place to walk at night. The building looked like it could benefit from a little paint.

He went inside and walked straight to the reception desk.

The Hispanic woman behind the desk looked up and smiled at him. She appeared to be in her late thirties and had short, curly black hair with a pink streak on the left side. Her large hoop earrings and chipped green nail polish added to the mystique. She looked like she wanted to make a fashion statement but didn't know what to say.

"Hi. My name is Robert Paige. I'd like to speak with the manager."

With surprising efficiency she picked up the phone and tapped a few buttons. "Ricardo, there's a Robert Paige here to see you."

Paige could hear a response but couldn't make out what he said.

"Please have a seat." She waved in the direction of a couch and some chairs on the other side of the room. "Mr. Diaz will be right with you."

The manager walked out before he could pick up one of the Spanish language magazines piled on the table.

"Hello, I'm Ricardo Diaz. How may I help you?" He extended his hand, a practiced smile on his face.

Paige shook it. "Hi. Robert Paige. I was a friend of Raul's."

Diaz quickly withdrew his hand, his expression altered to one of apprehension.

"I'll be direct. Can you tell me whether Raul was receiving threats?"

Diaz's expression turned from apprehensive to worried.

"Ah, Mr. Paige, I'm afraid I can't help you."

Paige sensed the man wanted to say more, but something prevented him from continuing. Paige could see it in his eyes. He was frightened. The silence made Diaz uncomfortable.

Diaz broke the silence. "Some FBI agents visited me this morning. They told me not to discuss the case with anyone. They said if I discussed the case I would be in violation of national security."

Diaz fell silent, shifted on his feet, and looked out the window. "They told me I couldn't even tell anyone about their visit." He glanced at Paige. "I'm sorry, but I can't talk about it. I've probably said too much already."

"Do you know who might have killed him?"

"He'd been getting threats for years, but I can't say any more. Sorry."

"I respect your position. Thank you for your time."

They shook hands and Paige left. Another dead end.

On his way out, he glanced at his watch. There was still time to pay a visit to the *Miami Herald*. Had the FBI been there as well?

6

The Miami Herald

Traffic started to pick up. It took about a half hour to get to the *Miami Herald* offices. Raul's boss was John Lasky. Paige didn't know what his title was, but he remembered Raul used to complain about him for being a spineless piece of shit. He'd killed several of Raul's columns because of fear they would offend somebody. Raul got incensed just talking about him.

Paige walked through one of the several front doors into a bustling lobby. A male and female receptionist sat behind a counter, chatting with each other.

He approached the one sitting on the left, a woman of retirement age with glasses and close-cropped graying hair.

"Hi. I'd like to see John Lasky."

"Just a moment." She turned to the directory on her computer screen. "He's on the third floor. You can take the elevator over there." She nodded toward the elevator bank to Paige's right.

A small group of people waited to get into the next car. As he stepped in line behind them, he smelled two distinctly different fragrances emanating from the women ahead of him.

The doors opened, and the group crammed in. The woman with the sweeter of the two fragrances moved over and stood next to him, which made for a more pleasant ride.

He squeezed out on three, leaving her behind to continue her journey. He looked around to get his directions and strode up to the first person he saw.

"Could you please tell me where I can find John Lasky?"

"His office is down the hall on the left," he said, pointing.

"Thank you."

Paige checked the names on the doors as he passed each office. It was much quieter and businesslike here. He felt like he'd stumbled into the middle of a beehive with everyone working silently in their little compartments. After seven or eight doors, he came to Lasky's office. A middle-aged pencil of a man with glasses sat behind a desk piled with papers in disarray. As Paige walked in, he glanced up from his galleys.

"Yes?"

"My name is Robert Paige. I know you must be busy. I'll only take a moment of your time."

"Yes, I am busy. I'm working on deadline. What do you want?"

He sounded a little gruff, much like Raul had described him.

"I was a friend of Raul Rodriguez. I'm hoping you could tell me something about—"

Lasky held up his right hand and cut him short.

"I can't talk about Raul. Is that it?"

Paige took one of the two visitor's chairs, sat down, and leaned back. "Well then, may I talk to the reporter who covered the story?"

"He no longer works here."

What? Raul had been dead for less than forty-eight hours. The Raul story must have been the last one he covered. "Do you know how I can contact him?"

"Nope."

"How can you not know how to contact him? He worked for you."

"As I said, I'm on deadline." He went back to reading his computer screen. Paige continued to sit silently in the chair, staring at Lasky. He thought hoping his presence and silence would trigger a response. It didn't work.

After about 30 seconds he realized he wouldn't be able to squeeze any useful information out of this guy.

"Good luck with your deadline."

"Thanks." He continued reading the screen as he said it.

Paige turned around and walked out. Something wasn't right. He didn't recall the name of the reporter who covered the story, but it would be easy enough to find. The article sat on his kitchen table at home.

As he returned to his car, he decided to give Priscilla a call before starting for home.

"Hello?"

"Priscilla. It's Bob Paige."

"Yes, I know. I could see your name on my screen."

She sounded scared. Her voice trembled.

"Bob, I can't talk to you. Please don't call again."

She hung up before he could reply.

Someone had to be monitoring the case. Everywhere he turned he got shut down. The two men he saw her with that morning were part of it. And their car had government plates.

He got in his car and started the drive back to his condo in Sunny Isles Beach, discouraged but not beaten.

***

As he pulled away, a dark blue sedan parked a hundred feet away started up behind him. It kept far enough back that Paige wouldn't observe its presence.

The driver looked over to his companion. "It looks like he's going home. We'll follow him anyway, in case he makes a stop along the way."

His associate turned off his iPad and looked straight ahead. He had been reading *Hunter* by Robert Bidinotto. The driver had already read it, a book about a vigilante who sought to do justice when the criminal justice system failed.

7

As soon as he got home, Paige grabbed the newspaper and turned to the Rodriguez article. Written by Leroy Witherspoon. It listed his email address below his name.

Paige sent him a brief email.

```
Dear Mr. Witherspoon:
My name is Robert Paige. I am an accounting professor at St. Frances University. I was also a friend of Raul Rodriguez. I would like to meet with you briefly at your convenience. Please let me know when and where it would be convenient.
```

He hit SEND, then took a brief nap before getting ready for dinner at Sveta's.

***

When he returned from Sveta's at about eleven, two email messages from Leroy Witherspoon were waiting for him. The first one said:

```
Thank you for your email. I am sorry, but I will not be able to meet with you.
```

Leroy

The second one had arrived fifteen minutes later. It had a different email address.

Dear Professor Paige,
Please disregard my earlier email. I can meet with you tomorrow at ten o'clock at the Starbucks down the street from the *Miami Herald*. I'll be the black guy with glasses wearing a white shirt.
Leroy

Paige sent him an email confirming the meeting, then went to bed.

The dark blue sedan parked outside his condo building pulled away, replaced by a black van.

8

Meeting Leroy

The Central Intelligence Agency owns anyone of any significance in the major media. William Colby (former Director of the CIA)

The next morning, Paige awoke at seven, had cereal with strawberries for breakfast, and did some leg and lower back stretching exercises. He practiced his karate forms three times a week, but this morning he wasn't in the mood.

He had been studying martial arts, on and off, for more than twenty years. He'd studied judo with Dick Adelman in Erie, Pennsylvania briefly in high school but couldn't afford the monthly payments. While he worked as a tax attorney in Manhattan, he studied Taekwondo with Henry Cho, and later studied Shukokai, a Japanese karate style, with Shihan Shigeru Kimura in Hackensack, New Jersey, along with his ex-wife and daughters. He'd continued his Taekwondo studies with Masters Brown and Cook in Fayetteville, North Carolina while a visiting professor at Fayetteville State University, and also studied Krav Maga. He still competed in tournaments on a regular basis but wasn't quite as sharp as he'd been in his thirties.

He arrived at Starbucks two minutes early. A slender black guy with glasses and a white shirt sat at a corner table facing the front door. He appeared to be in his mid-thirties. Witherspoon stood as Paige approached the table.

"Hello, professor. Please sit." He motioned to one of the chairs. "Would you like coffee?"

"Yeah, I suppose that would be appropriate for this place."

"I'll be here."

Paige stepped up to the counter and ordered a medium cappuccino. He usually preferred his coffee with a twist of caramel, either hot or iced, but this morning his taste buds hankered for a cappuccino.

He returned to the table with his coffee a few minutes later. "Thank you for agreeing to meet with me."

"No problem. Now that I don't have a job, I have time on my hands." He grinned, exposing a full set of crooked white teeth.

"Yes, I did have a question about that, if you don't mind my asking."

"I don't mind. Go ahead and ask."

"One day you're covering the Raul Rodriguez story, and the next day you're no longer working at the *Herald.* Is there a connection?"

"That's the reason I got fired, actually. John Lasky told me to drop the Rodriguez story and find something else to report on. I continued to interview people in my spare time anyway. I don't like being told what to do, especially when it comes to my job. I had a feeling there was more to the Rodriguez story, so I kept digging. Everyone I interviewed was afraid to talk about it. Someone must have been threatening them. I wanted to find out who and why."

"I guess you have a problem with authority, huh?"

He snickered. "Yeah, you noticed that?" He took a swig of his coffee and gave Paige another slightly crooked grin. A rebel and proud of it.

"It all goes back to my days in the army. They gave me a low-level journalist job, probably because they didn't trust me with a gun. I developed a liking for the work and a disliking for the army. After I left the army, I got a series of junior reporter positions in the Miami area and worked my way through the master's degree program in journalism at Florida International University. A few months before I graduated, I landed a job at the *Miami Herald*. I've been there ever since, until a few days ago. I didn't get where I am by backing down like some junior reporter."

"Did your boss give you any specifics about why they wanted you to drop the Rodriguez story?"

"Yeah, he was quite specific. My boss's boss's boss got a visit from the FBI. They threatened him as well as the newspaper. They said federal law gave them the authority to shut down the newspaper and arrest anyone they want if national security is involved, and that the Rodriguez case involved national security. They said any further reporting about Rodriguez might give aid and comfort to the enemy, which is treason."

"What enemy?"

"I asked Lasky that same question. He didn't have an answer. All he said was that I had become a threat to the newspaper and that I had to go."

"Didn't the newspaper raise any First Amendment concerns about free press and free speech?"

"Maybe they did. I don't know. I don't talk to the people that high on the food chain unless I have to. They're more concerned about the bottom line than they are about free speech or free press. I think most of them never even read the Constitution."

"So, what are your plans? What are you going to do about a job?"

He leaned back in his chair, pondering his response. "I don't know. If I stay in journalism, I'll probably have to leave Miami. The *Herald* is the only game in town. Anything else would be a step down."

Paige decided it was time to ease back to a more casual discussion. Right about now each of the others he'd interviewed had handed him his hat. He wanted to keep Witherspoon talking in case the journalist thought of something else to reveal.

"Are you married?"

"Yeah. My wife has a good job in one of the offices downtown. If we move, she'd have to quit and find another job that probably pays a lot less. And the kids would have to make new friends in a new school."

"Being a journalist with integrity can cause problems."

He chuckled again. "Yeah. Maybe I'll go to work for CNN—the Communist News Network. That way I won't have to have integrity. I can just report the news the government wants me to report."

"Oh, I forgot to ask. Why did you use a different email account for your second email?"

Witherspoon smirked. "You noticed that, huh? I think they're monitoring my main email account. Just to be on the safe side—I don't want to be one of those reporters who gets arrested, you know—I went to a local Internet café, created a new account just for you, and sent you the second email."

"Just for me? That's considerate."

"You're welcome. I probably wanted to meet with you more than you wanted to meet with me. Nobody else wants to talk about Raul Rodriguez. By the way, what's the next step for you?

Are you going to keep digging into this case? I exhausted all my leads before I got fired."

"It seems I've exhausted all of mine too. I don't know what I'm going to do next. But one thing I do know—I'm not ready to quit. Raul was a friend of mine."

They exchanged pleasantries for a few minutes, then got up and walked out, Paige to the left and Witherspoon to the right.

***

The two men parked in the black van across the street watched Paige as he exited Starbucks. Their electronic dish had monitored and recorded their conversation. The driver turned to look at the man operating the equipment.

"Did you get it all?"

"Yeah. Let's go home. I think Paige is done for the day."

9

Sunny Isles Beach

Paige and Sveta gazed at the Miami sunset from her terrace. He stood behind her, caressing her waist.

His cell phone rang.

"Hi, Bob. It's John Wellington."

"John, it's been a while. How are Sarah and the kids?"

"Fine, thanks. Bob, I'd like to get together for a little chat. What's your schedule like for next week?"

"I'm only teaching on Tuesdays and Saturday mornings this semester, so any other day is fine."

"Cushy job, Bob. Are you sure you're a full-time professor?"

"The university thinks so. Let's not tell them any different."

"I'll keep your little secret. How does Wednesday sound? We can meet for lunch."

"Sure. Which office will you be at on Wednesday?"

"Actually, I'd prefer not to meet you at any office. This isn't exactly going to be a Commerce Department discussion, if you know what I mean. How about the Rusty Pelican on the Rickenbacker Causeway? I like the panorama of Biscayne Bay from there. I'll make a reservation for noon. Maybe we can get a table with a nice view."

"I think all the tables there have a nice view, don't they?"

"Yeah, probably. It's nice to see that you're helping me spend taxpayer dollars efficiently."

"I do what I can. See you Wednesday."

Paige slid the phone back in his pocket and gave Sveta his "everything is fine" smile. He behaved normally, as though it were just a regular phone call.

"Who was that?"

"John Wellington. You remember him, right? My former MBA student who works for the Commerce Department. He has a consulting assignment for me."

"Yes, I remember him. Let's go to bed, honey. I want to cuddle."

Actually, she wanted to do more than cuddle, and so did he. After she had fallen asleep, he lay awake, forearm slung over his forehead, replaying the conversation he'd had with Wellington. Something in the tone of John's voice told him it wasn't a regular assignment.

That bothered him.

10

8:30 a.m.
Saint Frances University

Paige stood in front of his office door, flipping for the key. He felt tired just thinking about the long day ahead—two morning classes and an MBA class at night, with a lot of paper shuffling and meetings filling up the time in between. He'd work from nine in the morning until nine tonight. Then he'd be off until Saturday.

He used to work like that every day when he was a tax attorney in Manhattan. Paige smirked whenever he thought of his university schedule. Compared to his old Manhattan job, he was practically retired. Mentally, he divided his university salary by the number of hours he worked. On an hourly basis, he made more as a professor than he had as a tax attorney.

He pushed open the door and pocketed the key. A manila envelope lay at his feet. He picked it up, sat down, and opened it.

Out fell a folded piece of printer paper … and a photo of him and Sveta from last night, standing on her balcony.

Warily, he unfolded the paper. "Bad things will happen to you and your Russian slut if you keep asking questions about Raul Rodriguez. We can fill two new coffins if you like. Your choice."

A sudden chill ran up his back, causing him to jerk.

No one had ever threatened him before. He had felt fear as a kid from an occasional schoolyard bully, but his feelings at this moment were far more intense. His life had never been on the line before, and now Sveta's life also hung in the balance.

Maybe I should drop the Rodriguez probe. It just wasn't worth it. I don't want to put Sveta in harm's way.

He looked at the printout and photo again. Then became angry.

He never walked away from anything in his life before. He wasn't going to do it now. He decided to get the bastards.

The only problem was, he didn't know who they were.

He could keep asking questions about Rodriguez. If he did, they would come to him for sure. He wouldn't have to try to find them. But they would probably go after Sveta first. She was an easier target, and he wouldn't be able to protect her. There was no simple solution.

He couldn't warn Sveta. She wouldn't be able to take the news calmly. It would only make things worse.

He couldn't take the note and photo to the FBI. That would put him on their radar screen. They could possibly threaten to arrest him for interfering with a federal investigation, which would mean he would have two threats to deal with instead of one. Ever since 9/11, the FBI and other federal agencies had gone nuts. They saw terrorists behind every blade of grass, and they didn't mind shredding the Constitution to get them. He couldn't trust them. They had become as much of a threat to Americans' individual freedom as the terrorists. Maybe more so.

He wouldn't do anything for now. It was Tuesday, and he would be busy all day. He wouldn't have time to pursue Rodriguez's murder, and they wouldn't do anything to him until he started to ask questions again, or at least they wouldn't if they were men of their word.

11

9:30 p.m.
The Parking Lot

Class had finished at nine, but a couple of students wanted to ask questions after class, so he hung around for a half hour to answer them. He walked toward his car in the darkened, practically empty parking lot. Most of the evening students had already gone home.

He'd been distracted all day because of the photo and note. It's all he could think about. He couldn't focus on his work because of it.

He thumbed through his keys as he passed a black van parked two spaces from his car. The side door slid open.

His head snapped around. Two men stepped down from the van.

One moved off to Paige's left. The other walked straight toward him, sliding his hand into his right pocket. "You really need to stop asking questions about Raul Rodriguez. People could get hurt."

He pulled his hand from his pocket. There was just enough light in the parking lot to see that he had brass knuckles. The man picked up speed as he got closer.

Paige tensed up. Then he recalled the words Sensei Kimura had told him when he hesitated to attack. *"Take a chance."* Attack first.

Paige unleashed a powerful front kick to the guy's groin, followed immediately by a punch to the face, stepping forward as he launched it, putting all 180 pounds of his weight into it and letting out a blood curdling yell. Paige felt the guy's nose cartilage snap. As the attacker flew back from the impact of the punch, Paige gave him a round kick to the head with all he had, slamming the heel of his foot into the guy's temple.

The attacker dropped. His head hit the concrete like a coconut. He was out cold.

Paige spun around. A row of beefy knuckles flew at his face, grazing his chin. Paige slammed a side kick into his attacker's solar plexus, but couldn't fully extend his leg because he was too close. Paige was off balance. The guy's forward movement nearly knocked him to the ground.

This second guy was larger than the first. Paige moved to the side and regained his balance. The big guy just kept coming. Luckily for Paige, he was fairly slow on his feet.

Paige didn't want to spar with him. That would take time. The first guy might wake up any moment. It would be two against one. Time to do something he had never done in karate class, an illegal move that would have gotten him disqualified in a tournament.

He let loose with a kick to the stomach. The guy's hands dropped. Paige delivered a flurry of punches to his unprotected face. It wasn't enough to knock him down, but it was enough to disorient him long enough to set up a kick to the kneecap.

As the attacker raised his arms to protect his face from the punches, Paige let out a yell and slammed his heel into the guy's kneecap, causing the man's leg to snap backward.

His target screamed and dropped to the ground. He clutched his knee and rolled to one side. But he was still conscious. If he had a gun, he could still be dangerous. Even deadly. Paige had to knock him out, which meant kicking him in the head. Paige jumped to the side, positioning himself. He delivered it football style. If his head were a football, Paige would have just kicked a fifty-yard field goal.

Both of the aggressors were out cold, but they wouldn't stay that way for long. The parking lot was deserted. No witnesses. Paige could hear some cicadas chirping away, but other than that, the night was quiet. A light breeze wafted across his sweaty face.

What to do next? He thought about calling the police, but the pair could wake up before the police arrived. Besides, he was carrying a Glock in the door pocket of his car. In most states, including Florida, carrying weapons on campus was illegal, in spite of the Second Amendment's prohibition on infringing on the right to keep and bear arms. No Florida judge had had enough backbone to declare such restrictions unconstitutional. If the police decided to search his car, they could charge him with a felony.

He needed to know who they were. He searched them for ID and rifled through their pockets. They weren't carrying ID, but they did have guns, which he took.

Next he grabbed their right hands and rolled the barrel of the guns across their fingertips to capture their prints. Then he placed the guns in his briefcase, which he'd dropped.

He took out his handkerchief and dabbed it on their mouths to collect blood samples and DNA, making sure to use different corners of the handkerchief for each of his assailants. Then he snapped photos of their faces, the van and the license plate with his cell phone. He sent them to his email, just in case he lost his phone. Then he left.

On the way home he replayed the events of the parking lot in his mind. Sensei Kimura would have been proud of him, although he might have criticized the crispness of his technique, which had faded over the years.

Was it over? No, he didn't think so. It was strange that neither of them were Hispanic, since it was mostly the Hispanic community that got incensed over the Cuban embargo. They were just a couple of white guys in gym clothes.

He decided to start carrying a gun on his person. But it wouldn't be his Glock 17. Too bulky. He would carry his 9mm Makarov.

He had grown fond of Makarovs while working as a freelance CIA asset in Armenia, and later Bosnia, where he had been hired mostly to recruit new CIA assets. The Makarov had been a favorite of various Eastern bloc police and military forces ever since World War II. It was compact and easy to handle. The main drawback was that it only held eight rounds, less than half of what his Glock held.

He would give the photos, DNA samples, and the assailants' two pistols to Wellington when he met him for lunch. Wellington would know what to do with them. He was more than just a Commerce Department bureaucrat. Much more.

12

Paige's Condo, Sunny Isles Beach

After the parking lot incident Paige had trouble getting to sleep. He wondered about the next encounter he would have with those men. Maybe there wouldn't be another encounter. Maybe they would disappear if he dropped his private investigation. Or maybe they would plant a bomb in his car – or Sveta's. Or perhaps they would just shoot him, like they had done to Raul. There were all kinds of possibilities, and he didn't care to think about them. There was nothing he could do at any rate except wait for them to contact him again.

He got up, had breakfast, and graded some quizzes from his Tuesday night class. Then he shaved and showered to get ready to meet Wellington for lunch.

Paige had recruited him to be a CIA asset when he took Paige's MBA accounting class a few years ago. It turned out to be one of his most successful recruiting efforts. They had kept in touch over the years, and Wellington sometimes passed along freelance assignments.

Paige's involvement with the CIA began while he was working with the Armenian Finance Ministry as part of the USAID Accounting Reform Program to convert the country to

International Financial Reporting Standards. His job had been to determine which Finance Ministry employees were friendly toward the United States and which were not, then to recruit the friendly ones.

The CIA had wanted him to do some recruiting at the Armenian universities as well, both administrators and students, especially the smartest ones. When he returned to the United States, they gave him an assignment to recruit at whatever university he worked for.

Although Paige was curious to know what assignment Wellington had for him, he was more interested in telling him what happened in the parking lot and turning over the note, the photos, DNA samples, and pistols so that Wellington could have them processed.

Before leaving to meet with Wellington, Paige typed the guns' serial numbers into a Word document, took photos of both guns, scanned the note, and saved all of it in his hard drive. Then he attached the documents to an email and sent them to an email address of his that only a few people knew existed. He also copied them into a thumb drive.

Next he took a scissors to the handkerchief that contained the DNA blood samples, cut out the two bloodstained parts, then cut each of them in two. He placed one sample of each assailant's blood in an envelope and addressed it to himself at his university address. He placed the other two samples in another envelope to give to Wellington.

After gathering his things, he started to leave. He noticed something on the floor in front of the door. Another message. It read:

> "You were very impressive, Professor Paige. We underestimated you. However, you cannot outkick a bullet. Raul Rodriguez is dead. Stop asking why."

Paige lived in a secure building. There were guards at the front door and residents needed a special key to get into the building. Whoever stuffed the warning under his door must have special skills to circumvent the system. They had to be professionals, not average Cuban patriots. Perhaps not even Cuban at all.

Panic and relief hit him like two punches from opposite directions. Panic because his life had been threatened, and relief because it appeared he'd continue to breathe if he ended his investigation. He would think about his options and perhaps bounce a few ideas off Wellington.

Back at his computer, he scanned the second letter, saved it in his hard drive and thumb drive, and sent it as an attachment to his other email account. Then he placed it in the same manila folder as the first message and left. On his way to the car, he mailed the letter containing the DNA to himself.

13

12:32 p.m.
The Rusty Pelican

The Rusty Pelican. One of the nicer places to eat in Miami, although a bit pricy. Good food. Adequate parking. Spectacular views of Biscayne Bay and the Miami skyline.

An attractive hostess greeted him as he walked through the front door. That was one of the nice things about the Rusty Pelican; they always managed to hire hostesses and waitresses that aided digestion. This one was medium height, with long black hair and brown skin that highlighted the loveliness of her eyes.

"Good afternoon. Table for one?" She picked up a menu and motioned for him to enter the restaurant's dining area over the loud dining room chatter.

"No, I'm meeting someone." He spotted John sitting at a table near a window overlooking the bay. Paige motioned to John's table. "He's over there."

As he approached the table, John rose to meet him, shook his hand, and invited Paige to sit down. He looked like an Indiana prep school alumnus – six feet tall, mid-to-late-thirties, wavy dark blonde hair – expensive cut – and, of course, steel-framed glasses with round rims.

"You picked a good table, John."

"Yeah, I like to select the best whenever I entertain a taxpayer."

Actually, John didn't give a shit about taxpayers. He was a typical federal bureaucrat in many ways, although he was more energetic than most, which accounted for his rapid rise within the Commerce Department.

A waitress walked up to the table. "Would you like something to drink?"

Wellington replied first. "I'll have a scotch on the rocks."

Paige checked her out before responding. "Ice tea."

As the waitress turned around to leave, Paige leaned toward Wellington, a slight smirk on his face. "Don't you feel guilty having taxpayers pay for your booze bill?"

"Not really. The more booze they reimburse me for, the less money the government has to fund research on how cow farts deplete the ozone layer."

They both chuckled. Paige added, "You know, as a general rule I don't think federal employees should be reimbursed for more than the cost of a peanut butter sandwich, but you may have a point."

"Yeah, and all these sumptuous meals I've been buying you all these years lets you partially recoup some of the excess taxes you have to pay."

The waitress returned with the drinks and took their order. The restaurant was so noisy she had to repeat what they wanted, just to make sure she got it all. The table of twelve next to them had started to make a lot of racket. As she left, Wellington's mood grew serious.

"Bob, I've got an assignment for you, but the restaurant's a little crowded. We can talk about it in the parking lot after lunch."

"Is it a Commerce Department assignment?"

"No, it's a Company job, and it's right up your alley."

"Hmmm. Sounds interesting. Actually, I have something to discuss with you too. It's about a recent incident. I need your advice, and I'd like to tap into some of your resources."

"I didn't think accounting professors had *incidents*, but we can talk, after lunch."

***

After lunch, Wellington paid the bill, in cash, and they walked out toward the parking lot.

Wellington tilted his head toward the dock area. "Let's go over here. It has a much better view than the parking lot."

"Yes, I agree." As they walked toward Biscayne Bay, Paige went over in his mind what he would say. "Before we start discussing my new assignment, I'd like to tell you about what happened to me last night in the university parking lot."

He looked at Paige and smirked. "What? Did you get caught in the back seat with a co-ed?"

"Not quite." Paige related the details of the dead-end interviews with Raul's ex-wife and the others, and then concluded with the FBI involvement, the threatening notes, photos, and parking lot incident.

"I photographed their faces and the license plate on their van. I also took their guns and DNA samples. I have the stuff in the car. I'd like to give them to you. Maybe your people could get some fingerprints off their guns or the notes and find out who they were."

"I'll see what I can do, but I really think you should abandon the Rodriguez investigation. They sound serious."

"Yeah, I probably should let it go, but I can't seem to do it."

"But if you don't drop it, you might get hurt, even killed. And what about Sveta?"

Paige shrugged. "Maybe you're right. I'll have to think about my options."

"It seems like you don't have any options. All your interviews were dead-ends, and you have nothing to gain and a lot to lose by continuing with it."

"John, I hear you but I owe it to Raul to find out who's responsible. He was a friend."

"I can understand your loyalty, but Raul's gone. You need to move on."

Paige didn't respond. Instead, he looked out over Biscayne Bay. It was peaceful, with a few boats that seemed to be going nowhere in particular. Raul wouldn't be able to see that view any more. He was dead.

Wellington wanted to change the subject. "I'd like to talk to you about your assignment."

14

"The tyrant will always find a pretext for his tyranny."
Aesop's Fables

"… The people can always be brought to the bidding of the leaders. That is easy. All you have to do is tell them they are being attacked, and denounce the pacifists for lack of patriotism and exposing the country to greater danger."
Herman Goering at the Nuremberg trials

"In a time of universal deceit, telling the truth is a revolutionary act."
George Orwell

Wellington turned toward Paige. "Before I get into the details of your assignment, I'd like to give you some background.

"The NSA, CIA, FBI, and a few other agencies have a pretty sophisticated system for monitoring phone calls and emails. They have computer programs that search for certain words and word patterns. What you might not know is how they assign points. For example, if someone says *bomb* or *kill* or *president* or *jihad*, it's worth a certain number of points. If two of the designated words are in the same communication, the program assigns extra points.

If they're in the same sentence or within three to five words of each other, they get bonus points for that.

"A live agent reviews phone calls and emails that accumulate a certain number of points. It gets a little complicated if the person being monitored uses more than one phone or more than one email account, but if we determine that it's the same person using multiple accounts, we try to combine them into one file."

"Doesn't that kind of surveillance require a search warrant?"

"Not really. After 9/11, Congress passed some laws that let us do this kind of thing. Once in a while, if it looks like we've crossed the line and someone sues us, we find a judge who can backdate a search warrant for us.

"The system isn't perfect. A few months ago, some high school kids in Coral Gables were talking about a video game, and they kept using words like *kill* and *jihad* because that's what the game was about. Some of our guys paid a visit to their high school and grilled the principal about them. It turned out to be a waste of time. One of them contacted the Electronic Freedom Foundation, and they wrote us up in one of their blurbs. That led to some newspaper articles. We had to put out a couple of fires."

Wellington looked around to be certain no one was within earshot, then continued. "Some terrorists can get around the system by using throwaway phones or by encrypting their emails. Chuck Sherman and some other senators are trying to pass a law that would make it a felony to use a throwaway phone, but they haven't been able to get it through Congress because of the privacy issue, and because it discriminates against the poor and minorities."

"So, what you're saying is the only people the government is really monitoring are nonterrorists?"

"Yeah, that's about it, nonterrorists and terrorists who are stupid enough not to use throwaway phones and encrypt their emails. The Electronic Freedom Foundation is all over us for that, too."

"What is this Electronic Freedom Foundation you keep mentioning?"

"It's a group of civil liberties do-gooders who keep whining about our efforts to nip terrorism in the bud. We've been able to stop a lot of attacks on the United States with these methods. The EFF doesn't realize that what we do is in the best interest of America. Whenever they get wind of something we're doing, they send out an investigative reporter and post a story on their Web site about it. They're a real pain in the ass. They're one of the groups we're monitoring."

"What do you mean, we? I thought the CIA was limited to activities outside the United States."

"That used to be the case, and we really did follow that jurisdictional boundary, but that was before 9/11. Now we can do pretty much what we want, where we want."

"So, who is this joint operation with?"

Wellington looked out over Biscayne Bay, then observed the boats anchored on the dock. "Look, Bob, I probably shouldn't be telling you the details. It's on a need-to-know basis, but since you're my good buddy, I suppose I can tell you it's a joint CIA/FBI investigation. There are both foreign and domestic elements to it, so we would probably be able to justify it if anyone looked at it closely."

"So, why are you investigating the Electronic Freedom Foundation, actually?"

"Besides being a pain in the ass, they're a threat to national security because they publish what we're doing. The terrorists read that stuff, and they alter their behavior as a result. They're giving aid and comfort to the enemy, and they're getting a few members of Congress upset enough to try to cut our budget. We'd like to arrest them for treason, but so far the boss says no. He thinks we wouldn't be able to get a conviction. They're too high profile to liquidate or to arrest and send to Guantanamo. We've asked the IRS to audit them, but that's about all we can do, for now."

"But aren't they also trying to prevent you from shredding the Constitution?"

John's jaw dropped in disbelief. "What kind of talk is that? Don't you think we need to protect America from terrorists? You're starting to sound like one of those liberal college professors or left-wing journalists who see a Nazi behind every tree."

I don't like them violating the Constitution on a systematic basis, but I have to keep my mouth shut. I need John to believe I agree with what he's doing. I think I like the Electronic Freedom Foundation. I'll check out their Web site when I get home.

"They're on a watch list. We have a file on each of their employees and on anyone who writes studies for them."

"Don't you think that's being paranoid?"

"Sometimes a little paranoia is good. It prevents attacks against the United States."

Paige couldn't help but raise his eyebrows at that remark. "How does monitoring the Electronic Freedom Foundation prevent attacks against the United States?"

"You've got to see it from the big picture perspective, Bob. They tip off the enemy about what we're doing. They're a bunch of treasonous little bastards."

"Aren't they also trying to protect the Constitution?"

"Quit talking like that. Maybe I'll have to put *you* on the watch list." His voice sounded upset as he said the words. The sweat on his face had caused his glasses to slide part way down his nose. He pushed his right index finger against the bridge of his glasses to adjust them.

Paige thought, *I really need to keep my opinions to myself. I don't want him monitoring the phone calls and emails I have with Sveta. I'll just pump him for more information.* "Tell me about this watch list. Who's on it, and how do you determine who gets on it?"

"Well, I can't give you all the details because that's classified, but I can tell you what's already been reported in the press, more or less.

"Anyone who criticizes our efforts to win the war on terrorism is a potential addition to the list. If they do it often enough, they get on the list. If they appear on television or write newspaper articles about it, we give them bonus points. If some journalist interviews them, we assign points to both of them.

"We rank the terror threat based on the number of points they accumulate. If they accumulate more than a certain number of points, we tap their phone and look at their emails. We try to discredit the people who have the most points."

"How do you do that?"

"It depends. Once we start monitoring someone we gather information about their personal life. Sometimes we find out they're boinking their secretary. Then we find a way to make it public. You remember that story about Julio Sanchez, the councilman who had his mistress on the city payroll? We found out about the affair through a wiretap and got a friendly journalist to break the story. Now Julio is under indictment for misusing city assets.

"We don't limit the list just to people who criticize our efforts on terrorism. They get points for other reasons too."

"Like what?"

"Anyone who criticizes the TSA gets on the list. Anyone who punches a TSA agent for groping their groin gets bonus points."

"Does that happen a lot?"

"Yeah, quite a lot, but we can usually convince the local news media not to report it. If they report it anyway, they get some points. All those reporters chip away at our legitimacy and give aid and comfort to the enemy. Sometimes you need to grope a few groins to protect the country from terrorists. It's a small price to pay.

"People who criticize certain aspects of our foreign policy also get on the list."

"What is it they have to say?"

"Anyone who says we should pull our troops out of some country can get put on the list. If they say we should pull our troops out of Germany, they don't get as many points as if they say it should be some Middle Eastern country, because pulling troops out of Germany isn't a big deal. It's actually a waste of money having troops in Germany. That money could be put to better use in the Middle East, Asia, Africa, or Latin America. World War II ended in 1945. It's time Europe stood on its own feet. American taxpayers shouldn't have to keep subsidizing those socialist bastards." He cocked his head and smiled at Paige as he said it. "Anyone who says Israel should stop stealing Palestinian land gets put on a watch list. Anyone who advocates cutting off aid to Israel is also put on a watch list. Those kinds of statements give aid and comfort to the enemy. Israel is our strongest ally. We can't have people saying stuff like that against Israel. We also pass along that information to Mossad.

"Do you remember Professor Garcia at the University of Miami? He used to say stuff like that. He wrote a book about how people are disappearing and are being held without access to an attorney."

"It's true, isn't it?"

"Yeah, the Patriot Act and some other legislation let us do that, but that's beside the point. The point is that guys like Garcia chip away at our credibility and make it look like we're the enemy. They say we're more of a threat to America than the terrorists."

"Professor Garcia was caught with drugs, wasn't he?"

"Yeah. One of our guys planted some cocaine in his car, then arranged for the local police to find it. The university fired him. It was easy because he wasn't tenured. That took away his platform and his credibility. Who are you going to listen to, some professor from a prestigious university or someone who's unemployed and guilty of drug possession?"

"Don't you think that doing things like that shreds the Constitution?"

"You're not one of those guys, are you? Come on, Bob! We have to do these things to silence the people who are giving aid and comfort to the enemy. We're at war, and we have to do whatever it takes to win. We have to do what's best for the country."

Wellington had second thoughts about what he'd just said as soon as the words were out of his mouth. *I'd better take it down a notch. I think I'm alienating him, and I need Bob for this assignment. He's the only asset in my inventory who can do the job. I don't want him to decline the assignment.*

Paige noticed Wellington's body language. Shifting his weight from one foot to the other. Eyes darting around, from the ground to the bay and back, then to the boats docked alongside. Avoiding eye contact. *What's with John today? He's swaying back and forth like he's trying not to shit his pants.*

Paige tried to calm him down. "Well, I hear what you're saying." *But I don't agree. President Wilson imprisoned more than 10,000 people during World War I for speaking out against the war. Lincoln shut down newspapers and even issued a warrant for the arrest of a Supreme Court justice for saying something he didn't like. Roosevelt imprisoned more than a hundred thousand Japanese-Americans during World War II just to be on the safe side. John's sounding a lot like them.*

Wellington took a deep breath of the fresh bay. "By the way, you're probably wondering why I wanted to talk to you."

"Yes, that had crossed my mind."

"Do you know who Professor Saul Steinman is?"

"Sure. He teaches political science at Florida International University."

"That's what he does during the day. But in his spare time he criticizes our war on terrorism. He's on television just about every week. Last week he started circulating a petition to defund the TSA."

"I hadn't heard about that."

"He's starting to get signatures, mostly from his students. He also has some of them walking around the malls gathering signatures as part of a political science project. We put in a friendly call to the FIU provost to try to get him to stop, but the provost told us to go to hell."

"So did you put the provost on your enemies list?"

"Hey, I hadn't thought of that. Thanks for the suggestion." He gave Paige a devilish smirk.

"How did you find out about the petition?"

"We have one of his students giving us reports. The thing is, this guy's got to be stopped before he can do any more damage. He's a traitor. That's where you come in."

"I don't teach at FIU, and I don't teach political science. What do you want me to do?"

"That's not a problem. He meets with some other professors on a regular basis to plot strategy. We want you to attend those meetings and tell us what he's planning. Oh, one other thing I might mention. He's been funneling money to terrorists through a Palestinian humanitarian organization. We'd like you to find out more about that, if you can."

Paige looked surprised by Wellington's last statement. "But Steinman's Jewish, isn't he? Why would he funnel money to Palestinian terrorists?"

"Out of a misguided sense of humanitarianism. He's raising money to build housing for the Palestinian families who are being displaced by the Jewish settlements."

"But how is that funneling money to terrorists? They're just a bunch of innocent homeless people being evicted from their ancestral homes."

"They're also terrorists. Or potential terrorists. Here are Steinman's contact information and office hours." He passed a scrap of paper to Paige.

Paige glanced at it. "How do you plan to stop this guy? Are you going to report him for boinking one of his students?"

"No, we actually looked into that option, but we don't think he's fucking any students. Even if he were, that option would take too much time to be successful. This guy has to be shut down fast."

"How do you plan to shut him down? Are you going to liquidate him?"

Wellington looked out over Biscayne Bay, then gazed at the palm trees swaying in the breeze. He didn't want to look Paige in the eyes. "No, nothing that drastic. We just want to neutralize him so that nobody will listen to him or take him seriously."

"All right. What is it you want me to do?"

Wellington turned to Paige and stared directly into his eyes. "Just get invited to join his little professor group. Let us know when and where they meet, who the other members are, and gather whatever other information you can. We'll do the rest."

"Fair enough. I'll get into his group and get back to you when I have something to report."

"Great. That would be very helpful." Wellington looked at his watch.

"I have to get back to the office. Give me those items you were telling me about. I'll get my people to process them."

Some exotic birds were chirping in the trees as Wellington and Paige made their way back to the parking lot. Paige opened the trunk and gave Wellington the bag containing the guns, notes, and DNA samples, plus the flash drive with photos of the two men, their van, and license plate.

"I'll get back to you when I have something. It might take a few days."

15

“If you are afraid to say something on the internet because you fear your government then you may need a new government.”
Michael S. King

Paige had the rest of the afternoon free, and decided to take the scenic route back to Sunny Isles Beach. He rolled down the window so he could feel the breeze and smell the air, which was fresh in that part of Miami. Across the bay, the tall glass and steel buildings lined with palm trees were a far cry from his youth in Erie, Pennsylvania, which was just south of the Canadian border. Life was good.

He turned on the radio to get some music. Instead, he got a special news report.

> Nathan Shipkovitz, a law professor at the University of Miami, was found dead a few minutes ago in his car, which was parked in the university's parking lot. The cause of death appeared to be multiple gunshot wounds to the head. Shipkovitz had been an outspoken critic of the federal government's warrantless wiretapping and email monitoring program. He had written several papers on this topic for the Electronic Freedom Foundation. Sources say a

> note was found under the car's windshield wipers, but the police have not disclosed its contents.

The broadcast ruined his afternoon. He had never heard of the Electronic Freedom Foundation until that afternoon. Now it was part of the top local news story of the day. Could Wellington be behind the killing? Quite possible. Either he had set it up or he knew who did. It was too much of a coincidence.

Would Steinman be next? Was Paige's new assignment the first step toward setting him up for the kill? Should he tell Wellington he changed his mind? Should he at least confront Wellington, face to face, to check his reaction?

16

North Miami Beach

"The natural progress of things is for liberty to yield and government to gain ground."
Thomas Jefferson

"Political language ... is designed to make lies sound truthful and murder respectable."
George Orwell

Jim Bennett swiveled in his chair and gazed out his office window at the street below. He kept thinking about Santos. It bothered him that Santos shot Gabriella Acosta in the chest instead of the head. Assassins shouldn't become emotionally involved with their targets. They should make decisions that are in their best interests, not the best interests of their targets or their families. Being overly sensitive is a weakness. Having a weak partner can get you killed.

Jim Bennett—born Jaime Benítez—worked for the FBI out of its North Miami Beach office on Northwest Second Avenue. His parents came to Miami shortly after Fidel Castro seized power. His main job at the FBI was to keep track of the Latin American drug cartels. As a side job he kept the CIA informed of local FBI activities, for which he received a monthly cash stipend he neglected to include on his tax return. John Wellington also hired him to do freelance work from time to time.

The all-female Spanish-speaking staff at Super Cuts in Sunny Isles Beach liked seeing him walk through their door. Good looking and taller than average – a few inches under six feet with wavy, dark brown hair – they enjoyed flirting with him and he flirted right back.

He kept fit by jogging and going to the gym, although his body wasn't as rock solid as it used to be when he served in the military, where he learned to kill without thinking twice. On a few occasions, he had been part of a team that executed entire families in their homes, including women and children, up close and personal. That's why it didn't bother him when Santos killed Gabriella Acosta.

Seth Newman, a young attorney who started working for the FBI a few months after graduation, walked into Bennett's office and sat down in the plush leather chair next to Bennett's desk. "Jim, I just got back from that briefing on the new law that Senator Tom Garrett is sponsoring. I'm a little disturbed."

"Why's that?"

"I think major portions of it are unconstitutional. If it passes, we'll be in charge of enforcing an unconstitutional law."

Bennett shifted in his chair and leaned forward. His piercing brown eyes and thick eyebrows made people feel uncomfortable when he looked them directly in the eyes, which was what he was doing to Seth. "What else is new? Some provisions of the Patriot Act are unconstitutional too, along with most of the anti-terrorist laws that Congress has been passing. We can't let the Constitution get in the way of protecting America from terrorists. Which provisions are bothering you?"

Seth looked away to avoid eye contact. "The part about shutting down Web sites. The law would give us the authority to shut down any web site that *might* be engaged in copyright infringement or *might* be connected to people who are merely being labeled as terrorists. All we would need to shut down a web site would be for someone to merely allege that someone who is connected with the web site is a terrorist. We wouldn't be required to get a court order or anything. We wouldn't need proof. We could close them down preemptively. It could lead to abuse."

Bennett leaned back in his chair. "What's wrong with that? How else are we going to prevent people from stealing intellectual property like music?" He leaned forward again, for emphasis. "How else are we going to shut down terrorist networks?"

Seth glanced at him briefly, then looked away. "The law would allow us to do it without judicial oversight. We could shut down any web site we want for practically any reason we want. We could sign our own search warrants. We wouldn't need a judge to do it. We could use the intellectual property laws or the antiterrorism laws as an excuse to shut down anybody we want."

Bennett swiveled around in his chair, picked up his cup of coffee and took a whiff. It didn't smell too bad. He winced a bit as he drank it. It had been on the pot too long and had become bitter.

"Seth, I wouldn't worry about it. The laws are made to protect us from thieves and terrorists. Most of the people we shut down will be one or the other. The law Senator Garrett is proposing would just make it easier to do our job."

Seth leaned forward, looking briefly into Bennett's eyes before turning away. "The problem I have with it is that we don't have to prove guilt first. We could shut down *Amazon.com* for selling a book to someone who's on the terrorist list. All we would have to do is allege that they're aiding and abetting the enemy. We wouldn't have to prove anything until years later, after they're out of business."

Bennett looked visibly pissed. "If *Amazon.com* sells books to terrorists, they should be shut down." Seth and his ilk just didn't get it. "We're at war, Seth. We have to use all the tools at our disposal to shut down terrorists wherever we find them. Besides, isn't there a provision in the law that waives their right to judicial process as a condition of doing business in the United States?"

"Yeah, there is, and that provision bothers me too."

"Why's that?"

"Because doing business is a right, not a privilege that's granted by government. People shouldn't have to give up their constitutional rights as a condition of doing business."

"Seth, you're living in the past. Those days are gone." He flicked his wrist at the air as he said it, for emphasis. "We have to protect the people against terrorists."

"If all the law did was help us fight terrorism, I might not have a problem with it, but it does much more than that."

"Like what?"

"It allows us to shut down any web site that's linked to someone who's on the terrorist list. If some college student has a friend on *LinkedIn* or *Facebook*, we could block their web site just because of the link."

"What's wrong with that? If they're connected to a terrorist, they're probably giving them aid and comfort. The last time I looked, that was treason. We should do more than just block their web site. We should arrest them."

Seth became emboldened at that remark. "You know as well as I do that just because someone is on the terrorist list doesn't mean they're a terrorist. Grandmothers and infants get placed on that list by mistake all the time. A lot of the people on that list don't belong there."

"Yeah, I know. No system is perfect. You just have to try to be as accurate as you can. But it's better to have a few innocent people on the list than to omit a few guilty people."

Bennett's door was open. As the conversation became increasingly heated, it started to spill out into the hallway. Carl Johnson, another FBI attorney, overheard and decided to step in and join the conversation. Carl and Bennett were at the same pay grade but worked in different departments.

"Seth, I couldn't help overhearing your conversation. It sounds like you're upset with Senator Garrett's latest proposal."

"Yeah, I am. I think it's unconstitutional and sets a bad precedent. I see the country going down a slippery slope, and I don't like it."

"Well, I'm a little concerned too, but I'm also concerned that if we don't go a little bit down that slope, we'll lose the war on terrorism. Debbie Waterstein and Jack Lunn want to go a step further. Did you hear what their bill proposes?"

"No, I haven't heard."

Bennett perked up at the mention of Debbie Waterstein, the local congressional representative. Bennett or a member of his staff was sometimes assigned to protect her when she appeared at a public event in the Miami area. He had gotten to know her over the years, and he didn't like her. She was a phony, someone who would smile to your face and slip a knife in your back when you turned around. As she gained seniority in the House of Representatives, the power had gone to her head. She treated Bennett and his people like servants and barked orders at them. She never said please or thank you. She acted like a master rather than a public servant.

Carl sat down in the chair next to Seth. "Yeah, they're calling it the Patriot Reading Act. They're targeting anything that's anti-patriot—books, web sites, newspapers, anything in print. If it provides aid and comfort to the enemy, they want to shut them down. Any bookstore that sells anti-patriotic books would get shut down for giving aid and comfort to the enemy. Any credit card company that finances the sale would get shut down. Any advertiser that pays for an ad on an online web site that spouts anti-patriotic crap—shut down. The same with *Facebook*. Shut 'em down and arrest their owners.

Bennett started to smile, not because he approved of the proposed legislation, but because it showed that Debbie had gone over the edge. "It sounds like our friend Debbie is totally out of control. She's become drunk with power, much like Caligula and the other Roman emperors in the late phase of the empire."

Carl nodded in agreement. "Yeah, only she wears expensive designer clothes instead of a toga and drives around in a limo instead of a chariot. Senator Garrett says that if the bill passes in the House, he'll make sure it passes in the Senate. He'll have a voice vote on it, so the senators won't have to go on record as being for it. He'll declare that the ayes have it, regardless of how many votes it gets."

Bennett's smile turned into a smirk. "Ah, Senator Garrett. Now there's a prime example of rat puke rising to the top." He shifted his attention to Seth. "Seth, let's say that I assigned you to guard Debbie Waterstein or Senator Garrett the next time they were in town, and somebody tried to assassinate them. Would you step in front of them and take the bullet?" Bennett winked at Carl after he said it.

Seth squirmed in his chair and looked at the carpet. "Yes, I suppose I'd have to. It's my job."

"Well, then, you're the one who's going to get that assignment."

Carl and Bennett laughed. Seth did not.

The phone rang. Bennett swiveled around and picked it up.

"Jim? John Wellington. Can you talk?"

"Guys, sorry. I have to take this call. Seth, close the door on your way out." A few seconds later, he was alone. "Hi, John. What can I do for you?"

"I'd like you to stop by my office before you go home tonight."

"Which one? You have three of them."

"I'm at the downtown office today."

"Great. You want me to drive to downtown Miami at rush hour."

"Don't worry. Everyone else will be going in the other direction."

"Right. Until it's my turn to leave."

"Give me a call a few minutes before you arrive. I'll meet you in the lobby."

"I know the procedure. See you around five."

17

4:57 p.m.
Commerce Department

Bennett arrived a few minutes early. He called Wellington as he drove into the parking garage down the street. He didn't want to have to wait long in the lobby. His appearance—just under six feet with an athletic build and brown hair—made him standout in a crowd, especially in Miami, where most of the locals were short, and many were overweight.

Bennett walked through the front doors and saw Wellington on the other side of the lobby. He gripped a cloth bag in his left hand, which appeared unusual for someone who looked like an Indiana prep school graduate.

Wellington started walking toward Bennett. "Jim. Glad you could make it. I hope the traffic wasn't too bad."

"Not any worse than usual for five o'clock in Miami." Bennett wasn't used to being summoned to offsite locations. He was usually the one who did the summoning.

Wellington placed his hand on Bennett's shoulder and motioned toward the door with a nod of his head. "Let's go to my other office."

They went outside and turned left. A few moments later they turned left again, into the alley that separated the Commerce Department building from the one next to it. After going about fifty feet, Wellington stopped and turned toward the street, and Bennett.

"Here are some things our friend, Professor Paige, gave me his afternoon. He wants 'my guys' to process it." He related the story to Bennett. "Do it off the books. I don't want any paper trail."

"Got it. Do you want me to give you a written report?"

"Yes, but put it directly into a flash drive. Don't use your office computer at all. I want to show it to the boys and point out how they screwed up. Don't bother processing the DNA samples. We already know who they are."

Bennett smiled. "It's a good thing Paige didn't take it to the local police."

"Yeah, that could complicate our lives. Well, yours, at least."

18

Miami International Airport

"A hallmark of soft totalitarianism is the subjugation of the individual, all done in the name of personal freedom."
Atavus Ataraktos (John William McMullen, *Utopia Revisited*)

Santos Hernandez could be described as a lump of muscle on two legs. He was short, barely 5' 8", with massive arms and a chest that barely fit into his shirts. He had a round head with dark brown hair that was too short to comb. His neck was not clearly visible. It appeared that God set his head directly between his shoulders. He had the thick, full lips that women liked to kiss, although the only women he'd been kissing lately were his wife, Maria, and their nine year-old daughter, Rosa. On the surface they appeared to be a typical, hard-working Hispanic Miami family. But Santos had a dark side that even Maria didn't know about.

The dark side had remained hidden throughout high school and the two years he spent at Miami-Dade College. It didn't emerge until shortly after John Wellington recruited him to be a part-time CIA asset. Wellington thought he might be a useful asset because of his physical attributes and his job at the Miami International Airport, where he worked as a TSA agent. He was the

CIA's eyes and ears at the airport. He wasn't the CIA's only airport asset, but occasionally he did provide useful information and he had access to records that allowed Wellington to get information without going through official channels. It saved time and avoided the necessity of answering questions that Wellington didn't want to answer, since some of the projects he worked on were off the books.

It had been two weeks since he killed Raul Rodriguez and Gabriella Acosta. The public had mostly forgotten about it and moved on, but Santos Hernandez had not. The image of her face just before he pulled the trigger still haunted him. He wondered if he would ever be able to forget.

It started like a typical Tuesday afternoon at the gate entrance. The citizenry lined up like sheep, patiently waiting to go through the warrantless search process they had become accustomed to after 9/11. Santos watched a female TSA agent caress the breasts of one of the better looking female passengers, a job well suited for lesbians with deviant sex syndrome because it allowed them to legally grope hundreds of female passengers every day, and they could select the ones they wanted to grope. Before 9/11 it would have been considered sexual assault. Since then it had become just standard operating procedure in the fight against terrorism.

The passenger being groped reminded him of Gabriella. He still thought of her at least once a day. He couldn't forget the look of terror she had on her face as she realized she was about to die. He felt bad that he'd had to kill her.

Santos experienced a rare sense of guilt when he read her obituary. She'd left behind a son, a brother, and two parents. He could relate to that. He had a family, too. Usually when he snuffed someone he didn't think of them as a human being, just a target that needed to be eliminated. He preferred killing men.

An elderly woman in a wheelchair set off an alarm. Santos snapped out of his daydream about Gabriella and looked in the direction of the commotion. The TSA agent closest to the woman went into action.

"Ma'am, let's go over here." The female TSA agent motioned for her to go off to the side so that the other passengers could proceed to pick up their carry-on luggage. The woman looked startled. The man pushing her wheelchair chimed in. "She has dementia. She doesn't understand what's going on."

The agent blocked his advance with her right arm. "Sir, you have to wait here."

The physical contact caught Santos's attention. The man appeared to be in his early sixties. A little on the pudgy side, average height, thinning brown hair, pasty white skin and rimless glasses. From his appearance, one could guess that his ancestors came from Northern Europe or Ireland.

A second female agent roughly pushed him aside, startling the man. "We'll take it from here." She took control of the wheelchair, propelling it off to the right, toward the search area. The wheelchair slammed into a table. The tube connecting the elderly woman's urine bag and catheter caught on the edge of the table, causing the catheter to get ripped from her vagina. She screamed. Yellow liquid splattered onto the floor as blood began to ooze from her crotch.

The man who had been pushing the wheelchair started to protest. "That's my mother. She's got dementia. I need to go with her."

His mother turned around as best she could when she heard his voice. She couldn't see him because he stood behind her and the agent blocked her view. She had a pained look on her face. The blood continued to ooze. A few drops splattered on the floor. The

TSA agent continued to push the wheelchair toward the search area.

"James!"

The large female TSA agent tried to calm her down. She bent forward and spoke into her left ear. "That's all right, ma'am. This will only take a minute."

"James!" she exclaimed again, getting frantic.

Santos continued to watch as events unfolded. He noticed James becoming visibly upset by his mother's repeated calls. As James started toward her, the larger of the two female agents stepped in front of him, blocking his advance with her body. He continued to try to walk toward his mother, who was bleeding and screaming.

"James!"

By now, everyone in the screening area was watching the events as they unfolded.

The large, black female agent pushed him back as best she could, but she had trouble restraining him. Santos noticed, got up from his chair and walked toward them, briskly.

Santos grabbed him by the left arm and slammed him into the wall. He shouted, "You can't go in there! That's a restricted area!"

James resisted by raising his left arm. He broke the hold Santos had on him, accidentally slapping Santos in the face. Santos responded by slamming his right fist into his ribs, followed by a left to his face. The force of the second blow caused James's head to fly back. He hit the wall with a thud. Blood spurted from his nose as he slid to the floor.

The other passengers in the line gasped, unable to believe what they had just witnessed. Several of them took out their cell phones to record the event.

Santos could see that James no longer posed a threat, but he didn't stop. He kicked him, once to the face, then to the ribs. He could feel several of them break as his foot connected.

"You dumb fuck! I told you to stop!"

The other TSA agents watched as the event unfolded. Two of the male agents ran toward Santos and grabbed him before he could do any more damage. They eventually were able to restrain him. One agent handcuffed James. Santos and another agent lifted him up, causing his broken ribs to jab him in the side. He let out a scream. They led him away, dragging him past the line of passengers. He bled profusely from the face.

One of the passengers standing in line took a close-up photo of his bloody face and bulging eyes as the TSA agents dragged him past the line of gasping onlookers.

The two female TSA agents had stopped what they were doing to watch the altercation. His mother couldn't see what was going on, but she could hear the commotion. She tried to turn around to see, but the wheelchair pointed in the opposite direction.

The larger of the two female agents grabbed the wheelchair handles, rushed her into the screening room and closed the doors behind her. As the door closed, passengers could hear her screaming – "James! James! … Get your hands off me!"

19

The Olive Garden

"Is life so dear or peace so sweet as to be purchased at the price of chains and slavery? ... I know not what course others may take, but as for me, give me liberty or give me death!"
Patrick Henry

"Robert, did you hear what happened at the airport yesterday?" Sveta and Paige just sat down for lunch at the Olive Garden restaurant on Biscayne Boulevard and 181st Street in Aventura, a north eastern suburb of Miami. They liked eating there because of the salad and because of its closeness to her office. Michelle, their favorite waitress, placed the salad and bread on the table and left.

"Yes, I couldn't help it. The photo someone took of him being dragged away with a bloodied face made the front page of the *Miami Herald.* Did you see the pain on his face?"

"Yes. And someone took a video and posted it on the internet. I saw the whole thing on *YouTube* this morning. I heard it went viral."

Sveta took a sip of her ice tea. "I think it was terrible what they did to that man. Did you see it when that TSA agent kicked him in the face and the ribs? That's something they would do in Russia, but not in America."

"Yes. I heard the FBI questioned the person who took that photo of his bloody face. They're trying to decide whether to charge him with a crime because it puts the government in a bad light."

"Why would they go after him? All he did was take a photo."

"Yes, but publishing it makes it look like the government is more of a threat than the terrorists. It weakens their argument that no cost is too great to fight the war on terrorism.

The newscaster interviewed the TSA agent's boss. He said the investigation has already been completed and that the agent had been acting properly, just following procedure. They're going to prosecute the passenger for assault. The FBI is trying to get the *YouTube* video taken down because he said it provides aid and comfort to the enemy. They're also trying to find out who posted it."

"What enemy, Robert? Who is the enemy?"

"It's difficult to find one. I'm beginning to think the government poses more of a threat than the terrorists."

"I am thinking so too, Robert, but what can anyone do about it?"

"I don't know. Whenever some politician goes on TV to talk about national security, they all say the same thing: we need more funding, we need stricter laws, we need more surveillance cameras. It doesn't matter whether they're Democrats or Republicans."

"Robert, the condo board started putting more cameras in my building. Jason told me they got a federal grant to pay for it."

"Yeah, I read that there is a lot of government money for cameras. Did you notice there are now a lot of cameras all up and down Biscayne Boulevard?"

"Yes, and a lot of other streets too. The camera takes a photo whenever the light turns red. Hitler and Stalin could only dream of such a thing. I heard a news report a few weeks ago about somebody shooting out a few of them around 70th and Biscayne. I only heard it once, though. I wonder if the police pressured the TV station not to report it."

"I wouldn't doubt it. They're probably afraid of copycats. A lot of people don't like those cameras. I've read on the Internet that the government is putting pressure on the media not to report things that touch on national security."

Sveta stopped fumbling with her salad. "What do cameras on Biscayne Boulevard have to do with national security?"

"Nothing. That's the point. If the government can pressure radio and TV stations not to report on a few vandalized cameras, there's no telling what else they can do."

"They sound paranoid. People used to think like that in Russia too. You always had to be careful what you said or did. Before you know it, they'll be installing cameras inside our homes."

"They've already started to do that. A few months ago, one of the local newscasters reported on an incident at a local high school. The high school had issued computers to its students, paid for with a federal grant. The computers had cameras. The vice principal used to monitor them from home in the evening. Mostly they were just conversations between students talking about whatever teenagers talk about, but once in a while a student would leave the computer on when they undressed at night. On more than one occasion, he observed a student masturbating, mostly guys, but a few girls too."

"Robert, I've often wondered about that. Do guys masturbate a lot? I had a friend in Moscow who said her brother did it all the time. They lived in a two-room apartment that had thin walls and she could hear him doing it practically every day."

"Yes, it's not that unusual. It's almost part of their daily routine."

"Robert, did you masturbate a lot when you were a teenager?"

"Sveta, you're embarrassing me."

"I'm sorry, Robert, I was just curious."

"Actually, I got more sex when I was in the tenth grade than I do now, but I never had a partner in those days."

"That's because you're too busy, Robert. I would give you more if you weren't so busy."

"I'll keep that in mind."

Michelle approached the table. "Have you decided what to order?"

Sveta ordered first. "Yes, I'll have the linguine alla marinara."

"Sir, what would you like?"

"I'll have the chicken parmigiana."

"Thank you." She turned and left.

The noise from the packed restaurant made it difficult to carry on a conversation, so they spent most of their time eating. Paige's chicken parmigiana was good, but not as good as what they served at Trattoria Il Migliori in North Miami Beach. Not as large either. He could get three meals out of the Il Migliori parm. But the Olive Garden salads were larger and tastier, so it was a trade-off foodwise.

As they finished their meal, Paige continued to think about what was happening in America. He didn't like it.

"You know, Sveta, America's Founding Fathers would be appalled at what's happening in this country. If British soldiers had tried to do what the TSA and the camera installers are doing, they would have been tarred and feathered by the citizenry, or perhaps strung up. America has become a land of sheep. Someone should do something before it's too late."

20

Sunny Isles Beach

After saying good-bye to Sveta in the Olive Garden parking lot, Paige pulled out his phone and dialed Wellington from his car.

"Hi, John, this is Bob. Did you get the results yet?"

"Yeah, I did, but there's not much to report. I'm going to be in your neck of the woods this afternoon. Perhaps we can meet for a few minutes. Are you free?"

"Of course. I'm a professor. I only teach two days a week, and today isn't one of them."

"Thank you for reminding me. I sometimes forget that I work more in a day than you professor-types work in a week."

"Perhaps you should think about working less. The less you Commerce Department types work, the less damage you can do to the economy."

"Funny, Bob. You know we always have American consumers as our top priority."

"I know. That's why prices are so much higher than they would be in a free market. You're trying to protect American consumers from low prices."

"Precisely.... How does four o'clock sound? That's after your usual nap time, isn't it?"

"Yes, I'm usually done with my nap by then."

"Good. How about the Starbucks on Collins Avenue?"

"Sure. It's next to my gym. I can get in a quick workout after my nap and before dinner."

"See you then."

***

Paige entered the gym at about 2:30 in the afternoon, had a vigorous workout, and hit the showers at 3:45, which gave him more than the two minutes he needed to walk to Starbucks.

Ever since the incident in the parking lot, he'd been working out with more intensity than usual, combining weight training with martial arts. He also spent more time at the dojahng sparring with whoever was there. If he had another encounter, he couldn't afford to be as sloppy in his technique as he'd been the first time.

Paige arrived first and ordered a tuna croissant and cappuccino. He was hungry after his workout and wanted to ingest some protein. After picking up his order, he went outside and took a table in the northwest corner. That gave him a good view of Collins Avenue, while being far enough away that the exhaust fumes wouldn't assault his nostrils. It sat far enough away from the other tables that, with the street sounds, the other customers wouldn't be able to pick up their conversation.

A few minutes after four, Wellington walked over to Paige's table. He wore a short-sleeved white shirt and blue tie, but no suit coat. Miami was usually too hot to wear a suit coat outside.

"Hi, Bob." He reached out and shook Paige's hand. "I'll be right back. I'm going to get some coffee."

He returned a few minutes later, as Paige was taking the last bite of his tuna croissant.

After exchanging a few pleasantries, Wellington got to the point.

"My guys didn't find much. Their DNA isn't in the system. The van was stolen."

"What about fingerprints? Did they find anything on the notes or the guns?"

"No, they must have handled the notes with gloves on. There weren't any prints on the guns either."

Paige held in his look of surprise. He'd placed their prints on those guns himself. He eyed John as he tried to savor his cappuccino. "Were you able to trace the serial numbers on the guns?"

"Yeah. They belonged to some guy who died ten years ago."

"Hm. That sounds like a dead end. Pardon my pun."

"Funny, Bob. Someone probably inherited them, or maybe they were sold at auction or at a gun show. There's really no way to trace them without starting a paper trail, which we don't want to do."

"What about the photos? Did your face-recognition software find anything?"

"No. Apparently they aren't in the system."

"Seems a little strange. Anyone who has a driver's license is in the system."

"That's right, but nothing showed up. The face-recognition system isn't perfect."

"Or maybe their photos were taken out of the system because they have someone on the inside."

"Bob, you're being paranoid. They were probably just a couple of lowlife thugs."

The conversation gradually shifted. Wellington left a few minutes later. As Paige walked to his car, he replayed their conversation in his head. John lied to him about the fingerprints. When Paige searched their pockets, he found the van keys. Guys who steal cars don't have the keys. They have to hotwire them, and everyone who has a driver's license has their photo in the system.

Things didn't add up. He wondered why Wellington was lying to him.

21

James Young's Office

"If you want a vision of the future, imagine a boot stamping on a human face—forever."
George Orwell

"The truth is that men are tired of liberty."
Benito Mussolini

"There ought to be limits to freedom."
George W. Bush

James Young returned to work the day after Santos Hernandez had broken his ribs at the airport. It hurt to move, so he tried to stay seated at his desk as much as possible. His ribs felt slightly better today than they had yesterday, but they would take a few months to heal properly.

As he sat down, some Department of Homeland Security thugs pulled up to the building in two large, black vans shortly after two o'clock in the afternoon. They burst out of the vehicles simultaneously, guns drawn, scaring the hell out of the people on the sidewalk.

They crashed through the front door of the first floor office where James Young worked. "Where is James Young's office?"

The terrified young woman closest to the door pointed to the far side of the room, her hand trembling.

All eyes focused on the intruders, their black uniforms, Kevlar vests, and weapons. They were experiencing up close and personal the shock and awe that former Defense Secretary Donald Rumsfeld had been so proud of, except that Rumsfeld had intended the technique to be used against America's enemies, not its own citizens.

James heard the commotion and rose from his chair as quickly as the pain in his ribs would allow when he heard someone call his name.

The jackbooted DHS leader and two underlings marched into his office. "Step out of the room, Mr. Young."

He stood in front of them, slightly hunched over, speechless.

"I said get out!"

He didn't move fast enough to please the DHS agent. The man punched him hard in the solar plexus, then grabbed his right arm and twisted it, causing his broken ribs to separate, jabbing into his flesh. He let out a scream. His knees buckled from the pain and he dropped to the floor.

The leader motioned to his two accomplices. "Take the computer and files. Leave everything else."

They obeyed like robots. One of them stuffed the contents of his desk into a cloth bag. The other unplugged and dismantled his computer. Once Young's office was secured, the leader stepped back into the outer office.

As James struggled to get up, he could see one of them strut over to his secretary's desk. The clutter blocked access to the wires on the computer. The agent solved that problem by placing his left forearm on the desk and sweeping off everything on the desktop. Yanira Flores watched as the picture frame containing a photo of her family crashed to the floor, breaking the glass. James gritted his teeth. That's all he could do. He felt powerless to stop it. His ribs hurt so much he could barely stand.

Yanira stepped forward into the agent's personal space to confront him. "What are you doing!?"

He responded with an elbow smash to her face, causing her 110-pound, 46-year-old body to fly back against the file cabinet. The tip of his boot flew into her crotch as Tom Campbell, the company president, walked through the front door. James looked at Campbell, then the agent, then Yanira, who lay unconscious on the floor, blood all over her nose, mouth and chin.

Campbell strode toward the agents. "What's going on here!?"

The leader sauntered over to him. He looked drunk with power and placed his fists on his hips before speaking. It reminded James of photos he had seen of Mussolini, the Italian fascist dictator. "We're confiscating your computers and files."

The president's jaw dropped. His eyes narrowed. "Do you have a warrant?"

"We don't need a warrant. James Young has been classified as a terrorist for assaulting a government official. The Constitution doesn't apply to terrorists."

"Since when does assaulting a government official constitute terrorism?"

"Ever since I said so. The Department of Homeland Security has the authority to classify anyone as a terrorist, for any reason we think is appropriate."

James heard the words as they emanated from the leader's mouth. As he looked to his left and right he could see the other agents filling boxes with files and unplugging the other computers.

His colleagues stared at him in disbelief, as if to say it was all his fault that this was happening. He felt terrible. He looked around the office. It was trashed. The government agents had not been neat about it. Papers and other objects that had been on his colleagues' desks had been strewn across the floor. Everyone was looking at him.

22

Sveta's Condo

"Un-American activity cannot be prevented or routed out by employing un-American methods; to preserve freedom we must use the tools that freedom provides."
Dwight D. Eisenhower

"Private property was the original source of freedom. It still is its main bulwark."
Walter Lippmann

"I tell you, freedom and human rights in America are doomed. The U.S. government will lead the American people in — and the West in general — into an unbearable hell and a choking life." — Osama bin Laden

Paige and Sveta had just sat down to dinner in her kitchen when a television report caught their attention.

"The Department of Homeland Security raided the office where James Young works this afternoon. As you may recall from yesterday's news report, Mr. Young was arrested for assaulting a TSA agent at the Miami International Airport. He is being accused of domestic terrorism and is out on bail. The agents confiscated computers and files to determine whether Young might be connected to a domestic terrorist network."

"One of the employees who was in the office at the time of the raid recorded the following clip on his cell phone."

The DHS leader's image appeared on the screen, his fists on his hips. "We don't need a warrant to search property or to seize it. The War on Terror demands action."

The newscaster's voice broke in as the clip focused on Yanira Flores's bloodied face. "The Department of Homeland Security said that this employee, who has not yet been identified, assaulted one of their agents when he attempted to unplug her computer."

"Robert, can they do that? Can they just take property without any kind of warrant?"

"Apparently they can." The words stuck in his throat as he said it.

She clutched his forearm. "Why doesn't anybody do something?"

"My grandfather told me about the time he was walking down the street in Moscow. He saw some Soviet police beating a man. The man begged them to stop. One of the police took out his pistol and shot him. He was a neighbor of ours. Nobody did anything about it. Everybody was standing around watching, but nobody did anything."

23

9:17 p.m.
Florida Atlantic University

"We do not argue with those who disagree with us, we destroy them."
Benito Mussolini

Martin Kaplan emerged from his evening sociology class at Florida Atlantic University and started walking toward his car. It was a warm evening, like many in Boca Raton, but the ocean breeze helped a bit. Some kind of tropical bird made squawking noises in one of the palm trees.

As he entered the dark parking area, he vaguely noticed two men walking in the same direction, but didn't pay them any mind. He had been too busy thinking about the lecture he had just given to question their presence, or the fact that they didn't look like students. No books. No backpacks. Dressed more like delivery people than students. Older than most students.

"Professor Kaplan?"

The sound of the voice coming from his right side just a few feet away snapped him out of his hypnotic trance. As he turned he saw two men just a few feet away, one on the left and one on the right. They wore dark clothes. He couldn't make out their features clearly, but noticed they wore latex gloves. They came toward him at a quick pace and enveloped him, one on each side.

"Please, professor, don't panic. We just want to talk to you." The taller one grabbed his left arm firmly and led him to his car.

"Get in."

Kaplan wasn't accustomed to being treated like that. He wasn't used to people telling him what to do or touching him, especially in such a rough, forceful way. He looked around to see if anyone else was in the parking lot. There wasn't.

As he took out his keys and pushed the button on his keychain to open the door, he looked toward the Arts & Sciences building to see if there was anyone around but the two men blocked his view. They were so close he could smell their stale breath.

The taller one held the door open with his left hand.

"Get in." He continued to hold the door open so that Kaplan couldn't slam it and escape.

He sat down behind the wheel and looked up. "Should I fasten my seatbelt?"

"That won't be necessary." He reached into his pocket and pulled out a tubular object a little less than a foot long. He stuck it into Kaplan's ribs and pushed a small, red button, sending 1.5 million volts into Kaplan's side. He held it for two seconds, then pulled back.

Kaplan was paralyzed, but fully conscious. He could hear and see, but he couldn't move.

"You probably wondered why we paid you this little visit. It's because you're a traitor, you filthy piece of shit. Your investigation is weakening America and is giving aid and comfort to the enemy."

He stepped away from the car. Kaplan watched helplessly as the shorter guy stuck his head into the car and placed an envelope on the dashboard. He saw him reach into his left pocket and pull out a straight razor. He placed the palm of his right hand on Kaplan's forehead and pushed his head back.

"Bye-bye, you piece of shit." He placed the tip of the razor under Kaplan's right ear and sliced him from ear to ear. Kaplan could see his own blood spurting out onto the windshield and the envelope. Then everything went black.

They closed the door to Kaplan's car and a black van pulled up. They got in and drove off. The shorter one placed the razor in a plastic bag.

24

Paige didn't usually teach on Thursdays, but today was special. He'd been invited to present a guest lecture to a group of international business students about his accounting experiences in the former Soviet Union and Eastern Europe. He was heading in to do some paperwork.

Paige turned on the radio as he pulled out of his parking garage.

"Last night about 10 p.m., Martin Kaplan, a sociology professor at the Boca Raton campus of Florida Atlantic University, was found dead in his car on the university campus, apparently the victim of foul play. Kaplan, an outspoken critic of NSA data gathering, was a consultant to Representative Lois Klein, who is leading a congressional investigation into NSA's allegedly unconstitutional activities. Professor Kaplan headed up the task force for that investigation. An envelope was left at the scene, but authorities have not yet divulged its contents. Representative Klein could not be reached for comment."

Paige switched off the radio. His mind turned to the conversation he had with Wellington. He had assigned him to infiltrate Saul Steinman's study group, which consisted of professors who thought along the same lines as Martin Kaplan and Nathan Shipkovitz, both now dead. And not from natural causes. Murdered in university parking lots. Were the two guys who accosted him in his university's parking lot sent there to kill him? Was he on the same hit list as Shipkovitz and Kaplan? Was Wellington behind the hits? Did Wellington have plans to kill Steinman, and perhaps the other professors? And maybe him, too?

From his past experience with Wellington he knew he was a dangerous guy. John had lied about the fingerprints on the guns. Maybe he was lying about Steinman too. There were too many unanswered questions. He decided to play along. For now. Maybe things would become clear with the passage of time. The best thing to do would be to keep his eyes and ears open and his mouth shut. Wellington must not suspect that he was starting to connect the dots.

***

He arrived at the university and booted up his computer. He'd run a license plate check on the van. It was easy enough to do. Companies on the Internet would provide practically any public information for a few dollars.

While the computer booted, he rose from his chair and gazed out the window. Another beautiful Miami day. Co-eds walked to class, laughed, chatted, and talked on their cell phones, oblivious to what went on beneath the surface in their city.

From the faculty lounge down the hall wafted the pungency of the swill that passed for coffee. Maybe he would have a cup later. He didn't especially like the taste of the coffee that came out of that room, but it could become palatable if he added a little vanilla or caramel flavoring.

He sat at his computer and searched for Web sites that would give him the information needed. He selected the first option, read the instructions, input his credit card information, typed in the license plate, then hit the *search* button.

Up popped a name and address. The van belonged to George Heverly, thirty-four. The screen listed an address on Northwest 17th Avenue. No apartment number. Most likely a house. Single people usually lived in apartments, so he probably was married. Most married guys had kids. Since he was thirty-four, the kids were possibly still living at home.

Perhaps there was a photo of him online. He searched for *George Heverly Miami.* Nothing. Then he searched for *Facebook* and scored several hits. But no *Facebook* pages for George Heverly. However, there was one for Gwen Heverly. He clicked the link.

Up popped the main page. It showcased several family photos.

One of the faces belonged to the smaller of the two men who had assaulted him in the parking lot.

The girl in most of the photos, probably Gwen, appeared to be about thirteen. Some photos also included a younger boy of perhaps nine or ten, likely her brother. They'd be enrolled at an elementary or middle school near their home, unless they were home schooled.

He searched for schools within their zip code, viewed the schools' Web pages, and made a few phone calls to learn when school let out. The district generally dismissed students between two thirty and three. He checked his watch. Almost eleven. The MBA class didn't start until six. He had time to go back to his place, grab his camera, have lunch, and drive to northwest 17th Avenue before they got home.

He turned off his computer and left his office. The smell of coffee had grown stronger, but he wouldn't be having any today. Someone else would have to drink his share of that swill. He had a mission to complete.

25

Heverly's House

Paige returned to his apartment, picked up his camera, and left. He could have saved himself a trip by using the camera in his cell phone, but the one he had at home had much higher resolution.

On the way to the parking garage he wondered why Wellington had lied to him about the fingerprints and the other items of evidence. What was he up to? Who else was involved? Who was pulling Wellington's strings for this assignment? Were those two guys he met in the parking lot sent by Wellington? If not, who sent them? Were they sent just to talk to him, or to kill him? Would he be safe now that he had decided to drop the Raul Rodriguez investigation?

He found Heverly's house easily. Residential neighborhood. Close to a main highway. No one-way streets to complicate things. Several houses sprouted hedges in front. He could park in front of them to wait for the children to come home. If school let out between two-thirty and three, they would probably arrive home between two forty and three twenty.

At two-thirty he did a practice drive-by to get a feel for the neighborhood and to check out potential parking places that would not be too obvious. He pulled over and parked on the other side of the street about a hundred feet from the house, far enough away to not be too obvious but close enough to see what was going on. As he rolled down the window so that he could take clear photos, the heat of the sizzling Miami afternoon invaded his air-conditioned car. The smell of freshly cut grass filled his nostrils. It reminded him of his youth, when he used to cut his father's grass and earn some extra money cutting neighbors' grass. Now that he lived in a condo, he didn't have to do that anymore. The condo association had a staff of Haitians to do that work.

His mouth was getting dry. He popped in some gum and wiped the salty sweat from his forehead with his fingertips. It wouldn't be long now.

A block away, a group of children with backpacks walked in the direction of Heverly's house. At this distance he couldn't identify any as the kids from the *Facebook* photos.

The group of kids diminished as they peeled off to go to their respective homes. By the time they approached the Heverly house, just five of them remained in the pack.

Paige zoomed in and started snapping photos. Two of the kids, a boy and a girl, headed toward the side door, while the remaining three kids continued walking. He got the photos he wanted.

He started the car. A woman opened the side door as he passed by the house. He took one quick photo of the three of them.

26

James Young

James Young continued to go to the office, but there wasn't much work for him or anyone else to do. No computers. No files. His colleagues had empathized with him after seeing his bloody face on the front page of the *Miami Herald*, but now they kept their distance. The Department of Homeland Security had called him a terrorist.

Although his court date was looming on the horizon, his main concern at the moment was keeping his job. The company's customers kept calling to cancel their orders. With no computers, the company couldn't serve them. His colleagues spent most of their time taking cancellation calls. Every time a phone rang was like another nail in the coffin of the company. It would soon be out of business if they couldn't get their computers back.

He tried not to make eye contact. He tried not to talk to them. They stopped initiating conversations with him.

He looked at his watch. Quitting time. He glanced at Yanira Flores on the way out. Her broken nose had been reset. One of her eyes was still puffy from the elbow slam the DHS agent had given her.

On the drive home he pulled up to the ATM at his bank to make a cash withdrawal. He was declined. Twice. The bank was closed, but the drive-in teller windows were still open. He drove up to one of them.

"Good evening. How may I assist you?"

"I just tried to make a cash withdrawal on your ATM but was declined."

"I'm sorry, sir. Give me your debit card and a photo ID. How much would you like?"

"Two hundred dollars, please."

"Just one moment." She took the debit card and ID and started typing into her computer. A few seconds later she stopped.

"I'm sorry, sir. Your accounts have been frozen."

"What!? Why are they frozen?"

"I don't know, sir. All it says is that the Department of Homeland Security froze them this morning."

"What?" He shouted, gripping the car door to lean toward her. "How will I buy groceries?"

The teller stepped back from the drive-in window, startled by his sudden outburst.

He regretted the words as soon as he'd said them.

"Mr. Young, the bank is closed now. You'll have to come in tomorrow when the bank is open to straighten it out. I'm sorry, sir."

He grunted, but remained polite. It wasn't her fault that he couldn't make a withdrawal. "Thank you." He put his car in gear and left.

His wife had asked him to pick up a few things at the grocery store on the way home. He didn't need cash to do that. He could use his credit cards.

He pointed his car in the direction of the store, but couldn't concentrate on his driving. Every day seemed to add more problems to his already complicated life, mostly because of the inadvertent brush his hand had made to that TSA agent's face at the airport.

He arrived at the grocery store a few minutes later. He grabbed the items for his wife, then walked to the checkout. The cashier rang up the items and he slid his credit card through the card reader.

"I'm sorry, sir, the machine declined your card. Can you try another card?"

How was that possible? He made it a point to always pay his cards on time. He even paid a little more than the amount he owed so he could start the next billing cycle with a credit balance.

He tried another card. Declined. Then another card. Also declined. He only carried three credit cards with him. That had always been more than enough.

"I'm sorry, sir. I won't be able to finish processing your transaction."

"I'm sorry." He started picking up the items and placing them in his cart.

"What are you doing, sir?"

"I'm going to put them back on the shelves. You shouldn't have to do that. It's my fault."

"No, sir. You don't have to do that. It's store policy that one of our employees has to return items to the shelves."

"OK. I'm sorry for any trouble."

"That's all right, sir. Don't worry about it."

"Thank you."

He couldn't get out of there fast enough. He avoided eye contact with the other customers.

27

10:00 p.m.
Paige's Condo

Paige opened the condo door and tossed his keys on the kitchen counter. He plopped down on the couch and let out a sigh. His MBA students were generally smarter, more mature and motivated than his undergraduate students, but most of them didn't want to be in his class. They were mostly management or marketing majors and took his accounting class because it was a requirement for the degree. He had to try to teach them as well as entertain them to keep their interest.

He closed his eyes for a moment. The growling in his stomach told him to eat something, so he searched through the fridge and pulled out a Diet Pepsi and the ingredients for a ham and cheese sandwich. He grabbed the large bag of chips sitting on the counter and took everything to the kitchen table. He constructed and slowly devoured the sandwich and chips, then booted up his laptop and finished off the Diet Pepsi.

At his desk he put on latex gloves, opened a new packet of glossy photo paper, and printed the two best photos he had taken that afternoon. He set them aside. Next, he printed twelve copies of all the photos he took the night Heverly and the other guy accosted him in the university parking lot – their faces and guns, and the van's license plate – along with copies of the notes.

He reached over and took the packet of large envelopes he'd bought at Walgreen's on the way home. He inserted a complete set of photos, including the photos of Heverly's family into one envelope. He put a set of the parking lot photos, along with the photos of the guns and the copies of the notes into 11 other envelopes.

He then typed a note to George Heverly and a second note to the recipients of the 11 other envelopes. The note to Heverly said:

> Mr. Heverly:
> We know you assaulted Professor Paige and threatened his life and that of his girlfriend. If any harm comes to either of them, we will kill you. Neither you nor your family will live. We will also distribute copies of these photos and notes to the media and various government agencies so that your accomplices will be brought to justice. Back off or face the consequences.

He couldn't back up his threat, of course. He knew he was acting alone but Heverly didn't know that.

He printed his message and crammed it into one of the envelopes. Then he opened a new word processing document and began typing.

> You are reading this note because I, Robert Paige, have been murdered. As of this writing, I don't know who did it, but I can point you in the right direction. Last week I was assaulted by two men in the Saint Frances University parking lot as I was leaving to go home after my night class. Their photos are included in this envelope. One of my assailants was George Heverly. The enclosed photos of his van and license

> plate were taken at the same time, in the parking lot, along with the photos of the pistols I retrieved from them (which I gave to John Wellington for processing).
>
> Mr. Heverly threatened to kill me if I did not cease my investigation of the Raul Rodriguez murder. Threatening letters were later slipped under the door at my university and home (see enclosures). I do not know the identity of the other assailant, but he has a knee injury, which I inflicted in the parking lot. Perhaps you can learn his identity from the photo or by tracing the serial numbers on the pistols.
>
> I have reason to believe that John Wellington (currently employed by the U.S. Commerce Department) and the Miami office of the FBI may also be involved. If Svetlana Ivanova has been killed, the same people are responsible for her death as well.

Paige printed copies and inserted them into the remaining eleven envelopes. He addressed ten of them to various left-wing and right-wing media personalities, and to the Washington DC office of the FBI, then sealed all eleven envelopes and placed them in his briefcase, along with the envelope containing the note to Heverly.

Paige looked at his watch. Almost eleven. He took off the latex gloves, placed them in his briefcase, turned on the television, and watched the news.

At eleven forty-five he got up, put on a black T-shirt, black pants, black tennis shoes, and a black cap, grabbed his briefcase and Glock 17, and drove to NW 17th Avenue.

He arrived after midnight. His headlights broke the darkness to illuminate a neighborhood so still it might have been void of life. He parked a half block from Heverly's house, shut down the engine and switched off his lights.

He pulled on his latex gloves, pocketed the Glock and grabbed the envelope containing the note to Heverly. He closed the door silently and walked toward Heverly's house at a normal pace. A dog from a neighbor's house started barking. Someone shouted *Shut up!* The barking subsided.

In Heverly's driveway he walked to the right side of the van so he could approach without being seen. He slipped the envelope between the wiper and the windshield. A minute later he was back in the car. He started the engine, made a U-turn, and left.

28

George Heverly
The Next Morning

Gwen noticed the envelope on the windshield and she, her father and George Jr. walked toward the van. "Daddy, there's a big envelope on your windshield." George Heverly usually dropped his kids off at school on his way in to work.

"Thanks, honey." He removed it from the windshield and stared at it.

"Aren't you going to open it?"

Heverly hesitated. His gut told him not to open it in front of the kids.

George Jr. chimed in. "Yeah, dad. Open it. Let's see what's inside." Gwen clasped her hands and started jumping up and down in anticipation, her pigtails bouncing behind her.

"It's probably just something from work. I'll open it later." He'd been with the National Security Administration for more than ten years. They never left anything on his windshield. It would have been a breach of security.

"Please, Daddy, please!"

"OK. I'll open it and peek inside. If it's something interesting, I'll show you."

Gwen grabbed his forearm as he started to open it. The two photos Paige had taken the day before spilled onto the driveway, face up.

"Daddy, those are photos of us. And mommy's in one of them, too."

Heverly was stunned. He regretted his decision to buckle under and open the envelope in the presence of his children. He realized he had made a stupid mistake.

He had to say something. "I guess some nice man decided to share the photos with us." He grabbed the photos out of Gwen's hands and stuffed them back in the envelope as fast as he could.

"What else is in the envelope, daddy? Are there more photos?"

He had to end this conversation. Cautiously, he looked inside the envelope, making sure his kids wouldn't be able to see its contents. There were more photos. The one on top was of his accomplice, face bloodied. He figured it must have been taken at the university parking lot, where Paige knocked them both out.

"No, it's just some documents."

Gwen looked disappointed. He tried to hide the worried look that must have been on his face. They got in the van and started off for school. All Heverly could think about was the contents of the envelope. How did Paige find out who he was or where he lived? Was his family in danger? He would have to wait until he dropped the kids off to read the note he saw in the envelope.

He dropped the kids off, then drove a few hundred yards, pulled over and removed the contents of the envelope. He grabbed the note and started reading. He became more enraged – and worried – with each sentence. He should have killed Paige in the parking lot. Now it was too late. Killing him now would have consequences – for him and his family. What to do? He would have to tell his accomplice. And his boss, the one who sent him on the mission. But what then? Killing Paige was out of the question. What if his boss didn't see it that way? If his boss wanted Paige killed, a little note like the one he held in his hand wouldn't change a thing.

He took out his cell phone, called Wellington, and related the events.

"Hmmm. It appears we have a problem. Look, I'm on my way to work. Let's get together late this afternoon. I'll be at my downtown office. Bring Ed along too. Don't do anything we'll all regret. We have to find a way to cool things down."

"OK. I'll talk to Ed and get back to you."

"No need to get back to me. Just be here before four thirty. Call when you get to the parking garage."

They hung up. Heverly had calmed down somewhat. He still wanted to strangle Paige but Wellington wouldn't permit it.

29

NSA Headquarters

Heverly arrived at NSA headquarters, opened his office door, turned on the light and walked immediately to Ed Morris's office. He saw Ed fumbling with his keys in front of his door while trying not to drop the cane he had to use ever since Paige dislocated his knee in the university parking lot. Ed saw him approaching out of the corner of his eye.

"Hi George. What's up?"

"We need to talk about something. Got a minute?"

"Sure. Come on in." He opened the door and limped toward his desk. Heverly walked in and closed the door. Morris winced in pain as he attempted to sit down. He was a big guy. Placing his considerable weight on the leg with the injured knee was painful.

"How's the knee?"

"The doctor said I'll probably need surgery at some point. He reset it, but he said the meniscus is messed up. It's never going to get back to normal."

"Sorry to hear about that."

"I should have just shot that bastard Paige as soon as we got out of the van."

Heverly tossed the envelope onto his desk. "Yeah, probably, but now we've got another problem."

Ed looked at the envelope, then at Heverly.

"Professor Paige, or one of his buddies, dropped by the house last night and left that on the windshield of my van."

"How did he find out who you are or where you live?"

"I don't know. He must have found a way to trace my plates."

"Yeah, probably." Morris looked at the photos and read Paige's note.

"That fucker! We should have killed him."

"Yeah, but it's too late for that now."

"Maybe not." Morris had a frustrated look on his face as he tapped his empty coffee cup with a pen and bit his lower lip. "I'm not ready to give up yet."

"I called Wellington this morning and told him about it."

"Yeah? What was his reaction?"

"He sounded pissed. He wants to see us this afternoon."

"That's great. Like I have nothing better to do than drop what I am doing and drive downtown at rush hour for a chat."

"Yeah, I know. I feel the same way."

"OK. Let's plan on leaving around 4."

"Maybe 3:45 would be better. He said he wants to see us before 4:30. We might run into traffic."

"OK. Fine. We'll leave at 3:45."

30

An hour after Heverly opened the envelope, Paige arrived at his attorney's office with the other envelopes. Paige pulled into the office building's parking lot, got out, and looked around to see if anyone had followed him. He felt a little paranoid, and for good reason. He didn't know what Heverly's reaction would be after his midnight visit, but he had likely opened the envelope by now, and was probably figuring out what to do about it.

He pushed the elevator button to the second floor. It was shortly after nine. He took a left and walked to the office at the end of the hall. The office lights shone through the opaque glass. Someone had to be there. He tested the door knob. It was unlocked. He walked in and looked around. The secretary wasn't at her desk.

"Anybody home?"

Patrick Hamilton walked into the entryway, some files in his hand, his top shirt button unfastened. Patrick Hamilton was a good looking guy, in his early forties, an immigrant from Chicago who decided to escape the cold weather after graduating from the John Marshall Law School. He specialized in business law but practiced in a few other areas, too, depending on client needs.

"Hi, Bob. To what do I owe this unexpected pleasure?"

"Always the bullshit artist, huh, Pat?"

They both laughed and shook hands. Paige didn't need the services of an attorney very often. Their relationship consisted mostly of Paige giving Hamilton an occasional referral for legal and tax business that he no longer wanted to take.

"Come on in." He motioned toward his office. "What can I do for you? May I offer you some coffee?"

"No, I'm good." Paige took out all but one of the envelopes and placed them on Hamilton's desk. "I'd like you to mail these for me in the event of my untimely death."

Hamilton's jaw dropped. "What? You're kidding, right?" He looked Paige in the eyes, his mouth wide open. "Has someone threatened you?"

"You might say that." Paige gave him the short version of the story.

Hamilton picked up the envelopes and glanced at the names and addresses. "These are all media people. Is there something you're not telling me?"

"I left out a few details. The less you know, the better. I'm sure you can appreciate that as an attorney."

"Yes, it's probably better you don't tell me any more. But you're still my client. The attorney-client privilege applies."

"Yeah, I know, but sometimes it's better that certain things are left unsaid."

Hamilton nodded. "Should I bill you now, or should I wait until after I mail them?"

They both grinned. "If you bill me now, I can squawk about the exorbitant fee you're probably going to charge me. If you wait, I won't be able to protest."

"You're right. I'll wait."

They both laughed and engaged in some pleasant chit-chat to lighten the mood. After a few minutes, Paige left.

He got into his car and looked around to see if anyone was watching. He didn't notice anyone.

As he pulled out of the parking lot, he rolled down the window, took a whiff of the exhaust fumes on 163rd Street, and rolled it back up. Traffic was starting to pick up, and it was noisy. He wanted to drive without any noise or chemical pollution. He had things to think about.

Next stop - the bank. He always mentally cringed when he went to the Bank of America. Sometimes he got great service and other times it was appalling. He remembered one time when he had to get something notarized. The notary sat across from him in the office while the phone rang off the hook. She ignored it. After about 10 rings, he asked, "Aren't you going to answer it?" Her reply was, "No, we've decided we're not going to answer the phones today. We're short staffed."

He arrived a few minutes later. He walked in, started to sign in and, before he could finish, heard a young, female voice over his shoulder. "May I help you?" He turned around to see a 20-something blonde woman with a Russian accent.

"Yes, I'd like to put something in my safe deposit box."

"Have a seat. I'll get the key." As she walked away, he noticed a pleasant fragrance emanating from her direction. The scent intensified as she took him into the enclosed safe deposit box area. He went into the private room the bank provided, put the last envelope in the box and left. As he placed it in the box, he wrote "To be opened in the event of my death" on the front.

In the early afternoon he went to the gym to work the weight machines and practice his second-degree black belt form. As he finished, he decided to pay Wellington a visit. Part of him wanted to confront Wellington, but he decided against it. He was a dangerous man. It would be best not to tip his hand or let

Wellington know he knew he had lied about the parking lot incident.

31

Saul Steinman taught political science at Florida International University. He had achieved a small amount of fame in Miami because of his outspoken views on economic and political issues. The fact that he knew almost nothing about economics didn't stop the local television and newspaper reporters from asking his opinion on a wide range of issues. One of the main reasons they contacted him was because he always made himself available for interviews, and he was articulate. He took the World's Smallest Political Quiz on the Internet and found, to no one's surprise, that he placed solidly in the left liberal quadrant. He generally supported freedom of choice in personal matters but wanted government to regulate the socks off of business, both large and small. He liked the idea of confiscating the wealth of those who had earned it and giving it to those who had not.

He was a Jew, of sorts, but he was also an atheist. That's the thing about being a Jew. You could also be an atheist, if you liked. Catholics didn't have that option. Catholics could only be Catholics, but Jews could also be atheists, as long as their mother was a Jew. He usually kept kosher because of pressure from his wife, but developed a liking for bacon, lettuce and tomato sandwiches while serving in the army. He hadn't gone to temple more than a dozen times since his bar mitzvah.

He was a strong supporter of Israel and didn't have anything nice to say about Muslims, as a group, although he did have a sexual relationship with a Muslim girl for a few weeks while a graduate student in London. That experience wasn't enough to get him to change his mind about Muslims, although it did make him more sensitive to some of the human rights abuses the Israelis had perpetrated on the Palestinians. His Palestinian sleeping companion moved to London because the Israelis had confiscated her parents' home in Jerusalem. She had an uncle in London who took in her family until her father could find a job.

***

"Saul," the dean said as she walked into his office. "I got another complaint about you. It's about that interview you gave to Channel 7 yesterday."

Steinman stopped typing. As usual, Dean Joy Maximilien-Thomas didn't exude much joy. Her frown, however, had worn lines between and outward from her eyes. The sound of her voice grated on his ears. Her one redeeming feature was that she smelled nice. She wore far too much perfume, and left a trail behind her that lingered for hours, much like a skunk on a country road.

"What did they say?"

"I just got a call from some guy who wouldn't identify himself. He sounded like a redneck. He said that if you like Mexicans so much, perhaps you should move to Mexico. He doesn't want them in this country, and he definitely doesn't want to pay for their health care or the education of their children."

"Humph. Sounds like a Christian, probably a Baptist—always compassionate for the poor and downtrodden."

"Saul, it's the fourth complaint I've had about you in the last month. I realize you have a right to express your opinions, but you should try to ..."

"Be more diplomatic?"

"Yes, exactly. It's annoying getting these complaints. I have better things to do than come in here and have these discussions with you."

"Then don't have these discussions. You said it. I have a right to express my opinions, and I will continue to do it. Get used to it."

The nice thing about being a tenured professor was that you could tell the dean to go to hell and there wasn't much they could do about it. Unless you were caught screwing a student during class, you had a guaranteed job for life, and even then you might not get fired. A male professor who nailed a male student might merely be placed on probation and given a slap on the wrist. The administration would try to ignore it if a female professor was having an affair with a female student, even though doing so might expose the university to a sexual harassment lawsuit. It's not politically correct to challenge homosexual relationships.

The dean walked out in a huff. Steinman checked out her fat ass as she left.

32

Tomás Gutierrez was about 5' 10" tall. He had black hair and black eyes, and light brown skin. He served in the U.S. army in Afghanistan and Iraq. His parents, who fled Cuba shortly after Castro took over, were very proud of him. They didn't know what he did when he was in the army. They assumed he just worked with computers. They didn't know that one of the things he did while in Iraq was destroy evidence of a drone attack that killed 43 people who were attending a wedding party, including the video the drone recorded of the attack. Now he worked as a systems analyst at Carnival Cruise Lines.

His employee badge gave him practically unlimited access to the Ports of Miami and Fort Lauderdale. His skill as a systems analyst and his familiarity with the ports allowed him to gain access to a vast quantity of confidential data, which included passenger lists and ship movements. John Wellington had recruited him to work as a freelance asset for the CIA because of his position, access, and computer skills. At times he had been able to assist the FBI and CIA in drug busts that took place at one of the ports, without his employer's knowledge.

His ongoing assignment, when he could find time for it, was to plant viruses on the web sites of groups that criticized U.S. foreign or domestic policy. Since there were so many web sites to choose from, Wellington told him to focus his attention on the groups and web sites that gave the most aid and comfort to the enemy.

He usually had the authority to choose his own web sites, although Wellington occasionally made special requests. He also had a list of web sites and groups he was not allowed to infect. He gave Wellington a monthly report listing the sites he had infected. Occasionally he found one that he wasn't able to infiltrate. When that happened, he reported it to Wellington, who passed along the information to someone at the CIA headquarters in Langley, Virginia, where he had taken an intensive, one-on-one specialized course that gave him the skills he now had.

Usually he didn't infect *YouTube* sites while at work because most of them had audio, which would draw attention to what he was doing. He did it at home when his wife, Teresa, and his son, Julio, weren't around. That limited the amount of time he could devote to this ongoing project.

Last weekend he found a few *YouTube* videos that recorded TSA airport frisks of small children and a woman who'd had a double mastectomy. The quality of the videos wasn't good because they'd been recorded on cell phones, but they were good enough to enrage anyone who viewed them. He was able to infect all of them.

Viewers with good antivirus software wouldn't catch the virus. They'd merely be blocked out, but that was the purpose of infecting the videos, to prevent people from viewing them. And the people who did not have good antivirus software? Well, that would give them a wake-up call to get some.

"Tomás, are you looking at *YouTube* videos again? You know that Hank doesn't like us surfing the Net at work."

Jennifer Dawes, one of his coworkers, caught him in the act, although she didn't know that he was actually surfing to find his next target. Hank was their boss.

"I was just bored and had to take a break from debugging this new software Hank bought." He got up from his desk to refill his cup of coffee. He put a packet of hazelnut powder in the cup to enhance its taste and smell.

She smiled and looked him in the eyes as he returned to his desk. "Well, I suppose I won't report you this time."

She also surfed the Net at times. They used to joke about some of the things they found in cyberspace. He liked it when she stopped by to chat. She had a nice set of lips and teeth. She had good definition on her calves, too, which she got from playing tennis two or three times a week.

The time Tomás spent in Afghanistan and Iraq inspired his intense dislike for Arabs and Muslims. He took out his pent-up frustration by infecting web sites that had anything nice to say about Islam, although that wasn't part of his assignment. He didn't tell Wellington about it and didn't include those web sites in his monthly report, because he surmised Wellington probably wouldn't approve. He also suspected that some of those web sites were sponsored by the CIA and were being used to entrap potential enemies of America. After Jennifer returned to her desk he booted up another *YouTube* video.

33

Paige had started his workout with some warm-up exercises, then did circuit training, with extra work on his shoulders. His physical therapist had suggested extra shoulder work to strengthen his right rotator cuff, which he'd injured in a karate tournament a few years ago. He finished off by practicing the second degree black belt form, which consisted of more than eighty movements. He went through it twice, to build muscle memory, then hit the showers.

He was hungry and dehydrated after the workout, so he walked to the Starbucks on Collins Avenue and ordered a tuna croissant. He took it to an outside table, sat down, reached into his gym bag and pulled out a chocolate high-protein drink. It was tasty, even though it wasn't chilled.

The hedges between the tables and the street cut down on the traffic noise. The pollution from the exhaust fumes wasn't too bad at that time of day, mid-afternoon. It would get worse in about an hour.

After he finished, he took a look at his watch. 3:45. It would take 45-60 minutes to drive from Sunny Isles Beach to downtown Miami, so if he wanted to see Wellington before he left for the day, he had better get started. He still hadn't figured out how he would open the conversation, or what he would say, but he felt confident that the words would come after he showed up unexpectedly at Wellington's office and looked him in the eyes.

34

George Heverly stepped into Ed Morris's office. "Ready to go?"

"Yeah, let's go." Morris reached over to the right, picked up his cane, winced in pain as he got out of his chair, and started moving toward the door.

"You know, I've gained four pounds since I started using this cane?"

"Really? Why's that?"

"I've been eating more and exercising less. I've been sitting instead of walking. I'm not burning off the calories."

Heverly didn't know what to say, so he said nothing. Their walk down the hall to the parking garage was slow and silent. Morris had to hobble, and Heverly had to walk slowly to prevent getting ahead of him. As they walked into the garage, Morris pulled out his keys. "Let's take my car. That way I won't have to try to climb up into your van."

They both became immersed in their own thoughts on the drive to Wellington's office, with only occasional breaks in the silence. They pulled into the parking garage down the street from Wellington's office at 4:17. Heverly found a space, parked, and took out his cell phone to call Wellington.

"Hi. We're here. We just pulled into the parking garage."

"OK. Meet me in the lobby."

They got out of the car and walked toward the Commerce Department building on Southwest 1st Avenue. They arrived just as Wellington stepped out of the elevator. They waited for him by the front doors. Morris leaned slightly, keeping most of the weight on his good leg.

Wellington couldn't help but be amused, seeing Morris balancing on one leg and Heverly with a black eye and a splint on his broken nose.

"You guys look pathetic. You can't even beat up an accounting professor."

"Yeah, but he's no ordinary accounting professor."

Wellington smirked. "Yeah. I forgot to tell you he competes in karate tournaments. Sorry about that."

He motioned toward the front doors. "Let's go to my other office."

They knew what he meant. They walked through the doors, turned left, walked a few feet, and then turned left again, into the alley between the Commerce Department building and the one next to it. Wellington led the way. He stopped after they were about fifty feet into the alley. He turned around, ran his fingers through his longish, dark blond hair, and adjusted his round-rimmed glasses.

He tapped Morris's cane with the side of his leather loafer. "I suppose I should chew you guys out again, but it looks like you've suffered enough."

Wellington turned to Heverly and looked him directly in the eyes. "George, I don't know how Paige got your name and address, but it doesn't matter. What we have to do now is damage control. Killing him is out, for now, at least. We've got to calm him down so he doesn't expend any more energy digging into places where we don't want him to dig."

They nodded in agreement. Heverly started to speak. "I think what we've got to do is …"

"Shut up! You guys aren't paid to think. You're paid to do what I tell you to do." Wellington was getting animated. His pasty white face started to turn red. He looked Heverly directly in the eyes and stabbed his finger at him. "You're going to keep an eye on Paige, and you're going to be so good at it that he doesn't notice it. Got it?"

"Yeah, I got it."

35

Paige's otherwise pleasant drive to downtown Miami kept getting interrupted by thoughts of Sveta, who was in danger because of his investigation of Raul's murder. Should he just drop it? The meeting he was about to have with Wellington could stir things up even more. There was a reason Wellington lied about the evidence from the university parking lot confrontation with Heverly and that other guy. How was Wellington involved with Raul's murder?

Paige rolled down the front window and let the breeze flow over his face. It provided a distraction. He arrived at the parking garage and looked at his watch. Four twenty-two. Wellington would still be in his office. He seldom left before five, even if he had nothing to do. He had to lead by example.

The pungent smell of hot churros assaulted his nostrils as he exited the parking garage and headed toward Wellington's office. As he walked by the alley separating the Commerce Department building from the one next to it—Wellington's other office—he turned his head instinctively to check it out. The two of them had held numerous meetings there over the years.

He was startled to see Wellington, jabbing his finger at a man who looked like Heverly, with a bandage on his nose. He focused to get a better look. It *was* Heverly. There was a man standing next to him. Tall. Heavy-set. Leaning on a cane. Probably the other assailant he encountered in the university parking lot.

He felt the urge to get out of sight before they could spot him. He scurried to the side of the building and tried to listen in on the conversation. The street noise blocked out most of it. He could only hear a few words here and there – "slut ... better things to do ... Paige." He perked up at the sound of his name. He had heard enough. He had to get out of there. But he wanted to stay close by to observe what would happen next.

He looked around and noticed a variety store down the street, in the direction of the parking garage. He walked toward it, thinking about what to do next. He ducked in and looked around for the stationery section. When he spotted the sign, he walked over, selected the cheapest notebook he could find and a packet of pens. Then he walked toward the cash register located by the front door. The guy behind the counter looked Indian, or maybe Pakistani. Or Bangladeshi. Paige couldn't tell the difference by looking.

The candy counter was right by the cash register. He spotted a Hershey's milk chocolate bar with almonds and placed it on the counter, along with the notebook and pens. Good Pennsylvania chocolate, like the kind he used to eat as a kid.

He paid for his purchases, then walked toward the front door but didn't open it. He looked out the window toward the alley, took the chocolate out of the bag, opened it and began to nibble, while keeping his eyes focused on the alley across the street.

A few minutes later, he saw Wellington, Heverly and the man with the cane emerge from the alley. Wellington turned toward his office. The two men turned in Paige's direction and walked toward the parking garage. After they entered the garage, Paige exited the store and walked across the street, toward the garage. He gave them about 30 seconds, hopefully enough time to get out of sight.

Paige entered the garage and found a pillar close to the exit. It provided a good vantage point to watch the cars as they stopped to pay while keeping out of sight. The garage had just one exit, so they would have to stop at one of the two cashier stations that were now just a few feet away.

A few cars stopped to pay before exiting. Heverly sat in the passenger seat of one of them. There were two cars ahead of them in line, which gave Paige time to jot down the license number. He took out his cell phone and snapped a few photos of the car. After the injured man and Heverly drove off, he walked toward the elevator to get to his car on the second floor.

He thought about what to do with the new information. He couldn't take it to Wellington. All he knew was that Wellington had something to do with his attempted mugging, which explained why Wellington lied about the evidence Paige had given him.

How deeply was Wellington involved in Raul's murder? Had he ordered the hit, or merely been involved indirectly? Was he part of the hit team? That was unlikely. Wellington was more of a coordinator than participant, although, from conversations the two of them had had over the years, Paige was convinced that Wellington was capable to pulling the trigger.

The more Paige thought, the more questions he had. Was Wellington behind the Nathan Shipkovitz and Martin Kaplan assassinations? If so, could Saul Steinman be next? Wellington had assured him Steinman wouldn't be hit, but if Wellington lied to him once, he could very easily lie again. Steinman was the same kind of professor as the two who had been assassinated. They all were vocal in their opposition to some federal government activity.

As soon as he got home, he booted up his laptop and went to the same web site he'd used to obtain Heverly's information. He typed in the license plate. Up popped the name. Edward Morris, age thirty-seven, and an address on Southwest 22nd Street. There would be no need to go to *Facebook* to look for photos. He had the information he needed.

36

James Young stopped by one of the several law firms within walking distance of his office during his lunch hour. He had tried to find an attorney twice before but had been unsuccessful.

"I'm sorry, Mr. Young, I won't be able to help you. If the Department of Homeland Security placed a freeze on your bank accounts, you won't be able to pay me, and I don't work for free. Besides, if I took your case, they might do the same thing to me that they did to you."

"What do you mean?"

"The law allows DHS to confiscate the assets of anyone who provides aid and comfort to the enemy. I read of a few cases where they arrested the attorney who filed an appellate brief on behalf of someone who was accused of being a terrorist."

"But what about the right to counsel? And the right to a fair trial? And the right not to have property seized without a warrant and due process?"

"Those protections don't apply to people the government labels as terrorists. Look, Mr. Young, I'd really like to help you, but if I did, they might arrest me or confiscate my property, or both. They could shut down my office."

The other two attorneys he contacted told him basically the same thing. He was on his own.

"OK. Thank you for your time."

"I'm sorry I can't help you."

37

Paige sat in his university office, killing time before his Tuesday class. He usually didn't teach in Miami in the summer. He preferred to teach at a school in Asia, Europe, or Latin America, but the places where he usually taught weren't offering accounting courses this summer, so he'd decided to teach at Saint Frances University and pick up a few extra bucks.

Paige had to make contact with Steinman but didn't look forward to it. He picked up his pen and started to scribble on a pad of paper to postpone the inevitable. He could hear some students making noise in the hallway, so he got up from his desk and walked over to shut his office door.

As he started to close it, he looked into the hall. He saw Acirema and two other students carrying several large boxes of pizza. The smell wafted through the hall. It must be time for the Accounting Club meeting. Attendance usually spiked on the days they had pizza. Acirema generally got one of the highest grades on his exams. She was a diligent student and a hard worker.

Acirema was an unusual name. One day before class he'd asked her how she came to get such a name. She'd explained that it spelled America backwards. Her parents had escaped from Cuba and they'd wanted to give their daughter an American name because they loved their new country. What could be more American than Acirema?

The time had come. He had to make the call. He didn't care for the idea of targeting people just because they exercised their freedom of speech and press in ways the CIA or FBI found offensive. Maybe what Steinman said did provide aid and comfort to the enemy, but that was a small price to pay in order to protect free speech and press. Allowing the government to stifle dissent by discrediting, harassing, or assassinating American citizens was a much larger threat to freedom.

Steinman had office hours from two to four. It was two fifteen. He should be in his office.

Paige hesitated. He thought about backing out of the assignment, but decided against it. If he backed out, Wellington could replace him with someone who didn't have a problem setting up Steinman for extermination.

At least if Paige were the one setting up Steinman there might be an opportunity to do something to prevent killing him.

He made the call. Steinman picked up on the second ring.

"Hello?"

"Hello, Professor Steinman? My name is Robert Paige. I'm an accounting professor at Saint Frances University."

"Hello. What can I do for you?"

"I just called to let you know that I admire your work. I've seen you on television a few times, and I read your *Miami Herald* column."

Actually, Paige did like some of the things Steinman had to say. Steinman, being a far-left liberal, usually started from the wrong premise then proceeded to reach an illogical conclusion, but sometimes he arrived at the correct solution, although for the wrong reason.

For example, he argued that America should pull its troops out of most countries where it had troops, a position Paige agreed with. But Steinman thought we should do it because America was an imperialist nation. Paige thought we should do it because it wasn't in America's best interest to have entangling alliances like NATO, which required the United States to come to the defense of any member nation in the event of attack. Besides, there was nothing in the Constitution that permitted American troops to be stationed in foreign countries, at least when doing so harmed rather than fostered America's legitimate interests. Paige also thought that the massive expenditures needed to keep troops in so many foreign countries dissipated our national wealth and made the country weaker, which was not in America's best interest.

"I'm surprised. I thought all accountants were right-wing Republicans."

Paige chuckled. "Most of us are, but a few of us have seen the light." Paige winced a little as he said it. But he had to pretend he was on the same page as Steinman.

Actually, he didn't feel uncomfortable being labeled a right winger since his views on economic issues were similar to those of many right wingers, although he differed with them on some social issues. When he'd taken the *World's Smallest Political Quiz* online, his score had placed him solidly in the libertarian quadrant, which meant he agreed with liberals on some social issues and with conservatives on some economic issues.

Paige continued. "I was hoping we could have lunch sometime. I'd like to meet you."

"All right. How about next Friday?"

"Yes, that would be fine."

"Do you know where to find me? My office is on the fourth floor of the School of International and Public Affairs building."

"I'll find it. How does noon sound?"

"Noon is good. See you then."

Paige hung up and let out a sigh, relieved that the call was over, but apprehensive about what he was getting into. He never felt comfortable working for the CIA, even though it was part-time and sporadic. His training as a CPA ingrained in him the view that he should never lie or mislead. Whenever he received a CIA assignment, it seemed like that was all he was doing.

He started to think about his options.

38

"I'm sorry, Jim. I really am, but we have to let you go."

Tom Campbell and James Young had been friends for years. Tom knew what Jim had been going through ever since the incident at the airport two weeks ago. The Department of Homeland Security had just returned their computers and files, after holding on to them for two weeks.

"You know the problems we've had since the Department of Homeland Security confiscated our computers and files. You can't run a business without them. We lost a lot of business that we're not going to get back. We can't take the risk of keeping you on the payroll. If they come back again and confiscate our computers, we're out of business. You're putting all of us at risk."

Jim didn't want to look Tom in the eyes, so he looked at the floor. "OK. I understand."

Tom placed his hand on Jim's shoulder. "Jim, I really feel terrible about this, not only for you, but also because I don't like the direction this country is moving in. A government that can confiscate property without a warrant and without due process is a government out of control. I know you're not a terrorist. Everybody knows you're not a terrorist. But we have to let you go."

James didn't respond. He just continued to look at the floor. Tom broke the silence.

"Well, Jim, you know there is one little bit of silver lining in this situation."

"What's that?"

"We have exactly fifteen employees. If we let you go and don't replace you, there's a whole shitload of federal regulations we'll no longer have to comply with. A lot of federal regulations only apply to companies with fifteen or more employees. We'll be able to save thousands of dollars in compliance costs."

James smiled and looked up at Tom, who was also smiling. "Well, I'm glad I'm able to help you reduce the federal regulatory burden." They both laughed.

***

Jim left work early and went home to tell Janet. After she heard the news, she put her arms around him and gave him a big hug.

"Oh, Jim, I feel so bad, not so much for us as for you. I know how you must be feeling. All these things are happening to us and it's not your fault. If it wasn't for those TSA agents manhandling your mother we wouldn't be in this mess."

"Don't blame them. They were only doing their job."

"Doing their job? How can you say that? Punching you and kicking you isn't part of their job."

"It was just a misunderstanding."

"Jim, I'm worried. We haven't been able to draw any money out of the bank since they froze our accounts. Lucky for us my boss agreed to cash my paychecks instead of depositing my pay into our bank account, but I'm only working part-time. The company isn't hiring anyone full-time anymore because of the health care costs."

"Yeah, I've thought about that. And who's going to hire me, a sixty-three-year-old guy who's accused of being a terrorist?"

"I know. Let's not tell your mother. She doesn't know what's going on half the time anyway. Her dementia seems to be getting worse. Sometimes she doesn't recognize me."

39

"An elective despotism was not the government we fought for."
Thomas Jefferson

"When exposing a crime is treated as committing a crime, you are ruled by criminals." Anonymous

Paige got in his car. It was Friday, time to meet Professor Steinman. He felt apprehensive. He didn't like the idea of deceiving Steinman and he liked it even less that if he screwed up, Steinman would likely be dead. Too late to back out. If he walked away from the assignment, Wellington would get someone else who wouldn't fail.

Actually, it was an easy assignment in terms of logistics. Find out when and where Steinman's group met. Get the names and affiliations of as many group members as possible. Pass along the information to Wellington. The most difficult part of the assignment would be getting Steinman to invite him to join the group. The rest would be easy.

Gathering information about Steinman's Palestinian activities might prove more difficult, but it wouldn't be dangerous. It's not like trying to get information from the KGB or Nazis or other group that could kill any spies who got in their way. Steinman wasn't a threat. He probably didn't even own a gun. Most liberals didn't.

The drive from Sunny Isles Beach to Florida International University's main campus on Southwest 8th Street took a little less than an hour. Traffic was light and there weren't any accidents on Route 826 to halt traffic. Paige rolled down the windows and let the wind blow across his face.

He was fairly familiar with the Florida International University campus. He'd been there a few times before, once for a job interview. He didn't get the job because he published in the wrong journals. The FIU business school preferred hiring professors who published in the accounting journals that *real* accountants don't read. Manuscripts that had practical value in the real world got rejected by those journals. It was a joke among practitioners that professors who published in those esoteric journals got awards for trying to estimate the number of accountants who could dance on the head of a pin rather than for trying to solve real accounting problems.

Saint Frances University wasn't like that. They were pleased if their professors published in any journal. They didn't pay as well as FIU, but their professors didn't feel the pressure to publish or perish, which gave them more time to focus on their teaching.

Paige arrived fifteen minutes early, but it took twelve minutes to find a parking space. It was a pleasant walk from the parking garage to the Political Science Department. He arrived at Steinman's office a few minutes late.

The door was open. He peeked in and saw a man who appeared to be in his early sixties with thinning gray hair, slightly taller than average but with poor posture. He was walking over to a shelf to replace a book.

"Professor Steinman?"

"Professor Paige, please call me Saul." He walked over to shake Paige's hand. "Have a seat." He motioned to the only guest chair in his office.

"And you can call me Bob." His office smelled of books, old books. It was a smell the next generation of students probably wouldn't experience, as the traditional books made of paper would probably be replaced by e-books. Progress had a price, and losing the opportunity to experience the smell of old books was one of them.

Paige glanced over to the book shelf and noticed the book Steinman had just replaced was by Denise Levertov. She had been a well-known poet with an interesting background. Her father had been a Hasidic Jew who became an Anglican priest in England. Her husband, Mitchell Goodman, had been a major figure in the Vietnam anti-war protests in the 1960s. They had both signed a pledge not to pay taxes to support the war. Their son was a writer and artist who lived on the west coast. Their daughter-in-law was a famous artist in New Jersey.

Steinman's bushy black and gray eyebrows and black plastic glasses gave him an aura of authority and seriousness. The poor posture, probably the result of a back problem, made him appear more human and likeable. What would Steinman say if he knew the CIA probably had him targeted for extermination? Since he had a reputation for being unable to keep his mouth shut, he would probably hold a press conference to announce it to the world.

"So, which of my articles did you find most interesting?"

Steinman had a bit of an ego, like most professors. He'd asked the question out of more than just curiosity. He'd offered it as an opportunity for Paige to compliment him for his brilliant work.

"I don't have any particular favorites. What I like about your columns is your outspokenness. People like you help us keep the First Amendment alive."

"Ah, yes, we must exercise our right of free speech and free press. If we don't, the government will chip away at them until they're gone. The Patriot Act and some of the other laws they passed in the wake of 9/11 are doing exactly that. The government can monitor your telephone calls and emails and get away with it without obtaining a warrant, which makes it difficult for journalists to do their job, since their sources are no longer confidential. Sources of information will dry up quickly. It doesn't matter whether you're a liberal or conservative reporter. Have you heard what Senator Chuck Sherman wants to do?"

"No. What?"

Steinman sat down and adjusted his glasses. "He wants to pass a law that would only exempt *accredited* journalists from federal scrutiny. Everyone else would be subject to arrest and imprisonment if they revealed information that was embarrassing to the president or any member of Congress. And they would be held in contempt if they refused to reveal their sources."

"That's outrageous. Can he get away with that?"

"Actually, he already has. Well, not Senator Sherman, exactly. The federal government started arresting and imprisoning uncooperative journalists during the Bush administration. George W., that is. He and Cheney. They used the national security excuse to do it. The number of arrests has accelerated under the current administration. It doesn't matter if they're Democrats or Republicans. The line between the two parties has become blurred when it comes to free speech issues. It used to be that you could depend on the Democrats to protect free speech and free press from the rabid wing of the Republican Party, but that's no longer the case."

Steinman adjusted himself in his chair and leaned forward. "It violates the Fourth Amendment too, because it gives the federal government too much power to conduct searches and seizures without a proper warrant or judicial oversight. They demand library records to see who's reading what, which has a chilling effect on what people check out of the library. Senator Sherman loves that idea. One of the whistleblowers they arrested revealed evidence that they monitor Amazon dot com book purchases as well, not to mention which Web sites people are viewing. They can look at your medical records and even which movies you watch. They don't even have to label you a terrorist first."

Steinman picked up some papers and placed them on top of the pile on the left side of his cluttered desk. "Do you know that you can go to jail just for giving advice to certain groups to help them file legal petitions?"

"No, I didn't know that."

"Yes, the law states that you're guilty of a crime for providing material support to groups the government decides are terrorist groups. Material support could include whatever the government says it includes. That includes a lawyer who helps them file a legal petition. The Justice Department has argued in court that even filing an amicus brief in support of a group that's on the terrorist list is a crime. Presumably, even the accountant who keeps their books can be charged with a criminal act, which is something I am sure you can appreciate as an accounting professor."

Paige perked up when he heard that. Attacking accountants was something he wasn't aware of.

Steinman leaned back in his chair. "Just being placed on the list can lead to bankruptcy. How can a nonprofit organization raise any funds if the government can arrest anyone who contributes to them and can confiscate all their assets, including their bank account? How are you supposed to pay your mortgage or feed your family?"

"That's a good point. I didn't realize the government could do that."

"Yes, but that's not the end of the story. If you tell a member of the press what they did, or even if you just post it on a website, the government can threaten to arrest you or any journalist who reports the story if they believe that disclosing the information would be beneficial to terrorists. They call it giving aid and comfort to the enemy. It could also tip them off that the government is conducting an investigation that they want to keep secret. Once the word gets out that the government is seizing assets of some organization, all the other organizations engaged in similar activities or that have even loose ties to that organization will have time to hide their assets before the government can seize them as well."

Steinman let out a sigh. "I remember reading a case about a seventy-eight-year-old librarian who refused to recognize the authority of two government agents who came into the library demanding to see certain records about one of their patrons. She was prohibited from telling anyone else in the library about their demand. She told one of her assistants anyway. The government prosecuted both her and her assistant as felons for violating the Patriot Act. The only reason they withdrew their complaint was because the judge hearing the case was about to declare the Patriot Act unconstitutional and they didn't want to have to defend the Act at the appellate level."

As Steinman finished his story, Paige glanced at the bookshelves to his right. He noticed a photo of Steinman with some scruffy looking Arabs. It was an outdoor shot, probably taken somewhere in the Middle East, judging from the bazaar-type booths in the background.

Steinman noticed his interest in the photo. "That was taken in the Arab section of Jerusalem a few years ago."

"I didn't think you hung out with Arabs. They are Arabs, aren't they?"

"Very observant. Yes, they are Arabs, Palestinians, actually. Some Israelis say there's no such thing as Palestinians, so I thought I'd take a photo with them just to prove them wrong."

"For the last few years I've been trying to raise money to help them. Are you familiar with the term *collective punishment*?"

"No, I'm not, but I suppose I could guess what it means from the label."

"I'll save you the trouble of guessing. It's a practice the Israelis have been engaging in for years. When they identify someone they regard as a terrorist, they punish the family as well as the actual terrorist. One of the things they do is destroy their homes. But they're quite humane about it." His lips pursed into a sarcastic smile as he said it. "They have a group of soldiers appear at the front door of the alleged terrorist's home, knock politely, then announce to whoever answers that they have two hours to remove their possessions. Then they push over the house with bulldozers. It usually doesn't take long to do it, since most Palestinian homes are poorly constructed."

"Now that you mention it, I recall seeing something about that practice on television. But I didn't see it on American television. I think I saw it on a hotel TV in Europe or Asia."

"Yes, you're more likely to hear about it in Europe or Asia or the Middle East than you are in America. Amnesty International and the United Nations have condemned the practice of collective punishment. It's against the Geneva Convention. It's considered a war crime. But the Israelis don't care. They just list it as one of their weapons in the fight against terrorism.

"Well, some Israelis do care. A lot of them want the practice to stop. Some of them petitioned Caterpillar to quit selling their bulldozers to the Israeli military because they use them to plow over Palestinian homes and orchards. Caterpillar actually stopped the sales for a while.

"I've gotten in trouble for my views on the Palestinian issue, but I'm not the only Jew who doesn't like what the Israelis are doing to the Palestinians. A lot of other Jews feel the same way, but whenever one of us says anything negative about Israel we're accused of being anti-Semitic. The Israeli lobby goes ballistic whenever anyone accuses Israel of being an Apartheid state."

Paige adjusted himself in his seat. The metal chair was getting uncomfortable. "I suppose I can understand that. I feel the same way when someone calls the United States a racist country. I'm about as pro-American as you can get in most ways, but I don't approve of some of the things the American government has done over the years."

"Yes, I feel the same way about Israel. I am a strong supporter of Israel. I just don't like some of the things they're doing. But let me get back to my story. There are a few other points I want to make."

Paige shifted in his chair again. He was interested in what Steinman had to say, but his butt was getting a little numb from sitting in Steinman's metal chair.

"One way I've been helping the Palestinians is by raising money so that the families of those alleged terrorists won't be homeless. There are three organizations I know of that raise funds for this purpose, but two of them have gone out of business because the

Department of Homeland Security added their names to the terrorist list. As soon as that happens, no one wants to contribute. They were even 501(c) organizations, which means contributions are tax deductible. Anyone who contributes to those organizations can be arrested and put in jail for aiding terrorists, so the contributions have dried up. The last I heard, the organizations and their leaders were being audited by the IRS."

"That seems a little severe, don't you think? I suppose the Vatican could be placed on that list, since it also helps Palestinian refugees."

"Yes, it probably could, but I suspect the Department of Homeland Security wouldn't put the Vatican on the list of terrorist organizations because of the political fallout. They would have 80 million American Catholics upset with them and they would look even more ridiculous than they already do.

"Then there's the whole issue about building Jewish settlements on Palestinian land. Some Israelis say there's no such thing as Palestinian land because God gave the land to the Jews, but whenever I ask to see the deed, no one can produce it. When the president criticized the practice, Debbie Waterstein said he shouldn't interfere in Israeli zoning issues. What a ditz."

Paige smiled at that remark. He hadn't expected Steinman to criticize one of his own, a person whose political philosophy was basically the same as his. He was pleasantly surprised at Steinman's ability to think for himself rather than merely parrot the party line.

The more Steinman said, the more Paige became convinced that he must do all he could not to allow the feds to kill him. Even though Steinman was wrong on many of the issues, he was right on the most important issue, the trashing of the Constitution by the feds.

"Well, enough of my ranting and raving. Let's go to lunch. I'll drive, since I'm familiar with the area. What kind of food are you in the mood for?"

"Since it's Friday, I'd like a meat dish. It's a long story. I'll give you the details at the restaurant."

Steinman smiled at Paige's remark. "I can guess, but I'll let you give me the details. I know just the place."

40

Steinman drove through the arches at the main FIU gate, turned right on Southwest 8th Street, then made a left onto Southwest 107th Avenue. It put them in the Sweetwater section of Miami, one of the relatively poor parts of town. Paige noticed that a lot of the store signs were in Spanish. One of them quoted shoe prices. Paige, being the accountant that he is, calculated that someone earning the minimum wage would only have to work about thirty minutes to buy a pair of shoes in that store. He wondered what they must be made of or how long they'd last.

After a few minutes, Steinman turned right into one of the shopping centers. He turned his head toward Paige as he pulled into a parking space.

"This is a Nicaraguan place — Los Ranchos Restaurant, over there. It's a steak house. I've been here several times, usually as part of a group. The food is pretty good and the prices aren't bad. All the staff speaks Spanish as a first language but they can understand enough English to serve whatever's on the bilingual menu. A few years ago it won the Gourmet Diners Society's Golden Fork Award. The *Miami Herald* said it had the best steak in town, which may or may not be true, since Miami has a lot of good steak restaurants." Paige seemed pleased with the summary, and with Steinman's choice.

Steinman opened the door for Paige. The place smelled of fried meat, much like a Cuban restaurant. As they walked into the main room, Paige noticed a smaller room off to the right. On the walls it had a variety of artsy placards and enlarged versions of newspaper articles that had been written about the restaurant over the years. The white tablecloths gave the main room a nice touch.

One of the waiters led them to a table against the wall and took their drink orders. The menu had a fair selection of dishes, some of which Paige had never heard of. Luckily, the menu also provided brief descriptions in English.

Before the drinks arrived, a second waiter placed two small plates of garlic bread and a tray of condiments on the table. Paige picked up a piece of the bread and sampled it. It was thin, crunchy and tasty. He figured it must be some kind of Nicaraguan or Cuban bread.

Steinman placed the white cloth napkin on his lap. "I'm curious to know your views on the various issues. I don't have many conversations with accountants. I just assume they're all a bunch of knee-jerk right-wingers."

Paige chuckled. Steinman was only half wrong. He'd met some accounting professors over the years who were liberal Democrats. Socialist types tended to gravitate toward universities, perhaps because they didn't like the competition that existed outside the university's protected walls.

Paige took a sip of water and placed the glass on the table. "I suppose it would be fair to say that we agree on some issues and disagree on others." Actually, there was so little truth in that statement that it bordered on being misleading. Paige disagreed with Steinman on practically all the economic issues and on many of the social issues. The one issue they agreed on was their belief that freedom of speech and press, and even freedom of association, were in danger because of the federal government, not to mention freedom from unreasonable search and seizure and the right to a trial by jury, which the government had denied on several occasions.

"I'd like to think of myself as more than just an accounting professor. I have law degrees from Cleveland State University and Manchester Metropolitan University. I also have a PhD in politics from Sunderland University."

"Ah, that is unusual for an accounting professor. Most of the ones I've met are party-line conservatives who are totally uninformed about politics and philosophy. All they know about politics is what they hear on television."

Paige felt a sudden urge to strangle Steinman, but resisted the temptation. "Yes, I've met a few accountants like that." He had met some accountants over the years who fit that description, but he met even more accountants who were usually right on the issues, at least the economic issues, even though they hadn't had much formal training in the field. They applied common sense to the issues rather than Marxist theory.

"Why did you get all those extra degrees that had nothing to do with accounting?"

"I did them as part of my self-improvement program. I have this inner urge to keep busy and be productive. Going to Gannon University for my undergraduate degree is what started me down that path. They forced me to take a lot of liberal arts courses. I became interested and wound up getting minors in political science, philosophy, and history. After I graduated, I wanted to pursue all of those disciplines but didn't have the time. Years later, when my schedule eased up a bit, I decided to pursue them systematically."

"You like history? Me too. Did you ever think about getting a PhD in it?"

"Actually, I do have a PhD in history. Nineteenth century British and American economic history, to be precise. I got it from The Union Institute and University in Cincinnati. I did it as an external student living in New Jersey."

"That's amazing. I'm beginning to think you're crazy."

"You're not the first one I've heard that from."

A waitress came over to take their order. Mid to late forties, medium height. Slender but shapely, with brown skin and medium length black hair that had a few gray strands in it. Attractive for her age. The two features about her that caught Paige's eye were her high cheek bones, which served to emphasize the loveliness of her jet black eyes, and the fact that she had her belt pulled tightly around her waist, which made it appear that she had practically no waist beyond that required to connect the top and bottom portions of her body. Her shoes made noise as she walked. You could hear the click, click, click from thirty feet away.

Paige ordered petite mignonetas, which consisted of two grilled three-ounce beef tip medallions served with sherry wine sauce. Steinman ordered puntas casina—eight ounces of grilled tender tip beef with butter and sautéed onions.

"What are you doing, Saul? That's not kosher."

They both laughed. "I quit being kosher a long time ago, although there's a voice in the back of my head that says, 'Don't eat pork.' I think it's my mother's voice, actually. I don't mind having a little dairy with my meat."

Steinman paused for a moment, as though he was turning to the philosophy channel in his brain. "It's really ridiculous when you analyze it logically. Some guy thousands of years ago wrote in some book that God says you can't eat meat and dairy at the same meal. People just take his word for it and obey without questioning. They instruct their children not to do it either. Modern science tells us it's not any more detrimental to eat meat and dairy than it is to eat just the meat, especially if it's red meat."

Paige recalled some of his Jewish friends who still followed that tradition, and the famous line from the play/movie, *Fiddler on the Roof.* "Yes, it's the tradition."

Steinman looked a little surprised at Paige's comment. "So, you're familiar with Jewish plays?"

"Not all of them. I just happened to see *Fiddler on the Roof* at a time in my life when I was questioning everything. That line hit home."

"Have you stopped questioning?"

Paige was enjoying the conversation. As an accounting professor, he didn't have many opportunities to talk about this subject. Steinman's question caused him to have a flashback to the days when he attended Our Lady of Peace School in Erie, Pennsylvania. Whenever one of the students asked the nun a question about Catholicism that she didn't want to answer, she would say, "To question is to blaspheme." That always ended the conversation, since any student who dared to ask another question was sure to be on the receiving end of corporal punishment, not to mention a note to the parents.

"No, I haven't stopped, but I have slowed down a bit."

Steinman leaned back in his chair and smiled. "It's OK to slow down at our age. It's tiring to question everything, but questions keep the brain lubricated. Let me guess. You're Catholic, right?"

"I used to be Catholic. How did you know?"

"That comment you made about it's Friday and wanting a meat dish was a giveaway."

Although Steinman was an atheist, whose parents were Jewish, he enjoyed studying about religions. He was especially fascinated with Catholicism and Islam.

"When I was going to Catholic schools, the priests and nuns told us that we would go to hell for eating meat on Friday, which naturally led to several questions, like 'Why?' and 'What if we're eating meat and don't remember that it's Friday?'"

"What answer did they give you?" Steinman was curious. "In all my years of studying Catholicism, I never encountered any text that answered those questions."

"The answer to the first question is that it's because God says so. Jesus died on the cross on a Friday, and we should honor that day by not eating meat. That led us to ask, 'Where does it say that?' We knew it wasn't in the Bible, which the nuns discouraged us from reading because they said doing so might confuse us. Their answer was that, after Jesus died, rose from the dead and was about to ascend into heaven to sit at the right hand of his father, he gave the apostles some instructions. When he appointed Peter to be his successor, he gave him the power to forgive sins but also said he didn't have to forgive them if he didn't want to."

"And that's it? That's the justification they gave for going to hell for eating meat on Friday?"

"Yeah, pretty much. We have to extrapolate that Peter and all future popes have the authority directly from God to make new rules and new sins if they think it's appropriate, and that we are never to question their decisions."

"But that Biblical passage doesn't say any of that. I've read the Christian Bible cover to cover. I don't recall reading that."

"That's because it's not there. But we dared not point that out to the nuns, because questioning them would be blasphemy."

"What about the other point you raised … eating meat on Friday because you forgot it's Friday?"

"Ah, that's an easy one to answer. If you forget it's Friday, you're off the hook. Mortal sins are like intentional torts. You have to intend to commit the crime before you can be found guilty. But that's not the end of the story. Another question we asked, as budding little grade school Catholic philosophers, is 'What do you do if you remember it's Friday while you're chewing on a hamburger?' Since it's a sin to waste food, and since it's a sin to swallow a hamburger on Friday, what should you do?"

Steinman leaned forward. "That's a great philosophical dilemma. The level of philosophical discussion Catholic grade school students are exposed to is fascinating. Although the whole premise is bullshit, the reasoning process is somewhat sophisticated for a ten-year-old."

Paige nodded in agreement, then continued. "If you swallow, it's intentional, and therefore a mortal sin. But if you spit it out, you're off the hook. And you should rinse out your mouth and spit again, just to make sure you don't swallow any meat later. One question we never thought to ask is, 'Where does it say in the Bible that it's a sin to waste food?' It's too bad those nuns aren't here now to answer that question. They've probably all died and gone to hell by now."

Steinman smiled. "If I had said that, you'd accuse me of being anti-Catholic, or at least insensitive. But you can get away with it. Having a former Catholic say it makes it a valid topic for philosophical discussion."

Steinman took a sip of water. "That's a fascinating story. Growing up Catholic must have been quite an experience."

"Yes, it was. If you had a few more hours I could give you more details. As I think about it, some of those details are coming back to me."

"Actually, there's another spinoff to that meat-on-Friday story. Another question we asked is, 'Why is it that only Catholics go to hell for eating meat on Friday? Why don't non-Catholics also have to live by that rule?'"

"What was their answer?"

"It's an interesting one, and eminently logical if you buy the underlying premise. It's based on the Biblical passage that says, 'To whom much is given, much is expected.' Since Catholics—actually only Roman Catholics, since there are a few other kinds of Catholics—are the new chosen ones—the Jews used to be the chosen ones but they blew it by not recognizing Jesus as their savior—more is expected of them. One of those extra things is not to eat meat on Friday. Non-Catholics don't have that same burden. They can eat anything they want on Friday. Since they can't get into heaven anyway, it really doesn't matter what they do."

"Non-Catholics can't get into heaven? Does the Catholic church really teach that?"

"It did until they had one of their Vatican Councils. At the Council, the church leaders took a vote. They decided that non-Catholics would henceforth be technically able to get into heaven, although they would have to take the dirt path, while Catholics would be able to take the four-lane highway. I don't know if it was a simple majority vote or if they required a super majority."

"That's fascinating. You mean Catholics actually believe that bullshit?"

"Apparently, they do. Or at least the nuns did. But that's not the end of the story. The logical follow-up question was, 'What about all the non-Catholics who died before the vote? Can they now get into heaven?'"

"How did the nuns respond to that question?"

"They pointed out that the change was prospective only, not retroactive. Any non-Catholic who died before the vote was taken had to stay where they were."

"That's fascinating. I never read any of that stuff."

"I didn't either. You had to be sitting in a Catholic grade school classroom to get that information."

They both laughed and took sips of their drinks, which had just arrived.

"I still haven't explained why I like to eat meat on Friday, but you can probably guess. It's to prove to myself that I'm no longer a Catholic. I have to commit affirmative acts to prove it. Just thinking it isn't enough. In fact, I don't consider Friday to be a success if I haven't had meat."

"I'm sure the nuns would be pleased." Steinman sliced off a piece of tender tip with butter and sautéed onions and put it into his non-kosher mouth. "Bob, you seem like an interesting guy—for a goy, I mean," pointing his fork at him for added emphasis. "I'd like to invite you to a little unofficial gathering I have from time to time with a few friends of mine. We don't have any particular agenda. We just talk about anything that comes into our heads, which usually includes current events and how the government is turning the country into a police state."

Paige smiled. "That sounds like a pleasant topic."

"We haven't scheduled the next get-together yet. I'll let you know. If it's on a Friday, I'll try to remember to serve hamburgers."

"Thanks. And don't forget to put cheese on them."

***

They finished their meals, paid the bill, and headed toward the door.

Paige had enjoyed the lunch and the conversation. It was a success, from a business perspective, because he got himself placed on the list of invitees to Saul's next meeting. He achieved his goal, but he didn't feel happy about it. In fact, it spoiled his otherwise successful Friday. Wellington would be pleased to learn he had infiltrated the group, which probably placed Steinman one step closer to possible extinction.

Paige didn't want Wellington to kill Steinman. In fact, he was now more determined than ever to make sure that didn't happen. The problem was that he couldn't figure out a way to prevent it, unless he did something drastic.

On the way home he thought about his options and came up with an idea that might work, but it was extremely risky.

41

"I'm sorry, sir. I can't sell you that gun. You didn't pass the background check."

James Young was at one of the local gun shops. He'd finished looking at their inventory and decided which gun he wanted to buy. The guy behind the counter had just finished doing the background check required of anyone who wants to purchase a gun.

"Why didn't I pass? Did they give a reason?"

"Yeah. They said you're on a terrorist list."

James looked the dealer in the eyes. He swayed back and forth out of nervousness. "Do I look like a terrorist to you?" He saw his reflection in the mirror. White. Pasty-faced. Swaying back and forth. He didn't look like a terrorist, but he did look mentally unbalanced. He felt that way too. The last few weeks had put a strain on him mentally. Thc walls were closing in on him. He no longer lived in a free country. His own government was making his life miserable.

He had had enough. No more.

"Nah. You don't look like a terrorist to me. It's probably just a mistake. I read that there are a lot of people on the terrorist list who aren't terrorists.

"You might try getting one at a gun show. If you buy from a dealer you'll have to go through a background check, but you don't have to go through a licensed dealer. Some people go to gun shows to sell a gun. If you buy a gun from one of them, there's no background check. Or you could find one on the Internet."

"Thanks. I didn't know that." James hadn't fired a gun in more than forty years. He'd never had much of an interest in them. But that was before. Now it was the number one item on his list of things to buy. "Do you know when the next gun show's going to be? Where do they hold them?"

"You're in luck, my friend. The next one's at the Dade County Fairgrounds this weekend. Saturday and Sunday. It's on Southwest 24th Street. Do you know where it is?"

"Yeah, more or less. Thanks for the information."

42

Paige called Wellington's cell phone, since it was more likely to be secure than his phone at the Commerce Department. "Hi, Bob. Do you have good news for me?"

"Yes. The meeting went well. He invited me to their next get-together, which hasn't been scheduled yet. I'll keep you informed."

Paige felt apprehensive about making the call. Ever since meeting Steinman, he'd been thinking about how to make the mission fail, yet all his overt actions to date had been in the opposite direction – that Steinman probably would be killed, like Shipkovitz and Kaplan, in spite of Wellington's assurances to the contrary.

"That's great. Keep me posted."

***

Wellington was happy he could tell the Boss things were progressing as planned.

He decided to make a courtesy call to Mossad. Since Steinman was a strong and vocal supporter of Israel, he thought he should inform them that one of their supporters was about to meet with an unfortunate accident.

His local contact was Sergei Turetsky, a Russian Jew from Moscow who had moved to Brighton Beach, Brooklyn with his family as a child. During his high school years they lived in the Winston Towers complex in Sunny Isles Beach. A few years after he graduated from college, his mother moved around the corner to a smaller apartment in the Porto Bellagio building, where she still lived.

His main assignment was to make sure Islamic terrorists didn't attack any Jewish targets in Miami, one of the nine cities Al-Qaeda listed as being targeted for a nuclear attack if they could find a way to smuggle the devices across the Mexican border. His cover as a real estate agent gave him the flexibility he needed to move around. Mossad occasionally threw some business his way so he could show some legitimate income at tax time.

"Hello, Sergei? It's John Wellington. How are you?"

"Fine. Just enjoying another fine Miami day." He spoke from an outdoor café in South Beach, admiring the sights as they walked by, often in high heels and short shorts.

"I'd like to meet with you. Are you free around five this afternoon?"

"It sounds important. I have a ton of paperwork, but I think I can sneak away for a few minutes."

"Yeah, right. All that paperwork's from selling houses, I suppose."

"Of course. You know that's all I do."

"How about if we meet at Bayfront Park, by the Anton Cermak plaque?" Less than a mile from Wellington's Commerce Department office on SW 1st Avenue. A convenient walk for Wellington. He didn't care if it was convenient for Sergei.

"The Anton Cermak plaque? Are you trying to tell me something?"

Anton Cermak, former mayor of Chicago, got assassinated in 1933 at the site of the plaque while riding with the newly elected president, FDR. Giuseppe Zangara, an Italian immigrant, took aim at Roosevelt but missed. Historians speculate about what the United States might be like today if Zangara had been a better shot.

"Maybe. I'll let you speculate about it. It will give you something to think about besides shiksas."

"You're a funny goy … I mean guy. I'll see you at five." Sergei hung up, took another taste of his coffee and enjoyed the heat of the Miami sun on his face. But he felt a little worried. He had a feeling that whatever Wellington had planned would complicate his life.

Wellington arrived first. Turetsky arrived a few minutes later. Tall, just under six feet, slender and athletic looking, with short black hair, in his early thirties, he had a five o'clock shadow, which seemed appropriate because it was five o'clock. Wellington could hear the sound of traffic in the distance and smell the hot dogs and sausages being cooked by a vendor fifty feet away.

"Hi, Sergei." Wellington extended his hand.

"Hi, John. What's so urgent? Is something about to happen?"

Wellington looked serious. Turetsky sensed that he didn't want to hear what was about to come out of his mouth.

"I don't know quite when it will happen, but yes, something is about to happen. Do you know who Saul Steinman is?"

Turetsky's face lit up. "Of course. He's on television practically every week. Do you have something unfortunate planned for him?"

"Actually, we do. He's going to meet an untimely demise. We thought we should let you know, out of courtesy. It's not something that is negotiable." Wellington looked into Turetsky's eyes, checking his response.

"What did he do? Why are you targeting him?" He looked concerned, like they were about to kill a friend.

"The Company thinks he's a national security risk. That's all I can say."

Turetsky became animated. "A national security risk? He's a fucking professor!"

"Yeah, he's a professor on the surface, but he's also a national security risk."

In their own minds, Wellington and his Boss considered anyone who criticized the government's war on terror to be a national security risk. The fact that Steinman also tried to provide housing for the families the Israelis had made homeless as a result of their collective punishment policy merely bumped Steinman to the top of the list.

"You know my people won't like this. He's an outspoken supporter of Israel, although he's also a little quirky at times. We don't like our supporters getting silenced, especially by the American government." Actually, Turetsky had mixed feelings about Steinman. He was aware of his humanitarian work with the Palestinians, and while he didn't exactly approve of that work, he wasn't too strongly against it either.

"Yes, I know. It's unfortunate, but it's in Israel's best interest too. I'm not at liberty to tell you anything more."

"If it's in Israel's best interest, too, you had *better* give me more details. You know my superiors are going to ask. What am I supposed to tell them? They won't just let this slide."

After hearing that comment, Wellington regretted making the courtesy call. If they had just killed him without telling Mossad, they would hear the news at the same time as everyone else, be sad for a day or two, then move on to more pressing matters. They would never suspect the CIA, since the CIA doesn't kill Americans, or at least it didn't until recently. Recent laws and executive branch decisions now allowed the assassination of Americans on American soil without a trial or any kind of due process. It was one of the things Steinman ranted and raved about, because it pulled America further down the path toward totalitarianism.

"You'll have to trust me on this, Sergei. I'm really not at liberty to say anything else. If it makes it any easier, you can just forget we had this conversation. Your superiors don't have to know."

Unknown to Wellington, Turetsky was wearing a wire. The whole conversation had been recorded in a van a few hundred feet away. Sergei began to regret he told Mossad about their meeting.

"You know I can't do that, John. I have to report it. Maybe they'll just accept it, although I doubt it. How did you find out he's a national security risk?"

"We have a mole planted in his little discussion circle." Actually, the mole was Paige, and Paige didn't become a part of Steinman's circle until earlier that day. At this point he hadn't attended a single meeting. The Boss had decided that Steinman needed to be eliminated based solely on his television appearances, writing, and fund-raising for Palestinian refugees.

Sergei sighed. "OK." He pretended to accept the bad news. "Thank you for letting us know."

***

But he didn't just accept the news. As he walked away, he started thinking about how to make the plan fail. The problem was that he didn't know when or where it would happen. He decided to plant a mole of his own, although he didn't know if it might already be too late.

43

"Aaron, it's Sergei. I've got to talk to you." Sergei called Aaron Gelman, his boss at Mossad. Gelman's family came to New York from Belgium after World War II. They moved to Miami in the 1950s. Aaron was the product of a mixed marriage. His mother was an Orthodox Jew. His father was a Reform Jew.

"So talk, already."

"It has to be in person."

"Can't it wait?" Aaron looked at his watch. He wanted to go home.

"I suppose it can wait until Monday, but it will only take five minutes, maybe three. Are you in the office?"

"Yes, but I'm getting ready to leave."

"I can be there in ten minutes."

"OK, but hurry. Shona is expecting me home for dinner."

"OK. I'll be right there."

Sergei got in the van and instructed the driver to take him to Gelman's office, one of the tall, glass buildings in the Brickell section.

He arrived fourteen minutes later, took a seat, and related the details of the planned Steinman hit. Gelman fidgeted while Sergei spoke. His mind was on getting home to Shona before the sun went down. It would be Shabbos in a few hours. Sergei's story was complicating his life.

At the conclusion of the presentation, Gelman sat silently, clasping his hands together, his two index fingers together placed under his nose with his thumbs under his chin. "OK. We have three options. One, we can do nothing, in which case Steinman is dead. Two, we can kill the CIA guys who are planning this hit, in which case the shit will hit the fan. First of all, we don't know when it's going to happen or who's going to do it, so that option is out. Besides, if something goes wrong, my boss's boss will personally cut my balls off, and yours too. Three, we can do something else, but I don't know what."

Sergei shifted in his chair. "I like the third option."

"Me too. We don't know how much time we have, so we have to get started. Wellington said they have a mole. We need to have a mole of our own to track Steinman's activities, especially those meetings. Maybe we can use this opportunity to learn something about his funneling money to the Palestinian terrorists."

"How about Rachel Karshenboym? She's a sociology professor at Miami Dade College. She would fit right in with his group. I've worked with her before. Her family came from Saint Petersburg, with stops in Tel Aviv and New York. She received some weapons training while in the Israeli army."

"But she's a woman. Does he have any women in his group?"

"I have no idea."

"We have to try. Steinman likes women. I don't think he would be able to say no."

"Yeah, probably not. I'll contact her and brief her."

"OK. Keep me informed."

"Of course."

***

As they descended together on the elevator, Sergei had second thoughts about his choice of Rachel Karshenboym as a mole. She couldn't be controlled the way he liked to control his people. She had a mind of her own. He began to think he had made a mistake.

44

James Young arrived at the Dade County Fairgrounds at 10 a.m. The gun show had just started. Floridians liked gun shows. They treated them like a family event.

Two representatives from *Oathkeepers.org* had set up shop close to the entrance and distributed their literature. James walked over to have a look.

"Hello, sir. How ya doin' this fine morning?" He extended his hand to James and looked him in the eyes as he said it. He looked intimidating. Short. Shaved head. Tattoos. Scrawny. Wearing a T-shirt with a bunch of writing on it. The other guy wore a spiffy police uniform. Tall. Tanned. Muscular. They presented a stark visual contrast.

James shook his hand. He was afraid not to.

"Here. Please take our brochure. It will give you some information about our organization.

The scrawny one pointed to his shirt. "We're called the Oathkeepers. Our membership includes current and former police, military, and other first responders who've taken an oath to uphold and defend the Constitution against all enemies, foreign and domestic. But unlike the politicians in Washington, we take our oath seriously. We refuse to obey unconstitutional orders, like disarming the American people, conducting warrantless searches, or detaining Americans as enemy combatants in violation of their right to a jury trial."

James perked up when he heard that. He smiled. "I didn't know that guys like you existed."

He smiled. "Yes sir, we do. There are a lot of us, but we could always use a few more. Please consider becoming a member. Our brochure tells you how to join."

"Thank you." He took the brochure, then glanced at the guy's T-shirt. There were so many words on it that they had to be in small print in order to all fit.

He noticed that James was trying to read it. "This is our statement of principles." He stood up straight and gave James a chance to read it.

1. We will NOT obey orders to disarm the American people.
2. We will NOT obey orders to conduct warrantless searches of the American people.
3. We will NOT obey orders to detain American citizens as "unlawful enemy combatants" or to subject them to military tribunal.
4. We will NOT obey orders to impose martial law or a "state of emergency" on a state.
5. We will NOT obey orders to invade and subjugate any state that asserts its sovereignty.
6. We will NOT obey any order to blockade American cities, thus turning them into giant concentration camps.
7. We will NOT obey any order to force American citizens into any form of detention camps under any pretext.
8. We will NOT obey orders to assist or support the use of any foreign troops on U.S. soil against the American people to "keep the peace" or to "maintain control."

9. We will NOT obey any orders to confiscate the property of the American people, including food and other essential supplies.
10. We will NOT obey any orders which infringe on the right of the people to free speech, to peaceably assemble, and to petition their government for a redress of grievances.

It took him a while to read all 10 of them.

"Well, sir. You have a nice day. Please consider joining."

"Thank you. I will."

James walked over to the ticket booth, bought a ticket, and entered the building. He felt empowered. This was still *his* country. The politicians and bureaucrats hadn't taken it from him. Not yet, anyway.

He looked around to get his bearings. It was one large room, lined with rows of tables. Each table displayed something different. Some had pistols. Others had rifles or shotguns. A large red, white, and blue sign in the corner said AMMUNITION.

The guy at the gun shop told him to stay away from the licensed dealers. Look around for private individuals who were trying to sell guns. That way he wouldn't have to go through a background check.

They would probably be carrying a bag to conceal the gun, or it would be in a sheath if it were a rifle or shotgun. He wanted a pistol. Something that would be easy to carry and conceal. An automatic, with a large clip.

He saw a few people who fit the description. One of them had just approached a middle-aged man standing at a table that displayed a variety of semi-automatic pistols. He opened his bag and the man took a peek inside, then shook his head. Apparently not interested. The guy with the bag started to walk away.

James followed him. The guy walked fairly fast. Jim stepped up his pace. After a few seconds, he got close enough to make contact.

"Excuse me. Are you selling something?"

The guy turned around when he heard Jim's voice. He appeared to be in his fifties, slightly overweight with thinning gray hair.

"Yes. Would you like to take a look?" He opened a bag large enough to hold several weapons.

Jim looked inside. Two revolvers and one large semi-automatic pistol.

"How much for the semi-automatic?"

"I can give you a good deal on it. Three hundred and fifty, and I'll throw in an extra clip." He took it out of the bag and handed it to Jim. "It's an MPA 10SST. Holds thirty rounds, plus one in the chamber, .45 ACP."

Jim didn't understand half of what the guy just said. It was heavier than what he wanted, but it would fit his purpose.

"OK. I'll take it." A seasoned gun buyer would have counter offered. Anybody who sells guns at a gun show is willing to take less than the initial asking price, but Jim didn't know that. And he didn't care. He just wanted to buy something and get out of there. He reached into his pocket and took out a wad of cash. It was from the stash Janet had been able to save from her part-time job. She didn't know he'd taken it. She wouldn't approve. She didn't like guns, and they needed the money for food.

The guy took the cash and extended his hand. "Thank you. Nice doing business with you."

Jim turned and walked away. He had to carry it in plain sight since he didn't have a bag to put it in, but that wasn't a problem. He wasn't breaking any laws carrying a gun around at a gun show.

It would have been a problem if he'd tried to do that in a shopping mall.

Next stop, the ammunition table. Actually, he had several to select from. He chose the one with the big red, white, and blue sign, even though it wasn't the closest one. He liked red, white, and blue.

He stepped up to the table. Before he could open his mouth, the twentyish, good-looking woman standing behind the table said, "Hello, sir. What can I get for you today?"

He didn't know how to respond. The table had stacks of more than a dozen kinds of ammo. Some in boxes. Some in bags. He saw more large boxes and bags sitting on the floor behind her. Enough firepower to take over a village, or even a small town, if used properly. He didn't know what kind of ammo his new gun took.

He lifted up the gun so she could see it. "I just bought this gun. I need ammunition for it."

She took it from him and turned it around in her hands, almost fondling it. "This is a fine weapon. You can shoot a lot of home invaders with this one. What kind of ammo would you like?"

"I don't know. What do you recommend?"

"That depends." She picked up a box. "This one's good for target practice, but if you use it to shoot a home invader, it'll go right through him, through the wall, and into the next room, and maybe the neighbor's house. You shouldn't use these except for target practice."

She picked up another box. "These are hollow points. They're more expensive, but they're the only thing you should be using for home defense. They hit and splatter. They don't come out the other side, or if they do, they leave an exit hole the size of a baseball, since their energy's already spent by the time they exit.

You don't have to worry about them going through the wall and hitting a loved one."

"I'll take the hollow points."

"How many would you like?"

"I'll take a hundred."

"If you want a hundred, I can sell you a bag of them. They're cheaper by the bag." She reached to her right and picked up a bag. "Here you go, 100 .45 caliber ACP."

"Thank you." He reached into his pocket, pulled out his slightly depleted wad of cash, and paid.

"Thank you, sir. Here's our card. Stop by and see us when you run out."

"Thank you. I'll do that."

He turned and walked toward the exit door. He had all he needed.

45

"If liberty means anything at all, it means the right to tell people what they do not want to hear."
George Orwell

Wellington turned toward the group. "Can you suggest anyone else to add to our list?"

John Wellington, Santos Hernandez, Jim Bennett, and Tomás Gutierrez relaxed in Santos's family room, chatting over beers. The wife and kids weren't home.

Gutierrez answered first. "I don't think we should be killing professors and journalists. All they're doing is exercising their First Amendment rights of free speech and free press. I didn't go to Afghanistan to protect American freedom so I could see it taken away in my own country."

Wellington looked downright startled at his response.

Before he could say anything, Santos Hernandez chimed in. "Tomás, you can't believe that!? What they say is giving aid and comfort to the enemy. That's the definition of treason. They're traitors. We have to execute them before they can do any more damage to our country." He spoke with a thicker than usual Cuban accent. It came to the surface when he got emotional.

Bennett added his two cents' worth. "Santos is right. We can't let the likes of Shipkovitz, Kaplan, and Steinman continue to give aid and comfort to the enemy. They're either with us or against us, and they've chosen to be against us."

Tomás began to squirm in his seat. He started to think he shouldn't have expressed his opinion. He tried to backpedal in order to get off the hot seat. Maybe a further explanation would do that. "I'm not saying that they aren't giving aid and comfort to the enemy. All I'm saying is that we shouldn't execute people who are merely exercising their Constitutional rights. We should be targeting people who do overt acts to destroy our country. I …"

Santos interrupted him. "But I thought we all agreed that professors and journalists should be included in our list because they're giving aid and comfort to the enemy?"

"I've changed my mind on that. I don't think we should be targeting them."

Wellington, Hernandez, and Bennett looked at each other in disbelief, not knowing what to say.

Wellington tried to smooth it over. "OK, let's do this. We won't add any journalists or professors to the list. We'll just target those idiots in Washington who are destroying the country with their excessive spending, high taxes, overregulation, and welfare programs. And maybe some of the bureaucrats who enforce the rules they make."

Bennett turned toward Wellington. "But what about Steinman? What should we do with him? He's already on the list."

"We'll keep him on the list, but we won't kill him just yet. Let's see what Paige can find out about what Steinman's up to and how he plans to continue his humanitarian aid to the Palestinians."

Gutierrez looked at Wellington, who could feel his piercing stare. That stare always made him uncomfortable. A piercing stare from a regular person is one thing. A piercing stare from an assassin is something else, even if it's a friendly assassin. Wellington thought the lie would pacify him, at least for the moment. He realized it was a short term solution, and that he would have to confront Tomás's opposition at some point.

Tomás continued. "I don't think we should include whistleblowers on the list either."

They all straightened up on hearing that remark. Santos put his beer on the table and started waiving his hands. "What do you mean, we shouldn't have whistleblowers on the list!? Those fuckers are giving more aid and comfort to the enemy than professors and journalists! They're exposing our tactics. They alert the terrorists that they need to change the way they do business. It makes it harder for us to get them."

Tomás tried to justify his position. "Those guys are exposing corruption in the government. If government officials are violating the Constitution, the people have a right to know. They're helping to make the country stronger by rooting out corruption. They—"

Bennett interrupted. "What about that guy who disclosed all the stuff the NSA was doing? Don't you think people like that need to be stopped? He was definitely giving aid and comfort to the enemy. He was also disclosing national security secrets."

Tomás replied, in a nervous voice. "I think that people who expose unconstitutional conduct are heroes. The people need to know what their government is doing. If we allow government officials to systematically violate the Constitution, it won't be long before we aren't any better than our enemies. If we don't have a rule of law, we don't have anything."

Hernandez, Bennett, and Wellington looked at each other in disbelief. Wellington tried to pacify the situation, which had gotten out of hand. "Look guys, we can agree to disagree on this point.

Let's keep journalists, professors, and whistleblowers off the list, for now. There are plenty of politicians and bureaucrats who need to be on our list. Would that make everybody happy?"

They all nodded, but actually no one was happy. Before Tomás had opened his mouth they all thought they were on the same page. Now the group seemed deeply split, and there didn't appear to be a solution that would return things to normal. They all felt uncomfortable at that point. They finished their beers and made excuses to leave. As Wellington left, he decided to arrange a meeting with the Boss to inform him of the conversation they just had.

46

"You did the right thing bringing this to my attention. Tomás has become a problem. We may have to eliminate him." The Boss was responding to Wellington's summary of the conversation that took place over beers at Santos's house.

"Yes, I was thinking the same thing. But let's wait and see if this thing blows over. Maybe he'll come to his senses."

"I don't think that will happen, but there's no harm in waiting to see how things evolve. If he can get back on track, there's no need to get rid of him. He's been a valuable asset."

"I agree. I'll keep you posted."

47

"Yeah, I know Saul Steinman. He's a schmuck." Rachel Karshenboym voiced her opinion of Saul Steinman to Sergei Turetsky as they walked outside her office at the Kendall campus of Miami Dade College. He had just finished briefing her on the assignment. The sound of her voice always annoyed him, but at least he could enjoy the breeze and the sight of the palm trees swaying on both sides of the sidewalk as they walked toward the parking lot. It was much better than Moscow.

"He says he's a strong supporter of Israel, but he's totally against U.S. Middle East policy. He's funneling money to the Palestinians. Killing people who funnel money to terrorists and who oppose U.S. Middle East policy would be doing both Israel and the United States a favor. I think we should coordinate our efforts to make sure he gets eliminated as soon as possible. We need to silence him and stop him from funding those Palestinians."

Sergei had expected some resistance. His prior dealings with Rachel had always been less than pleasant. Would Steinman feel comfortable even being in the same room with this woman, let alone inviting her to join his group? Could she keep her private views to herself? He doubted it. That would seriously compromise the mission.

"All I'm asking is that you infiltrate his study group and keep us informed of what's going on. I don't know what Aaron has planned for him. Maybe you'll be pleasantly surprised."

Sergei was talking out of his ass and he knew it. Although he didn't know precisely what Gelman's plans were, he knew they didn't include killing Steinman. He had to say something to calm her down because he could feel she was going to refuse the assignment.

That seemed to pacify her. There was a change in her facial expression. Sergei noticed it.

"OK, I'll take the assignment, but I have mixed feelings about it."

"That's fine. I understand. I'll tell Aaron you have mixed feelings."

"You do that." She didn't like Aaron Gelman and she made no attempt to hide her feelings. She thought he was a politician who cared more about covering his ass than doing what was right for Israel.

Sergei walked back to his car both relieved and anxious—relieved because he would be able to tell Gelman that she had accepted the assignment, and anxious because of fear she would screw up. He began to think of a backup plan.

48

James Young sat on the side of his bed, thinking about his predicament. It had been exactly three weeks since Santos Hernandez pummeled him at the airport. Less than three weeks since the Department of Homeland Security goons punched him, froze his bank accounts and credit cards, and got him fired. His broken ribs still hurt.

The assault case the TSA filed against him would go to trial in a few months. He couldn't get an attorney to represent him. They were all afraid of what would happen to them if they defended someone accused of being a terrorist. They could be accused of aiding and abetting.

His mother's brain was melting away from dementia. His wife had been cut back to part-time at work to avoid being subject to the federal health care regulations. They were practically out of money. The cash his wife brought home from her job wasn't even enough for groceries.

He felt under attack, isolated, and alone.

He walked over to the bedroom closet, took out his gun, slapped in a fully loaded clip, and tossed it into a large cloth bag, along with the extra clip. When he picked it up by the handle, he noticed the outline of the gun barrel and the end of the clip were visible. They poked the cloth bag from the inside. That would draw too much attention. He walked to the bathroom closet, took out a bath towel, and wrapped it around the gun. That would soften the angular features so they wouldn't be too prominent.

He got in the car and headed for the Miami International Airport.

49

If you can't kill the general, kill the foot soldiers.

James felt dead inside as he drove to the airport. His mind. His spirit. The federal government had killed him with its laws. Everything but his body. His elected representatives and their cronies had betrayed him. They had betrayed the trust of all Americans. They were safely ensconced in Washington, but the foot soldiers, the enforcers, were in Miami.

Some of them were at the Miami International Airport. And they were vulnerable, especially if you didn't care about getting away after you did what needed to be done. He didn't care about getting away.

He pulled into the Dolphin parking garage and took the first space he saw. He didn't try to get a space near an exit or an elevator. He didn't plan on making a quick escape.

He turned off the ignition. Grabbed the extra clip from the bag. Put it in his pocket. He picked up the MPA 10SST. Checked to make sure it had a shell in the chamber. Rewrapped it in the bath towel. Returned it to the bag. He got out of the car and started walking toward the terminals. It was a large airport. It would take a while to get to his destination, but time was no longer a factor for him. No job. No cash. Pending court case. No attorney. No hope. All because the TSA assaulted him and his mother.

He passed a few TSA agents along the way. He resisted the urge to kill them on the spot. That would derail his plan. He had a specific target in mind.

A few minutes later he arrived at the same terminal he had been at three weeks before. The terminal where the TSA had whisked his mother away in her wheelchair. The place where Santos Hernandez beat him. He would have to show his ticket to the TSA agent posted at the podium before he could gain entrance to the search area. He didn't have a ticket. He would present his MPA 10SST instead. No photo ID needed.

He got at the end of the line, and waited for his turn at the podium. The line was short. It would be his turn soon. He looked over at the search area as best he could. His view was partially obscured by the machines and the people ahead of him. He could see the woman who had pushed him aside and wheeled his mother into the private screening room. He couldn't see Santos Hernandez.

He spotted two TSA agents with side arms, both off to the left just beyond the electronic scanners. There could be more. A few wore Kevlar vests.

They'd started wearing the vests and carrying firearms shortly after one of them got shot by a disgruntled patriot at the Los Angeles airport. There had been a few other shootings since then, and the frequency was starting to increase, but not to epidemic proportions. Most Americans still didn't protest the warrantless searches and the verbal and physical abuse. Most still preferred to give up a little liberty in exchange for temporary security. But the TSA had started to get blowback from the small segment of the population that had had enough.

He didn't know much about shooting people, but he did know that shooting someone in their Kevlar vest was a waste of time. Those people had to be shot in the head. He would shoot the ones carrying firearms first.

The woman ahead of him had just had her ticket and ID checked. He was next.

"Ticket, sir?" The TSA agent at the podium held out her hand to take his ticket. She looked Hispanic. Dark eyes. Black hair. In her early thirties. TSA uniform neatly pressed.

He reached into the bag, pulled out the pistol, and pumped a round into her chest. – BAM! — splattering her blood and flesh on the people behind her.

Everyone screamed. Panic. Scattering like cockroaches.

James ran through the scanner, setting it off, then turned to the left. The two armed agents stood there, in a panic, trying to draw their guns.

He aimed at the head of the closer one and squeezed the trigger. BLAM! He missed. He corrected his aim and squeezed off another round. This one hit him just below the left eye. His head exploded into red mist. James shifted his aim to the other agent. The shot caught him in the throat, just above his Kevlar protection.

The immediate threat was over, but it wouldn't be long before other agents with guns would appear. He had to act fast.

Some travelers were still screaming.

"Don't worry, folks. I'm only killing TSA agents today."

The screaming stopped, but the looks of terror on their faces remained.

He looked around, trying to spot Santos Hernandez.

He turned to one of the male agents, pointing the gun at his face. The gun was getting heavy. He held it with both hands. In a slow, deliberate voice, he asked, "Where is Santos Hernandez?"

"He's not here today. I don't know where he is."

Damn. I was really looking forward to killing that bastard. After all he did to me and my family. Well, I came here to kill as many TSA agents as I can. They're all the same anyway. Just like cockroaches. It doesn't matter where you start. Kill the closest one first.

With that, he took aim at the agent standing in front of him and squeezed the trigger. The agent's brains splattered all over the agents next to him. Then he turned to the female agent who had pushed him aside three weeks earlier to grab his mother. He aimed the gun at her head. He focused on the spot between her eyebrows, just below her bangs. "Remember me?"

She looked puzzled by the question. She didn't remember accosting him or his mother. She had assaulted so many people over the years that she no longer realized she was violating their rights.

"Three weeks ago you assaulted me and my mother. I came back to celebrate our anniversary."

He squeezed the trigger again, but as he squeezed, she moved to the right. He missed her. The bullet caught the agent standing behind her in the shoulder, causing her to scream and fall to the floor. He turned toward her again, took aim, and fired two rounds into her chest.

He still had more than twenty rounds left in the first clip and another thirty rounds in the clip in his pocket. There were six agents remaining in his immediate area. He took them out one at a time with shots to the torso, going from right to left. Then he walked up to each of them, aimed at their head, and squeezed the trigger again.

He noticed the agent he had shot in the shoulder accidentally was still alive. Very much alive. She was propped up against the wall, holding her shoulder and whimpering. Staring at him in terror. He walked over to her and looked her directly in the eyes. She was in her early twenties, skinny, light brown skin, short black hair, a little kinked. Some kind of mixed race. Caucasian and something else. Maybe African. Maybe Haitian. Maybe part Hispanic. She was the new generation of American. She had a soft look about her. Not hardened like the other TSA agents.

"Don't worry. I'm not going to kill you. I've done enough killing for today."

She nodded her head. She looked a little relieved by what he had just said. Just a little.

"You need to quit this job. Don't work for the federal government."

She nodded her head vigorously, still staring him in the eyes. "OK. I'll quit."

Just after he finished his sentence multiple shots rang out. Something struck his back. James saw his chest explode as the four rounds the TSA agents had fired into his back exited his chest. The force of the rounds propelled him forward. He landed next to the girl. She faded away into darkness, and peace finally came.

50

Paige and Sveta were having dinner at her place when they heard the news on television. It was the lead story, not only in Miami but nationwide. The reporter provided some background information, but gave an incomplete and biased account.

"Shortly after 11 a.m. this morning, a person identified as James Young entered Terminal D of Miami International Airport and opened fire on several TSA agents, killing 10 and wounding one. Three weeks earlier he had been accused of assaulting an agent in that same terminal. Information is sketchy at the moment. The police said that he had recently been placed on the terrorist list, but have not given any further details. The investigation is ongoing. He is survived by his wife, his mother, two children and three grandchildren."

"Robert, isn't that the same man who got beat up by a TSA agent at the airport? The one whose bloodied face was on the front page of the *Miami Herald*?"

"Yeah, I think it's the same guy."

"How can they say he assaulted a TSA agent when the photos and film taken at the scene clearly showed that the agent was the one who assaulted him?"

"I don't know. Maybe some government censor wrote the script for her. Or maybe they're afraid to give the whole story. If they say anything positive about someone who's on the terrorist list, they could be accused of aiding and abetting the enemy and arrested for treason."

"But Nelson Mandela was on the terrorist list until he was ninety, long after he became president of South Africa. People said lots of nice things about him."

Paige picked up his fork and took a stab at his salad. "That's different. Nelson Mandela had a following. James Young didn't. Nobody's going to get arrested for saying something nice about Nelson Mandela."

Sveta leaned forward to make a point. "But Nelson Mandela shouldn't have been on the terrorist list."

"James Young probably shouldn't have been on it either. Even if he did assault a TSA agent, that's no reason to be put on the list. That's not an act of terrorism. It might be an act of patriotism. Those guys have been abusing people and conducting warrantless searches since 2001. They need to be smacked around from time to time." Paige picked up his knife and sliced off a piece of steak. "I heard that a lot of people are on the terrorist list who aren't terrorists. They can't get on airplanes. Sometimes they can't get jobs. Some of them are babies or children. One U.S. senator was put on the list by mistake. The government refuses to publish the list for national security reasons."

Sveta was getting animated. "Robert, I'm upset. This is starting to sound more and more like Soviet Russia. You get accused of something but you can't confront your accuser because it might compromise national security."

"Yes, the country does appear to be going in that direction. One reason we have the right to a jury trial is to prevent abuses by government, but if the government merely alleges that the defendant is a terrorist, the right to a jury trial goes out the window." Paige sat back in his chair. "Somebody needs to do something."

51

"Hi, John. What kind of protectionist crap is the Commerce Department pushing these days?" Paige was taking Wellington's call on his cell phone.

Wellington smiled. He knew it was a well-known joke within the business community that the Commerce Department did more to block trade than facilitate it. He adjusted his glasses.

"Is that any way to speak to a humble public servant?" He knew the criticism was valid. He did what he could to facilitate trade, but he had to comply with the various anti-trade policies the Commerce Department foisted upon its all-too-willing employees.

"Bob, I'd like to chat with you about developments. Are you free for lunch tomorrow?"

"Sure. I'm giving a guest lecture at the University of Miami tomorrow afternoon. Perhaps we can meet before my lecture."

"Sure. Can you recommend any restaurants in the area?"

"Yeah. One of my favorites is *La Palma*. Sometimes I go there either before or after I give a guest lecture. It's on Alhambra Circle in Coral Gables. Do you know it?"

"No, but I'll find it on the internet. Shall we say twelvish?"

"OK. If it's sunny, I'll be outside. If it's raining, I'll be inside." The outside section especially appealed to Paige. The white table cloths and the architectural design had a southern European caste, but one couldn't tell which country. Although Italian in cuisine, all the waiters spoke Spanish. Whenever Paige would go there, he could almost be certain that he wouldn't hear a single word of Italian, which detracted slightly from the place's authenticity.

***

Paige arrived a few minutes early. He decided to leave home in plenty of time because of the traffic. He usually had trouble finding *La Palma* because the streets in that section of Coral Gables weren't set up in a strict grid pattern. Some of the streets ran one way and they didn't all have proper street signs. The street names painted on stones at ground level were impossible to read after dark, and difficult to read during the day.

Wellington walked into the courtyard at 12:20. His preppy appearance fit right in with the upscale nature of the restaurant.

"Hi. Sorry I'm late. I couldn't find the place and my GPS didn't help much. It told me to turn left instead of right."

Paige laughed as he shook Wellington's hand. It was a fairly firm handshake. He knew exactly what Wellington meant. Whoever designed the streets and street signs in Coral Gables should be shot. The waiter took their drink order and they began to chat.

"Anything new with Steinman?"

"No. He told me he would let me know when the next meeting was scheduled but he hasn't contacted me yet."

"Bob, the reason I wanted to chat with you is to let you know I have informed Mossad of our plans to infiltrate Steinman's little group."

Paige looked surprised and a little concerned. "Why did you do that?" He remembered something his mother had told him as a kid

– too many cooks spoil the broth. He thought the fewer people who knew about the plan, the fewer complications they would encounter. But on second thought, maybe spreading the word would be a good thing. He wanted the plan to fail, especially if Wellington planned to kill Steinman, and the more people who knew about it, the higher the probability of failure.

"As a courtesy. Steinman has been a strong supporter of Israel, and I thought it would be the right thing to do, especially since he's funneling funds to the Palestinians."

"How did they react? Did they support the idea?"

"Yeah, pretty much. They don't like the fact that he's funneling money to the Palestinians, and they would like to know if he's up to anything else."

Although Wellington had assured him that Steinman wouldn't be killed, Paige didn't believe him. Paige wondered if the real reason Wellington met with Mossad was to inform them of the planned hit, and whether Mossad would just look the other way or try to prevent it. Wellington thought the same thing, although he didn't say it.

52

"What do you think about what Tomás said the other day? Do you think he's become a problem?" Santos Hernandez and Jim Bennett were sitting in Bennett's car, staking out a potential future target. Bennett raised the issue. His stare always made Santos feel uncomfortable. Santos looked straight ahead at the building they were staking out to avoid eye contact.

"Yeah, I think maybe he has, but I don't want to think about it."

Bennett kept his eyes focused on the apartment building. "Me either. It seems like he's not one of us anymore."

Santos glanced at him briefly. "Maybe he never was one of us. Maybe we just assumed he was."

"Yeah. I'm beginning to believe that, too. What do you think we should do about it?"

Santos hesitated before responding. "I don't know. I don't want to think about it."

"I don't, either. Let's wait and see what happens."

"You don't think he'll blow the whistle on us, do you?" Santos sounded worried.

"No. He's in too deep. He'd be cutting his own throat if he did that."

"Yeah, you're right. Let's wait and see what happens."

53

Rachel Karshenboym had made an appointment to meet Saul Steinman in his office. As she took the elevator to the fourth floor of his building at FIU she battled in her head what she would say. She had to be on her best behavior and not show her true feelings for him. She detested his weak views on U.S. foreign policy.

As she walked into his office he was seated at his desk.

"Hello, Professor Steinman? I'm Rachel Karshenboym."

He rose from his chair to shake hands.

He motioned to the chair in front of his desk. "Please, sit down. And call me Saul."

Her nostrils drew in the scent of old books. It reminded her of the many hours she spent in the libraries in Russia and Israel … and also her uncle's parlor in Odessa, where she visited a few summers as a child.

She wore a low-cut, black and white blouse that revealed enough of her breasts to make people notice from 20 feet away. She made sure she bent forward as she placed her purse on the floor. He noticed, and she noticed that he noticed.

"What can I do for you, Professor Karshenboym?" She noticed his eyes were bouncing back between her eyes and breasts.

"Please, call me Rachel. I just wanted to meet you. I've seen you on television and enjoyed some of your articles. I thought that since we live in the same city, I should meet you."

"You have an interesting accent. Russian, I presume?"

Yes, is it that obvious?"

"Well, the name also gives it away. If it were German, it would be Karshenbaum."

"It's the Yiddish version. It means cherry tree."

"Ah, our families come from the same part of the world, although mine was a little West of yours, in Berlin."

As Steinman jabbered away, Rachel glanced at the photo of him posing with the Palestinians. She tried not to cringe.

Her mind snapped back to the conversation. She replied, "Actually, the most recent generation of my family came from Saint Petersburg, but I think their roots were in Germany."

"Saul, I was thinking. I know a number of professors in the Miami area who are concerned about the direction the country is moving in. I wonder if we might assemble some of them into a study group to discuss the issues. It would be a good opportunity to meet with like-minded people and it could be fun."

"That's a good idea. Actually, I've already formed such a group. Would you like to join?"

"Sure. I'd love to." She feigned surprise, but the whole purpose of the meeting was to get him to ask. She didn't have a Plan B in the event he didn't ask.

Saul sat back in his chair. Although he didn't respond immediately to her quick acceptance, the look on his face betrayed what he was thinking. His expression and body language were saying, I wish I hadn't invited her to join my study group. His expression reminded Rachel of what her Mossad handlers had said, that his group was an all-boys club, and he probably wanted to keep it that way. Maybe he was having second thoughts, but it was too late for him to back out. Had had offered and she had accepted.

He leaned forward. "Great. I'll let you know when the next meeting's going to be."

"Thanks, Saul. I'd better be going now. I know you're a busy man. Here's my card. It has my contact information."

"Not a bother. Glad to meet you."

She bent forward to pick up her purse as she got up from the chair, giving him another opportunity to look at her breasts, which he took. She wore a tight skirt that caused her to waddle a little as she walked out. She could feel his eyes on her ass. She felt her visit had been a success.

54

Think Globally, Act Locally

Wellington had just ended a meeting at his Commerce Department office by the airport when his cell phone rang. It was the Boss. "John? Hi. We need to meet. It will only take five minutes. When can you get to the Starbucks on West Flagler?"

"I'm not at the downtown office today. I'll have to come after work."

"That will be fine. How's 5:30?"

"I can be there. What's so urgent?"

"It's not urgent. It's just that I'll be busy for the next few days and late this afternoon would be convenient for me."

"OK. I'll see you then."

Wellington was curious but not overly concerned. The Boss told him it wasn't urgent, so he put it out of mind and went back to work.

***

Wellington always got annoyed when he had to sit in Miami's rush hour traffic. What a hassle. But the Boss wanted a five-minute conversation. Hopefully the Boss wouldn't increase his workload.

His Commerce Department job kept him busy. He had enough work already.

He arrived at 5:26. Probably the worst time to be in that part of downtown Miami. The rush-hour traffic produced exhaust fumes faster than the ocean breeze could blow them away.

The Boss was already sitting at a table, sipping coffee. The smells emanating within the Starbucks coffee emporium cleansed Wellington's nostrils of the exhaust fumes.

"Hi John. Let's take a walk outside and talk. It's too noisy in here."

They walked out the front door and turned right.

"John, I'll be brief. After we neutralize Steinman we have to continue getting rid of traitors. We can't have our own citizens criticizing the government. It gives aid and comfort to the people who want to destroy us. I want to give you and your crew a little homework assignment. Have each member of the team identify two more trouble makers in the Miami area— professors, journalists or others — who deserve to be eliminated. We'll start a list. As we eliminate them, we'll add others to it. Let's arrange to meet in a few weeks, probably on a Saturday. I'll reserve a private room at the Versailles and let you know the day and time."

"Should I invite Paige to join the group?"

"No. I don't trust him. Let's keep this close to the vest."

"Your wish is my command."

"Yes, I know."

Wellington looked left and right to see if anyone was within earshot. "There's something else I'd like to discuss. Tomás has expressed reservations about executing professors and journalists."

"Reservations? What the fuck does that mean?" Wellington knew the Boss didn't like having his orders challenged, but he had to let him know what was going on within the group.

"You know. He doesn't think we should be killing professors and journalists just for exercising their right of free speech and press."

"Oh, he doesn't, huh? Maybe you need to remind him who's in charge."

"He knows who's in charge." Wellington lowered his voice. "His hesitancy to kill professors and journalists might become a problem."

"If he hesitates to carry out my orders, he's the one who'll have a problem." The Boss became agitated. He took a step toward Wellington.

Wellington continued. "What should we do if he refuses to snuff someone on the list?"

"Do you think that's a real possibility?"

"It might be. I got the feeling that he's really against the idea of assassinating journalists and professors."

"Well, I suppose we'll have to cross that bridge when we come to it. But I'll tell you this. We can't have people picking and choosing who they're going to kill or which orders they're going to obey."

"Yeah, I know. But what should we do if he refuses to kill one of the people on our list?"

"If he disobeyed a direct order in the military, he'd be court-martialed, or maybe shot on the spot, depending on the circumstances."

"Yeah, but we can't court-martial him. He's not in the military any more, and even if he were, a court-martial would be out of the question in this case. There's about a one hundred percent chance it would make the press, which is exactly what we don't need."

The Boss took a deep breath and gazed across the street as he thought about the options, exhaled, then turned and looked directly into Wellington's eyes. "If he refuses to obey a direct order, he becomes a threat to the team. We can't afford to have threats to the team. Do you understand what I'm saying?"

"Yes, sir. I do."

The Boss was so close that Wellington could feel the Boss's breath on his face each time he exhaled. The Boss poked Wellington hard in the chest with his right index finger, one poke for each word. "TAKE – CHARGE – OF – THIS – GUY."

"Yes sir, I'll do that."

"Good. Keep me posted. Let me know if he gives any further indications of having less than total loyalty."

As he finished his sentence the Boss noticed a mother and daughter walk past them wearing burkas. He looked at Wellington and jerked his head in their direction.

"You see that? They're all around us. Her husband might be planning an attack on America as we speak."

Wellington could only see their backs, since they had already passed by on the sidewalk. He felt the urge to say something positive. "They're not all bad. Some of them are patriotic Americans. They're here because they didn't like what's going on in their country. They hate militants more than we do. A few of them are free lancing for us to infiltrate the local mosques."

"Yeah, I know, but you can't really trust them. They point toward Mecca five times a day. How many times do they point toward Washington?"

The Boss looked at them again, then turned toward Wellington. "Did I ever tell you the story about when I was in Tikrit?"

"No, I don't think so."

"Actually, it was a little village outside of Tikrit, about 90 miles northwest of Baghdad. We went into the village to see if we could find any insurgents. All we saw were women and children. No men."

"Where were they?"

"Probably hiding under some rock, waiting to shoot us." He started to smile, one of those dirty, evil smiles a pervert gets as he is about to do his thing.

"We gathered up about a dozen women and children and took them into one of the houses, a one-room hut, actually. Then we proceeded to introduce them to some enhanced interrogation."

Wellington noticed the evil smile on his face. "What kind of enhanced interrogation techniques did you use? Did you waterboard them?"

"No, nothing as mundane as that. We wanted to give them a memorable experience. Well, actually I was the one who wanted to give them a memorable experience. The other men in the platoon were against the idea, but I was in charge, so they did what I told them to do.

Do you know what female circumcision is?"

"Yeah. It's disgusting. They cut off the woman's clitoris, and sometimes the labia. It's a common practice in Africa. They do it in some Muslim countries, too."

"Yeah. The Muslim men don't want their women to get too much pleasure from sex. They cut off their clit so they don't get tempted to fuck the other guys in the neighborhood. They usually do it when they're young, before they reach their fifth birthday. Sometimes they use anaesthesia and sometimes they don't."

"Is that what you did to them?"

"Please, let me finish. I don't want to spoil the ending. It's an interesting story."

The Boss looked around to see if anybody was listening before continuing. "We gave them an opportunity to tell us what we wanted to know. I had our interpreter ask them where the men were. First he asked them as a group, but nobody said anything. A couple of the girls started crying. So I had him ask them one by one. The mothers and the daughters. Still nothing.

"I started to get pissed. If I didn't find out where the men were, we would all be in danger, not just us, but all of our men in the area. I had to get the information. I had a responsibility to my men.

"So I grabbed one of the girls and dragged her to the bed in the corner. Then I told four of my men to take an arm or a leg to hold her down. I started ripping off her clothes and told one of the men to go into the truck and get a pair of pliers. When he gave them to me, I took out my knife and clamped her clit with the pliers. By then all the women and children were screaming so loud it was hurting my ears. My men were having trouble holding the girl down. She was only about 50 pounds, but she was yelling and twisting like crazy.

"I told the interpreter to ask them one last time where their men were. Before he could even finish his sentence they all pointed north. They were jabbering away, spilling their guts out. The interpreter said the men were a few kilometers north of town.

"What did you do then? Did you let her go?"

"No, I figured that since I already had my knife out I might as well finish what I had started. I sliced off her clit and tossed it on the floor."

Wellington gasped. The Boss smiled, reminiscing. "She was bleeding like a stuck pig. We couldn't stop the bleeding. I wanted to light up a Koran and cram it between her legs to cauterize the wound, but the general told us we shouldn't burn Korans, so I told one of the men to go to the truck and bring me a newspaper.

When he came back, I lit it and stuffed it between her legs. It worked. The bleeding stopped.

"Then we left and headed north. We found the men from the village, about 20 of them. We ordered an air strike, which got most of them. We took care of the rest of them ourselves."

The Boss looked at his watch. "It's getting late. I've got to go. I have a date tonight."

With that, the conversation ended. They walked toward the parking garage without saying another word. Wellington wondered what he should do if Tomás refused to obey a direct order. The Boss wasn't used to that. It was obvious to Wellington that he wouldn't tolerate his authority being questioned.

As they approached the entrance to the garage, they saw a young girl walking a small Chihuahua on a leash. She appeared to be about 12 years old, with pigtails, and wearing clothes that looked like hand-me-downs. All of a sudden, the dog stopped, squatted and made a brown deposit on the sidewalk just ahead of them. After finishing its business, the girl and the dog continued walking.

The Boss saw what happened and became enraged. "Hey! You! Get back here and pick that up! Didn't your parents teach you anything?" He increased his pace and started walking toward her quickly.

"I'm sorry, sir, but I didn't bring any paper with me. I can't pick it up."

The Boss's yelling and aggressive movements caused the dog to become defensive, thinking its master was being attacked. It started yapping at the Boss. The girl had to hold the leash tight to prevent it from taking a bite out of his ankle. He stepped forward and kicked it in the side, hard, causing it to yelp and fly a few feet into the air. The girl screamed and ran to comfort her dog, which was cowering and limping on its right side, its brown eyes sadly looking up at the Boss.

"If you can't clean up after your dog, you shouldn't have one."

"I'm sorry, sir, I'll bring paper next time."

Wellington remained silent as he saw what happened. He knew better than to confront the Boss when he was angry, which was often.

Wellington had some apprehension about the plan. Now he also had to worry about the possible problems Tomás might cause if he refused to obey a direct order. Although Wellington agreed with the general idea – to get rid of traitors – they would be turning up the heat by adding multiple targets to the list. At some point, the local police and FBI would start to see a pattern and would devote extra resources to finding out who the serial killers were. Their contacts within the police department and FBI might be able to give them some information and alert them when they were getting too close, but it was a risky business. He started to get nervous about the Boss's plan to ratchet up their mission.

55

"Sarah, may I help you with something?" Paige and Sveta were having dinner at the Wellington's home on the edge of the Everglades. It was more or less in the country. The air smelled fresh and the birds chirped, but the area had been getting built up in recent years. In a few years, it would probably be in the middle of a suburb. It took Wellington less than an hour to get to downtown Miami, even during rush hour.

"Oh, no thanks, Sveta. Everything's under control. On second thought, maybe you can make the salad." She pointed to the left. "The ingredients are all on the table over there."

Sarah, John's wife, was medium-height with brown eyes and dark blonde hair that came partially out of a bottle. A few pounds overweight. Her body morphed from firm to soft over the last decade, like many suburban housewives in the late stage of their child-bearing years.

She had taken a liking to Sveta since Paige started seeing her a few years ago. They got together every few months. Sarah didn't know that John met with Paige on a more regular basis. She thought of Paige as just a nice accounting professor and John as just one of Paige's former students who worked for the Commerce Department.

Sveta walked over to the table and picked up the freshly rinsed arugula and romaine. "How did you and John meet?"

"We met while we were undergraduates at the University of Florida. John was a political science major. I studied French."

Paige overheard the conversation and decided to chime in. "So, Sarah, do you keep up with your French?" Paige fancied himself a bit of an amateur linguist. He picked up some French, German, Portuguese, Russian and Spanish over the years, enough to hold a conversation, and was curious to know how other people learn languages.

"Not really. I read some things on the internet in French once in a while and I subscribe to some electronic newsletters, but that's about it. With the kids and work, I really don't have much time to read. I haven't read a French novel in years."

"That's too bad. It's nice to maintain skills in a second language, especially French. It's the language of diplomacy."

"Yeah, about two centuries ago," Wellington chimed in, chuckling. He liked to make jokes about the French and he liked hearing them.

Wellington continued. "Other than the literature, I don't know what about the French is worth studying. They're a bunch of socialists. Their economy and culture are falling apart. It's not even a good place to visit anymore."

Paige didn't exactly disagree, but he did manage to find a few positive things to say about the French. "That's not quite true, John. The history and architecture are quite interesting, and the food, too. And I almost forgot, they did save our ass during the American Revolution."

"Yeah, you're right about that. If it weren't for the French, we would be speaking English today. And if it weren't for us, they'd be speaking German." Wellington smirked at his comment about speaking English. He thought it was clever.

Sveta was curious about Wellington's statement. Her eyebrows furrowed as she asked, "John, why do you say that it's not a good place to visit anymore? I was in Paris when I was in transit to America and I thought it was a nice place."

"It's swarming with Muslims. They're trying to cram their views down the throats of the French people. They want the French judicial system to adopt Sharia law. They block traffic on Fridays by praying in the streets. It's illegal, but they defy the police to do anything about it. They insult French women who wear short skirts or who don't wear a scarf, and call them whores. The police are spineless. They're too afraid to do anything.

"They've reached a critical mass, especially in the big cities. They're starting to take over. And their birth rate's higher than the local population. Between popping out Muslim babies and liberal immigration, it won't be long before they control France."

Paige added, "You have a point, John. It's tough to have the kind of secular society the French people want if they allow a group of outsiders to call the shots."

"The problem is, they're not outsiders any more. They become French citizens, although their loyalty is to Mecca or to their religion. They speak French, but they prefer the language of their home country. They refuse to obey French law if it conflicts with Sharia law. The French nation as we know it is dying."

Sarah got depressed listening to their conversation. "OK, guys. Dinner's ready. Come to the dining room."

Wellington and Paige walked into the dining room. Sarah and Sveta put the food on the table. Jack and Alicia sat at their assigned places, waiting to start. Jack, their 12-year-old son, was into baseball. He played in a league. Wellington volunteered to be one of the coaches and tried to get to as many of the games as he could. He couldn't be the head coach because his job prevented him from being at some of the games, but he did what he could.

Alicia, their 6-year-old daughter, had brown hair and brown eyes like her mother, and pasty white skin, like her parents. She took dance lessons. Sarah drove her to and from lessons.

Wellington led the brief prayer. Paige was an agnostic. He abandoned Catholicism years ago and never replaced it, but whenever anyone started a meal with a prayer, he kept his mouth shut and went along with it out of respect for their beliefs. He always managed to say *amen* at the end if called for.

When Sveta first came to America, she thought it was a strange practice to speak to God before meals, or at any other time. Atheism was the official religion of Russia during the communist era and the government suppressed talk about religion. She grew up with no religion, although she wasn't quite an atheist. She wondered what the truth was when it came to religion but didn't make an effort to read up on it. All she knew was that being a Christian in America was good and being anything else was bad. She wondered why people who called themselves Christian sometimes disagreed on which version of Christianity was the best one. She had read that, a few hundred years ago, people used to kill each other over that question.

"Jack, take off your cap. We're eating." Jack liked to wear his baseball cap everywhere, even in the house. Wellington tried to break him of the habit, at least at the dinner table. He removed it and hung it up on his chair post.

"Jack's team won yesterday, 26 to 21. It was a real pitching duel."

"Yeah, it must have been." The score reminded Paige of his days of playing sandlot baseball. It was easier to get a hit than to strike someone out. If anyone got out it was because they hit a fly ball that someone caught. There weren't many strikeouts in sandlot ball. They usually didn't even bother to keep score. They just played for the fun of it.

Sarah chimed in. "John's been coaching the team whenever he can. He goes to most of the games."

"Yeah, they've won two games so far this season."

"How many games have they played?"

"About seven, I think. We try not to emphasize the win-loss ratio because it might damage their self-esteem."

"Yeah, I've heard about that."

"Yeah, we also give everyone on every team a trophy at the end of the season."

"Really, why do you do that? Doesn't that destroy the value of a trophy?"

"The people who make the rules don't think so. They think that giving out a bunch of trophies boosts their self-esteem. I might also add that each member of the team that has the most wins gets a second trophy, which is larger than the other trophies."

Paige smiled. "Well, I'm glad to hear that. I wouldn't want them to turn into a bunch of egalitarians."

Wellington chuckled. He understood where Paige was coming from. He thought the same way himself. It reminded him of something he read on the internet.

"Did you know that some high schools in California nominate everyone in the graduating class to be valedictorian?"

"No, I didn't know that. Why do they do that?"

"It's partially a self-esteem issue and partially to help their graduating seniors get into college. If it's on their transcript that they were valedictorian, the principal thinks it will boost their chances of getting admitted somewhere and getting a scholarship."

"Isn't that a sham? Even fraudulent?"

"Yeah, I suppose it is. But I read that most college admissions committees know which California high schools do that, so they disregard it when they make their decisions about who to admit or give scholarships to."

"Doesn't that discriminate against the best students, the ones who could have actually been the valedictorian?"

"Sure, but the people who make the rules in the California high schools don't think that's important. It's more important to help *all* students than to recognize the achievement of the best students."

Paige smirked. "I don't think Ayn Rand would approve."

Wellington smiled. "I hear you." He was somewhat familiar with Ayn Rand and her philosophy. He had read *Atlas Shrugged* in a college literature class and had read portions of her *Capitalism: The Unknown Ideal* and Rothbard's *Egalitarianism as a Revolt against Nature* in a political science class. He wasn't a big fan of egalitarianism, in spite of the indoctrination he received from his professors as an undergraduate.

He also rejected most of the corporate social responsibility gibberish his management professors tried to cram down his throat as part of his MBA program. He believed that, as a private club, a corporation's main duty was to its club members – shareholders - and that corporations should try to maximize profits any way they could, as long as they didn't break any laws or resort to lying, cheating or stealing. That's the position Milton Friedman, the Nobel Prize winning economist, took, and he agreed with it.

"Jack, what did you learn in school this week?" Sveta was curious to learn what students were being taught in American schools. When she was Jack's age in Moscow, she was learning math, science and Marxism for kiddies. Paige once told her, half jokingly, that American kids learned the same things, except without the math and science.

"I learned that Florida's going to be covered with water in 50 years because of global warming and that smoke stacks kill people. I want to move but daddy doesn't want to."

Sveta was shocked. She didn't expect to hear that. She didn't know what his reply would be but she didn't expect that.

John chimed in, "Yeah, that's the kind of stuff they're teaching in school these days. The teachers are telling them the government has to do something to prevent us from killing the planet. We're thinking of sending him to a private school, but doing that would be expensive."

Paige suggested, "Maybe the Florida legislature will get around to passing a voucher law that will let you decide where to send Jack and Alicia."

"Yeah, but I don't see that happening any time soon. The teachers' union's against it. They don't want to have the government break up their little public school monopoly. They're in favor of choice when it comes to abortion but not when it comes to educating your own kids. They think they know what's best."

"That's just a little hypocritical, don't you think?"

"Sure, but they never let logic get in the way of pushing their agenda. I don't like it, but there's nothing I can do to stop it."

"Maybe you could move to France." They both laughed.

After dinner, Wellington and Paige started to walk out to the patio in the back yard while Sarah and Sveta cleared the table, picking up some of the food and dishes and depositing them in the kitchen along the way.

Sarah saw them picking up a few plates. "Don't do that. I'll take care of it."

Since they already had some dishes in their hands, and since they were going in the direction of the kitchen anyway, they decided to continue walking toward the kitchen. Although Sarah appreciated the thought, she preferred to be in charge of the kitchen, including the before and after details. She was a bit of a control freak when it came to food and the kitchen. John never put the stuff where she would have put it, which required her to search for the leftover food before putting it back in the fridge.

After they were on the patio and out of earshot, Wellington turned toward Paige. "Do you have anything to report on Steinman and his merry little band of commie bastards? The Boss likes to keep informed."

Paige smiled. They both knew they weren't communists, just a bunch of well-meaning social democrats and socialists, although Wellington wasn't nearly as sympathetic toward them as Paige. Whereas Paige regarded them as misguided, Wellington saw them as enemies of the state.

"Maybe I should talk directly to the Boss. After all, it's on a need to know basis, and I don't know if you're authorized to have this kind of information. What's his phone number? Maybe we can invite him for a beer."

"Nice try, Bob." Wellington saw right through Paige's ploy, which was more of a joke than a suggestion. Paige knew that Wellington would never set up a face-to-face meeting with the Boss.

"What's his name, again? I forgot."

Wellington just smiled. Paige continued.

"What color hair does he have? Does he even have hair? How tall is he?"

"He's just tall enough that his feet reach the ground. And yes, he has hair, but I'm not going to tell you the color. I'm not going to tell you the color of his eyes, either, although I can tell you that he has two of them."

"Well, that's a start. At least you're not stonewalling me."

"I try to be helpful when I can."

"Does he ever wear high heels on weekends?"

"No. You're getting him confused with J. Edgar Hoover."

Paige knew he wasn't going to get any information out of Wellington, but he did wonder who the Boss was and how active he was in this project. Failure to know the Boss's identity might cause problems for him later and he knew it. He just hoped that failure to know wouldn't prove to be fatal.

56

Paige picked up his phone. "Hi, Bob? Saul here. I'm going to have a little get-together tomorrow evening. Can you make it?"

"Sure. What time?"

"How about 7?"

"That will be fine. Your place, right?"

"Yeah. It's not Friday but I might have some meat anyway, probably sandwiches."

"Fine. See you then." Paige hung up and immediately called Wellington.

"John? Hi. It's Bob."

"Hi. Do you have some news for me?" Wellington stood by the window of his Commerce Department office, giving instructions to his assistant. She sensed it was a personal call and left the room.

"Yes. I just got off the phone with Steinman. He's going to have his next meeting tomorrow night."

"You know what to do. Let us know what he's up to and get the names of the people who attend. Use that pen I gave you."

A few months ago, Wellington gave Paige a pen that took photos and could record up to three hours of conversation.

"OK. Will do." Paige didn't feel comfortable spying on his new friend, yet he continued to commit overt acts that would put Steinman one step closer to extinction, like telling the CIA about the meeting. He didn't like what he was doing, but he kept doing it anyway. He was in too deep to back out now.

After they hung up, Wellington placed a call to his Boss to inform him of the meeting.

Steinman also called Rachel to invite her to the meeting. He hoped to get another look at her … assets. She immediately called Turetsky to give him the information.

"Sergei, it's Rachel. I just got off the phone with Saul Steinman. He has invited me to his next meeting. It's tomorrow night." She was squeezing a pen in her other hand. She was tense, but it was a good kind of tense, one borne of excitement.

"That's great news. Try to determine who the mole is. Get as much information on him as you can, where he works, where he lives, anything else that would be useful."

"Can I also ask him how they plan to kill Steinman? Maybe I can lend him my gun."

"Not funny, Rachel. Try to be cordial to everyone in the room. I know it'll be a stretch for you. Don't draw attention to yourself."

"Yes, I know. I'll learn what I can." After she hung up, she took a deep breath, then exhaled slowly. Her breath was stale, but there was no one else in the room, so it didn't matter. Exhaling gave her the opportunity to taste her breakfast a second time. She looked out the window, more or less in a day dream. The tops of the palm trees were swaying in the breeze. It was another sunny day in south Florida. Life was good.

Rachel Karshenboym thought along the same lines as John Wellington and his Boss when it came to Steinman and his kind. She thought the world would be a better place without them and their ilk. People who gave aid and comfort to the enemy were guilty of treason, like vice president Cheney said after 9/11. They should be liquidated. But she decided to bide her time and limit her involvement to collecting information and passing it along … for now.

57

"An evil exists that threatens every man, woman and child of this great nation. We must take steps to insure our domestic security and protect our homeland."
Adolf Hitler, 1933, on the creation of the Gestapo, the Nazi secret police.

"Arms discourage and keep the invader and plunderer in awe, and preserve order in the world as well as property... Horrid mischief would ensue were the law-abiding deprived of the use of them."
Thomas Paine

People began drifting in to Saul Steinman's place around 7 p.m. for the get-together. By 7:30 everyone had arrived. There were ten people in attendance altogether, Saul and his wife Rona, six professors from various universities in the Miami area, Paige and Rachel Karshenboym. They were engaging in small talk when Rona walked into the room.

"OK everybody. The sandwiches and coffee are ready. They're in the kitchen. Help yourself."

"Bob, I'd like you to meet my wife, Rona."

"Pleased to meet you." He held out his hand to shake.

She didn't feel comfortable shaking a man's hand but she did it anyway. The Orthodox Jewish family she grew up in had a rule forbidding women from touching a man other than their husband. She drifted away from orthodoxy after marrying Steinman, which caused some tension within her family. They had two rabbis preside at their ceremony, one Orthodox and one Reform. She tried to keep a kosher home, but it was difficult because Saul liked bacon, lettuce and tomato sandwiches. She refused to make them. He had to make them himself, using a separate fry pan for the bacon.

"I won't be participating in the meeting, but I'll be in the kitchen if you need me."

Paige turned toward her. "Oh, why aren't you participating?"

Saul chimed in. "She's bored with politics and economics. The things we talk about depress her."

"I'm a librarian. I like to talk about literature. Saul prefers talking about current events."

"Ah, a librarian. Some of my favorite people are librarians. Where do you work?"

"At the North Miami Beach Public Library. It's a schlep but I enjoy it." Saul and Rona lived in southwest Miami, close to the main campus of FIU. The North Miami Beach Public Library was in the northeastern part of town, about 30 miles away and close to the Orthodox temple she used to attend before she married Saul.

She looked like a librarian, short gray hair and frumpy, with rimless glasses. Her smile gave her a certain sex appeal, though.

Paige noticed one wall was lined with bookshelves. As he walked closer, he took a whiff. He liked the smell of books, but the smell from these books wasn't as strong as the smell in Steinman's university office, probably because there weren't as many of them and because the living room was a more open space than his cramped, cluttered office.

Most of the titles were in political science and political philosophy. He recognized a few of the titles, mostly by left-wing authors. But one shelf was different. It was filled with art books. Paige was curious and decided to ask.

"I noticed that one shelf of your book case has art books. Is there an artist in the family?

Rona stepped closer to the book shelf and adjusted one of the books. "That would be me. I studied art at Brown University as an undergraduate. I thought about going to the Rhode Island School of Design for an MFA but decided to become a librarian instead. It's a steadier paycheck, you know."

"Yes, as an accountant I understand completely."

"I've maintained my interest in art, though. I order the art books for the library, and I have a small art collection."

Paige noticed a few paintings and prints hanging on the far wall. She saw he was looking at them.

"Come on over and I'll show you my collection." She motioned to the left side of the wall. "I did these two after I graduated from Brown." She pointed to two autumn landscape scenes. "I have a few others strewn about the house, but these are the only ones I feel comfortable enough about to display in the living room."

"They're very good. I like the way you use color." Actually, Paige did like them, although he was no expert. They were oil paintings, not water colors. The paint was mostly smooth, not too lumpy. He didn't know much about painting styles, but he knew that van Gogh and most of the impressionists were lumpy painters. They spread the paint in thick layers. He concluded that lumpy was ok, since they were lumpy painters and they became famous, partly because of the lumps.

"Thank you." She motioned to a large print that appeared to be the centerpiece of the collection. "And this one over here has a story."

"Ah yes, I remember it well," Steinman interjected. He could hardly get a word in edgewise. Once Rona got started talking about art, it was difficult to shut her up.

"One Saturday afternoon, or maybe it was Sunday, I don't recall, Saul and I were attending an art exhibit in Manhattan and some of Irina Urumova's work was on display. I really fell in love with her work and I mentioned it to Saul. I thought he wasn't paying attention. He doesn't really appreciate art. But when I went to the ladies' room he approached one of the staff and bought it for me. He had it shipped here to Miami. It arrived a few days before my birthday."

Saul chimed in, "I'm quite proud of that purchase. One of her art friends told me it's gone up in value about 500 percent since I bought it."

"Oh, Saul, you shouldn't look at art as an investment. He's always like that." Paige could relate to his viewpoint. Paige didn't know much about art either, and tended to form his opinions based on market value.

After everyone returned from the kitchen, Saul made the introductions. Paige reached for the outer pocket of his sport coat and clicked a button on the pen that Wellington had given him. It started recording the introductions. The chip in the pen could store up to three hours of conversation. It could also take photos.

"Ladies and gentlemen, we have two new members this evening. Since we have one of each, I'll introduce the lady first." Steinman extended his arm in her direction. "This is Rachel Karshenboym." She was seated on a metal folding chair, bent slightly forward with a plate of food on her lap. She brought her boobs to the party and they were tastefully displayed, to the enjoyment of everyone. As the only woman in the group, she had the best boobs in the room.

One of the men asked, "Welcome Rachel. What do you do?"

She was happy to reply. "I'm a sociology professor at Miami Dade College."

"You have a lovely accent. Where are you from?"

"I'm from Saint Petersburg, Russia. I also lived in Israel for a while." She deliberately failed to mention that she also spent some time in the Israeli army, where she learned some very efficient killing techniques that she fantasized about using on some members of the group.

"Welcome to the group."

Paige took notice, not only of her boobs but also the fact that she was a new member of the group and that she had an Israeli connection. He discreetly clicked the button on his pen to take her photo. He planned to send it to Wellington after he returned home.

Then he motioned in Paige's direction. "The other new member is Robert Paige. He's an accounting professor at Saint Frances University."

Rachel perked up when she heard *new member.* She suspected he might be the CIA mole when she saw him click the button on his pen. Her suspicions were confirmed when Steinman revealed that he was a new member of the group. She had her man. She knew where he worked. Now all she had to do was find out where he lived. Mission accomplished, more or less.

She leaned forward in her chair. "Where do you live?"

"In Sunny Isles Beach. Do you know where it is?"

"Yes, of course, just north of Miami Beach. It's a Russian neighborhood. I've been there many times."

"Yes, sometimes I feel like I'm in Odessa when I walk out the door."

"I know what you mean. Everyone there speaks Russian."

Actually, Rachel's statement wasn't quite true. Some residents of Sunny Isles Beach also spoke Polish and a few other Eastern European languages as well as Spanish. The Brazilian woman who lived down the hall from Paige spoke Portuguese. Some of the snowbirds who inhabited his building in the winter were from Quebec and spoke Canadian French. The service personnel spoke Haitian Creole. The language on the beach and on the sidewalks was mostly Russian.

She tried her best to be cordial but took an instant disliking to Paige. She didn't like Americans as a general rule. She thought they were undereducated, uninformed, naïve and uncultured. She made exceptions for some of the Americans she met in New York. She felt more comfortable with Jewish doctors, lawyers and professors. Most of the men she had slept with over the years had come from one of those three categories, although she once had a Catholic lover who could give her multiple orgasms.

Steinman called the meeting to order. "OK, let's get started. Although you're free to discuss any topic, I'd like to start by discussing the TSA and its Gestapo tactics."

Most of the group nodded in agreement. Rachel was appalled. She thought what the TSA did was necessary to protect the country from terrorists. Giving up a little freedom was necessary in the interest of national security. Then she remembered she was there as an observer. Keep a low profile. Don't do or say anything that would draw attention. She kept her mouth shut and pretended to go along, while every fiber of her being screamed to say something to defend the TSA and its actions.

"As you know, the TSA has been in the news a lot lately for its abusive search policies at airports. Last night there was an item on television about them strip searching a woman who had a double mastectomy. She was wearing some kind of temporary metallic support device to keep her skin stretched, pending implant surgery."

Daniel Harris added, "Yeah, I saw that on the news. A few days before that they ran a story about a TSA agent who squeezed a guy's urine bag, causing it to leak piss all over the guy's pants and the floor. He had to get on the plane with wet pants." Daniel Harris taught philosophy and theology at Barry University, one of the local Catholic universities. Although he was no fan of the Constitution — he wanted to do away with the Second Amendment's right to bear arms — he got outraged whenever some government official conducted a warrantless search without probable cause.

Keith Martin chimed in, "I saw a story about them forcing a 90 year-old woman in a wheelchair to take off her diaper. We need to respond to that sort of tactic and make sure things like that get publicity. The public has to be aware of what's going on in this country." Kenneth Martin was an English professor at Saint Thomas University, another Catholic college in Miami. Although he liked the fact that the courts were dismantling the First Amendment protections on free speech by punishing people for saying things that offended women, minorities or any other protected group, he got upset whenever the feds violated the Constitutional protections against unreasonable searches.

Eduardo Garcia quickly added, "I'll tell you something that hasn't been reported in the news. The FBI is going around to the TV stations threatening to arrest reporters who report on the TSA abuses. The reason I know is because my daughter-in-law works for

Channel 4. They came in and told Lourdes Martinez they would arrest her if she reported any more TSA incidents. They told her she was guilty of treason for giving aid and comfort to the enemy and that she could be charged with violating the Patriot Act. They said they would take her away to an undisclosed location where she wouldn't have access to a lawyer. She wouldn't even be able to call her husband or kids. And they would give her a private trial with no reporters and no jury." Eduardo Garcia taught anthropology at Florida International University. He had been a friend of Steinman's for more than 20 years. They met at a faculty union meeting.

Rachel started to fidget in her seat. She had all she could do to restrain herself from screaming at them. She wanted to scream at the top of her lungs - Couldn't they see that the government was doing what was necessary to protect us from terrorists? They should spend some time in Israel, where the population is surrounded by terrorists, many of whom are walking freely in the streets of Israeli cities because the government doesn't know who they are. Rather than reporting TSA incidents, Lourdes Martinez should be reporting on terrorist cells in the United States. Journalists have a duty to support their government, not report news stories that tear down government credibility. If she didn't like what the government did, perhaps Lourdes Martinez should move to Cuba, where her family came from.

Brian Lewis added, "OK, I agree that we should do something to publicize this kind of activity, but what should we do?" Brian Lewis was an assistant professor of psychology at Florida Atlantic University. Although he didn't know it, his dean was plotting to sabotage his application for promotion and tenure because of his views supporting gays in the military.

Kevin MacPherson suggested, "One thing we could do is organize protests inside and outside airports. We could make signs and maybe disrupt the lines at the security checkpoints to draw attention to the issue. We should make sure to notify the media before we do it to make sure we get maximum press coverage." Kevin MacPherson taught law at the University of Miami law school. He had become known in legal circles for writing some law review articles comparing President Bush and Vice President Cheney to Hitler and Goebbels and for comparing some of the Nazi legislation in the 1930s to the post-9/11 legislation in the U.S. Congress. One item he deliberately failed to report was Hitler's confiscation of privately owned guns shortly after assuming power in 1933.

Mitchell Fisher asked, "Couldn't they arrest us and do the same thing to us that they threatened to do to Lourdes Martinez? And what makes you think the media would come? If the FBI has been threatening to arrest them, they probably would be too afraid to cover the story." Mitchell Fisher was a humanities professor at Lynn University. He appeared visibly nervous at the direction the discussion was going. Although he didn't like the direction the country was moving in, he was afraid to do anything about it.

MacPherson pointed out, "Rights are like muscles. If you don't exercise them, you lose them." It's a point he made often in his law classes. "We can make sure the message gets out. We can have a few people recording it with their cell phones and iPads and have them post it on the internet."

"We could also write letters to the editor and post blurbs on various internet sites. We could call in on radio talk shows, expressing our concern – no, outrage – about what is happening to freedom in America." Daniel had made calls to talk shows in the past. The conservative talk show hosts sometimes hung up on him, but not before he was able to voice his opinion about some issue of the day.

Steinman suggested some long-term activities that would help push the message. "As educators, we have a duty to educate the younger generation. One thing we could do that would affect the long-term would be to assign term papers on some aspect of these issues. We could have our students write term papers comparing some of the acts of Hitler's brown shirts to the stuff the TSA is doing today. Kevin, you could have your students research the civil liberties and free speech and free press implications of some of the legislation that's been passed in recent years, and the constitutionality of arresting American citizens on American soil and holding them without access to an attorney or a public trial."

Brian suggested that, "We could give students an incentive to put a lot of effort into it by offering to select the best papers for publication in an edited book, which would be edited by us, of course."

Daniel leaned back in his chair. "Clever, Brian. Trying to beef up your publications for your promotion and tenure package?"

His comment triggered a smirk from the group. Rachel became more disgusted by the moment. She and Paige were the only ones who hadn't made any suggestions or comments yet.

Paige actually liked the direction the conversation was taking. Although the room was filled with a bunch of lefties who took a cafeteria approach to defending the Constitution, he thought they were right on this issue. The discussion energized him and made him even more determined to see to it that Wellington's team wouldn't kill Steinman. He was starting to like the other members of the group, too, with the exception of Rachel. He sensed she had some hidden agenda, although he couldn't figure out what it might be. He could tell she wasn't enjoying the conversation from her silence, fidgeting and facial expressions.

Paige felt the need to say something. He had to join in on the conversation to become an active participant in the group. "All of these suggestions are good, but they don't have to be mutually exclusive. We could do several of them at the same time. Rachel, what do you think?" He really didn't care to hear Rachel's opinion. He just wanted to make her uncomfortable by putting her on the spot.

He succeeded. She seemed startled and taken aback by his invitation to participate.

"I … I really don't know. I suppose we could do all of those things." She actually hoped they wouldn't do *any* of those things. She really didn't have a problem with what the TSA did, although she would prefer they focus their attention on Muslims, since targeting low risk targets like shiksa grandmothers in wheel chairs and goys with urine bags gave the TSA bad publicity, which was counterproductive.

The discussion continued for a few more minutes. Some members started having separate conversations with other people in the group. When Steinman felt he had lost control of the discussion, he suggested taking a short break.

Some members of the group used the opportunity to take a pee or a smoke break or to refill their plates. Rachel took the opportunity to start up a conversation with Paige. Although she had an instant distaste for him, she felt compelled to approach him. She shot up out of her chair and started walking toward Paige as fast as her fat little legs would carry her. She hadn't thought about what she would say. All she knew was that she had to get closer to him to get a better assessment of the threat he posed.

Her decision to approach Paige saved him the trouble, since he had also decided he wanted to get closer to her, to assess her threat potential.

"Professor Paige, may I call you Robert?"

"Yes, of course." Actually, most people called him Bob, but Russians and other East Europeans usually preferred to call him Robert, so he went along with it.

"Robert, I was wondering, what is an accounting professor doing cavorting with political science and philosophy professors? I didn't think accounting professors were interested in this kind of conversation." Actually, she couldn't care less what his response would be. She knew he was CIA connected. Much more than just an accounting professor. Her experience with Mossad had taught her that anybody can be a spy. Accounting professors were as capable of being patriots or traitors as anyone else in the general population. She just needed an opening line. That one seemed as good as any.

"I wasn't always an accounting professor. I majored in social sciences as an undergraduate, with a concentration in economics and minors in political science, philosophy and history." What he said was true. What he didn't say was that he started off as an accounting major and changed majors after three semesters because he failed Intermediate Accounting I. He didn't return to accounting until after graduation, when he took a job as a bank auditor. He felt compelled to go back to take some night school classes because he didn't know what he was doing during the day.

"Ah, that's interesting. Where did you go to school?" Actually, she didn't give a shit where he went to school. She just wanted to find out as much as possible about him. She regarded him as the enemy, and it was always a good idea to learn as much about the enemy as you can, since it might help to defeat him.

Paige knew what she was up to. It was obvious to him she was attempting to gather information. He decided to go with the flow and not resist. Resisting might alert her that he was on to her. Besides, everything he was about to tell her about his education was already posted on his university website, which he was sure she would look at before she went to bed that night. He had planned to do the same thing with her website.

"I went to Gannon University in Erie, Pennsylvania for my bachelor's degree. Have you heard of it?"

"No, I haven't. I'm sure it was a charming little place."

He didn't know whether she was being polite or sarcastic.

"Yes, it was a charming little place, come to think of it, although at the time I was too busy working and studying to enjoy its charm."

"And for graduate school?"

"I got my master's in taxation from DePaul University in Chicago and my law degree from Cleveland State University in Ohio. I also have a PhD in accounting from the University of Warwick in England and a DPhil in finance from the University of the West of England."

"Ah, you've been to several different places. Which one did you like best?"

He laughed, temporarily forgetting she was the enemy. He was enjoying the conversation.

"As far as geographic location is concerned, I suppose I liked England, since it has much less snow than Cleveland, Chicago or Erie. For intellectual stimulation, I think Erie would be my choice. I spent a lot of hours holed up in the Gannon library reading books and staying warm in the winter. There wasn't much else to do there for six months a year, so I stayed inside and read."

"Da, I know what you mean. I'm from Saint Petersburg."

"Did you study there?"

"Yes, I studied sociology and political science at Saint Petersburg State University. I got my PhD in sociology from New York University."

She had taken the path of many immigrants, taking a degree or two from a university in the home country, then getting a PhD from an American or British university. Saint Petersburg State University was generally regarded as the second best university in the former Soviet Union, after Moscow State University. Her comment about Gannon University being a charming little place probably had some snobbery attached to it.

"You mentioned you spent some time in Israel. How long were you there?"

Her body visibly stiffened. She could feel the conversation turning more in the direction of interrogation. She hesitated and thought for a moment, which people often do when they're about to tell a lie.

"Oh, I was only there for a couple of years. I spent my time mostly in a kibbutz." Her answer was partially true. She did spend some time in a kibbutz. She hoped her answer would satisfy his curiosity. It didn't.

"If you were there for a couple of years, then you probably spent some time in the Israeli army, too, didn't you?" One of Paige's former Jewish students told him a story about being drafted into the Israeli army after spending a few months in a kibbutz, so he knew it was a distinct possibility.

She seemed unsettled by the question, but quickly recovered, as best she could. "Yes, I was in the Israeli army for a few months." Actually, she was in for more than a year.

"What did you do in the army?"

"Nothing much, just dug some irrigation ditches." Actually, she had taken some courses in security procedures and participated in several enhanced interrogations of Palestinians who didn't have proper credentials and who were suspected of plotting to plant a car bomb outside a crowded street in Tel Aviv. One of them tried to sue her and her colleagues for torture in an Israeli court. The case was dismissed for lack of evidence.

"So, it was mostly like being on vacation."

She let out a small laugh at his comment. "Yeah, mostly."

Although she was enjoying the conversation, her main focus was on gathering more information about Paige. As the conversation continued, she made mental notes to help her remember the details she would put in her report of the meeting. Paige did the same thing.

The meeting broke up around ten-thirty. On the way out, Rachel made a point of striking up a conversation with Paige and walked him to his car. She wanted to see what kind of car he drove and get the license number, which she wrote down as soon as he got in the car. When she got into her own car she immediately scribbled down all that she could remember, so she wouldn't forget anything. After she got home she added details to her notes and checked out Paige's university web page, where she was surprised to learn that he also had a PhD in political science from the University of Sunderland, another British university and a certificate in Intelligence Studies from American Military University. She put all the information in her report, which she gave to Sergei Turetsky.

Turetsky gave Paige's name and license plate number to a contact he had at the Division of Motor Vehicles and learned Paige's home address and other information. He downloaded and printed the online copy of Paige's driver's license and placed it in his file, along with a printout of Paige's university web page. Both documents included a photo of Paige, which he enlarged and distributed to his boss and several of his subordinates, along with a summary report. He decided to have Paige followed.

58

"That's quite an interesting story." Wellington was commenting on the data dump Paige had just given him of the Steinman get-together. They were having lunch at *The Chart House* in Coconut Grove. Wellington chose that restaurant because it had tasty seafood and he was in a seafood mood.

Their outside table overlooked the boats in the marina. A speed boat went by, a little too fast. Its wake caused one boat to slam into another boat, making a small noise. The sun glistened off the water. A sea gull landed and perched on one of the docking posts. The smell of the salt air added to the ambiance.

Wellington took the chip from Paige's pen that had recorded the events of the meeting. "I'll file your report and make copies of the photos you took. You can attach names to the photos after I print them out."

Paige leaned forward and looked Wellington in the eyes. "I think Rachel Karshenboym's going to be a problem. I could feel it. I got the distinct impression that she's much more than just a sociology professor. She made a point of coming up to me during the break. I felt like I was being interrogated."

"Yeah, she probably is much more than just a sociology professor and you probably were being interrogated. I'll run her name through the system and see what I can find. If you managed to get a good photo of her, we might be able to pick something up with our facial recognition software. She might have done some work using other names. We'll treat her as a threat for now, but a friendly threat. After all, she does work for the same team, more or less."

"Any idea why Mossad might have planted her?"

Wellington's eyes narrowed, his lids almost closed as he replied. "I don't know. I guess they're just interested in Steinman for the same reasons we're interested in Steinman."

As he uttered the words, Wellington was thinking something entirely different. Mossad knew that Steinman was going to get hit, but Paige didn't know. Mossad's options were limited. It was unlikely they would try to prevent the hit. They probably just wanted to monitor the situation for now, and maybe learn something about the aid he was funneling to the Palestinians.

Wellington wanted to change the subject slightly. "By the way, do you think any of the professors you met at Steinman's should be put on the list for further investigation? Do you think any of them are a sufficient threat to national security?"

"Nah. They're just a bunch of namby pamby professors. Karl Marx probably wouldn't even bother talking to them." Wellington smirked. He found the comment to be especially funny, coming from a professor. Paige didn't want to have any of them investigated. He took a liking to some of them and he liked most of the ideas they came up with to draw attention to the TSA abuses.

Wellington wanted to pursue the issue. "I'm a little concerned they might organize some demonstrations to protest the TSA's policies. That kind of thing could catch on like it did with the Occupy Wall Street protests."

"Yeah, but those protests were organized and funded by outsiders. These guys are unorganized and unfunded and they don't have any ties to groups in other cities."

"Yeah, like Martin Luther King. He wasn't organized or funded at first, either, but it didn't take much funding for him to have an impact. All he had were a cause and people who were willing to march in the streets. And being unfunded today doesn't mean they'll be unfunded tomorrow. All they need is one guy like George Soros to take an interest in their cause and they could be funded overnight."

Wellington paid the bill in cash. He didn't want to use his Commerce Department credit card. He didn't want to have to answer any questions from the bookkeeping department. He could tap into his CIA slush fund without the need for much more than a receipt. They finished their meal and headed toward the parking lot.

Wellington got in his car. He took out his cell phone and called Jim Bennett, his contact at the FBI, who was also on the CIA payroll.

"Jim, I'd like you to run a background check on Rachel Karshenboym. She's a sociology professor at Miami Dade College. Yeah, it's K-A-R-S-H-E-N-B-O-Y-M. I might be able to send you some photos later. Do a facial recognition scan."

"Who is she? What am I supposed to find?"

"I'll tell you after you do your check. I want to see how good you are."

"Thanks a lot, fuck face. You know the FBI always gets its man … or its woman, in this case. We'll find something on her even if there's nothing to find."

"On second thought, I think I should give you a few hints, since this search is a little out of the ordinary. She was born in Russia and spent some time in the Israeli army."

"Hmmm. I think I see where this is going. Am I to assume I shouldn't ask for Mossad's assistance with this search and that I shouldn't use a Jewish agent to do the search?"

"That would be a very good assumption. I'm sure you don't have any Mossad moles in your office, since they are completely trustworthy and don't have a history of spying on the United States, but there's always a first time." He smirked as he said it.

"Yeah, right." They both knew it was a joke. A few months previously, the *New York Times* reported that several Israeli spies had been discovered working at the State Department. It was an open secret that Mossad had spies in sensitive U.S. government positions and that the United States had spies within the Israeli government. It wasn't considered a big deal, since they were allies. Most of the time the press didn't even report on it. The *New York Times* article was an exception. Apparently, something had slipped through the cracks. The usual modus operandi was for someone from the government to suppress the news before it could see the light of day.

Paige got into his car and drove away. He started to think about what the next few steps might be. He didn't trust Wellington's admonitions that Steinman wasn't on their hit list, although it was plausible that Wellington just wanted to keep apprised of Steinman's activities. But Professors Shipkovitz and Kaplan had been hit for doing and saying things that weren't much different from what Steinman had been doing and saying for years. If Wellington was interested in Steinman, maybe he was also interested in Shipkovitz and Kaplan. Maybe interested enough to silence them. And the two guys who accosted him in the university parking lot apparently worked for Wellington, based on what he saw of their conversation in the alley by Wellington's Commerce Department office building. There were too many unknowns. He decided to go along with the plan. For now.

59

"Thank you for your report. I think you've identified the CIA mole. Anyone who would have a pen in his pocket that is capable of taking photos isn't an ordinary accounting professor." Sergei Turetsky was commenting on the report of the Steinman meeting Rachel Karshenboym had just given him orally. They sat in Turetsky's real estate office, along with his Mossad boss, Aaron Gelman. It was after 9 p.m. All the other real estate agents had gone home. They were alone. It was quiet. The air conditioning put a chill on the room. Rachel noticed it.

Gelman didn't usually get involved in minor projects, especially in the early stages. The fact that he was physically present at the meeting indicated that he didn't regard the Steinman project as something minor.

Turetsky turned toward Gelman. "Do you think we should alert Tel Aviv about this?"

"No, not yet. That would be premature. Let's find out some more information first." Gelman hesitated to pass along the information to his superiors for several reasons. For one, they might dismiss it as nothing and accuse him of being paranoid, which they had done on several other occasions. He didn't want to appear to be incompetent. He had an image to protect, an image that was damaged due to a few errors of judgment in the past. He didn't want to have another incident added to his file.

His other reason for not reporting was that Tel Aviv might consider this series of events to be so important that they would take over the project, taking it out of his hands. That would result in another loss of face for him. He could always alert them of this planned hit later, when he had more details.

Gelman looked at his watch. "What are our options?" He was getting nervous about the time. His wife, Shona didn't like it when he was out late and it was getting late. Luckily, he always had a built-in excuse. He worked for Mossad and she knew it, although she didn't know the details. His job prevented her from asking the questions that most wives ask when their husband came home late without a good reason. He had used this built-in excuse to dally with high-end prostitutes from time to time. His preference was non-Jewish blondes from Eastern Europe or the Midwest.

"Sergei, what do you think?"

"One option would be to do nothing. Just let it happen."

Rachel practically jumped out of her chair to respond. "I like this option. Steinman is a piece of shit. He's doing things that undermine U.S. security, and that means Israeli security."

Gelman was a little startled by her response to the question, and by her enthusiasm. He was accustomed to more reasoned discussions. He also didn't know about Rachel's volatility. He wasn't used to dealing with personnel a few levels lower in the chain of command. He almost never dealt with private contractors or part-timers. Rachel was a part-timer.

She continued. "We should assist them to make sure they do the job right. If we let him continue doing what he's doing it would not be in Israel's best interest."

"I think that's overstating the case." Turetsky was beginning to think he had made a mistake by bringing Rachel into this case, or for letting her stay to participate in the discussion. Perhaps he should have thanked her and asked her to leave after she finished giving her oral report.

Turetsky continued. "Steinman's a mixed bag. Although some of his present activities don't help the cause, we mustn't forget that he's a strong supporter of Israel, and that he's vocal about it in the media. I think his support counterbalances his other activities."

Gelman chimed in, "This whole thing would never have happened if the TSA had adopted the techniques we use to screen passengers. Rather than strip search nine year-old boys and grandmothers with colostomy bags, they should focus their attention on the real threat, which is Muslims."

"Yeah, but the Americans are overly sensitive about profiling people. They'd rather strip search a thousand grandmothers than offend a single Muslim." The Americans' lack of logic on this point baffled Turetsky. He had difficulty understanding the American view that all people should be treated equally.

Gelman interrupted. "We could talk all day about the way Americans do things but that wouldn't get us any closer to resolving this problem." Although everyone in the room was an American citizen, they were also Israeli citizens. From the tone of their conversation, it was clear that their ultimate loyalty was with Israel rather than the United States.

Gelman continued. "What are our other options? Let's make a list. Let's think of everything we can possibly do, even if it doesn't sound realistic at first. We can always cross those options off the list later." He looked at his watch. It was approaching 10 pm.

"Make sure that assisting them to execute Steinman is one of the options on the list."

"Yes, Rachel, we'll include that on the list for now." Turetsky said it, but he had already crossed that option off the list in his mind, both because he thought Steinman needed to be saved and because the CIA didn't need any help killing a professor. If they needed help with such a low level target, he thought there was no hope for western civilization.

Rachel turned toward Turetsky. "We should also consider liquidating all of them, since they are all a bunch of little Steinmans. We could let them kill Steinman or we could execute all of them ourselves. I can do it at the next meeting." Rachel's energy level had increased, in sharp contrast to the other people in the room, who were sitting and trying to have a rational discussion of the options.

Gelman had to say something. Rachel was getting out of control. "I don't think that's a realistic option. We shouldn't be in the business of snuffing every person who advocates doing something that's not in Israel's best interest. All options involving killing Steinman are off the table."

Rachel became visibly upset, but she hadn't given up on the idea.

Turetsky felt compelled to end his silence. "One option would be to warn Steinman. If he knew he was a target he could do things to protect himself. He could take some defensive actions." He was talking off the top of his head. This option had just popped into his head. He hadn't had time to think out the details.

Gelman turned toward Turetsky. "What defensive actions could he take? He doesn't know when or where it would happen. He doesn't know who would do it. The only realistic thing he could do would be to get out of town, and I don't think he'd consider doing that." Gelman was thinking logically. Although he had never met Steinman, he put himself in Steinman's shoes, thinking about what Steinman would do in the situation.

"What's more likely is that he'd hold a press conference to broadcast the fact that he is being targeted, and use that as an opportunity to push his agenda." Turetsky had studied Steinman enough to be able to predict his most likely reaction. "On second thought, I don't think telling Steinman he's being targeted would be a good idea. He couldn't really do anything to protect himself, but he could complicate things for us. My contact at the CIA expects us to keep this information to ourselves. He told us in confidence, as a courtesy. If Steinman held a press conference, they could guess where he got the information."

"Another option would be to liquidate the CIA people who are trying to snuff Steinman. If we kill the killers, Steinman and his band of little shits could continue to live." Rachel was half joking. It was a way for her to vent her frustration.

Gelman responded quickly. "Rachel, that's not a realistic option. Targeting CIA people would be counterproductive. Besides, we don't know which CIA people to target, and even if we did manage to kill the right people, they'd be replaced by people we probably don't know."

"Not to mention the fact that the CIA wouldn't let us get away with wasting their people… and they'd do much more than merely file a protest, if you know what I mean."

"You have a point, Sergei. That option is off the table. One thing we could do is protest to the CIA one or two levels up the chain of command. Maybe we could have a meeting with some of them and try to persuade them not to do it."

"That's an option. However, I don't think it would be effective. From the discussion I had with my CIA contact, I got the feeling that there was no room for negotiation or conciliation on this hit. They merely informed us as a courtesy."

"You're probably right. So it looks like our plan for now is to do nothing, but to keep our eyes and ears open. Maybe we can come up with something. If not, Steinman's small potatoes. We can't allow this incident to interfere with the fairly good relations we've built up with the local CIA office." Gelman spoke like a leader, seeing things from the broader perspective, much like Meyer Lansky did in *The Godfather* when the Corleones told him about their plans to terminate two of his low-level soldiers.

Gelman continued. "Let's put a tail on Paige. See what he's up to and who he's spending time with. I think we have some time. Let's see what we can find out."

"OK. I have someone in mind. I'll get right on it tomorrow morning."

Gelman looked at his watch. "It's getting late. I think we've made some progress. Let's go home."

They got up and left. Turetsky turned off the lights on his way out. Rachel was extremely upset. All the options she favored had been crossed off the list. She thought she might have to take matters into her own hands.

60

Sveta and Paige were having lunch at the *Olive Garden* in Aventura. He liked the *Olive Garden* for several reasons. The food was pretty good, the prices weren't bad, and if he ate there, he wouldn't have to cook. Besides, it was close to where Sveta worked, so he wouldn't have to eat alone. One possible negative - you couldn't smell the food. The ventilation system sucked up the smells of the food before it could reach your nostrils.

Another negative was that it sometimes took 30-45 minutes to get a table. That wasn't the case today, though, which was a good thing, because Sveta had to get back to work.

"Robert, you seem a little distant lately. Is there something wrong?"

"Oh, it's nothing. I was just thinking about a project."

"You've been thinking about projects a lot lately. You've been especially quiet for the last few weeks."

Usually, when Paige thought about a project, it was a writing project. He always worked on several articles as well as a book or two at the same time. It was a built-in excuse he always had, although this time he was thinking about the Steinman project, and how he had to find out if Wellington intended to have Steinman killed.

Sveta was right. Ever since he met with Wellington about his new assignment, he had been more contemplative than usual. Sometimes he thought about getting out, resigning his position with the Company. He was only a part-timer, anyway. He wasn't that valuable an asset to them. He could probably be replaced easily. He might even be able to help find his own replacement. Sveta didn't know about his part-time job with the CIA. No one did.

"Sorry. I'll try to be more attentive. I'll try to think of my projects only when you're not around."

"You shouldn't have to try to be more attentive, Robert. It should come naturally."

"You're right. What I meant to say was ..."

"Robert, you should quit while you're behind." She smiled as she said it. She caressed his hand as she continued. "You don't have to try to sweet talk me. It's not like you're trying to get into my pants. You've already been there, and I may let you in there again if you would say a few nice words now and then." Her Russian accent made the words sound especially cute.

Actually, he often got to say only a few words now and then. Sveta always did most of the talking. He liked that about her. He enjoyed being with a woman who could carry on a pleasant conversation, even if most of it came from her end.

"What kind of project were you thinking about? Is it something that I can help with?"

Paige had discussed his projects with her before, on many occasions. She could almost always understand the gist of them, and could often offer insights that he hadn't considered. Although her main subject in school was mathematics, the Russian curriculum also included mandatory courses in philosophy, history, economics and sociology, all from a Marxist perspective. It was part of the indoctrination process the Soviets imposed on their people.

"I'm doing a series of articles on the ethics of tax evasion. I'm looking at some of the arguments that have been used historically to justify tax evasion on moral grounds."

"Tax evasion is always justified in Russia, but never justified in America. The government here is good. We need to support it. Why do you need to do a series of articles about it? Two or three sentences should be enough." Sveta was very patriotic and appreciated the opportunities that America had to offer, in spite of her worries about the direction the country was taking.

"It's a little more complicated than that. What if the government's engaged in an unjust war? Is there a moral obligation to pay for it just because you live in America?"

"Like the war in Iraq? That was a really stupid war. There weren't any weapons of mass destruction. Al-qaeda wasn't in that country until after we got rid of Saddam Hussein. We shouldn't have gone in there." Sveta got especially upset about the war in Iraq because she knew someone whose son got killed there.

"Yes, that's one example. During the Vietnam War years, some people protested and refused to pay taxes to support the war."

"But how could they do that? Taxes are taken out of their paycheck before they even see the money."

"That's right. That's one reason why their efforts failed. They did it mostly to publicize their opposition to the war."

He continued. "I have an even better example of when tax evasion can be morally justified. If you're a Jew living in Nazi Germany and Hitler is the tax collector."

"Of course. You could even argue that Jews had a moral duty *not* to pay taxes to Hitler. And non-Jews, too."

Paige shifted in his chair. "How do you feel about paying Social Security taxes so that the elderly can have pensions?"

"Social Security is a terrible investment. I have to pay and young people have to pay, but the system will be bankrupt before I retire. I won't get any of my money back and neither will the young people."

"Would you evade paying for it if you could?"

"Of course, there's no moral duty to pay such taxes, but it's not possible to evade them."

Paige responded, "That's one of the nice things about philosophy. You can ask theoretical questions without having to come up with solutions."

"Robert, I think you've taken too many philosophy classes. It's a good thing you also studied accounting or you would be starving."

Perhaps it was true. In addition to his studies in accounting, taxation and law, Paige had also taken a PhD in philosophy at the University of Bradford in England as part of the self-improvement program he had imposed on himself. It wasn't as marketable as an accounting PhD, but that didn't matter. He had never considered being a philosophy professor because of the massive pay cut he would have had to take. He liked philosophy for its own sake. He took a PhD in ethics at Leeds Metropolitan University for the same reason. He was able to do both degrees as an external student.

The waitress came over to take their order. Their favorite waitress, Michelle, wasn't on duty that day, but the waitress they had was pretty good, and more than fairly attractive. Graciela was tall for a Puerto Rican, or Boricua, as they call themselves. She had brilliant white teeth, made whiter by her dark brown skin. Her medium length black hair, black eyes and eyebrows gave her a sensual and mysterious look. Her long French manicured nails made her look like a fashion model. She liked waitressing at the *Olive Garden* because it provided the flexible schedule she needed to attend classes at the Florida International University law school.

The room was chilly. The air conditioning was cranked up too high. Sveta put on a sweater. She usually carried one with her when she went to the *Olive Garden* because of the air conditioning.

As the waitress walked away, Paige noticed someone looking at him from two tables away. As soon as they made eye contact, this mysterious person looked away, picked up his fork and started fumbling around with the food on his plate. He was sitting alone.

Not the kind of person who stood out in a crowd. In fact, he was hardly noticeable and not at all threatening. He appeared to be in his early forties, with thinning hair and pasty white skin, and a rather large nose that supported rimless glasses. Apparently he had been avoiding the sun all his life. He looked like an accountant, the kind the firm would keep in a back room with a pencil and calculator, away from the clients. Paige's former Yiddish speaking clients would probably refer to him as a nebbish.

Paige thought there was something familiar about him, like he had seen him before, but he couldn't remember where. Maybe at a continuing education seminar of the Florida Institute of Certified Public Accountants. He would fit right in.

Paige and Sveta continued their conversation and finished their meals. Paige had some kind of Cajun fish. It was tasty, but also a little on the spicy side. He usually had to blow his nose once or twice whenever he ordered it because of the effect it had on his nostrils. Sveta had ordered a salad with two or three kinds of lunchmeat slices in it. Her clothes had been fitting a little tighter than usual lately, which gave her the signal she needed to lose a few pounds.

Sveta looked at her watch. "Oh, I'd better go. I have to get back to work." She had an hour for lunch but no one really kept track of how long she was out. She put in more than the required 40 hours a week anyway, so she didn't feel guilty about taking a long lunch occasionally. One time, shortly after starting at her current employer, her boss mentioned that she came back late from lunch and suggested that she not take more than the allotted sixty minutes, at which point she suggested that maybe she would start going home at precisely five o'clock from that point forward. He got the message and never raised the issue again.

They walked out the door and Paige escorted her to her car. She gave him a little peck on the cheek and caressed his arm. Then she whispered into his ear, "Call me this evening. I won't be too busy."

As Paige turned around and started walking to his car, he saw the little nebbish looking at him again. He stood about 50 feet away, just outside the restaurant. As soon as Paige spotted him, he looked away rather guiltily and started walking toward the next line of cars.

Paige wondered if he was being followed and who might have placed the tail on him. His first thought was Wellington. He decided to confront him. He picked up his phone and dialed him up. He was on speed dial.

"John? Hi. It's Bob Paige. Can I stop by this afternoon? There's something I'd like to talk to you about. Which office are you at today?" He tried not to sound angry, but couldn't conceal it completely.

"Bob, you sound upset about something. Anything we can talk about on the phone?"

"No, this is something we should discuss in person. It's probably nothing, but we shouldn't discuss it over the phone."

"I agree. I'm at the downtown office today."

"OK. I'll be there in about 45 minutes." It usually took him that long to get to downtown Miami from Aventura, sometimes less, depending on traffic. He had to go to the Commerce Department office on SW 1st Avenue. He really didn't want to waste two hours of his day going back and forth, but he didn't see any alternative. He forgot to check which car the nebbish had gotten into. A professional wouldn't have made that mistake, but he wasn't a professional.

Since he didn't know what kind of car to look for, he did the next best thing. As he turned onto Biscayne Boulevard, northbound, he shot into traffic, then turned into the first gas station he could find. He filled up his tank, which was already about three-quarters full. If the nebbish were following him, he would probably be waiting for him in the next mini mall on Biscayne Boulevard. Rather than getting back onto Biscayne, he took a side street, then a few more side streets, meandering toward I-95. After a few minutes, he got on I-95, heading south.

He pulled into the parking garage closest to the Commerce Department's offices 53 minutes later. As he got into the elevator he thought about how he should open the conversation. Maybe a punch. But he wasn't sure that Wellington was guilty. Even if he was guilty, he might not admit it. He could be a shifty character when he had to be. A good trait if you work for the CIA.

61

"Hi Bob." Wellington held out his hand for the customary handshake. "You sounded upset about something. What is it?"

Wellington looked genuinely concerned. Paige was more than just a part-time underling. He was also a friend, not to mention the person who recruited him for the CIA. He motioned for Paige to sit down as he walked toward the door and closed it.

"Someone was observing Sveta and me at the *Olive Garden* today. Did you send him?"

"No, why would I do that?"

Wellington looked and sounded genuinely surprised, first because Paige was being followed and secondly because Paige had accused him of being the one to put the tail on him. He looked Paige directly in the eyes and leaned forward in his chair, placing both elbows on his desk.

Paige gave him the details as Wellington listened intently. From his expression and body language, it appeared that this news was a surprise to him.

"If you are being tailed – and that may not be the case – my guess is that it's Mossad. Since they care enough about what we're doing to plant a mole in the Steinman meetings, they might be interested enough to gather information and look into what you're doing, too. Have you been banging anyone's wife? Maybe it's a jealous husband or a private investigator hired by a jealous husband."

"Very funny. Why couldn't it be a PI hired by the lesbian lover of the woman I'm banging? Ok, maybe I'm projecting with that one."

They both chuckled. "Sorry, Bob, I should've been more all-inclusive." They chuckled again.

Wellington stood up and looked out the window. Not much of a view from his downtown office, but better than nothing. Mostly other buildings, with a thin slice of the Atlantic Ocean a few blocks away.

He stroked his chin, deep in thought. "OK, let's do this. I'll get a couple of my men to follow you from a distance the next time you go out. I'll give them a description of the guy you mentioned. If he turns up again, they'll take him aside and have a little chat with him. How about that?"

"That sounds like a good plan. It might be nothing. Maybe I'm just being paranoid. But I think he was following me."

"OK. We'll see soon enough. How about going to the Aventura Mall tomorrow afternoon? Go to a movie. They have a 24-plex there. There's a large open area in front of the ticket booth and a few private offices inside the theater. I know the manager there. I'll tell him we might want to use one of their offices for a few minutes. Just let me know what time you plan to leave your place."

"What makes you think I'm free tomorrow afternoon? I have to work for a living, you know."

"No you don't. You're a professor. You only work nine hours a week, with summers off."

"Very funny, John. You know I have to spend my spare time doing research."

"Yeah, right. Debits have been on the left since at least the fourteenth century. Unless the feds change the rule, they'll still be on the left tomorrow and the next day." They both smiled.

As Paige left, he started to think about what might take place at the movie theater. Maybe the guy would follow him there, maybe not. Maybe Mossad had a tag team that would take turns following him, which would make it more difficult to detect whether someone was tagging along because he didn't know what the second guy would look like. Or maybe the second person would be a woman, although that's not likely. A woman would be easier to spot, since men tend to focus on them, especially if they're attractive. Men generally don't pay attention to other men.

Would John's agents do their job? Would they be professional or would they act like thugs? How would the Mossad guy react? Would one of them start an altercation or would they proceed quietly to one of the rooms Wellington had mentioned?

If Mossad had assigned someone to tail him, what was their plan? What did they have in mind? Would they try to interfere with Wellington and his crew, and if so, how? Would they be willing to resort to violence? That would be a mistake, but Mossad had made mistakes in the past. One couldn't be content thinking logically when it came to Mossad or any other spy agency. Whenever people are involved, there's always the possibility of irrational behavior, especially if someone feels physically threatened. Paige was sure Wellington wouldn't send two of his smallest guys. They would probably be ex-military and probably on the large side.

As Paige drove back to Sunny Isles Beach he began to get a little worried. Would he be in any danger? Would Sveta? Should he start carrying a gun, just to be on the safe side? He was going to do it after the university parking lot incident, but changed his mind.

His Glock 17 was too big to put in his pocket. Perhaps his 9mm Makarov would be a better choice, unless he wanted to wear a holster, in which case the Glock would be better because it held 18 rounds, compared to 8 for the Makarov. He decided not to think about it anymore. Tomorrow would be another day. It could be a day that changed the course of his life.

62

As Paige approached the door to his condo, he noticed a small circular object mounted above his neighbor's door across the hall. It pointed at his front door. It looked like a camera. He didn't notice it the day before. Perhaps it was installed recently. Small, about a half inch in diameter, hardly noticeable, not the kind the building's board of directors would install. The fifty or so cameras they installed as part of their security system were much larger and noticeable and they were installed in public areas, not above people's doors.

The first thought that came to his mind was Mossad. Now he was sure that the nebbish at the Olive Garden had been following him. The camera had confirmed it. Or maybe Wellington's crew had put it there, although he doubted it. It had to be Mossad. It couldn't be anyone else. He decided to play along and pretend he hadn't seen it.

He turned on his computer as soon as he walked through the door. After it warmed up, he checked to see if any changes had been made to any of his files or if any of them had been downloaded. They hadn't. He didn't keep any incriminating evidence on his computer anyway, but he was curious to see if someone had taken a look. He typed in a three-character message and sent it to Wellington's personal email account – 1 p.m.

Wellington would know what it meant. He would leave the condo for the Aventura Mall at 1 p.m. the following day. He decided to take his 9mm Makarov with him, although he didn't expect to use it. It had been the standard military firearm in the Soviet Union for about 40 years before its collapse. He had taken a liking to the Makarov when he worked as a consultant for USAID in the Ukraine. It was the same caliber as the Glock 17 but lighter to carry.

***

The next day Paige left his condo a few minutes before 1 p.m. and went to his car in the parking garage. Would the nebbish be waiting for him somewhere down the street, or would the nebbish be replaced by someone he didn't recognize?

If the nebbish were lurking in the shadows, he probably wouldn't be parked on 174th Street. That would be too obvious. The most likely place would be in the parking lot at the intersection of North Bay Road and 174th Street. The local police often parked there to lie in wait for people who didn't make a full stop at the stop sign. It was a good choice to observe the passing traffic.

Many of the locals resented the Sunny Isles Beach police because they harassed motorists. They set up speed traps as part of their daily routine to catch the 80-year-old residents going a few miles over the speed limit, yet they didn't hesitate to zip in and out of lanes without giving a signal, and crashed red lights on a regular basis. They thought the laws didn't apply to them.

Paige turned his head to the right as he passed through the intersection at North Bay Road. He always did that to check whether a police car was waiting to pounce on someone who failed to come to a full stop at the stop sign. What he saw was a late model white car pull out of the parking lot. There was nothing extraordinary about it. White was the most popular color for cars in Miami, probably because white reflected heat, whereas black and the other dark colors absorbed it. Paige couldn't tell if the nebbish was behind the wheel. The car was too far away.

He decided to conduct a little test to see whether the car was following him. After turning north onto Collins Avenue and going a few blocks, he suddenly turned left into one of the shopping centers, pulled up to the drive-in window of the local McDonald's and ordered a small diet Coke. The white car also turned into the parking area but stayed back about 100 feet. Paige didn't want to seem obvious, so he didn't look at the white car again until after he got his Coke and continued north on Collins Avenue, toward the Aventura Mall.

He could see the white car pull onto Collins Avenue. It stayed five or six car lengths behind him. As he approached NE 192nd Street he got into the left lane to go to the mainland. Looking through the rear view mirror he could see the white car moving into the left lane. He picked up his cell phone and called Wellington.

"I've got a visitor. He's in a white car. He's staying about a hundred feet back. I'm on Route 856. I'll be at the mall in a few minutes."

"OK. Gotcha buddy. I'll tell the boys to expect you."

63

The mall had a lot of empty spaces at that time of day, which made it easy to find a parking place. Paige parked a couple hundred feet from the entrance closest to the 24-plex. As he got out of the car, he checked his right front pocket to see if the pistol was there. He knew it was, but he checked anyway.

He looked for the white car but didn't want to be obvious, so he took out his cell phone and pretended to make a call. As he put the phone to his ear he saw the car pull up, staying far enough back to be inconspicuous. The driver pulled into a space but didn't make any attempt to get out, which made it impossible for Paige to get a good look at him. He decided to keep walking toward the mall entrance. Paige could feel the warmth of the sun beating on his forehead.

He walked slowly to give his tail a chance to step out of the car and get closer. He went through the entrance door, walked a few feet, stopped and counted to five slowly to give his tail some time to catch up. When he got about half way up the escalator, he pulled out his cell phone again and turned around to see if any of the faces behind him were familiar. Sure enough, it was the nebbish, wearing a dark blue, short-sleeved shirt. The nebbish hadn't spotted him yet. He was looking to the left and right, but it would only be a matter of time before he saw Paige, since he had about 30 more feet to get on the escalator, and it was moving slowly. He used the opportunity to call Wellington and give him a description of the nebbish, dark blue shirt and all.

"OK. I'll relay the message. My guys are waiting for you, sitting at an outside table at Johnny Rocket's. You know where that is, right?"

"Yeah, I know." Johnny Rocket's was a 1950's style diner, complete with classic rock music playing on the sound system. The waiters and waitresses wore 1950's style uniforms. The menu consisted mostly of burgers and hot dogs, with a choice of fries, onion rings, shakes and Coke products. Sveta and he had eaten there several times, either before or after taking in one of the movies at the mall. It was located across from the theaters.

"Go into Johnny Rocket's. My guys will intercept him when he gets close enough. After they intercept him, they'll take him into one of the offices in the mall. There's a security guard standing by the theaters who'll give you directions, or you can just tag along with them, if you like. I've already talked to the mall manager. They have a room prepared. We won't have to go into the theater."

As Paige walked toward Johnny Rocket's he saw two beefy guys sitting at one of the outside tables close to the door. They wore sun glasses and were sipping what appeared to be Cokes. They both faced in the direction of the foot traffic, just looking, not engaging in any conversation. The sun glasses made it impossible to see their eyes, which was the main reason they wore them. It enabled them to observe the nebbish or anyone else without drawing attention.

It wasn't unusual to see people wearing sunglasses inside a shopping mall, but two beefy guys wearing sun glasses and sitting, both facing out at an outside table in the middle of the afternoon, when there was not too much foot traffic, made them stand out. The one with the shaved head looked intimidating.

Paige passed right by them as he walked into Johnny Rocket's. Their table was so close to the door that they could have tripped him if they wanted to. The nebbish appeared, but stayed back until the hostess seated Paige at one of the inside tables. Then the nebbish resumed his approach toward the entrance. As he passed by the beefy guys on his way into the restaurant, they stood up and walked toward him. The bald one took a position directly behind him while the other one walked around to his left, blocking his escape. The one with hair said, "Hi. We'd like to have a little chat with you. Come with us and don't try anything stupid."

The hostess, who was standing directly in front of him and about to greet him, had a shocked expression on her face. She was a small, thin, white teenager, probably just out of high school, with a few pink zits on her face. Each of the beefy guys probably outweighed her by about a hundred pounds. They towered over the nebbish.

The one with the hair turned toward her. "He won't be needing a table." He flashed a badge, probably fake, since CIA operatives don't carry badges. It had the intended effect. It calmed her down. Since she thought they were police, there wouldn't be a need to call the police.

As they turned to exit, the nebbish asked, "Who are you?"

The bald one replied, "We'll talk in a few minutes. Just follow us," at which point the nebbish slid his glasses back to the bridge of his nose with his right index finger.

As they escorted him out of the diner, Paige got up and followed them.

The nebbish looked a little nervous, but not as nervous as a civilian would be. His training helped him maintain a calm demeanor. Besides, he was in a shopping mall in a friendly Florida city, being escorted by two guys who didn't appear to be Arab or

Muslim. He knew he wasn't going to be liquidated or harmed. He figured they were probably with one of the federal government agencies, most likely the CIA, since the case he was working on involved that agency.

He felt more embarrassed than anything. Getting caught meant he wasn't doing his job properly. He must have slipped up. Otherwise, no one would have suspected he was tailing Paige. A minor mistake. It wouldn't result in any injuries or deaths, just embarrassment with his superiors, and perhaps a joke or two aimed in his direction.

They went down the escalator and turned left. The two beefy guys resumed their positions, one on each side of the nebbish. Paige followed a few feet behind. They didn't touch him. That would have drawn too much attention. They just kept close enough to make him think twice before trying to run.

A mall security guard stood by the door of the office they would be using.

He grabbed the door handle and opened it. "Here you go. Be sure to close the door when you leave. It locks automatically."

The guy with hair said "thanks" and they proceeded to select chairs around a large, oval-shaped table.

The bald guy pointed to the chair at the end of the table. "You sit over there." Recording equipment had already been set up to record the event, aimed at the place where the nebbish would be sitting.

The bald guy sat to the right of the nebbish. The bright overhead lights shined off his head. The guy with hair sat on the nebbish's left. Paige sat next to the guy with hair.

The nebbish turned toward the bald guy. "I don't suppose I could have an attorney present, huh?" He said it half jokingly, but looked a bit nervous. It was a little intimidating to be in a closed room with two big guys ordering you around.

The bald guy looked at him, half smirking. "Nah, no need for that. We just thought you were a cute little fella. We wanted to welcome you to the Aventura Mall."

That remark lightened the otherwise tense atmosphere. The bald guy did most of the talking. "My name's Tom." He pointed to his partner. "My friend's name is Jerry. You already know Professor Paige, since you've been following him."

"Before we begin our little chat, we'd like you to stand up, empty out your pockets and place your hands against the wall."

He did what they suggested. He emptied his pockets on the table and assumed the position, as they say. He didn't have to be instructed to spread his legs as Jerry searched him for weapons and recording devices. He was clean.

"OK, you can sit down." Paige watched intently. It was like viewing a television show in 3-D where you could reach out and touch the actors.

The nebbish sat down, looking a little nervous. "I don't suppose I can see some ID. I don't think your real names are Tom and Jerry."

"No, you can't see some ID. We're just here to have a little chat."

Jerry chimed in, using an obviously fake New York accent for comic effect. "I feel insulted that you would cast aspersions on our integrity, accusing us of lying like that."

Tom continued the conversation as Jerry picked up his wallet and searched for ID.

"Who do you work for and why are you following Professor Paige?"

He responded with an exaggerated Yiddish accent and inflection. "What? You're not going to ask me my name?"

Tom looked a little embarrassed. He had forgotten to ask.

Jerry volunteered the answer. He leaned back in his chair and looked at the nebbish's driver's license. "His name is Simcha Rosenstein. He has a Florida driver's license and a Miami Beach address."

"So, Simcha, nice to meet you. Who do you work for and why are you following Professor Paige?"

As Tom asked the questions, Jerry spread out the documents he found in Simcha's wallet and took photos of them individually with his cell phone. When he finished, he sent them to Wellington. A few miles away, another CIA team removed the camera aimed at Paige's front door and swept his apartment for bugs. They didn't find any.

"What makes you think I'm following the distinguished Professor Paige?"

"Actually, we think we know who you're working for. We just want to hear you say it. With a name like Simcha Rosenstein, our guess is that you're probably not working for Al-Qaeda."

"That would be a good guess."

Jerry took out a portable scanner and placed it on the table. "Simcha, we'd like to do a scan of your fingerprints…with your permission, of course."

"Of course." He realized that agreeing would be the best choice. Mossad would do the same thing to Tom or Jerry if they were caught in a similar situation. He placed his fingertips on the scanner glass, right hand first, then left. They also scanned his thumbs.

Jerry took out a long stick with a ball of cotton attached at the end. "One more little request. We'd like to take a little swab of saliva. Open your mouth, please."

"And if I refuse?"

"Then we'll have to cram it up your nose, but we might push it too far. If it goes into your brain, it could kill you … accidentally, of course."

His words sent a chill across the table. He knew they were serious.

He opened his mouth without saying anything and let them take the swab.

Jerry placed the cotton end of the swab into a small electronic machine and sent the results to Wellington.

"Would you like to put on some latex gloves and give me a prostate exam, too? Or maybe, a colonoscopy?" He said it in a sarcastic manner. He was no longer amused by the welcoming committee.

"Not this time. But if we catch you following Professor Paige again, we'll reconsider."

"Message received, loud and clear." His voice cracked slightly as he said the words. Simcha got the impression that Tom might actually enjoy giving such an examination. He could see in his eyes that he was capable of inflicting torture, or even death, without thinking twice about it. Some of his co-workers at Mossad were made of the same material.

"We don't like it when people follow our people around. Not that he's one of our people, you understand."

"Of course, I would never think of following him around, even though he's not one of your people."

Jerry got a text message from Wellington. HE'S MOSSAD. LET HIM GO. TELL HIM TO GIVE OUR REGARDS TO SERGEI.

He showed it to Tom, who nodded, then turned to Simcha.

"OK, you can go. Give our regards to Sergei."

"Yes, I will do that. Have a pleasant afternoon, gentlemen."

He got up and left.

After the door closed behind him, Tom turned to Paige. "Well, I don't know what we just learned, other than the fact that you're being followed by Mossad, which we could have guessed before this meeting."

Jerry turned toward Paige. "I think it's more like communicating a message than a learning opportunity. We want to tell Mossad to stop following Professor Paige around."

Tom turned toward Paige, who was getting ready to leave. "So, Professor Paige, can you tell us what's going on? Mr. Wellington didn't tell us anything, other than to pick this guy up, find out who he is, and ask him why he's following you."

"Sorry boys, you know how it is. Need to know basis. Besides, I don't know much more than you do. Thanks for your help."

They seemed a little disappointed at Paige's response, although they understood the protocol. If Wellington had wanted them to know more, he would have told them.

Paige walked around the mall for a few minutes before returning to his car. He didn't want to run into Simcha in the parking lot. Although relieved that the matter was apparently resolved, he still wondered what Mossad had up its sleeve. They'd probably back off after this encounter, but if they didn't, then what? It would mean they weren't going to let it go. That could only mean trouble … and maybe danger. Maybe they suspected Saul Steinman had been marked for extermination and wanted to prevent it. If so, they probably thought Paige was part of the plan to make it happen, when in fact Paige also wanted to prevent anything from happening to Steinman. He concluded that he would have to wait to see how events played out.

64

"Sergei? Hi, this is John Wellington."

"I thought you might be calling."

"Yeah, there's something we need to talk about."

"We got your message."

"Yes, I know, but I think we should meet anyway. My Boss insists. You know how bosses are."

"Yes, I understand. Same place?"

"Yes, that would be fine. Same time?"

"OK, five o'clock. See you then."

They had arranged to meet at Bayfront Park, by the Anton Cermak plaque. Wellington enjoyed the short walk from his downtown office. It was another warm afternoon in Miami. He enjoyed the feel of the sun on his face, a pleasure he didn't get by staying in his air conditioned office.

Sergei arrived a few minutes early. This time he didn't inform his boss and he didn't carry a wire. He figured he would give Gelman a briefing later. Wellington showed up right on time.

"Hi Sergei."

Sergei shook his hand and they proceeded to walk together. It was a pleasant afternoon, not too hot with a slight breeze. They passed by some Hispanic children kicking a soccer ball. A young mother, presumably belonging to one of the boys, pushed a baby carriage a few feet behind them.

"Sergei, we're a little concerned that you were following Professor Paige. We informed you of our intentions out of courtesy. Do you plan on doing anything that would complicate both of our lives?"

"We're sorry about that. Aaron was just curious. He wanted to learn a little bit about Professor Paige, so he had him tailed."

"So, you've decided to drop it?"

"Yes."

Actually, Sergei didn't know what his boss intended to do about the proposed Steinman hit, but one thing he knew for sure was that no decision had yet been made about what to do, if anything. Mossad had limited options. From a utilitarian perspective, it appeared the cost of doing something exceeded the benefits.

"That's what I was hoping you'd say."

"Have you decided to go through with the hit, or did you change your mind? Steinman's small potatoes on the war on terror."

Wellington smiled. "Well, maybe he's small potatoes, but as far as I know, nothing has changed."

"Have you decided when to do it?"

Wellington thought that Sergei was asking too many questions. If Mossad truly had decided not to interfere, perhaps he shouldn't be asking so many questions.

"No, it's not an urgent priority. It's just on our list of things to do."

Sergei laughed. "I'd love to see that list."

"I'm sure you would. Well, I'll let you get back to whatever you were doing." Wellington extended his hand and Sergei shook it firmly. They took off in opposite directions. As Wellington passed by the hot dog and sausage vendor, he took a whiff of the grilled meat and fried onions that were assaulting his nostrils, stopped for a few seconds, turned around and approached the stand.

"Sausage, please. With onions, sauerkraut and mustard." It had been a few years since he had tasted a vendor sausage. He was usually too busy with work to enjoy these small pleasures. He took a bite. The taste of the sausage, merging with the fried onions, sauerkraut and mustard reminded him of the times his father used to take him to ball games and parks when he was a kid.

As he stood there, consuming his sausage, he started thinking about his encounter. Sergei appeared a little too curious about the CIA's plans for Steinman. Maybe the time had come to start worrying.

65

Bob and Sveta decided to take a walk around the neighborhood in spite of the broiling sun. The Winston Towers complex, comprised of seven buildings, sat in a comfortable section of Sunny Isles Beach, filled with young and old, representing an array of ethnic and age groups. On Saturdays, the sidewalks were populated by Hasidic and Orthodox Jews walking to or from services, often pushing a baby cart. They had to live within walking distance of their synagogue because the rules forbade them to drive on Shabbos.

Another area resident, a gorgeous and exotic looking Asian woman from Kazakhstan, strolled by them, pushing a cart with two seats, one for each of her twins. As she passed them, Sveta took notice. "Her babies are adorable, don't you think?"

They were adorable, with thick black hair, just like their mother. But whenever he would see her with them, he never really focused on the babies. She was stylish and stunning, and looked more suited for Park Avenue in Manhattan. But she actually did fit in, culturally at least. She spoke Russian, as did her Ukrainian husband.

"Yes, they are cute." Although physically present, his mind drifted far away, bouncing back and forth between the accounting article he started writing that morning and his recent experience at the Aventura Mall. He wondered if Mossad was really done with him, or if they had future plans that included him.

Sveta motioned to the park on the left. It was a small patch of lawn shared by the Winston Towers community. "Let's go in here and sit for a while." As they entered the park, she took his hand and dragged him behind her. They found an empty bench and sat down.

She started caressing his fingertips. He liked when she did that. It awakened his senses. He liked to caress her fingertips, too, usually when they were on her couch or when he was on top of her in bed.

Paige was enjoying the silent caress, but decided to break the silence. "You haven't talked about work lately. Are you working on anything interesting?"

"Not really, it's pretty much the same old stuff. Robert, I do have one question. It's about taxes."

"Sure, what is it? I don't know if I can give you the right answer off the top of my head, but I can look it up for you."

"There's no need to look it up. We pay people to do that. I'm just curious. Do you remember that parcel of land I told you about? We have an option to buy, but we can't finalize the deal until we get an environmental impact study."

"Yes, I remember. You told me about it. That was months ago. You haven't bought it yet?"

"No, it's been seven months and the government still hasn't started doing the study. We're paying $30,000 a month to keep the option open, which means we've already spent an extra $210,000 for land we might never purchase."

"That's outrageous! What a waste of money."

"Yes, I agree. And there's absolutely no need for the study. It's just a piece of land."

Paige had heard about the high cost of environmental regulations like this before, but it was the first time it impacted someone close to him.

"My question is this … How should we account for those monthly payments? Should we take them as a deduction on our tax return, or do we have to add them to the cost of the land when we finally exercise our option? And what happens if the government doesn't let us buy the land? How should we treat all those payments then?"

"Hmmm. I really don't know the answer to that question. As I said, I could look it up."

"I know you could look it up, but don't bother. As I said, we have people who can do that. I was just curious."

As Paige thought about how stupid and costly the federal government's environmental regulations were, Sveta added, "We really don't need any more deductions. All the regulations the government has been slapping on us the last few years have eaten up most of our profits. The owners are really getting fed up with it."

They needed a break from talking. They took it. Sveta put her head on Paige's shoulder, let out a sigh and caressed his forearm. They continued to hold hands in silence for a few more minutes.

Eventually, it was time to move on.

Sveta lifted her head off his shoulder. "Let's walk some more."

They stood up and resumed their stroll. As they exited the park they turned left, toward the 700 Building. It was hot and they were parched. Sveta suggested a solution.

"Robert, let's go back to my place. I'll make some iced tea."

"Sounds good to me." Actually, Paige had been thinking of suggesting they go to one of the restaurants or cafes on Collins Avenue for a cold drink, but hesitated to make the suggestion because it would have entailed additional time walking in the broiling sun.

As they walked through the front entrance, Milla, the Haitian desk clerk, had just come on duty. She stood behind the front desk unpacking her things. Apparently, she was working both the afternoon and evening shifts that day.

"Hello Miss Svetlana. Mr. Robert. It's a hot one today, isn't it?"

"Yes, it is." He liked Milla. She always seemed cheerful, even though she didn't have much to be cheerful about. She earned just above minimum wage, raising two kids with a husband who mostly ignored her, living in a country where she had to function in English, her third language, after Creole and French, with little prospect of improving her lot much in the future. Still, she was much better off in America than Haiti, and she knew it. She was happy to be here.

A lot of Americans complain about immigrants, speaking funny languages and taking away their jobs, but most of them are hard workers. They have to be to survive. They're willing to leave their homeland and family and take jobs that Americans don't want, and they don't just take, they also contribute to society. As economist Peter Bauer used to say, "Immigrants not only have a mouth; they also have two hands."

Watching Milla at work caused Paige to reflect on a comment his undergraduate economics professor, Bill Dargan, made in class one day. "They should pass a law that requires people to leave after three generations. By then, they become soft and lazy. If we let in more immigrants, our growth rate would increase because they work harder than the people whose ancestors have been here for a few generations."

The class of impressionable Gannon University freshmen and sophomores were shocked by his statement at the time, but now

Paige could understand exactly what he meant by it. If everyone worked as hard as Milla, the American rate of economic growth would be higher.

Paige and Sveta walked into the elevator and started to hug, swaying back and forth slightly and caressing each other's fingertips. Paige bent forward and nuzzled her neck. He breathed in her scent. Her perfume, mixed with her perspiration aroused his senses. As the elevator approached her floor, Sveta squeezed his hand, gazed into his eyes and smiled. Maybe she was thinking about giving him more than just iced tea.

66

They arrived at the door to her condo. As Sveta dug into her purse for her keys, Paige noticed a small camera above the door of the apartment across the corridor. It looked just like the camera across the hall from his apartment. It aimed directly at her door. He briefly thought about pointing it out to her, then decided against it. She didn't know anything about his part-time CIA job. He didn't want her to know she was being monitored, probably by Mossad. She had come from a totalitarian state where everyone watched everyone else. Informing her of the camera would do much more than just spoil the moment.

Her condo was always spotless, more or less. She liked to keep a clean place, in contrast to Paige's condo, which varied between being messy and very messy. His was the epitome of "the bachelor pad." Mail and open take-out containers everywhere. He usually decided to clean the kitchen when the counter tops started getting sticky. Sometimes he would borrow George and Florence's maid for an hour or two. They lived one floor below him and emigrated from Brooklyn a few decades ago.

Sveta visited his condo occasionally, but she preferred her place. Whenever she visited him she got the urge to clean, and she didn't want to do any cleaning when she was with him.

The tea had been chilling in the fridge for hours. She usually kept a quart or two on hand so she would have something cold to quench her thirst when she came home. She grabbed a bright yellow lemon, cut it in half, then squeezed both halves into the pitcher and stirred.

While she freshened up the drink, Paige retrieved the glasses. The galley kitchen was cramped. With the glasses stored in the cabinet directly in front of Sveta, brushing up against her was unavoidable, but she didn't mind, as evidenced by the smile she gave him as he did it. She filled one of the glasses and gave it to him. He took it and gazed into her eyes as he took a sip. She gazed back. The fragrance of the lemon was reinvigorating and the cool liquid alleviated the dryness in his mouth.

She motioned to one of the chairs in the kitchen. "Robert, why don't you have a seat?" Although she had a nice, large living room, they didn't spend much time in it. Their interludes were usually split between the kitchen and the bedroom. She turned on the sound system and selected "So Much To Give" by Lydia Canaan. It was one of her favorite Lydia Canaan songs.

The couple sipped their refreshments for a few minutes, all the while engaging in small talk and playing footsie under the table.

"Robert, I'm feeling a little icky from walking in the heat. I'd like to take a shower. Care to join me? I could really use some help washing my back."

He grinned. "Well, I was always taught to help a woman in distress." She smiled at him, turned, and led him to the master suite.

Once in the bedroom, she spun around and looked up at him. Standing on her tip-toes, Sveta and Robert shared a soft kiss, then continued on to the master bath. The room was a sizable space, yet comfortable. It looked like the kind of master bath one would see in magazines that showcase the most luxurious resorts and spas from around the world. She had it custom made shortly after buying her condo as a present to herself, and as a way to permanently celebrate her escape from the Soviet Union.

The décor provided a tranquil setting which included a large, stand-alone shower, surrounded by blue-gray slate tile. Shampoos and body wash sat on top of a built-in sill in the back of the stall. Sveta turned on the shower faucet and water began to sprinkle down like rain. Paige's eyes scanned his Russian beauty before landing on the front of her white blouse. One by one, he unfastened each pearl button. After reaching the last in the row, he slowly took the silky garment down her right side and kissed the exposed skin. His lips traveled up and down her smooth neck. It wasn't long before she assisted in *his* disrobing.

The two kissed tenderly and embraced while waiting for the water to heat up. Robert again inhaled her scent. Light, sweet flowers with a hint of vanilla. She always smelled great.

Once the water reached a good temperature, they stepped into the shower and found some soap. Each took a turn lathering up the other. First, Sveta ran her hands over Robert's back, tracing his spine and massaging him lightly. Next, they faced one another. She rubbed his chest as he looked into her clear green eyes.

Wrapping his arms around her, he washed her back. She lifted her arms toward the ceiling and reversed her position, now facing away from Robert. As he kissed her creamy shoulders and long, delicate neck, she let her hands fall onto his head and twisted her fingers around in his hair. Then he started caressing her chest with soft smooth strokes and well placed pinches as he rhythmically pulled her body closer to his.

Robert continued to hold her tighter as he moved his right hand lower and lower, until he reached her sweet spot. Tenderly, he slid his fingers inside of her and set off a chain reaction of sighs and moans. After allowing her a few minutes to enjoy his caring touch, he decided to turn it up a notch.

He pinned her against the wall and gyrated against her as he continued to manually explore her. The feel of the cold slate against her body gave her goose bumps, while the hot, wet steam of the water warmed her inner core, heightening her pleasure. Each time she squeezed his hand, he nudged her closer and closer to the back of the shower. When he finally got her where he wanted her, he helped her assume a bent over position using that well placed shelf feature. Decorative *and* functional. With his left hand sliding smoothly up her back, from the crack of her ass up to the nape of her neck, he removed his fingers and replaced them with his member, completely joining the two of them as one.

It was what she was waiting for. The whole day she had fanaticized about this. It was one of their favorite positions. He surrounded her hips with his hands and pulled her in tighter, against his lower body. She took him in all the way. He made her so freakin' hot! They continued until they both reached their peak of excitement, culminating in an explosion of their genitals.

After a moment of recuperation, he withdrew and she turned to face him. They held each other and she kissed his chest while he smoothed his hands over her back. They let the water rush over them as if caught under a waterfall in the far-off jungle rain forest. After a couple minutes, he kissed her and motioned to leave the shower.

"You go ahead, Robert. I'm going to stay in a little longer."

"Okay."

Paige left the shower and dried himself off. He dropped the towel onto the floor toward the corner of the room and walked over to the toilet. Not thinking to close the door to the separate water closet, he relieved himself, then continued on to the bedroom.

A couple hours later Paige awoke to find Sveta snuggled up to him with her hand resting on his chest. He tried to get up without disturbing her, but she was a light sleeper and opened her eyes the moment he slid to the edge of the bed.

Paige got dressed and Sveta put on a black and red embroidered silk robe she received as a gift from a friend who travelled to China. After finishing another helping of iced tea, Sveta walked Paige to the door. He kissed her softly, turned and walked down the hallway. He headed toward the elevator, not forgetting about the camera across from Sveta's. He wanted to remove it, but would have to wait until Sveta closed her door. She thought he had a nice butt and enjoyed watching him walk away. After ten or so paces, he heard the click of her lock.

He turned around, walked back and quietly removed the camera. He put it in his pocket and walked toward the elevator. After he pushed the button and waited for the elevator to arrive, he took the camera out of his pocket, removed the chip, placed the camera on the floor and stepped on it. He could hear it go crunch. He picked it up and tossed it into the waste container by the elevator.

He suspected Mossad had planted it and wondered why they were still interested in him. Since it was Saturday, he would have to wait until Monday to pay a visit to Wellington's office.

As he walked through the lobby he took out his cell phone and called Wellington to schedule an appointment. Milla sat at the front desk, chatting on the phone, too busy to notice him. He thought she looked cute that day. Her smile revealed a slight gap between her two front teeth. She was always smiling. That's one of the things he liked about her.

"Hello, John? This is Bob Paige."

"Hi Bob. To what do I owe the pleasure of this call? Did you get tired of reading financial statements?"

"Yeah, I had to take a break, and since talking to you is only slightly less exciting than reading financial statements, I thought I'd give you a call."

"Ouch! That hurt, Bob. I thought I was one of your favorite students."

"You were, but now you're just another former C student."

"Ouch again! You're really on a roll. What can I do for you?"

"I need to stop by and see you on Monday. Where will you be?"

"I'll be at the downtown office. It sounds serious."

"Well, maybe it is and maybe it isn't. We can decide that on Monday."

"OK, but let's not meet in the office. Call me on my cell phone when you arrive and we'll meet in the lobby. Any time after nine-thirty will be fine."

"OK, I'll call around nine-thirty."

"OK, I'll see you then."

Paige closed his phone and tried to put the matter out of mind, but in the back of his head he wondered whether postponing the meeting until Monday was a mistake.

67

Sunday

The rest of the weekend was uneventful. Paige and Sveta had breakfast at Denny's on Sunday morning. Sveta went to visit her sister. Paige worked on a manuscript he was under contract to submit to a book publisher. He thought about the camera a few times and what it might mean. He decided its presence meant Mossad hadn't finished with him and that he should be more alert whenever he went out of the building. Did they still have a tail on him? Why did they still have an interest in him? It probably had something to do with Steinman, since that was the only company project he was involved in at the moment.

The fact that Mossad still had an interest in him led to a few spin-off ideas. Was the extent of their interest limited to a few cameras or were they also tapping his telephone and monitoring his emails? Did they plant a tracking device on his car? Was Wellington going to whack Steinman in spite of his denials, and if so, was Mossad prepared to stop the hit on Steinman, and if so, what were they willing to do to prevent it? Who else might they be tracking? Was Mossad also tracking Wellington and Steinman? They were bigger potatoes than he was. It would make sense that if they were watching him, they would also be watching Wellington and Steinman. How deeply was Rachel Karshenboym involved? Was she just spying on Steinman's meetings, or was she assigned to do more than that?

***

Monday

Monday morning. Paige looked at his watch. Nearly eight-thirty. If he left his condo now it would take about an hour, more or less, to get to Wellington's downtown office. Lots of traffic flowed in that direction at rush hour. He decided to wait fifteen minutes to give traffic some time to thin out. He used the time to check his email and reply to a few of the more urgent messages. Actually, he seldom received urgent messages, but he liked to reply to student emails as soon as he could. One of the questions on the evaluations that students filled out at the end of the semester asked if the professor responded quickly to student emails. He wanted to make sure he got positive evaluations.

After fifteen minutes he left the condo, got on the elevator and took it to the parking garage. He got into his twelve-year-old Nissan Sentra and headed out. He bought the Sentra shortly after arriving in Miami ten years before, after completing an assignment for the company in Bosnia.

The first few cars he owned were Chevys and Fords. They always gave him trouble. He had to keep taking them in for repairs. After a few years he got tired of the hassle and has been buying Japanese and Korean cars ever since. Technically, the Nissan was an American car, since it was made by non-union workers in Tennessee, but it was made to Japanese specs, so it was the best of both worlds.

He first became acquainted with the auto union shortly after completing his undergraduate degree. He had moved to Warren, Ohio and the General Motors assembly plant was just down the road in Lordstown. He used to drink beer on weekends with some of their workers, who bragged about how they put beer cans in the door jambs to see if they'd pass inspection, which they always did. The doors wouldn't start rattling until the car reached a speed of five miles per hour and the cars were driven off the assembly line at three miles per hour. No one noticed any rattles until some customer bought the car or took it for a test drive.

Waiting the extra fifteen minutes paid off. The traffic on I-95 was still heavy but it moved fairly quickly until about a half a mile from the downtown exit. Paige parked in the parking garage down the street from Wellington's Commerce Department office shortly after nine-thirty. He called Wellington as soon as he got out of the car to give him some time to get down to the lobby. Wellington was waiting for him when he arrived. The glasses, gray suit, dark blonde hair and tall, slender figure always reminded Paige of what an Indiana prep school graduate might look like 20 years after graduation.

"Hi Bob, let's go outside." The short walk from the quiet, air conditioned lobby to the hot, noisy streets of Miami was a contrast in decibels, smells and textures. Even though it was not yet ten o'clock, the concrete started to heat up. The smell of auto exhaust fumes mixed with those of churros and doughnuts from the shop down the street provided a certain atmosphere, similar to that found in some New York City neighborhoods and a number of Latin American cities.

After exiting the building, Wellington turned left and Paige followed. When they came to the alley, they turned left and walked for about 50 feet into the alley before stopping. "You sounded concerned about something on the phone. What is it that's important enough to come down here?"

"When I went to Sveta's on Saturday, I noticed there was a camera over the door of the neighbor across the hall. It pointed at Sveta's apartment. It's the same type of camera you guys removed from my neighbor's door. After I left I took it down." He pulled an envelope out of his pocket and gave it to Wellington. "Here's the chip I pulled out of it."

Wellington had a puzzled look on his face. "Hmmm. Sergei told me they would lay off. I guess he changed his mind."

"Or maybe he was just lying to you. People in your profession aren't exactly known for telling the truth when it doesn't suit them."

Wellington looked annoyed by the comment but let it pass.

Paige continued, "If they're expending resources to monitor my activities, they must be monitoring Steinman as well … and maybe you, too, since you're a bigger fish than me."

Wellington looked concerned. "I'll have to confront Sergei about this, but I doubt he'll tell me the truth. It'll be interesting to watch him squirm. Maybe I can learn something from his body language and eye movements. I doubt the bastard will look me in the eye when I confront him. I'll have someone look at the chip to see if there's anything interesting on it. Thanks for bringing this to my attention."

With that, Wellington gave Paige a slight pat on the shoulder, turned and started walking back to his office. As he left, Paige wondered if Wellington knew more than he was letting on.

68

Wellington pulled out his cell phone as soon as he walked into the lobby and called Jim Bennett. He figured the FBI had the equipment and the expertise to see what was on the chip. No one in his Commerce Department office had the skills or the equipment, and even if there were someone on staff, he wouldn't use staff resources for this assignment.

"Jim, this is John. Could you stop by sometime today? I want to give you something."

"It sounds important. You know I'm a big shot FBI guy who doesn't have time to spend on trivial matters."

"Yes, I know, that's why I'm going right to the top." They both chuckled.

"How about three? I have to be downtown for a meeting anyway. I assume you're at the downtown office today?"

"Yeah, I am."

"OK. I'll call you when I arrive."

"See you then."

***

Traffic in the downtown area was a little heavier than usual that afternoon, and there wasn't much of a breeze on the side streets, which meant the ocean breeze couldn't blow away all of the exhaust fumes. The smell of the churros from the street vendors had to compete with exhaust fumes and street noises. The side streets were a little dirtier than usual, too.

Bennett arrived on time, which was a little unusual. Miami was on Latin American time, which means three could also mean three-thirty. As he walked into the lobby, Wellington was there waiting for him. After shaking hands and exchanging pleasantries, Wellington got right to the point. He related the conversation he had with Paige and handed over the envelope.

"I can probably have something for you tomorrow morning. I'll give it to one of my guys and tell him it's important."

"Thanks. I appreciate it."

Neither of them expected to find anything of importance, just Sveta coming and going. What they found surprised them.

69

Bennett had the results the next morning. He put them in a flash drive and called Wellington.

"John, this is your favorite FBI guy. I have something for you. Where can I drop it off?"

"I'm at the Rickenbacker Causeway office today. Is that convenient for you?"

"No, it isn't. Why is it you Commerce Department fucks get all the nice offices overlooking Biscayne Bay while *real* Americans like me have offices overlooking a parking lot?"

"Funny, Jim. I'll tell J. Edgar Hoover the next time I see him."

"You do that. I really can't get away before four. I can send it with a messenger, but not one of our guys."

"OK, that'll be fine. Thanks."

The messenger arrived around three with the envelope. Short. Hispanic. Probably in his early forties. Tattoos on both arms. Apparently he forgot to put on deodorant that day. From his appearance and smell, he would fit right in with one of those police lineups they show on television. Maybe he wasn't a poster boy for the American free enterprise system, but he served a valuable function. Wellington's secretary signed for the envelope. She noticed the odor and his dirty fingernails.

"Mr. Wellington, a package just arrived for you."

"Thank you." He opened it and looked inside after she left. The envelope contained a flash drive and a note on plain white paper with just one word – Jim. The return address on the outer envelope was completely phony.

He plugged the flash drive into his laptop. The first few seconds recorded the installation and a brief shot of the face of the person who did the installation – Rachel Karshenboym. It was all the evidence he needed to confront Sergei. He printed a copy of the frame with her face in the camera and put it in an envelope. Then he took out his cell phone and called Sergei.

"Hello, Sergei? This is your favorite Commerce Department official. How's commerce in your neck of the woods?"

"Hi John, the Miami real estate industry's a little slow these days. I only sold two properties this week, but the week's still young. Maybe things will pick up." He took a sip of his mojito. He was ensconced at an outside café on Lincoln Road, the walking street on South Beach, people watching. He had just finished a meeting with some of his Mossad colleagues.

"I'll be at my downtown office tomorrow. Let's get together for a little chat."

"I like our little chats, John. They're always nice and short, and after them I always have more work to do."

"This one won't be any different. Same place? Around five-fifteen?"

"OK."

"See you then."

As Sergei put the cell phone back in his pocket he noticed two young, scantily-clad women walk by his table. One white, one black. The black one had long, slender legs, tight shorts and platform high heels. The white one had sandals and a cut-off shirt that revealed a silver piece of jewelry in her belly button.

After they passed, he motioned to the waiter for the check. He wondered what the meeting could be all about. He thought the Steinman thing had been settled. He took out his cell phone, called his boss, Aaron Gelman and filled him in.

"Sergei, I don't know what's going on, but it's not good. The Steinman thing's behind us as far as Wellington knows. The fact that he's scheduled a meeting isn't a good sign."

"I know. I'll keep you posted."

"You do that."

He hung up and went back to his people watching while he waited for the check. He watched some people more than others. He specialized in people in high heels and/or short shorts or skirts. Usually they were women but some of the people who wore high heels and short shorts in South Beach were of another persuasion. He liked to watch them, too, but only out of curiosity. They didn't have anything like that in Moscow, at least not on public display.

***

They met at the appointed time, at Bayfront Park by the Anton Cermak plaque. Sergei arrived first.

Wellington extended his hand. "Hi Sergei, always nice to see you."

"Same here, John."

Actually, they were both just being cordial. Whenever they met, it always made more work for both of them. They really didn't like seeing each other.

"I have a photo I'd like to show you."

"Oh, John, you didn't catch me with those Mexican midget twin sisters, did you? I can explain. It's not what it looks like."

"No, Sergei, I have those photos in my personal archive. I'm saving them for a rainy day."

"Whew! I'm relieved."

Wellington opened the envelope and took out the photo. "This photo came from a camera that someone installed across the hall from Bob Paige's girlfriend's apartment." Wellington checked Sergei's reaction as he showed it to him. He looked genuinely surprised.

"You recognize her, of course? She's the little mole you planted …"

Before Wellington could finish his sentence, Sergei interrupted, "Of course I recognize her, but I don't know what she was doing by Paige's girlfriend's apartment. What she did was totally unauthorized."

"Well, if what you say is true, you need to have a talk with her. We don't like it when our allies are spying on our girlfriends. We take it personally."

"Of course, I understand completely. Some things are off limits. I'm really sorry this happened. I'll have someone talk to her about this indiscretion. She's completely out of line."

"And you can guarantee that it won't happen again?"

"Yes, of course."

"You can keep the photo … in case you run out of toilet paper."

The comment took Sergei by surprise. Wellington turned and walked away before he could respond. Wellington wasn't in the mood for shaking hands or being cordial.

Sergei called Aaron Gelman and related the conversation he had with Wellington. Gelman was furious.

"That bitch is out of control. I had reservations about using her right from the start. Call her and ask her what's going on. And make it very clear that she's off the case." Gelman didn't like to get involved with details, especially when it included someone lower on the food chain. He didn't like dealing with women in general, especially the ones who were confrontational. Dealing with his wife, Shona, was enough.

Sergei called Rachel on her cell phone but she didn't answer. That wasn't like her. The only time she turned off her cell phone was when she was in class or on an op, and she didn't have any classes this late in the day. He wondered what she was up to.

70

"Let's go to Hollywood Beach for dinner. That Thai place."

Sveta was referring to the *Sushi-Thai* restaurant on the Boardwalk in Hollywood Beach. It had both inside and outside dining and was right across the Boardwalk from the ocean. It was toward the end of the two-mile Boardwalk, so there wasn't as much foot traffic as in the middle, and the chance of finding a parking place was better.

"OK. We haven't been there in a while. Let's go."

Paige liked Thai food. He had been to Thailand several times, usually in the summer. He had a short-term summer teaching gig in Bangkok for each of the past six years.

They were already in the car, going north on Collins Avenue. As they approached 186th Street a car pulled up next to them on the left. Paige sensed something. He looked left. Rachel Karshenboym was in the car, pointing a gun at him from the driver's seat. He slammed on the accelerator, just in time. He saw a muzzle flash, followed by two loud noises. BLAM! BLAM!

He heard the back window shatter. Hitting the gas had turned out to be a smart move. It thrust the car forward just enough to throw off her aim. He instinctively sped into the right lane and accelerated even more, slamming the gas pedal to the floor and zigging and zagging in and out of traffic like the Company had taught him to do as part of his training at the Company farm in Virginia some years back. Sveta was screaming.

Karshenboym also accelerated. She wanted to get in a few more shots but Paige was too far ahead. She decided to abandon her plan to kill Paige, for the moment at least. She turned left at the fork in the road, across the bridge to the mainland. Paige didn't notice. He kept on speeding through traffic, changing lanes to avoid crashing into the cars ahead of him. He didn't have the option of turning onto a side street because there weren't any. That section of the island was too narrow. There were only a few hundred feet separating the intercoastal waterway on the left from the ocean on the right.

He kept up the pace until he reached Golden Beach, which was just north of Sunny Isles Beach. Shortly after crossing the border he heard a siren. He looked out his rear view mirror and saw a police car. He had crashed through the trap the Golden Beach police set up to catch speeders. It was a major source of revenue for the small bedroom community. They didn't have much else to do, so they expended most of their resources pulling over speeders.

Paige was somewhat relieved, and pulled over. He was concerned that Karshenboym might still be in pursuit, but he hadn't seen her in his rear view mirror for many blocks. He figured she had probably abandoned the mission.

The policeman pulled in behind Paige, got out of the car and started walking toward them. His hand was on his pistol, which was still in its holster. A second police car pulled in behind the first one. The Golden Beach police usually work in teams. Most people who speed in Golden Beach are only 5 or 10 miles over the 35-mile limit. Paige was clocked at over 90. They were treating it as a special case and were taking extra precautions.

As the officer approached the driver's side of the car, Sveta started screaming before either Paige or the officer could say anything.

"Someone just tried to kill us! Look! They shot out the window!"

She continued to try to explain what had happened. The excitement in her voice was drowning out the words. Her Russian accent, which was usually so slight you could hardly notice, was getting thicker by the second. She was more interested in telling what had happened than in proper pronunciation.

The officer looked at the window and took his hand off his pistol.

"Driver's license and registration, please."

Paige handed them over.

"What happened, sir? Did someone try to shoot you?"

Paige explained what had happened. All he told the cop was that it had been a woman and that he didn't know who she was or why someone would want to shoot him. Paige suggested that it might be a case of mistaken identity.

If it would have been up to Paige, he wouldn't have reported it to the police. He just would have called Wellington and let him deal with it. Wellington could have found someone to discreetly replace his shattered window without notifying the police and he could have sent some of his boys to pick up Karshenboym, if they could find her. But it was too late for that. Sveta was with him, and now the police were involved. He had to feign ignorance of the person and motive.

"You'll have to come to the station with us. We need to write a report."

Paige followed the first police car to the station, which was only a few blocks away. The second police car followed Paige. It took nearly two hours before they were finished interviewing both of them. Paige wanted to call Wellington to tell him about the incident but decided against it. If either the police or Sveta overheard the conversation it would raise questions he didn't want to answer. He couldn't take a chance on calling Wellington from the men's room. He had to wait. He wondered if his decision to wait would turn out to be a mistake.

71

Rachel Karshenboym was frustrated that she had failed to kill Paige. It wasn't like her to screw up such an easy mission. All the people she had whacked for Mossad had been liquidated without any major problems. Maybe if someone else had been doing the driving, she would have been able to concentrate on the job, but she had to do this job alone, since Mossad hadn't authorized it.

After taking the bridge to the mainland she started thinking about what to do next. She couldn't go home because Paige had probably recognized her. If there wasn't someone waiting for her at home, it wouldn't be long before someone would show up, and it wouldn't be the local police. She decided to pull into the Aventura Mall and call Sergei. She wasn't looking forward to the conversation but she couldn't think of anything else to do.

She found a parking space a few hundred feet from the shops and pulled in. She took out her cell phone and called Sergei. He picked up on the third ring.

"Hello, Sergei? This is Rachel."

"Rachel, I've been trying to contact you. We need to talk."

"Sergei, just listen to what I have to say. I just tried to kill Paige and that little blonde slut of his but I missed. I think he recognized me."

"What!? Why did you do that? We didn't authorize a hit. What were you thinking?"

"Paige needs to be eliminated. And so does Steinman. I wanted to get Steinman, too, later this evening, but now I can't. What should I do?"

Sergei thought for a few seconds.

"I have half a mind to bring you in and turn you over to them. You've really caused a lot of problems for us."

"Yes, I know, and I'm sorry, but I felt strongly that they both needed to go."

"No they don't. Steinman's small potatoes, and Paige is one of them. Do you realize what could happen if we start executing CIA assets?"

"I'm sorry. I wasn't thinking." She was shaking as she held her cell phone.

"Well, it's too late to do anything about it, but we can work on damage control. You have to get out of the country. Do you have your passport with you?"

"Yes, I always carry it with me."

"Good. Go to the airport and fly to Tel Aviv. If you can't get a direct flight, get a connecting flight. Get there as fast as you can. Once you're in Israel you'll be safe. But I'll have to try to clean up your shit."

"OK, I'll go there right now. What about my car and the gun?"

"Park it in one of the airport garages. When you get there, call me and tell me where it is. Leave the key under the mat on the driver's side and leave it unlocked. Leave the parking stub there, too. I'll have one of my guys pick it up. Put the gun in the trunk, or in the glove compartment, if it'll fit."

"OK, I'll call you."

"You really fucked up big time, Rachel."

"Yes, I know. I'm sorry." Her voice cracked as she said it. She was near tears.

***

Sergei called one of his guys and told him to take a taxi to the airport and wait for instructions. Then he called Aaron Gelman, his boss. He wasn't looking forward to the conversation but it couldn't wait until morning.

Gelman picked up on the second ring. Sergei could hear Gelman's wife, Shona in the background.

"Aaron, who could be calling you this late?" she shouted from the next room. "Tell them you'll talk to them in the morning."

"Shona, I have to take this call." He walked into the bedroom and closed the door.

"What could be so important you're calling me at home at this hour? You know Shona doesn't like me to get calls at night."

"Yes. I know. I'm sorry, but this couldn't wait."

Sergei related what had happened. Gelman wanted to scream at him but couldn't because Shona would hear.

"OK, we'll find a way to deal with this. Call our people in Tel Aviv. Tell them to pick her up when she arrives. Tell them what you just told me, so they'll know what this is all about. They'll find out anyway. It's better if they hear it from us first. If Wellington calls you, pretend you don't know anything about it."

"OK, will do."

Gelman hung up. As he walked out of the bedroom, Shona asked, "Who was that?"

"Wrong number."

Gelman spent the rest of the evening thinking about his options. He was hoping that Paige hadn't recognized her but he proceeded with the assumption that he had. Luckily, no one had been killed or injured. If someone had, there would have been hell to pay. He was hoping the whole thing would blow over in a few days or weeks, but he knew that hoping wouldn't change the reality. The next few days would be the worst. Then things would calm down, or so he hoped.

What he didn't know was that the failed attempt would lead to a response that would make his life much more complicated.

72

After Paige and Sveta finished their interviews with the police, they were exhausted.

Paige turned to Sveta. "Are you hungry?"

"Yes, a little, but I'm not in a mood for Thai food or Hollywood Beach. Let's just go back home. We can stop at Denny's."

Paige thought that was a good idea. He was anxious to call Wellington. Time was precious and he wanted to tell Wellington what had happened before Rachel Karshenboym could get out of the country, since Paige suspected that was what she would do.

It took them less than 10 minutes to arrive at Denny's. It was past the normal dinner hour and there were lots of available tables. One of the waitresses seated them immediately.

"I'm going to go to the men's room. I'll be right back."

"OK. I'll be right here."

Upon entering the men's room, Paige checked to see if anyone was there. He was alone. He took out his cell phone and called Wellington, telling him what had happened as quickly as he could. He didn't want anyone to walk in and listen to the conversation.

"Thanks for telling me about this right away instead of waiting until tomorrow morning. Maybe we can catch her before she leaves the country, assuming that's what she plans to do. I'll get back to you as soon as I have something."

Wellington hung up and immediately called one of his contacts at Miami International Airport. He would have preferred calling Santos Hernandez, his TSA contact, but Santos was working the day shift and had already left the airport grounds. Contacting anyone else might raise questions he didn't want to answer.

"Hello, Sam? This is John Wellington. How are you?"

"Fine, John. To what do I owe this pleasure?"

"I think a certain person of interest might be flying out of Miami International in the next few hours and I would like you to detain her, if possible...unofficially, of course. We don't want any paperwork."

"Ah, I don't know if I can do that, John. We have to follow protocol, you know. All these new regulations require us to fill out paperwork every time we wipe our ass."

"Yeah, I know. But this is important and it's not something that should get on the radar, if you know what I mean. National security."

"Yeah, yeah, that's what you guys always say. Give me some information. I'll see what I can do."

"Her name is Rachel Karshenboym. I'll fax you a photo and some details."

"Where's she flying to?"

"Probably Tel Aviv or some other Israeli city, but it's just a guess."

"Well, that complicates things a little, because there aren't any direct flights to Tel Aviv from here. She'll have to book a connecting flight."

"Yeah, that does complicate things. Check the international flights. My guess is that she'll want to get out of the country as soon as possible, so she probably won't book a flight to Cleveland or Detroit."

"Are you sure she's coming to Miami International? She might go to the Fort Lauderdale airport instead."

"Actually, I'm not sure if she's going to any airport. I'm just assuming, and I think Miami International would be her first choice, since it has more international flights."

"Well, if it's any consolation, the Fort Lauderdale airport doesn't have any direct flights to Tel Aviv, either. She would have to get a connecting flight there, too. Send me the information. I'll see what I can do."

"Thanks, Sam. I appreciate it."

Wellington hung up and looked at his watch. The clock was ticking, and time was not on their side. He called his contact at the Fort Lauderdale airport. The conversation was about the same. About an hour later, Sam called back.

"Hi John. I got the information you wanted. She left for Tel Aviv about a half hour ago. She took British Airways with a stopover in London. Do you want me to contact the people in London to detain her?"

"No, that won't be necessary. Thanks, Sam. I owe you one."

"Yeah, I know. And I won't forget."

Getting any more outsiders involved is the last thing Wellington wanted. The whole professor-whacking project was under the radar and he wanted to keep it that way. If someone outside the loop got involved, there would be questions and probably paperwork. He decided to drop his pursuit of Karshenboym. Extradition was out of the question, for at least two reasons. He didn't want the visibility and Israel doesn't extradite its own people anyway, with very limited exceptions, and only in high profile cases. The last thing he wanted was for this case to become high profile. He would deal with the situation locally.

By this time, Wellington was both tired and fuming. If the Israelis were willing to whack Paige, what else were they willing to do? What were their plans? He needed to know.

He looked at his watch. It was after 10pm. He called Sergei. He didn't want to wait until morning.

"Sergei, you fucking son of a bitch."

Sergei was in the living room of his apartment, with Carla, a young Cuban woman he had picked up at one of the bars in South Beach. Wellington's call broke the mood.

"John, why all the hostility? We're allies, remember?"

"Allies don't go around trying to whack allies."

"What do you mean? Nobody's going around whacking anybody."

Carla perked up when she heard him say that. Wellington was screaming into the phone so loudly that she was able to hear both sides of the conversation. She wondered what she had gotten herself into. Who was this guy, anyway? He had told her he worked in real estate. She decided she should be more careful deciding who to go home with in the future, although the conversation she was hearing did arouse her sexually. She wondered what he would be like in bed. She felt a slight swelling in her crotch.

"Rachel Karshenboym tried to whack Robert Paige earlier this evening. I suppose you don't know anything about that, do you?"

"No, of course not. We would never authorize anything like that." He tried his best to sound surprised and sincere. He had been expecting the call.

Sergei became alert to his surroundings. He was standing in front of the couch. Carla was sitting, leaning forward, looking up at him, her eyes practically bulging out of her head, her mouth wide open, listening intently. He decided to move into the bedroom. He closed the door.

"I want to see you and Gelman tomorrow at ten o'clock. You need to explain why you targeted Paige."

"We didn't target Paige. We would never do that. What Rachel did was completely unauthorized."

"Yeah, well you can tell that to my face tomorrow at ten. Same place."

"OK. I'll call Aaron and arrange the meeting."

"You do that." Wellington hung up.

Sergei looked at his watch. It was too late to call Gelman. He knew better than to incur the wrath of Shona. He decided to send him a text message instead.

"We have a meeting tomorrow at 10 with W. It's about Rachel."

A few minutes later he received a reply. "OK. Pick me up at 9:30."

***

The next morning, Sergei drove to Gelman's office in Brickell. He arrived a few minutes early. Gelman was outside waiting for him. No need to find parking. The drive to the Anton Cermak plaque would take a few minutes. They talked on the way.

"What did Wellington say exactly?" Sergei related the conversation he had with Wellington the night before. He left out the fact that Carla had overheard the first part of the conversation. It was a breach of security Gelman didn't need to know about.

Carla's eavesdropping did have its benefits. She was very excited in bed. Although he made the first move on the couch, she initiated sex the next three times. He was shooting dust by the time she was done with him the next morning. He promised to call her.

"We have to convince him we had absolutely nothing to do with this."

"Yes, I know. I don't know how easy that will be, though. After all, she did work for us. By the way, she's in London, waiting for a connecting flight to Tel Aviv."

"Well, at least you have some good news to report."

They arrived at Bayfront Park, parked the car and walked to the Anton Cermak plaque. Wellington was waiting for them.

Gelman and Sergei extended their hands to shake as they approached. Wellington kept his hands in his pockets.

"I'll get right to the point. Why did you try to whack Paige and what are your future intentions regarding Paige and Steinman?"

Gelman did the talking. "I'm very sorry this happened. Rachel Karshenboym was acting totally on her own. We would never authorize such a thing."

Wellington didn't know whether to believe them or not. It didn't matter. She was out of the country and out of the picture. They wouldn't dare try again. He was a CIA asset, and they knew there would be consequences if they tried again.

"Then you can assure me that Paige is not in your sights?"

"Absolutely!"

"And that you won't place surveillance on him or his girlfriend?"

"Absolutely!"

Wellington turned to Sergei. "Is there anything else we need to discuss?"

Gelman interrupted before Sergei could say anything. "No. I would just like to say again that we're very sorry that this happened. It will not happen again."

"It had better not, or there will be consequences."

With that, Wellington turned around and walked away. Sergei and Gelman did the same. After dropping Gelman at his office, Sergei went back to his apartment and took a nap.

73

Friday night. Paige and Sveta were at the Steinman's, having dinner with Saul and Rona. They'd had dinner with them a few times in the last month. Paige and Saul were becoming friends and so were Sveta and Rona. Although they came from different backgrounds, they enjoyed each other's company. Sveta had suggested having dinner at her place but Rona politely declined, and offered to have dinner at her place instead. The reason she declined was because Sveta didn't keep a kosher kitchen, although Rona didn't say that when she declined Sveta's invitation.

They were sitting in the living room. Sveta had just finished telling Saul and Rona about what happened earlier in the week. Both Saul and Rona had been listening intently.

Rona leaned forward. "Who do you think could have done it, and why?"

Paige interrupted. "We really don't know. It doesn't fit the usual modus operandi of a drive-by shooting. For one thing, it was a middle-aged white woman."

Saul interjected, "And it was in a Jewish neighborhood, Sunny Isles Beach! Nobody's safe anymore."

Paige turned toward Steinman. "I think it was a case of mistaken identity. She didn't look like any of my students."

Saul and Rona laughed. Rona got up and started walking toward the kitchen. "I think the brisket is ready." It smelled delicious. The aroma was wafting into the living room.

A few minutes later she emerged to announce, "Dinner's ready." They all walked into the dining room and sat down, while continuing their conversation.

"This is a typical Friday night kosher dinner," Rona explained, "brisket, chicken soup with matzo balls, challah and potato kugel."

Saul replied, "I told Rona years ago that I'm an atheist but she still thinks that if she feeds me kosher meals, I'll become Jewish again."

Saul continued. "There's a special story behind the challah. When the Jews made their exodus from Egypt and wandered in the desert for 40 years, God dropped manna from the sky so they would have something to eat, but he didn't drop any manna on Shabbos, so he dropped twice as much manna on Friday. That's why we have two loaves on the table."

Rona interjected. "Saul, you forgot to tell them the most important part. Tell them why the Jews wandered in the desert for 40 years. It's because men never ask for directions."

They laughed and started eating. After a few minutes the conversation turned toward politics and current events.

Saul turned toward Paige. "Did you see any drones yet?" He was referring to the unmanned aircraft the federal government had started flying over Miami as part of its anti-terrorism program.

"No, I haven't seen them but I heard about them on TV."

Saul leaned forward. "What do you think of them?"

Rona interjected. "I don't see anything wrong with them. They're using them to protect us from terrorists."

"That's bullshit ... pardon my French." Saul was visibly upset. He was practically shouting. "I saw one flying over Florida

International University last week. FIU doesn't have any terrorists."

Paige tried to calm him down. "Some people are upset about it. I read on the internet that some guy in Dallas got arrested for trying to shoot one down with a rifle. He demanded a jury trial but the feds aren't going to let him have one. They say he can't have a public trial for national security reasons and because it would give aid and comfort to the terrorists."

Saul put down his tea cup. "Who are these terrorists, anyway? I think the feds are becoming the terrorists. I read that some guy in Coral Gables got arrested for illegally watering his lawn and that the local police found out about it because of a drone. It took photos that the police are going to use in court. We're headed toward a police state and nobody seems to give a shit."

Rona interjected. "Saul, calm down. We're trying to have a peaceful dinner."

The rest of the dinner was pleasant, as the conversation shifted to less controversial topics. When dinner was over, Rona and Sveta started taking the dishes into the kitchen. Saul and Paige walked into the living room and continued their conversation.

"Saul, do you ever worry that some of the stuff you say might get you in trouble?"

"Sometimes I worry a little, but not enough to shut me up. I'm tenured and I have the First Amendment to protect my right to free speech."

"Did you know that some members of Congress want to amend the First Amendment so that people who speak out about the federal government's anti-terrorist activities aren't protected?"

"Yeah, I heard about it but that's never going to happen." Saul seemed quite confident.

Paige was less certain. "During World War I, President Wilson had 10,000 people arrested for speaking out against the war. During the Civil War, President Lincoln shut down newspapers and had a warrant issued for the arrest of a Supreme Court Justice. What makes you think they can't do that again?"

"That was before television and the internet. They wouldn't dare do that now. There would be riots in the streets."

"How can you be so sure? After the federal massacres at Waco and Ruby Ridge the people didn't do anything. They killed a bunch of people who were minding their own business. Their main crime was that they didn't like the federal government. If the feds can execute dozens of innocent people, including women and children, and get away with it, what makes you think they'll get upset if the feds arrest a few left-wing academics?"

"I hear what you're saying. Most of the people are asleep, and the millions of right-wing nut cases mostly approve of what the feds are doing. Which reminds me, did they ever catch the guy who assassinated Raul Rodriguez?"

"No, I don't think so. I haven't heard anything."

That comment got Paige to thinking about the reason he first approached Steinman for a meeting. He felt guilty about what he was doing, spying on someone who had become a friend and reporting back to Wellington. He sometimes felt like he was a spy for the Gestapo, the Nazi secret police.

"Don't you ever worry about getting assassinated? You hold the same position on the Cuban embargo that Rodriguez held, and your views aren't much different than those of professors Shipkovitz and Kaplan, either."

"Yeah, I know, but you can't go around being paranoid about being assassinated. I feel that I have to speak up when I think something is wrong. Nobody's going to shut me up."

"Saul, you mentioned that most of the right-wing nut cases approve of what's going on, but some of them don't."

"Like who?"

"Timothy McVeigh, for one. He got so upset about what the feds did in Waco and Ruby Ridge that he *did* something about it. There are a lot of others who felt the same way. They just didn't do anything about it."

"Yeah, that's the point. They didn't do anything about it. At least I have the guts to speak up. You don't have to blow up federal buildings with day care centers to make your point."

"Do you think that speaking up is enough? What if your words fall on deaf ears? What if the millions of low-information voters we have in this country continue to elect the same politicians we have in Washington now? Do you think that, at some point, targeted assassinations might be more effective?"

"We haven't reached that point yet, and I hope we never do."

Paige continued. "Timothy McVeigh considered targeted assassinations. He wanted to assassinate the attorney general for approving the Waco and Ruby Ridge massacres and the federal judge who put his stamp of approval on the Waco murders, but decided against it because it would be too difficult. He went to Plan B, which was blowing up the federal building where he thought some of the federal agents who took part in Waco and Ruby Ridge had offices."

"I don't approve of any assassinations, targeted or not. We live in a democratic country where we can change things peacefully without taking human life. You sound like you approve of political assassinations."

Paige hadn't fully formulated his views on the issue, but he had decided that Steinman should not be an assassination target, whether by the feds or a private party who disagreed with him.

Paige continued. "Sometimes words may not be enough. Germany was a democracy in 1933, when Hitler assumed power through the democratic process. Don't you think the world would be a better place if someone would have assassinated that democratically elected leader in 1933?"

"Without a doubt, but that's an exception."

"Do you think there could be exceptions that apply to present-day America? Are there any cases where targeted assassinations might be morally justified?"

"No, I don't think so. We're going in the wrong direction, toward a totalitarian state, but things haven't gotten that bad yet. We have a long way to go before any kind of assassination is justified."

Paige wanted to push the envelope to see where Steinman thought the red line should be drawn. "Do you think that shooting down a drone or two would be justified? Nobody would be killed, since they're unmanned?"

"Yeah, that might be justified. We shouldn't have drones flying over universities."

"How about shooting out some of the cameras they're installing on our highways? Do you think that could be morally justified?"

"Yeah, I think George Orwell and Aldous Huxley would approve."

"But drones and cameras can be replaced. We wouldn't solve the problem by destroying them. We would only be increasing government spending because they would replace them."

"Yeah, but we would be sending a message."

"But if mere words won't change anything, what makes you think that shooting up a few cameras would be any different?"

Steinman was curious as to where the conversation was headed. "Then what do you suggest?"

"What if those right-wing nut cases started targeting the people who control the drones and the people who install the cameras? Do you think that would send an effective message? You know what they say ... Nothing changes until there's a body count."

"Well, that certainly would send a message, but do you really think that's the way to go?"

Paige pondered for a moment to consider his response to Steinman's question. "Sometimes one little act can have a disproportionate effect on the feds' behavior. Like that guy who tried to blow up an airplane with explosives in his shoes. Ever since that incident, the feds have been making us take off our shoes at airports. Maybe if a few right-wing nut cases, as you call them, would target a few of the foot soldiers who install cameras or fly drones, they would get the message."

Steinman was getting visibly upset. He was beginning to think he was talking to one of the right-wing nut cases he so strongly disapproved of.

Paige continued. "Let's take it a step farther. Rather than going after the foot soldiers, why not go after the politicians and bureaucrats who made the decision to install the cameras and fly the drones over universities?"

"You're starting to scare me, Bob. Are you serious or are you just pulling my chain?"

"Let's change the facts a little. Let's say that we were in Nazi Germany in the 1930s and Hitler's goons started flying drones over some university in Berlin and put up cameras to track the movements of Jews."

"That's an entirely different situation."

"How is it different?"

"Well, I don't know. But it's different."

"Would killing their goons be justifiable? Would it be a patriotic act? Wouldn't it be an act of self-defense?"

"Yes, I think so, but the situation in the United States is different."

"How is it different?"

"We are a democracy. We elect our leaders."

"Hitler was elected."

"You keep pointing that out." Steinman smiled. He thought Paige put up some pretty good philosophical arguments for an accounting professor. He was enjoying the discussion, even though he strongly disagreed with the direction Paige was taking it.

Rona and Sveta walked back into the room. Rona was carrying a bowl of sliced fruit. Sveta was carrying small plates and forks.

Saul noticed as they entered the room. "What, no ice cream?"

Rona feigned a disagreeable expression on her face. "We just had brisket and you know it. I'm not going to give you dairy after you just ate meat. As long as you live in this house you're going to eat like a good Jew, even if you're an atheist."

Paige was enjoying the conversation, too, but he was also getting upset by it. He wanted to tell Steinman that he had probably been targeted for assassination, even though he wasn't quite sure because of Wellington's repeated denials. He wanted to scream it out so the whole neighborhood could hear. But he kept silent, just like the masses kept silent after Ruby Ridge and Waco. But, unlike the masses, he planned to do something. He just didn't know what to do – yet.

74

"No people and no part of a people shall be held against its will in a political association that it does not want."
Ludwig von Mises

"Governments are instituted among Men, deriving their just powers from the consent of the governed ... whenever any Form of Government becomes destructive of these ends, it is the Right of the People to alter or to abolish it, and to institute new Government."
U.S. Declaration of Independence

Late afternoon. Steinman and Paige sipped coffee at Starbucks on the FIU campus. It was raining heavily in Miami, too heavily to go outside. The pitter patter of the raindrops against the windows was soothing, almost hypnotic. One could smell the ozone in the air. They decided to stay inside and wait until the rain stopped. A week had passed since Rachel's attempt on Paige's life.

Earlier that day, Steinman had given a lecture in his political science class about secessionist movements in nineteenth century America. A few of his students raised some questions about recent news reports that discussed the possible secession of California.

Steinman expressed concern about the secession movements that were popping up all over the country.

"Bob, what do you think of these secession movements? Legislatures in Florida, Louisiana, Texas and Kansas have voted to secede, and the California legislature is talking about scheduling a vote on it next week."

"I like the idea. The federal government is out of control. They're racking up multi-trillion dollar deficits every year and are borrowing the money from China. My children and grandchildren are going to have to pay that debt unless we either declare national bankruptcy or secede."

"Do you think national bankruptcy is an option? That's never been done before."

"Sure it's an option. Other governments have done it. We can, too. The alternative is to have our children and grandchildren burdened with the debt that our incompetent representatives have created."

"Don't you think we can pay it off by cutting spending and raising taxes?"

"No, I don't. The national debt has grown too large for that. Besides, Congress is incapable of cutting spending, and for every extra dollar they raise in taxes, they spend an extra dollar and a half. Even if the feds confiscated 100 percent of the assets of the richest five percent of the population, it wouldn't be enough to fund the government for more than a few months. And they could only do that once. What would they do next year?"

"You're a lawyer and a CPA. Can't you think of a better solution?"

"Actually, secession is a better solution."

"Why is that?"

"We could pay off the debt by printing money, but that would destroy savings and the value of the dollar. Or we could declare national bankruptcy, but if we did that, we would still have the Patriot Act and all those other laws that take away the right to an attorney or a jury trial and that allow warrantless searches, wiretaps, monitoring emails and drones flying over our homes. If we seceded, we would get rid of the debt and the Patriot Act at the same time."

"But wouldn't that lead to a civil war? That's what happened the last time states tried to secede."

"Not necessarily. The fifteen Soviet republics seceded from the Soviet Union without any problem. We could do it, too. We could follow the lead of our Soviet comrades."

Steinman leaned forward to emphasize his next point. "Funny, Bob. But this is serious stuff. What would happen to the smaller states? I think that the larger states like California and Texas could survive as independent nations, but what about Rhode Island?"

"I don't think it would be a problem for the smaller states. Rhode Island's economy is about the same size as Luxembourg or Slovenia. They're doing fine as independent nations. Rhode Island could survive.

"And it wouldn't have to survive alone. The states that seceded could set up a free trade zone like the European Union did. And it doesn't have to be a 50-state secession. There's a two-state option. The Democratic blue states could form one independent nation and the Republican red states could form another nation. States that are evenly divided could choose which new state to join. States like Florida that are split 50-50 could divide into smaller units. Miami-Dade County and the other Democratic strongholds could join the Blue Republic and the rest of the state could join the Red Republic. There's no need for the political units to be contiguous.

If Alaska and Hawaii can be hundreds or thousands of miles away from the mainland and still be part of the United States, Miami-Dade County can be a few hundred miles away from the rest of the Blue Republic. I don't see it as a problem."

"Hmmm. I never thought of that. You make it sound so easy, but I'm uncomfortable with it. I'll have to think about it some more."

"Most people are uncomfortable with the idea of secession at first. They thought the Civil War ended discussion of secession once and for all, but there have been lots of successful secessions all over the world. If other countries have done it successfully, so can we."

"Well, I'll have to think about it. I still feel uncomfortable with the idea."

"Sure. Go ahead and think about it. And while you're thinking about it, you can also think about how you're going to apologize to your children and grandchildren for burdening them with the debt they're going to have to pay and for the freedom they don't have because you allowed the government to pass the Patriot Act."

Steinman had a serious look on his face. He wanted to counter Paige's arguments but he couldn't think of a way to do it.

"Bob, I'm in a bit of a quandary. I want to refute your arguments, but I can't think of any good counter-arguments. That never happens to me. I can always think of good counter-arguments, but the way you just put it seems to make sense."

Paige picked up his coffee cup and took a sip. "Yeah, it's tough to refute logical arguments that are backed up by facts."

75

"All that is necessary for the triumph of evil is that good men do nothing."
Attributed to Edmund Burke

"There comes a point when the only way you can make a statement is to pick up a gun." Sara Jane Moore (attempted to assassinate President Gerald Ford)

"Every normal man must be tempted at times to spit upon his hands, hoist the black flag, and begin slitting throats."
H.L. Mencken

"John, we can start with you. Tell us about your two choices."

The team had assembled at the Versailles Restaurant to give their presentations. Each member was given a homework assignment by the Boss to select two individuals who were a sufficient threat to national security to be terminated.

The Boss had called the meeting to order. He chose the Versailles Restaurant for symbolic reasons. It had deep historical significance. It was the restaurant in Miami where Cuban-Americans met to discuss politics, especially how to overthrow Castro. Politicians went there to pander for the Cuban vote.

Television crews went there whenever there was news about Cuba so they could interview real live Cubans. It was in the heart of Little Havana, on Calle Ocho between 35th and 36th Avenues. The Boss saw it as a fitting place to plot to kill people who were threats to national security. He'd rented a private room so the general public wouldn't be able to listen in on their conversation. It was noisy outside, but most of the noise got blocked out when the doors were closed. The closed doors also served to prevent the aroma of the four bouquets of flowers that had been left by the last party to escape. They waited until the waiters had delivered the drinks.

"My first choice is David Reynoso. He's a law professor at Florida International University. He's one of the leading advocates for allowing American courts to use United Nations mandates and European Union law as precedent in American courts. He also thinks that Sharia law should be recognized in Muslim divorce settlements and contract disputes."

"Good choice. People like that are undermining the fabric of American society. Who is your second choice?"

"Alfredo Cardera. He's the dean of Arts & Sciences at Nova Southeastern University. He has an avowed policy of hiring far leftists. He hasn't promoted any white males in five years. He sees them as the oppressor class. One of the black female professors he hired had to be fired by the provost for gross incompetence. She lied on her resume about having a PhD."

"Another good choice. People like that undermine our educational system. People should be hired solely on the basis of merit. Jim, who are your choices?"

"My first choice is Fabio Perez. He's a journalist. The kind of stuff he writes could just as easily be published in Havana. His main theme is conflict between the proletariat and the bourgeoisie. He advocates class warfare."

"OK, that's a good choice. Who else?"

"Carlos Tapanes. He's a philosophy professor at Florida International University. He gives his students assignments to apply Karl Marx's ideas to social and political issues."

"Another good choice." The Boss was starting to fidget. Actually, he thought most of their choices were mediocre. He had other ideas and a more bold approach, but he wasn't going to unleash it on them until they had finished their presentations. He cleared his throat.

"Santos? You're next."

"I have four people. My first choice is Francisco Guzman. He's a Unitarian minister. He preaches one-world government and gives speeches about why we should allow the United Nations to tax us."

"My second choice is Brett Frantoff. He's the anchor for the 6 o'clock and 11 o'clock news. He chooses stories that show a left-wing bias. He never has anything good to report from a conservative perspective. Besides, my wife has the hots for him."

That caused the group to laugh and lightened the atmosphere in the room. They stopped their discussion as a waiter entered to take their orders. After the waiter left they resumed.

"My third choice is Jorge Cardona. He's a senior editor at the *Miami Herald*. He writes about Latin American law and advocates adopting laws similar to what Hugo Chavez pushed through in Venezuela before he died."

"My fourth choice is Yanisledy Cruz. She's a political commentator and journalist. She's a propagandist for every left-wing cause in the United States and Latin America."

"Well, I'm glad to see that you chose a woman, finally. I was beginning to think you were a bunch of sexist pigs."

The Boss's remark drew a smirk from the crowd.

"Tomás?"

"I don't want to spoil the party, but I don't think we should be assassinating professors and journalists. All they're doing is exercising their First Amendment rights of free speech and free press. I think we should only kill people who do more than just talk about doing things that would harm America."

The room grew silent. The other members of the team knew about Tomás's view on this point, but what he just said was a direct challenge to the Boss, and the Boss didn't tolerate challenges to his authority. Their eyes shifted to the Boss, waiting to hear his response.

The Boss's face turned red. The veins on his neck looked ready to pop, and everyone in the room noticed. He had just been challenged in public, in front of his team members. He couldn't ignore it. He had to reassert his authority in as strong a manner as possible. He took a deep breath and hesitated for what seemed like an eternity before responding.

"Tomás, I hear what you're saying, and I agree – in theory. The problem is that those people are giving aid and comfort to the enemy with their words and actions. Giving aid and comfort to the enemy is treason. They have to be punished, and stopped. However, we need to prioritize. Tomás, I think you will like what I am about to say.

"The assignment I gave you was to choose two individuals who were worthy of extermination because they were a threat to national security, or because they gave aid and comfort to the enemy, which is basically the same thing. Since I gave you that homework assignment, my thinking has changed. Well, not really changed. Rather, I've improved on my initial idea. Although all of the people you chose are worthy of extermination, we must prioritize. We must eliminate the worst people first, the ones who pose the most immediate danger, the ones who could cause the most damage if we allowed them to continue living. So, I've made up my own list."

They looked startled. It came as a surprise. They were expecting the Boss to verbally rip Tomás apart and they were anxiously anticipating exactly how he would do it. The Boss noticed the expressions on their faces.

"I didn't say we wouldn't eliminate the people you selected. I'm just saying that we should cancel some other people first."

They looked relieved to see that the Boss had been able to so skillfully get around the challenge Tomás just made.

"Gentlemen, the biggest threat to national security is the debt. We must punish those who got us into this mess and kill them before they can do any more damage. If you study history, you'll find that every great empire or civilization crumbled from within before it was invaded or overthrown by an external force. That's precisely what's happening today in America.

"Anyone who advocates big spending programs is a candidate for the list. Politicians who advocate the biggest spending programs go to the top of the list."

Santos interrupted him. "That includes just about every politician, and they're all in Washington. You told us to limit our targets to people in South Florida."

"Yes, that is correct. However, we don't have to assassinate all of them. All we have to do is kill a few of them in order to send a message to the rest. You know what they say … Nothing changes until you get a body count.

"We can adopt the same technique the Islamic fundamentalists use. Whenever anyone publishes an image of Mohammed, they execute the person who did it and blow up the offices of the offending newspaper. We can do the same. We can target one of the biggest advocates of big spending in South Florida, liquidate him or her and blow up their campaign headquarters or local office and execute as many of their staff as possible. Then we make sure the press knows why they got targeted. Once the word gets out, politicians will be very hesitant to support any more big, wasteful spending programs, especially if we tell the press that we plan to continue targeting big spenders."

Tomás looked concerned. His wife was an occasional volunteer for local politicians. "I don't like the idea of executing civilians."

The Boss replied, "They aren't civilians if they work for an enemy of America."

Jim Bennett interjected. "Actually, I think Tomás makes a good point. Executing civilians would give us bad press, just like it does when the Islamic nut cases kill civilians."

The Boss hesitated a moment before responding. "Hmmm. Yeah, I suppose you're right. OK, let's not whack any civilians unless it's absolutely necessary. We don't need the bad press. It would be counterproductive."

"All those Islamic groups have names," John pointed out. "Should we give ourselves a name, too? It would make for good press."

"How about the Sons of Liberty?" Jim suggested. "The American patriots who dumped the tea into Boston harbor used that name."

"Good idea. Let's use it. Let me continue. I want to explain the reasoning behind my choices so you can better understand why I made the choices I did.

"Think of the American republic as a structure made of wood. The structure is being attacked by termites. It is a slow process, but if it's allowed to continue, it's just a matter of time before the structure will collapse. The termites in this case are people who advocate policies that undermine the American system and any politician or bureaucrat who helps to implement those policies. I have some politicians on my list, but they're not all politicians. People in the private sector are also undermining the structure of the American system. From now on we'll refer to these people as termites, because that's what they are.

"It's too late to kill people like FDR, who gave us Socialist Insecurity, the biggest Ponzi scheme of all time, or LBJ, who gave us Medicare and a bunch of other socialized medicine programs, but we can waste some of their successors and clones here in South Florida. We can send a message to Washington that the line has been drawn."

Santos looked at Tomás, who was visibly pleased with what the Boss had just said.

76

"Democracy ... is two wolves and a lamb voting on what to have for lunch. Liberty ... Is a well-armed lamb contesting the vote."
Attributed to Benjamin Franklin

"OK, it's time to start making the assignments. John, I want you to figure out the logistics and find a way to make this happen. Jim, Tomás and Santos will report to you and you'll coordinate things. I'll assist you any way I can.

"The first person on my list is Nelson Fuller. He's the chairman of the Miami Branch of the Federal Reserve Bank of Atlanta. The Fed is helping to finance the massive deficits and is undermining the currency. It would be better to target the Chairman of the Fed in Washington but he's too far away and too hard to get at. We can accomplish our goal of sending a message by targeting someone local. Their offices are on NW 36th Street. John, you're in charge of this guy. Jim, use your resources at the FBI to find out his schedule and find a weak spot, then pass along the information to John.

"Senator Tom Garrett is next on the list. His major crime against humanity is pushing through the various bailout packages that are bankrupting America. He also defended Fannie Mae and

Freddie Mac when some of the more enlightened members of Congress called for their abolition. He was instrumental in convincing Congress to bail out the European banks, which forced American workers to pay for European pensions and health care costs. John, you're in charge of this one, too. Jim, get his schedule and give it to John. Try to choose a good time and place to make it happen."

Two waiters walked in as the Boss was about to give the next assignment. He waited for them to take away the dishes before continuing. The shorter one smelled like cheap cigar smoke. He probably had a smoke just before coming in to remove the dishes.

"Jim, this one's for you. It's Representative Debbie Waterstein. Her main crime against humanity is getting up in the morning."

The comment drew a chuckle.

"Everything she does undermines the republic. This fucking termite has got to be stomped on, and hard. She's against ending the Socialist Insecurity Ponzi scheme and replacing it with a privatized system. She wants to expand the socialist medical system and force the rich to pay for it. She's slapping regulations on businesses so fast they're getting punch drunk. She wants to outlaw red meat in the schools. The cattle industry in Texas will thank us for this one."

Jim interrupted. "She's a big supporter of Israel. Do you think we should get Mossad's blessing on this one first?"

"Fuck Mossad. If we had to get Mossad's approval before whacking a member of Congress, we wouldn't be able to whack anybody. They're all supporters of Israel. We have to do what's right for America. Besides, anyone we whack will be replaced by another supporter of Israel, so there won't be any net loss of Israel supporters. If we do this right, it will look like a group of patriots did it. It won't have the CIA's fingerprints on it."

"Why do you guys always insist on taking all the credit?" Jim asked. "Don't forget, the FBI is helping you guys."

Tomás added, "I'm sure J. Edgar Hoover would be proud of you."

"Not to mention the Commerce Department," John added.

"And the TSA," Santos added.

"And the private sector. Don't leave Carnival Cruise Lines out of this." Tomás liked the idea of private sector involvement.

"OK, guys. Enough.

"Jim, I have one more assignment for you. I think you'll like this one. It's Representative Jack Lunn. This guy is a class warfare specialist – rich against the poor, whites against blacks, young against old, workers versus welfare cheats. Tax the rich. The top 1 percent is already paying more taxes than the bottom 95 percent and he thinks that's not enough. He comes back to Miami practically every weekend. It shouldn't be difficult finding the right time and place."

Santos began to fidget. He knew his assignments would be coming soon and he was less than enthusiastic about what they might be.

"Santos and Tomás, I have four guys for you, which you can share, but first let me explain why they need to be terminated so you can understand why it's so important.

"Are you familiar with the eminent domain laws?"

Tomás shifted in his chair. "I've heard of them but I don't know exactly what they are."

"I'll give you a brief summary. The U.S. Constitution and some of the state constitutions give government the authority to confiscate private property for public use – public parks, roads, stuff like that. The problem is that in recent years the government has been confiscating private property for private use. Let me give you an example.

"A few years ago, Daniel Frumpton, the big New York real estate billionaire, was building a hotel, condominium, restaurant complex in Fort Lauderdale. The problem was that he needed more land to do what he wanted to do and there was a little old lady who didn't want to sell her home. It was on the spot where he wanted to build a restaurant. He went to the city council and convinced them to condemn the property and turn it over to him so he could build.

"The little old lady had lived in that house ever since a few months after she got married fifty years before. She raised her family there. All her memories were in that house. Her husband had died and the kids had left home. It's all she had.

"The council gave its approval. It went to court and the judge gave his approval for the confiscation. She was paid a pittance for the property and most of what she received went to the attorney who defended her. She died a few months later of a broken heart. Frumpton stole all of her memories while he lined his pockets, but what's worse, he pissed on the Constitution to do it. It's an abuse of the eminent domain laws but, unfortunately, it's not the only abuse. This kind of thing has become more common in recent years, especially since the U.S. Supreme Court held that this kind of abuse doesn't violate the Constitution."

Santos looked shocked and angry. "They said that? How could they do that? I want to kill that Frumpton fucker, and the members of the Supreme Court, too." His Latin temper had been aroused. Castro had confiscated his family's property in Cuba. He was taking it personally. Maybe he couldn't whack Castro, but he could whack this guy.

"Actually, that is your first assignment. Frumpton, I mean, not the Supreme Court, even though there are a few of them we could do without. He has a place in Palm Beach that he visits on a regular basis. That will put him within range. Find out when he's coming to sunny Florida, pick a time and place, and do it. As a TSA agent, you have access to flight records."

"That's one guy. You said you have four for us."

"Yeah, Santos, I do. The other three are connected to Frumpton and the eminent domain laws."

Santos and Tomás smiled. They weren't apprehensive about their assignments any more. They could see that they were being given an opportunity to do a good deed for America and they were looking forward to it.

"Frumpton's pulling the same stunt for some property in Aventura. Keith Ross, the city manager, is pushing it because he says it will create jobs and increase tax revenue."

"But the purpose of government isn't to create jobs, it's to protect property," John added.

"That's right. I'm glad you weren't absent from civics class the day they taught that lesson.

"The case went to court and was recently decided against the four families who will have their homes confiscated."

"So who do we whack? Keith Ross, I hope?"

"Yes, Santos, he's one of the people on the list. The others are Jules Rapaport, the judge who gave them the OK, and Jerry Goldman, the attorney who represented Frumpton. Ross and Goldman should be easy to whack. The judge might be more difficult, especially if he thinks he might be a target. That's why I want you to get the judge right after you get Frumpton."

"It will be our pleasure." Santos smiled when he said it.

"Those are the eight termites we need to exterminate first. We can add more to the list later. We have to start sending the message that America won't stand for this kind of behavior and abuse of power."

Jim was curious. "Are you thinking about some other names for the list?"

"Yes, I'm thinking about it all the time. My current thinking is that we need to kill more lawyers. Members of the plaintiff's bar."

"Like who?"

"I don't know. I'm still doing my research. The tort system in this country is out of control. Remember that McDonald's case, where the woman got a multi-million dollar settlement for spilling hot coffee on her crotch when she placed the coffee cup between her legs while driving through the drive up window?"

"Yeah. I remember reading about it. It was all over the television, too. McDonald's got sued because they failed to warn her the coffee was hot."

"I want to target the termite lawyers who file that kind of lawsuit. They're making America the laughing stock of the world. They make doctors perform a lot of unnecessary tests just to protect themselves from lawsuits. Some of them are closing up shop because they can't afford the malpractice premiums.

"They cause drug prices to skyrocket because the drug companies have to raise their prices to pay multi-million dollar claims and liability insurance premiums. That causes the government to step in to regulate drug prices, even though it's the government's fault the drug prices are so high because they refuse to rein in the lawyers."

"Yeah, because the plaintiff bar is one of the largest contributors to politicians' reelection campaigns."

"That's right, Jim. Again, we don't have to exterminate all of them. If we target a few, then broadcast to the world why we did it, that will send the message that they must stop engaging in that kind of activity or face severe consequences. Those who don't get the message can get whacked later."

John interjected, "What about Saul Steinman? Are we going to terminate him first? Where does he fit in the lineup?"

"Let's put him on the back burner. We can always get him. Have Paige keep attending the meetings to let us know what's going on with his group."

"Should I tell Paige about our decision?"

"No. I don't trust Paige. He's a professor and no professor is completely trustworthy. They all have their heads up their asses. Just let him keep reporting for now. Besides, he doesn't know we plan to whack Steinman. He thinks we just want to learn what goes on at his meetings."

"Should I tell Mossad the heat is off their boy?"

"Fuck Mossad. They always need something to worry about. Let them worry about Steinman. Besides, the heat isn't really off. We can get Steinman a day or two after we get the others. Think of Steinman as the dessert after the main course."

Tomás and Santos had been listening in on the conversation. They couldn't help it, since they were sitting across the table. They liked their assignments as well as the assignments their colleagues received, but Tomás wondered if he could do anything to stop the Steinman killing, since he didn't think professors and journalists should be executed just for exercising their First Amendment right of free speech and press. He also wondered whether Santos would be willing to help him.

77

Nelson Fuller

"The incorporation of a bank and the powers assumed (by legislation doing so) have not, in my opinion, been delegated to the United States by the Constitution. They are not among the powers specially enumerated."
Thomas Jefferson

"Banking establishments are more dangerous than standing armies; and that the principle of spending money to be paid by posterity, under the name of funding, is but swindling futurity on a large scale."
Thomas Jefferson

"We must not let our rulers load us with perpetual debt."
Thomas Jefferson

Nelson Fuller got his PhD in economics from the University of California at Berkeley about 20 years ago. He was a firm believer in the Keynesian economic theory that a country could spend its way out of a recession through deficit spending, in spite of the overwhelming evidence to the contrary. He fully supported the

Federal Reserve Board's policy of pumping money into the economy, even though the effect was to increase inflation and thereby rob people of the purchasing power of their savings. In fact, he supported any Federal Reserve Board policy that increased its control over the economy.

In his mid-forties and of average height, he had orange hair, which was fairly long but thinning. Physically, he was not well suited for Miami. His pasty white skin started turning pink after being in the sun for five minutes. He had the kind of skin that was prone to skin cancer. He was better suited for Bellingham, Washington, the city that had the least number of sunny days in the country.

His job as Chairman of the Miami branch of the Federal Reserve Bank of Atlanta was mostly administrative. He was just a branch employee at one of the 12 regional Federal Reserve Banks.

The people in Washington didn't much care for his opinion. He was upset about that, but planned to remedy that situation soon. He was ambitious and planned to use his current position as a stepping stone that would place him closer to the seat of power. He was the favorite to assume the chairmanship of the Atlanta Fed when the current chairman retired next year. In the meantime, he was enjoying the fringe benefits, one of which was having access to insider information about when the Fed was going to change interest rates. He also used the fact that the Fed had never been audited to enhance his personal wealth.

The nice thing about knowing when interest rates were going to change was that it didn't matter whether they were going to go up or down. You could make a killing either way, as long as you knew the direction of the change.

A few years ago, shortly after assuming his current position, he set up a series of offshore accounts under phony names so that he could trade on his insider interest rate information. He had been able to pile up enough cash that he no longer had to work, but he had no intention of retiring. He was making too much money on the side for that, and he was into it for the power more than for the money. Once he made it to the Atlanta Fed chairmanship, he would be one of the 50 most powerful men in America; maybe one of the top 20.

Nobody but a select few knew who the Fed was lending money to or under what terms and conditions. The fact that the Fed had never been audited since its founding in 1913 had allowed this corruption to fester. There were many opportunities to skim a little off the top here and there, especially when the Fed made loans to banks in Latin America, Asia and Africa. The people on the receiving end had been treating him very well. He set up a second group of offshore accounts to deposit their gifts.

He followed a regular routine. He got to work shortly before 9am and left around 5pm. Some days he didn't have a lot to do, but he made a point of always arriving on time and never leaving early unless he had a good reason so that he could set a good example. He ate lunch at the same three or four restaurants.

He never flirted with the female staff. He followed a strict policy of *don't shit where you eat.* He didn't want any sexual scandals to derail his career path. He was married, with two sons, 17 and 20. He hadn't cheated on his wife in more than 15 years.

As an undergraduate at Princeton he experimented with homosexuality. His roommate in his junior year was a jock, who used to refer to him as his fuck cushion, because he was fat at the time and preferred to be on the bottom.

***

Jim Bennett didn't have much difficulty learning Fuller's schedule. He almost always went to lunch between 12:50 and 1:10. He liked going around 1pm because it made the afternoon shorter. He seldom took more than an hour for lunch because he wanted to set a good example. Most of the restaurants he chose were within walking distance. He usually ate alone, although sometimes he used lunch as an opportunity to have a meeting. He liked to multitask.

About a week after Bennett received the assignment to get information about Fuller's schedule, he and Wellington met in the lobby of Wellington's downtown office building.

"Hi John," he said, extending his hand. They shook, and Wellington said, "Let's go outside. It's a beautiful day and I don't want to talk in the lobby in front of all these cameras."

They walked out the front door, turned left and stopped about 50 feet later. They stopped a few feet short of the alley because there was a truck there loading merchandise and making a lot of noise. The alley was also a little smellier than usual because the garbage hadn't been picked up yet.

Jim reached into his pocket, pulled out a flash drive and handed it to Wellington.

"Here, John. This has all the information you'll need. It's password protected but I didn't make up a password for it. I figured that if you did it you might be able to remember what it was."

"Good thinking, Jim. I'll try to think of something I can remember. What kind of stuff is in here?"

"Fuller's going to be an easy hit. He's regular. He follows a pattern. Comes and goes at the same time. Goes to lunch around one o'clock at the same restaurants, usually alone. Most of them are close to a parking lot or on-street parking. I have it all written down, with photos and my personal suggestions."

"Thanks, Jim. The Boss will be proud of you."

"Thanks, John. I appreciate that."

They shook hands and said good-bye. Wellington went back to his office, plugged the flash drive into his laptop and skimmed it for content. There was more than enough information to complete the task. Since a good password contains both letters and numbers, he chose one that had both – F6211212518, which included the first letter of Fuller's last name, plus the numerical equivalent of his name. F was the 6th letter of the alphabet, U was the 21st, L the 12th, E the 5th and R the 18th. He slipped it into his pocket and went back to his Commerce Department work.

78

Wellington looked over at Paige. "Pass the meat loaf, please." Paige picked it up and passed it to him. As he placed the palm of his left hand under the plate he could feel the heat. As it passed beneath his nose he could smell it as the steam rose. Paige and Sveta were at the Wellingtons, having dinner.

Sarah picked up a bowl and passed it to him. "Don't forget the potato salad." He took it and put a few dollops on his plate, just enough to satisfy Sarah. It was her mother's recipe. John didn't especially like it. He told her that several times over the years but she didn't get the message, so after a while he stopped mentioning it. He just ate enough of it to keep her happy. He would much have preferred mashed potatoes today. They go much better with meat loaf, but Sarah didn't know that. Although she was a pretty good cook, some of her food combinations left a lot to be desired.

Alicia, their six-year-old daughter, was wearing a pretty yellow and blue dress. She sat politely at the table, waiting for the food to come to her. Sarah sat next to her, helping her put it on the plate.

Wellington noticed that his son, Jack was wearing his baseball cap at the table again, which was not unusual. During the summer it was usually welded to his head. "Jack, take off your cap, please. We're at the dinner table." Jack responded by silently hanging it on the post of his chair, to be retrieved as soon as dinner was over.

"So, Sveta, what kinds of food did you eat growing up in Russia?" Sarah was curious to learn about what people ate in other countries. Although she read about it in books, it was always better to get a first-hand description.

"One of my favorites was borscht, especially in the winter."

"I've heard of that but what is it?"

"It's a kind of vegetable soup. The main ingredient is beets. My mother used to make it by chopping up beets, onions, carrots, celery and tomatoes and adding some spices like crushed garlic, sugar, a few pints of beef stock, a bay leaf, salt and pepper. Maybe she would put in a little red wine vinegar, too. Sometimes it would actually have chunks of beef in it, and maybe a chopped up boiled potato. Then, when it was nearly ready to serve, she added some sour cream. It was delicious. It goes very well with thick, Russian black bread, too."

"That does sound delicious."

Wellington added, "It sounds like a lot of work to me."

"Oh, John, it's not work when you enjoy cooking. You wouldn't know because the only cooking you've ever done is pushing the button on the microwave."

"Do you still make it?"

"No. John is right about the work. It is much easier just to buy it at *Kalinka.* It's a Russian deli on Collins Avenue in Sunny Isles Beach. I sometimes add a little something to it after I get home, like sour cream, which I can also buy at *Kalinka.*"

Alicia was sitting quietly, listening and absorbing every word of the conversation. Although she had met foreigners before, they were almost all Spanish speaking. She went to school with some of them. Sveta was the only Russian she had ever met. She was fascinated by her accent.

Alicia's curiosity finally got the better of her. "Did they have supermarkets in Russia? And microwaves?"

"No, they didn't, not while I was growing up. All those things came later."

"Then where did you buy your food?"

Sveta smiled. "We bought it on the street or in small shops." She didn't want to go into further details, like the fact that there were sometimes shortages of basic goods, or that you often had to bribe a store keeper to sell you something. Some store keepers deliberately kept their shelves empty. It provided them with opportunities to earn extra income by selling food and other products under the table – or out the back door. The shortages were the result of central planning. Bribery was the natural result of market forces, trying to match supply and demand at a market clearing price.

"Alicia had a dance recital yesterday. Tell Sveta about it."

"Yeah, I had a dance recital yesterday. It was kinda fun."

Sarah went on to give the details, but only Sveta was paying any attention. Wellington was thinking about the assignment the Boss had given him to assassinate Nelson Fuller, and Paige was thinking about how he could prevent Wellington and his boys from executing Steinman, assuming that that was their plan. He wondered if Rona, Steinman's wife, was also on the hit list. Both he and Sveta had grown to like them after having dinner with them a few times. They had become friends.

Paige liked Wellington and his family. They were good parents. Their kids seemed well-adjusted, although that could all change as they hit their teen years. He wondered how Wellington could be a family man and a cold blooded killer at the same time. But more importantly, Paige wondered whether he had the ability or the will to stop him from executing Steinman, if it came to that. Time would tell.

79

Today would be Nelson Fuller's last day on earth, or at least it would be if John Wellington had anything to do with it. Wellington looked at his watch. It was 12:57pm. Three of the four restaurants where Fuller ate were in the same general location, so there was a 75 percent chance Fuller would be walking by soon. He planned to whack him when he was about a block from the restaurants. Fewer witnesses that way.

Wellington waited for him, dressed in a white t-shirt with no identifiable characteristics, wearing a black baseball cap, also with no identifiable markings, old looking blue jeans and sneakers. He wasn't wearing his regular glasses. He had on sun glasses instead. He had left his suit, dress shirt and black leather shoes in the trunk of his car, which he parked around the corner, pointed toward a side street for a quick getaway. He would change into them later, before returning to work.

The car had a phony license plate on it, just in case. He had a small supply of them, which he collected as part of his work. He would replace it with his real plate later, in a dark, indoor parking garage a few miles away.

He wore transparent skin-hugging plastic gloves. He didn't plan on touching anything, but he didn't want to leave any finger prints, just in case. He was carrying his Beretta Model 92 Custom

Carry 9mm in a cloth bag. The attached suppressor made it too bulky to tuck into his jeans.

Wellington didn't want to look conspicuous just standing there, so he stopped to look into a few store windows, keeping his hands in his pockets so no one would notice his transparent gloves. Occasionally he would look in the direction where Fuller would likely be coming from. After about a minute, Fuller appeared. He crossed the street and was about a hundred feet away, walking directly toward Wellington.

Wellington stepped to the next store window and pretended to be looking at the merchandise. He transferred the cloth bag to his left hand, reached in, clicked off the safety and waited for Fuller to pass by. As Fuller walked by, he reached into the bag, pulled out the Beretta, assumed the firing position with both hands on the gun, pointed it at the back of Fuller's head, who was now about five feet in front of him, and stopped.

Two women had emerged from the store and were directly in his line of fire. One of them saw the gun pointing at her and screamed. She just stood there, staring at him, not moving. Her friend looked to her left and saw Wellington pointing the gun. They both just stood there, frozen. They were blocking his line of fire and Fuller was getting farther away.

The woman's scream caused everyone within ear shot to turn in her direction to see what was going on. There were a half dozen people on the sidewalk, on both sides of the street, all looking at Wellington. Fuller, who was now about 20 feet away, also turned around to see what the commotion was all about.

Wellington took a side step, which put Fuller within his line of fire. Fuller was too far away for a good head shot. Those should be done at close range. Since the head was a small target, he needed to be really close to make sure he could hit it. Wellington's adrenalin was pumping. He was nervous. His hands shook. Although he had killed before, he could never get rid of the shakes immediately before a hit. He had to be closer.

The women's sudden appearance and scream threw off his plan and his concentration. Rather than make a single shot to the head, he decided to pump a half dozen rounds into Fuller's torso and let the hollow points do their job. If he didn't die immediately, he would probably bleed out before he could get to a hospital.

It didn't really matter whether he killed him or just wounded him. The point was to send a message to Washington. He would make his point whether Fuller lived or died.

The first two rounds hit Fuller in the torso, knocking him backwards. The third round tore into his right thigh just before he hit the pavement, ripping through the main artery and shattering his leg bone. The last three shots missed. Wellington wasn't a great assassin, but he was good enough. Fuller died on the way to the hospital.

His original plan had been to plant one hollow point in the back of Fuller's head, watch his head explode like a melon, then pick up the shell casing and run to his car to make his escape. In all the excitement, he forgot to pick up the shell casings. After firing six rounds he turned around and ran to his car. No one followed. They were all too stunned by what they had just seen. After a few seconds, all that remained were the spent shell casings and the smell of gunpowder.

Leaving the shell casings behind wasn't a good move. They provided ballistics evidence, but it probably couldn't be traced back to him, unless they found the gun in his possession. He made sure to load the clip with gloves on so he wouldn't leave any finger prints on the shell casings.

He pulled into the dark parking garage a few minutes later, changed his clothes and the license plate and headed back to the office. His hands were still shaking. The adrenalin was still pumping. He was reliving the scene in his head, again and again.

***

He had sent the message to Washington, so to speak, but they wouldn't be able to understand what it meant unless he spelled it out for them, so he pulled into one of the mini mall parking lots along the way, took out a laptop that he had purchased under a phony name, and connected to an anonymous server so they couldn't know where he was located. He typed out the message.

> "Those who debase America's currency will pay a heavy price. Nelson Fuller was the first to pay. There will be others. No one who works for the Federal Reserve Bank will be safe."
> Sons of Liberty

He sent it to at least one news person at each of the major television and radio stations in Miami as well as a few in Washington, DC. Then he sent it to a dozen patriot web sites as well as the *Huffington Post* to make sure the feds wouldn't be able to suppress the message.

It went viral. All the radio talk shows were talking about it during the evening rush hour. It was the top story on the evening news. That night, Fox News tried to have a fair and balanced debate on the issues it raised, but they couldn't find anyone who would take the side of the assassin. Supporting the assassin could be construed as advocating the violent overthrow of the government, which was treason. The assassin was immediately labeled a terrorist. Anyone who had anything positive to say about what the assassin had done could be arrested for giving aid and comfort to a terrorist.

The message started to cause a panic at the Federal Reserve Banks throughout the country. There weren't any plans to assassinate any more regional Fed chairs, but they didn't know that. All the regional Fed chairs thought they were being targeted. It didn't change their monetary behavior, of course. They continued to debase the currency. They continued to make secret loans with secret terms to secret people in secret countries, some of which were enemies of the United States. But it was no longer business as usual. They knew they wouldn't be audited, but they didn't like the increased visibility.

80

"When in doubt, tell the truth."
Mark Twain

When Paige heard the news about Nelson Fuller he suspected immediately that Wellington had something to do with it. Over the years, they had had several discussions about how the Federal Reserve Board was able to work in secret for more than a hundred years without an audit, and speculated about what kind of criminal activity might be discovered if it ever was audited. Paige used to talk about it in his financial accounting class every semester, including the semester when Wellington took his MBA class. He wondered whether his class discussion of several years ago had led Wellington to the conclusion that something had to be done about the Fed.

He decided to schedule a meeting with Wellington and bring up the subject to check his reaction. He was also curious to know why Wellington was talking to George Heverly and Edward Morris in the alley shortly after they assaulted him in the university parking lot, and why he lied about the fingerprints on the guns and the stolen van that turned out to belong to Heverly. Depending on how the conversation about the Fed went, he might confront him about Heverly and Morris.

"Hello, John? Bob Paige here. I was wondering if I might stop by in the next day or so for a little chat."

"Sure. Is everything alright? Do you have something to report?"

"No, nothing like that. I'd just like to bounce some ideas around."

"OK. I'm going to be in my downtown office the rest of the week. Which day is good for you?"

"How about tomorrow afternoon around four? I'll call when I get to the parking garage."

"OK. That will be fine. I'll meet you in the lobby."

"See you then."

Wellington was curious to know what ideas Paige might want to bounce around, but didn't think much about it, and went back to work. Paige was starting to get nervous about what he would say and what Wellington's reaction would be. He would have to wait until tomorrow.

***

The next day, Paige left his condo at around 3:15 pm. If traffic was normal, he would pull into the parking garage by Wellington's office around four. He arrived at 3:57 pm. He drove a little faster than usual because he was nervous. He didn't know quite what he was going to say or how he was going to say it, but he was anxious to see the expression on Wellington's face, and wondered whether he would be truthful or would continue to lie.

He picked up his cell phone. "Hi, John? Bob here. I just pulled into the garage."

"OK, I'll see you in a few minutes."

Paige walked into the lobby and didn't have to wait more than a few seconds before Wellington got off the elevator. Wellington walked toward him and extended his hand. Paige reciprocated. They shook hands. Paige opened the conversation.

"Hi John. Sorry to pull you away from your important Commerce Department work, but I had a few questions for you."

"Fine." He motioned toward the front doors. "Let's go to my other office." They went outside, turned left, as usual, and then left again, into the alley. After about 50 feet, they both stopped and looked behind them to see if there were any curious onlookers. There weren't.

Paige took a deep breath to calm his nerves. "John, when I heard about the Nelson Fuller assassination, the first person I thought of was you."

"Me? Bob, I'm flattered, but as I recall, you're the one who always talked about the Fed and how something had to be done." Wellington was caught off guard by the question. He had expected the conversation would revolve around Steinman, or Mossad, or perhaps both. Raising the topic of the Fed threw him off balance. Paige could sense it by the tone in his voice.

"Well, yes, I have been saying for years that something had to be done about the Fed, but I was thinking more along the lines of an audit."

"Are you upset that someone decided to assassinate a high-ranking local Federal Reserve Board official?"

"No, not really, but I would have preferred an audit. Killing a Fed official won't change anything. Having an audit probably would."

"Hmmm. I get your point. Well, I wasn't too upset when I heard about it, either."

Paige decided to push a bit. "Is that all you did was *hear* about it?"

"Of course. What are you implying?"

"I know you and your crew would like to cleanse America of certain elements that are weakening the country. I was just wondering whether you decided to do more than just talk about it."

"Bob, you know I have to deny that I had any involvement in that assassination even if I did it myself, since something like that would be on a need to know basis."

"Of course. I understand completely. I think you've already answered my question. I'd love to ask who else might be on your list, but I know you wouldn't tell me, and probably wouldn't even admit there was a list."

"You know the rules, Bob."

"Yes, I do, and I understand the reason for the rules. You can't go around telling people who you've whacked and who you plan to get next."

"That's right, and Commerce Department employees don't go around killing people anyway. They only kill potential trade deals." Wellington was referring to the many trade deals that were killed as a result of federal regulations that restricted or prohibited trade. With tariff rates dropping, the favorite tools of the protectionists had become the antidumping laws and the environmental and labor standards that were included in most trade agreements, all of which prevented otherwise good trade deals from becoming reality. Paige smirked as he heard the words coming from Wellington's mouth.

"Well then, let me ask you another question. Why did you send George Heverly and Edward Morris to rough me up in the university parking lot?"

Wellington was blind-sided by the question. He thought that Paige might suspect something because Paige was able to find Heverly when he apparently could not, but he had put that question out of mind because he was busy focusing on the people who were being placed on the hit list.

"Ah, ah." He stammered because he didn't know what to say or how to respond. He decided to feign ignorance. "Who are George Heverly and Edward Morris?"

"They're the two guys I saw you talking to in this very alley a few days after they paid me a visit. One of them was leaning on a cane. The other one had a splint on his broken nose, a nose that I broke, by the way."

Wellington knew he wouldn't be able to feign ignorance any longer. He took a deep breath, then exhaled. His mind was racing, trying to figure out what to say and how to begin. He decided to tell the truth, or at least as much truth as it would take for Paige to stop asking questions.

"OK. Here's the deal. It was the Boss's idea. I tried to talk him out of it, but he insisted. He was getting nervous about your investigation of the Raul Rodriguez assassination."

"And why would he give a shit about my investigation unless he was somehow involved? Did he order the hit? And was Gabriella Acosta part of the deal, or was she just in the wrong place at the wrong time?"

"Bob, you know I can't answer that question."

"I think you've already answered it. And what about the professor Shipkovitz and Kaplan assassinations? Was he behind those, too? Why were they executed? The only common element is that they spoke out against the government. Is that sufficient reason to kill them?"

Wellington was looking at the ground, swaying back and forth, placing the weight first on his right foot, then the left, with his hands in his pockets. Finally, he said something.

"Yes."

"What? Merely criticizing the government is sufficient reason to get you killed? What kind of bullshit is that?"

"It wasn't just what they said. It's the effect what they said had."

"What do you mean by that? Please explain. I don't get it."

"The things they were saying were impeding the government. They were making the government's job harder. They were also giving aid and comfort to the enemy. What they were saying was treasonous." Wellington had stopped being on the defensive. He went on the attack.

"You don't really believe that, do you?" Paige was practically screaming.

Wellington's voice became calm. He looked Paige directly in the eyes. "Yes, I do."

Now it was Paige who didn't know what to say. He could tell from the look in Wellington's eyes that he meant it, and that there was more to come.

A light bulb came on in his head. Now he understood where Wellington was going with the Steinman assignment. Steinman had been doing the same things that Rodriguez, Shipkovitz and Kaplan had been doing. He was destined for the same fate. He already knew the answer to his next question, but felt compelled to ask it anyway.

"Do you intend to add Steinman to the list of recently deceased?"

Wellington looked him straight in the eyes.

"Yes. He's as guilty of treason as they are. He deserves the same fate. But first we'd like to learn more about what he's doing and what he has planned. We'd also like to learn more about the other members of his group."

"Do you plan to whack them, too?"

"Maybe. That hasn't been decided yet."

Paige knew he couldn't continue to assist them in their venture, but he also knew that if he resigned from the assignment, they would only get someone else to replace him, and his own life could be in danger if he quit. He couldn't quit, but he couldn't continue either.

"Well, are you with us or against us, Bob? We need to know."

Paige knew his answer to that question could determine his fate. He had to stall. He had to have time to think about his options, none of which seemed good. He also knew that he couldn't allow Steinman to join the list of recently deceased.

"Well, Bob, I'm waiting for your answer."

Paige had to say something. He didn't have a choice. He knew what he had to say if he wanted to stay alive.

"OK, I'm with you, but I think you're making a mistake. You should be going after bigger fish. Professors and journalists don't do nearly as much damage as some of the people in Washington. They're the ones you should be going after."

He hoped what he said convinced Wellington he was a loyal member of the team. If Wellington wasn't convinced, he would still be in danger.

"That's a good suggestion. I'll tell the Boss. However, the people in Washington are too far away. Although we think globally, we have to act locally."

Paige hoped he had convinced Wellington of his loyalty. What he said bought him some time, but time was running out for Steinman. He had to figure out a way to prevent Steinman's killing while keeping himself alive.

81

Tom Garrett

"When you see that in order to produce, you need to obtain permission from men who produce nothing—when you see that money is flowing to those who deal, not in goods, but in favors—when you see that men get richer by graft and by pull than by work, and your laws don't protect you against them, but protect them against you—when you see corruption being rewarded and honesty becoming a self-sacrifice—you may know that your society is doomed."
Ayn Rand

Tom Garrett had represented Florida in the U.S. Senate for more than 20 years, long enough to acquire sufficient seniority to chair several important committees. With seniority comes power, but even Senators without much seniority had a certain amount of power. Sometimes they abused it. Senator Garrett started abusing it during his first term.

"Frank, I really think you need to get with the program. If you want me to help you, you're going to have to help me. I don't think a million dollars in a suitcase is beyond what you're capable of. After all, you run a goddamn bank."

Garrett was speaking to Frank Carbone, the president of one of the ten largest banks in America. They were in Garrett's Washington office. Carbone's bank wanted to open dozens of branches in Florida and Georgia. Getting permission would be worth hundreds of millions of dollars. Garrett was using his influence to block the approval process. Carbone was visiting Garrett to try to persuade him to change his mind. It was not his first visit.

"I'm sorry Senator. I just can't do that. It would be too risky. I couldn't just go into the vault and take it. I'd have to get other people involved. I don't know who I can trust. One of them might blow the whistle. Besides, the auditors might catch it. We have pretty good internal controls."

"Well, I'm sorry you can't do it, Frank. Maybe one of your competitors will be interested in expanding into Florida. It's a great state, you know." Garrett took a puff on his cigar, then placed it in his ashtray. It smelled like an expensive brand. Smoking in the office was prohibited everywhere else in America, but not in his office. Senators didn't have to obey the laws like the rest of us. He got out of his chair and walked Carbone to the front door.

As he passed by the reception desk on the way back to his office, he said, "Betty, please tell Ken I want to see him." Ken Tolleson was Senator Garrett's special assistant. His main task was to make things happen. He was very good at it.

Ken walked in a few minutes later. "Ken, close the door and have a seat."

"Frank Carbone isn't being cooperative. We need to convince him to change his mind."

"I suppose you have an incentive plan you would like me to present to him?"

"Yes, I do, actually, but not directly to him. He has to go out of the country two or three times a month on bank business. He's negotiating a big merger in Western Europe. He has to fly back and forth. I want you to see that his passport gets revoked."

"Uh, how can I do that without raising a lot of eyebrows at the State Department?"

"It's simple. You don't have to go through the State Department. We snuck in a provision as part of a highway bill that allows the IRS to revoke a passport if someone is involved in a tax dispute. Call our contact at the IRS and have them start a tax dispute with him. Make sure that they revoke his passport as part of the deal. Do it today. I want to get this ball rolling … and tell them not to notify him about any of it. Not the tax dispute. Not the passport revocation. Let's let him find out about it the next time he goes to the airport. It will be a nice little surprise."

Ken smiled. "I'm sure it will."

"After it happens, give him a call to make sure he knows who pulled the plug and what he has to do to get it unpulled. You might also point out that we are being kind to him. We could have waited until he was out of the country before revoking his passport. If it's revoked when he's out of the country, he wouldn't be able to get back in. If he takes it to court, it will take years to resolve. The bank will fire him long before that because he won't be able to do his job. Point that out to him."

The Senator sat back in his cushy, black leather chair, took a puff on his cigar and smiled. Ken smiled back. "I'm on it." As he got out of his chair he gave the Senator a thumbs-up, turned around and left. The fact that the passport law deprived citizens of the right to travel without due process didn't seem to faze either of them. Nor did the abuse of power. They merely saw the law as a tool to be used to get what they wanted.

82

"Injustice anywhere is a threat to justice everywhere."
Martin Luther King

"Teach your kids about taxes. Eat 30% of their ice cream."
Unknown

"I'm sorry Mr. Carbone. Your passport has been revoked. I have been instructed not to return it to you."

It was the supervisor at the American Airlines desk at the Miami International Airport who gave Carbone the bad news. When Frank Carbone attempted to check in for his flight to Brussels, the computer kicked up a message that his passport had been revoked by the Internal Revenue Service and that it was to be confiscated.

Carbone's jaw dropped when he heard the news.

"That can't be. There must be some kind of mistake. Does the computer say why it was revoked or who revoked it?"

"All it says is that the Internal Revenue Service revoked it because of a tax dispute. The notice doesn't say anything about taking you into custody. You are free to go. You should check with the IRS to resolve the problem. I'm sorry, but you will not be able to get on the plane to Brussels today."

Carbone was both furious and worried, furious because the IRS was abusing its power and worried about the consequences of not getting on the plane. Not being able to attend the meeting in Brussels could prove to be disastrous for the planned merger. He could send one of his senior vice presidents but it wouldn't be the same. The bank needed to send its top guy. Sending someone lower on the corporate echelon would send the wrong message and would greatly weaken the bank's bargaining position.

If the word got out that the bank president's passport had been revoked, it would send a chill through Wall Street. The Securities and Exchange Commission and the Federal bank auditors would be fighting it out over which of them would be in charge of the bank audit, which there surely would be. The bank's stock price would drop. Merger talks could be cancelled. He would be under pressure to resign. He couldn't let that happen, but he didn't know what to do.

He started to sweat, even though the airport air conditioning made the place uncomfortably chilly. He wiped the perspiration from his forehead and wiped his hand on his expensive suit jacket. The main lobby was busy and noisy, but he didn't hear any of it. He was too busy thinking about what had just happened, and what he could do about it.

As a stopgap measure, he took the cell phone out of his pocket and called Nick Botten, the senior vice president who was most familiar with the merger negotiations.

"Nick, this is Frank. Do you have your passport with you?"

"No, I don't carry it with me. I keep it at home. Why do you ask?"

"I've run into a problem at the airport. They won't let me get on the plane. Some kind of administrative glitch. You have to go to the Brussels meeting in my place. Book the next flight out, go home, get your passport and get your ass to the airport. Call me as soon as you get your passport and I'll brief you on the strategy I planned on using at the meeting."

"OK. What should I tell the people in Brussels? They'll be asking why the president couldn't make it."

"I don't know what we'll tell them. We'll think of something. We can talk about it later."

"OK. I'll book my flight and get my passport."

"Have your secretary book your goddamn flight. We don't have a lot of time to waste. If you don't get your passport and get on a plane in the next few hours, you'll have to wait until tomorrow, and that will be too late."

"OK. I'll call as soon as I have my passport."

Carbone was worried. He didn't want to think about the problems his lack of a passport would cause. He didn't know how to fix the problem. He didn't even know the IRS was investigating him or that he had a tax problem. Someone in the bank's tax department always filed his tax return for him as a courtesy. If someone screwed up, there would be hell to pay, but that was the least of his worries at the moment.

He didn't know what his next move should be. He knew that contacting the IRS should be high on the list, but calling their direct number would probably put him into an endless loop. He didn't know who to talk to and whoever would be on the other end of the line probably wouldn't know, either. He hadn't had to deal with this low level administrative crap in years. One of the nice things about being the president is that you can delegate such details to underlings. That's what he decided to do.

He took out his cell phone and was about to call the vice president who was in charge of tax matters, but before he could push any buttons, his phone rang. He looked at the screen. It was Ken Tolleson.

"Hello, Mr. Carbone? This is Ken Tolleson, Senator Garrett's administrative assistant."

"I know who you are. What do you want?" Carbone's voice was more than a little hostile. He wanted to strangle someone but didn't know who. Maybe Tolleson would be a good first choice, followed by the esteemed Senator. Unfortunately, they were both out of his grasp at the moment.

"The Senator has heard that you are having a tax problem. He would like to help."

Son of a bitch, Carbone thought. The cat was out of the bag. Now he knew who was causing the problem.

"Oh, he did, did he? That's very interesting because I didn't know I had a tax problem until a few minutes ago."

"Well, as you know Mr. Carbone, you are one of the Senator's favorite people and he wants to see that you are taken good care of."

"Tell the Senator that I appreciate his concern."

"I'll be sure to convey that message to the Senator. By the way, the Senator has a message for you."

"Oh? What's that?"

"The Senator suggests that you visit Washington sometime next week, whenever it's convenient for you. He won't be able to meet with you because he's too busy, but he suggested that I meet with you to welcome you to the city."

"That's very thoughtful of him. Will you be picking me up at the airport?"

"No, that won't be necessary because you won't be arriving by plane. The Senator thinks that carrying a suitcase full of paper with photos of Ben Franklin on them might be difficult to explain to the TSA in the event they should decide to search your luggage." He was referring to hundred dollar bills. "Perhaps Amtrak would be a good alternative. You can catch it from Penn Station in New York. It's a pleasant ride."

"Yes, I'm sure it is."

"Good. Then we're agreed?"

"Yes." Carbone didn't have much of an alternative. If he didn't comply, his career would be ruined. It was also in the best interest of the bank to go along. He didn't know how he would get a million dollars in cash but he would find a way. He had to. "I'll call you after I book my ticket."

"That would be great. Talk to you soon."

83

“When injustice becomes law, rebellion becomes duty.”
Thomas Jefferson

Jim Bennett had been able to learn Senator Garrett’s schedule. It was an easy task for an FBI agent. Santos Hernandez used his TSA position to get his flight information. All that remained was for Wellington to carry out the assignment. He was looking forward to it because he thought Senator Garrett was scum, although he didn’t know the full extent of his sliminess.

He was being targeted primarily because of his support for bailouts, which were bankrupting America, and for pushing the Fannie Mae and Freddie Mac agenda, which caused the American mortgage market to collapse, and with it, the loss of millions of American jobs. His enthusiasm for deficit spending was watering down the value of the dollar and causing America to become disrespected internationally, not to mention making more Americans dependent on government handouts. There was no doubt in Wellington’s mind that Garrett was one of the biggest termites gnawing away at the American infrastructure. Killing him wouldn’t solve the termite problem but it would be a step in the right direction.

He needed a wing man or, more precisely, someone to drive so he could get a better aim at the Senator. He had already decided how to do it. He would wait until the Senator left the airport and follow his car. He would decide when to pop him based on traffic patterns.

He considered Bennett but decided against it. Bennett might be busy. He never knew in advance when his FBI schedule would have an opening, and ever since Nelson Fuller got whacked, he had a full plate. He was assigned to the team to find the assassin.

Santos Hernandez worked shifts at the TSA. He usually knew in advance what his schedule would be, and he was scheduled to work the night Senator Garrett was to arrive. He wouldn't be available, unless the plan to take out the Senator was postponed. Wellington didn't want to postpone it. He wanted to take care of the Senator as soon as practically possible so he and his team could move down the list and add more names.

The only one left was Tomás Gutierrez. He was mostly a 9-to-5 guy. His job at Carnival Cruise Lines didn't require much overtime. He got off at 5pm and the Senator wasn't scheduled to arrive until shortly after seven. He could check the plane's arrival on his cell phone. He knew approximately where the Senator would arrive and where he would get in the car that would be waiting for him. He even knew what the car would look like, since Senator Garrett followed a regular pattern. The same car and the same driver were usually assigned to pick him up whenever he flew to Miami.

The plane was scheduled to arrive at 7:05pm. He probably wouldn't have any check-in luggage, since he had a home in Miami and he was scheduled to return to Washington in two days. Wellington wanted to make sure he wouldn't be using his return ticket.

***

Friday night. Wellington looked at his watch - 6:45. Garrett would arrive in 20 minutes if his plane was on time. Gutierrez sat behind the wheel. Wellington waited in the back seat. He had more flexibility there because he could shoot out the left or right side, depending on which was more suitable, given the circumstances.

The plan was to follow him out of the airport, pull up next to him and shoot him when the time seemed right. His home was in Coral Gables, so he would likely be heading in that direction after leaving the airport. If things went according to plan, he would be picked up by a late model black Lincoln Town Car, one of the cars the taxpayers leased for his Miami office.

Wellington checked the arrivals on his cell phone. It was scheduled to arrive on time. They waited in a parking area just outside the airport. Ten minutes before the plane was to land, Gutierrez pulled out and drove toward the terminal where the senator's car would be waiting. There were a few empty spaces just before the door where Senator Garrett was expected to exit. Gutierrez pulled over and they waited.

Wellington was going to use a shotgun to do the job. He hid it under a blanket on the floor of the back seat to hide it from view, in the event that one of the traffic cops at the arrivals terminal wandered by and peeked inside. They were both carrying FBI badges, in case someone in uniform told them they had to move.

The shotgun he had chosen wasn't a regular shotgun, and neither were the shells he planned to use. The AA12 was a military grade, 12 gauge shotgun, capable of firing up to 300 rounds per minute. The shells were Frag 12s. They weren't really shotgun shells at all. They were more like miniature grenades that had a 9 foot burst radius. They exploded on impact. You didn't have to actually hit the target to be effective. You just had to come close.

He wasn't planning on using more than one or two of them. That was all he would need to do the job. The blast would likely take out the driver as well, but he figured that anyone who worked for Garrett probably needed to be exterminated anyway. It wasn't a problem for him. He just had to pick a place where there wasn't much traffic, and that wouldn't be easy to do on a Friday night. He didn't want to kill any civilians when the car started careening out of control at 60 or 70 miles per hour.

Wellington and Gutierrez waited just before the gate. The black Lincoln Town Car wasn't anywhere to be seen. It must not have arrived yet, which was unusual because the Senator didn't like to be kept waiting. The driver would have to face a flurry of verbal abuse if he didn't get there before the Senator. The Senator didn't know how to treat the help. He verbally abused them on a regular basis. His office had a high turnover rate as a result.

After ten minutes, the town car still had not arrived. Senator Garrett emerged from the gate, carrying nothing but a briefcase, and got into the front seat of a red Toyota waiting for him at the curb.

"What the fuck!" Gutierrez exclaimed. "Are things so bad in Washington that even Senators have to cut back on expenses and buy Toyotas instead of Lincolns?"

"I don't know what's going on here, Tomás. Let's follow him and see where he goes. After we get out of the airport, pull up alongside him and see who's driving. This is highly unusual."

Garrett's car left the airport and turned toward Coral Gables. At least he was headed in the expected direction.

"Pull up on his left side so we can get a good look at the driver, but not in the lane next to him. Pull two lanes over."

Gutierrez stepped on the gas and changed lanes. Wellington hit the lever to open the back window. As they drew parallel to the red Toyota, Wellington removed the blanket and placed the gun on his lap. It was his weak side. He was right handed but, from this position he would have to fire like a left hander, but it wouldn't be a problem. All he had to do was come close. The Frag 12s would do the rest. His mouth was dry. He needed a drink of water, but now was not the time. He had a job to do first. He caressed the shotgun as he continued to look at the red Toyota.

As Gutierrez pulled up, Wellington could get a clear view of the driver. "It's a woman."

Gutierrez turned his head toward the back seat. "Who is she?"

"I don't know, but then I don't know anyone from his staff."

"Maybe it's his girlfriend."

"Or his wife."

"Or his daughter."

"Yeah, it could be any of them, but I don't think it's his wife. Too young. She looks like she's in her 20s. Draw back and let me think about this for a minute. There's too much traffic here anyway. Let's follow them for a while until I can figure out what to do."

Gutierrez turned his head toward the back seat again. "What is there to figure out? Just whack them so we can go home."

"I don't want to shoot if it's his daughter. I don't want to waste civilians if I can help it. Besides, killing his daughter would give the Sons of Liberty a bad name. It would cause some people to be against us, maybe even label us as terrorists instead of patriots."

Gutierrez volunteered to help him in the thought process. "If it's a staffer, it's no big deal. If it's his girlfriend, it would add a little spice to the news reports – Senator Garrett and girlfriend killed on the way to a tryst."

"Yeah, that would make for good press, but it would also dilute the message we want to send – that the termite squad is on the job and that we won't stop until all the termites in America are exterminated."

He knew his statement wasn't true. They wouldn't be able to kill all the people who were tearing at the fabric of America. But he also knew he wouldn't have to assassinate all of them to be effective. All they needed to do was send a message that those who were tearing America down with their collectivist ideas and abuses of power were being targeted.

"Let's abort."

"What? He's only a few feet away. Let's get him now."

"No, we can do it another time. Let's try for Sunday when he takes the flight back to Washington. Maybe he'll have another driver."

Wellington had decided. Garrett could wait.

84

"We live in a dirty and dangerous world. There are some things the general public does not need to know, and shouldn't. I believe democracy flourishes when the government can take legitimate steps to keep its secrets and when the press can decide whether to print what it knows."
Catherine Graham (former publisher of the Washington Post)

Sarah took the spoon out of her mouth and turned toward Sveta. "I really like your borscht, Sveta. It's very tasty." The Wellingtons were having dinner at Sveta's in Sunny Isles Beach.

"Oh, it's nothing. I bought it at Kalinka's and just added a few things."

Wellington dabbed his mouth with the cloth napkin Sveta had provided. "Yes, it's very good. You'll have to show us where this Kalinka place is. Bob, you're a lucky man. I think she's spoiling you."

Sarah immediately gave him a dirty look. She wasn't pleased by his comment. He noticed and decided to shut up.

Someone knocked at the door.

"Robert, would you get that, please? I'm busy in here."

"Sure." Paige walked to the door, and looked in the peep hole. It was Milla. In addition to her job at the front desk she also had a part-time catering business specializing in Haitian food. It helped supplement her income, since she and her husband never seemed to be able to generate quite enough money to pay all the bills. When she could fit it into her schedule, she worked a third, part-time job at Piman Bouk, a restaurant on NE 2nd Avenue and 59th Street in Little Haiti.

"Hi Milla. Come on in."

"Hello, Mr. Robert. Where is Miss Svetlana?"

He motioned in the direction of the kitchen. "She's in the kitchen."

Milla knew where the kitchen was. She had delivered Haitian food to her many times over the years. She walked in and placed the bags of food on the table.

"Hi Milla. I'd like you to meet my friends. This is John and Sarah."

"Pleased to meet you."

Sveta reached into her purse and came up with some money. "Thank you for the food, Milla." She took it without making eye contact. "Thank you, Miss Svetlana."

Milla turned around and walked toward the door. "Good-bye, Mr. Robert."

Paige opened the door for her and closed it after she left. Paige and Sveta both felt good about doing business with her. She was a good cook and they knew she could use the money. She was always smiling and cheerful.

Sveta took the food out of the bags and started putting it on serving dishes.

Sarah picked up one of the dishes and started carrying it into the dining room. "Let me help you."

Wellington took a whiff as Sarah placed the dish on the table. "Hmmm. That smells good. What is it?"

As Sveta walked into the room, she volunteered an answer. "That's called griot. It's deep fried pork chunks. I like the way Milla makes it. Crispy on the outside and moist on the inside." She placed the bowl on the table. "And here are the rice and beans." It was red beans and rice, cooked together, giving the rice the appearance of being red.

Wellington took a sip of his Heineken beer, straight from the bottle, and leaned back in his chair. "Ah, this is a truly international meal – Dutch beer, Russian borscht and Haitian pork, rice and beans."

Sarah chimed in. "I don't think I'm going to get on the scale for a few days."

As they ate, the conversation turned to current events.

Paige turned toward Wellington. "Did you hear about the whack job on that Federal Reserve guy?"

Wellington perked up and adjusted his glasses with his right index finger and thumb. "Yeah, I heard about that."

Paige decided to have a little fun with the topic. "What do you think about it?"

Sveta jumped in. "I think it's terrible. This is America. They shouldn't be assassinating people."

Paige continued. "The mainstream media hasn't said much about it, just that he got whacked and that there was a note or something."

Wellington couldn't keep his mouth shut any longer. "Yeah. Actually, it was a message spread on the internet. He got whacked for debasing the currency. The Sons of Liberty took credit for it."

Paige was not surprised that Wellington knew so many of the details. He wondered how much detail he knew and how involved he was in the killing.

"I don't think those details were reported on TV. Where ..."

Before Paige could finish his sentence, Wellington cut him short. “I read about it on the internet. It’s the source of all truth, you know.”

It was a joke Paige and Wellington had about the internet. Since the mainstream media had practically become the propaganda wing of the administration in Washington, most people no longer trusted what got reported by the mainstream media. They got their news from cable stations and the internet.

Wellington looked a little nervous. He fidgeted and didn’t look Paige in the eye. He looked like an Indiana prep school student about to be reprimanded by the principal.

Paige picked up on it but didn’t say anything. He wanted to probe a little, without being too obvious. “Do you think there will be other assassinations? This Sons of Liberty group sounds like it has an agenda. Do you know anything about them?”

“Just what I read on the internet.” His fidgeting became more intense. “Nobody seems to know who they are or where they’re coming from. Maybe they’re a rogue spinoff of one of the private militias in Florida.”

One of Paige’s undergraduate minors was history. He especially liked American revolutionary history. “I’m familiar with the name – Sons of Liberty. That’s the group that dumped British tea into Boston Harbor a few years before the American Revolution. Do you think they’re connected to the Tea Party?”

“Nah, I don’t think so. The Tea Party isn’t into violence. It’s not a homogeneous group. The only thing they have in common is the belief that the federal government has become too big. They take pride in being peaceful. I don’t think assassination is part of their platform, although maybe some individual members might like the idea.”

Paige became more curious by the minute. He perceived that Wellington wasn't telling everything he knew, but the dinner table wasn't the place to push the point. He decided to wait until a more appropriate time and place. One thing Paige was especially curious about was why Wellington seemed so nervous talking about the subject. It wasn't like him to get rattled so easily. He would push a little, but not now. He wanted to find out how deeply Wellington was involved.

85

"Rebellion against tyrants is obedience to God."
Benjamin Franklin

"We sleep safe in our beds because rough men stand ready in the night to visit violence on those who would do us harm."
George Orwell

Sunday night. Time to kill Senator Garrett. Tomás Gutierrez would be Wellington's wing man again. Jim Bennett needed a rest after a week of overtime at the FBI. His main assignment that week was to find Nelson Fuller's assassin. It was the Miami office's top assignment and they were getting heat from Washington to find the assassin before he could strike again. He had to go through the motions.

There weren't any solid clues, but if one turned up, he would try to throw the other investigators off the trail. All they knew was that the assassin was a man. The witness reports were conflicting. Some said he was tall. Others said he was of medium height. Some said he was Hispanic. Others said he was Anglo. It's not unusual for eye witnesses to report incorrect information. That worked to Wellington's advantage.

Wellington liked working with Gutierrez. He was calmer and less prone to emotional outbursts than Santos Hernandez. He was easier to control and didn't challenge orders, although he was worried that Gutierrez might balk at an order to assassinate a journalist or professor. He would cross that bridge when he came to it.

Senator Garrett's plane was scheduled to leave Miami at 8:07 pm. If he were a normal person, he would have to get there more than an hour early to go through security, but since he was a member of the privileged Washington elite, he could get there pretty much any time he damn well pleased. The airport staff would just have to deal with it. On several occasions, they had to hold the plane for him because he was running late. He always flew first class. Taxpayers would just have to pick up the extra $150 cost for his two and a half hour ride. He couldn't be bothered flying in coach with the rabble he was representing.

Since they didn't know when he would be leaving for the airport or where he would be leaving from, they would have to guess and take their chances. The best guess was that he would be leaving from his home in Coral Gables in a black Lincoln Town Car with his regular driver about 90 minutes before flight time, but it was just a guess. If the woman who had picked him up in a red Toyota on Friday night was the one to pick him up today, Wellington had decided that they would abort the mission again and wait until his next trip to Miami, which would be a week or two later. He didn't come home every weekend.

Wellington and Gutierrez didn't want to wait any longer. They wanted to cross him off the list tonight. They didn't want to waste any more of their time on him. He was taking time away from their families. They resented it. The fact that Garrett also had a family and that his wife and children might miss him never entered their minds. You can't think about those things if you want to be an effective assassin. If you think of your target as a human being you have already lost the fight. You have to think of them as an inanimate object, just a target that has to be hit on the first attempt.

They started their mission two hours before flight time, just to be on the safe side. It paid off. They saw a black Lincoln Town Car drive past them a few blocks from the Senator's home 97 minutes before flight time. Wellington saw it first.

"There's the Town Car. Let's follow it just to make sure, but stay back so they don't notice they're being followed." Gutierrez pulled out and followed, keeping about a hundred feet behind. A few minutes later it pulled into the Senator's driveway. They drove by and parked a few blocks away, between the Senator's house and the airport, and waited.

The Town Car passed by five minutes later, going a few miles over the speed limit. Gutierrez turned toward Wellington. "It's not far to the airport, and the closer we get, the more traffic we'll run into. We've gotta do it soon."

Wellington rolled down both back windows and gripped the AA12 firmly. Then he shifted to the right and rested the gun butt on his left thigh. "Let's get him on a side street, before he makes it to the highway. Pull alongside him when you get a chance, but keep some distance. I don't want to get any blowback from the Frag 12s."

Garrett's Town Car turned left, toward Le Jeune Road, which was only a few blocks away. Time was running out. Wellington could sense it. He started fidgeting in the back seat.

"We have to get him before he gets to LeJeune Road. If we don't, there'll be too much traffic. We might get caught in a traffic jam."

"Gotcha, boss." Gutierrez swung left and accelerated until they were alongside Garrett.

Hopefully, the blasts from the Frag 12s wouldn't cause Garrett's driver to jerk to the left. They were positioned a little too close for comfort. Some of the blast might bounce back in their direction. It's a chance they would have to take.

Wellington caressed the AA12 shotgun and waited for the right moment. His mouth was dry. He stuck the barrel out the right rear window just as Senator Garrett turned to look at their car, which was hovering a few feet away. Wellington placed the gun butt on his left shoulder. It was his weak side, since he was right-handed, but it didn't matter. At this close a range, he couldn't miss.

He squeezed the trigger. The blast from the shotgun in the enclosed quarters was deafening. Gutierrez jerked instinctively and slammed on the gas pedal. They didn't think to wear ear plugs but it didn't matter. In a few minutes they would be able to hear normally again, perhaps with a slight ringing in their ears.

The shot hit its mark. The Frag12 exploded on impact with the window, causing it to shatter, and ripped off the Senator's head. The explosion also took off the back of the driver's head. The Town Car swerved to the right and went off the road into someone's front yard. Some fragments from the blast hit their car but didn't cause any damage. Gutierrez took the next right turn. They made a clean escape. It all happened so fast that none of the people in the other cars were able to give a clear description of them or their car. They rolled down the remaining windows so the smell of the gunpowder could dissipate.

***

"Government does not create wealth; it redistributes it. Whatever you receive from government was taken from someone else."
Robert W. McGee

After driving a few miles, and after making sure they weren't followed, Wellington told Gutierrez to pull over. Wellington took out his laptop and sent a previously composed message to all the radio and television stations in the Miami and Washington, DC areas, as well as some political websites, explaining why Senator Garrett had been killed.

> Senator Tom Garrett was exterminated because he was guilty of crimes against the American people. His support of Fannie Mae, Freddie Mac and corporate bailouts wasted trillions of taxpayer dollars and helped destroy home ownership in America. He also set a bad precedent, that redistribution of wealth is an acceptable policy. It is not. Let this be a warning to the other members of Congress who waste taxpayer dollars and who advocate taking the wealth of those who have earned it and giving it to those who have not. We will deal with you, too. You are on our list and you will be exterminated ... at the time and place of our choosing. The only way to remove yourself from the list is to resign.
> Sons of Liberty

The assassination and the note to the media caused an uproar that resounded throughout Washington and the nation. The Garrett assassination proved that Nelson Fuller's killing was not random. It was part of a larger scheme that probably involved other people, although it was not possible to say how many. The FBI suspected that the assassinations were localized, since they both took place in Miami, but they feared the executions would spur copycat killings in other cities. The frustration expressed by the Sons of Liberty was widespread. Millions of other Americans felt the same way. Many of them had guns. Several members of Congress resigned, but not Debbie Waterstein or Jack Lunn, who were next on the list.

86

"The limits of tyrants are prescribed by the endurance of those whom they oppress." Frederick Douglass

Senator Garrett's assassination caused problems for Frank Carbone, the bank president with the passport problem. He had found a way to get the million dollars Senator Garrett demanded but now he didn't know what to do with it.

There was no way in hell he was going to give it to Ken Tolleson, Garrett's snotty assistant, since Tolleson didn't have any power of his own. He was practically out of a job. Whoever was appointed to replace Garrett would probably want his own people, which meant Tolleson would soon be fired.

He still had the IRS problem to deal with. Now that Garrett was gone, there was no one to get the IRS off his back and there was no way to get his passport back, other than by going through the normal process, which could take years. He would be fired long before then.

He didn't know what to do with the money. It was risky to take it out of the bank. It would be risky to try to return it.

He figured his best bet would be to approach Florida's other Senator, Marco Emeraldo. He had a reputation for being squeaky clean. If he told him his story, perhaps he would understand and would be able to do something without the necessity of bribing him. He decided to hold on to the money until after he met with Senator Emeraldo, just in case. If he could get his passport back without paying a bribe, he would find a way to return the money to the bank.

87

Debbie Waterstein

"To compel a man to furnish funds for the propagation of ideas he disbelieves and abhors is sinful and tyrannical."
Thomas Jefferson

"They are not to do anything they please to provide for the general welfare, but only to lay taxes for that purpose ... Certainly no such universal power was meant to be given them." Thomas Jefferson

"The government is merely a servant—merely a temporary servant; it cannot be its prerogative to determine what is right and what is wrong, and decide who is a patriot and who isn't. Its function is to obey orders, not originate them."
Mark Twain

Debbie Waterstein was one of the more visible members of Congress. She never missed an opportunity to put her ugly face in front of a camera. The Congressional leadership was grooming her for bigger and better things. She was on a power trip. She didn't have to be convinced that in order to get along, you have to go along. She was more than willing to go along with any legislation the Congressional leadership wanted to pass, as long as it increased spending or taxed the rich.

She never saw a spending program she didn't like. She thought up a few of her own. She believed that the government owned one hundred percent of the people's income, and that she and her colleagues were gracious enough to let them keep some of it. The Boss had listened to some of her speeches. That was what got her on the list.

"Marta, contact that guy in New York who wants to outlaw table salt in restaurants. I forgot his name, but you can find it on the internet. He's a member of the New York State delegation in Albany. I want to ask him about his strategy."

"Yes, Debbie. I'll get right on it."

When she first took office eight years ago she winced whenever a staff member called her by her first name. She preferred to be called Ms. Waterstein or Congresswoman Waterstein, but decided she would appear to be a woman of the people if she allowed them to call her Debbie instead. She has since gotten used to being called Debbie. It was part of her strategy to be seen as just one of the little people, a vanguard of the proletariat.

One way she kept her finger on the pulse of the little people is by renting slum properties. She didn't collect the rent herself, of course. She didn't want to actually meet the people she rented to. She hired people to do that for her. Her rental properties were all listed under corporate names. Her tenants didn't know that she was their landlady. She preferred it that way. If they knew she was their slum lord, they might not vote for her.

She thought the state legislators in Albany were doing some good things and wanted to learn more. They and their colleagues in New York City had managed to outlaw smoking in restaurants.

She and New York Senator Chuck Sherman had co-sponsored a bill to do the same thing nationally but it got tied up in committee. She didn't care that prohibiting smoking in restaurants violated the property rights of the restaurant owners. She thought some things were more important than property rights. The fact that Congress didn't have the Constitutional authority to regulate smoking never entered her mind. She believed the Commerce and General Welfare Clauses gave Congress carte blanche to do whatever it wanted.

She was frustrated that she couldn't ban smoking nationwide, so she decided to go after table salt. It caused high blood pressure, it was unhealthy, and it increased medical costs. That was all the excuse she needed.

After she got rid of table salt, she planned to outlaw red meat in any school that accepted federal funding, which meant most of them. She fully believed that red meat made children aggressive and caused people to become fat. She believed it was her mission as a member of Congress to regulate people's lives. She didn't think the average American was capable of making informed decisions. Her mission was to do that for them.

At the other end of the spectrum, she wanted to prevent fashion magazines from using thin models who appeared to have eating disorders, but the First Amendment's guarantee of free press was getting in her way. She sponsored legislation to carve out an exception to the First Amendment that would allow Congress to regulate magazine advertising. There were already some prohibitions on alcohol and tobacco advertising. She wanted to expand those prohibitions, but hadn't figured out how to do it and still keep below the radar. She didn't want the magazine industry to have time to gather opposition against her proposal. She would try to sneak the bill into another piece of legislation on a totally unrelated topic, perhaps a transportation bill or something like that. Members of Congress seldom read the bills they vote on. She might be able to get away with it. Once a bill became law it was difficult to repeal, even if it was a bad law. She knew that and used that fact to her advantage.

In the meantime, she would target models under 18, since that would allow Congress to accuse editors of contributing to child abuse. The mere thought that magazines could be targeted would put a chilling effect on them. They would be very hesitant to hire thin models, especially if they were under 18. But she didn't know what to do with thin models who were over 18. Perhaps for purposes of this law, the bill could define a child as anyone under 21 or 25. Or perhaps magazine editors could be arrested and fined for contributing to a hostile work environment for pressuring models of any age not to eat.

She didn't want to move too fast. One thing at a time. If she went after salt, red meat, sugar, carbonated soft drinks, junk food, pizza in the schools, obesity and thin models all at once, it would dissipate her resources. She would be spreading herself too thin. It would also make it easier for the property rights and individual responsibility crowd to see a pattern. She preferred to work under the radar, in the shadows.

The fact that most of her constituency didn't care about those issues didn't bother her. She felt it was her job to do what was best for them whether they wanted her to or not.

The fact that the Constitution didn't give the federal government the authority to make laws in those areas didn't bother her either. She figured it was all covered under the Commerce and General Welfare clauses. She thought the people who advocated repealing those provisions of the Constitution were crazy, although she sometimes worried that their idea might pick up enough supporters to become a real threat to what she wanted to do.

Being a member of Congress allowed her to push her personal agenda. That's why she ran for Congress. She thought being a member of Congress was the best job in the world. She couldn't wait to get up in the morning. She never thought that her mornings might be numbered because of her agenda.

88

Jack Lunn

Jack Lunn was a member of Florida's congressional delegation. His district was just north of Debbie Waterstein's. They were colleagues and worked together on some projects of mutual interest.

Jack was more practical than Debbie. He didn't go to Congress more than 20 years ago so he could push his personal agenda. He didn't have one. He went so he could drink in the power.

He was in the pockets of every special interest group that was politically correct. There were a lot of elderly people in his district, so he decided to become a strong supporter of government-funded Social Security, even though it was a Ponzi scheme rip-off. He wasn't concerned that the young people would have to pay for it and that it would go bankrupt long before they retired.

He was against increasing the retirement age or reducing benefits, two solutions that would postpone its inevitable bankruptcy. He preferred tax increases for the rich to fund it, even though the rich wouldn't qualify to receive benefits under his plan and even though taxing the rich wouldn't solve the problem, since the Social Security deficit was a hole that was far too deep for the rich to fill. Even if the rich were taxed at 100 percent of their marginal income, it still wouldn't be sufficient to save Social Security from bankruptcy. He had heard that argument from economists many times but ignored it. You can't get votes by telling old people their Social Security is going bankrupt. You have to give them hope, at least until after the next election.

Whenever anyone advocated getting government out of the pension business and privatizing Social Security he went on the attack, accusing them of being insensitive, heartless and in favor of throwing grandma under the bus. His strategy had been effective. He kept getting re-elected to Congress every two years.

"Steve, I want you to get a copy of the latest Congressional Budget Office report on tax revenue. Read it and come up with some arguments to increase taxes on the rich. They're not paying their fair share. We have to find ways to increase their taxes."

Steve Waldron was Jack's Congressional assistant. He had a Master of Public Administration degree from Harvard and never worked in the private sector. He preferred working in the government sector, preferably in Washington because that's where the action is. He preferred redistributing income to generating it.

"That might be an uphill battle, Jack. Their last report showed that the top 1 percent already pay more than the bottom 95 percent."

"Yeah, I know, but I'm sure you can find some arguments. The top marginal tax rate in the 1950s was 94 percent. We're not anywhere near that now. There's room for an increase."

Jack's facts were a little off, but that never stopped him from making his argument. The 94 percent rate was in effect in 1944-45, toward the end of World War II. The top rate declined a bit after that but remained above 90 percent until 1964, when it dropped to a mere 77 percent.

"OK, I'll get right on it."

He called Yolanda, one of his Congressional staffers, into his office. Yolanda had beautiful brown skin. She was an African-American, Puerto Rican mix. He'd had a brief affair with her but ended it when his wife smelled her perfume on one of his shirts. Yolanda stopped wearing perfume in the office after that, just in case he wanted to resume their relationship.

"Yolanda, I'd like you to check on that radio station in Palm Beach, the one that has that loud mouth conservative talk show host. See when their license is up for renewal. Maybe we can get the Federal Communications Commission to find some irregularities."

Lunn didn't like most of what that guy said. He had a funny name. Jack could never remember it. All he knew was that the station was hampering his reelection campaign. Maybe if the FCC could find some irregularities, he could pressure the station into firing that guy in exchange for getting its license renewed. As a representative of the people, he thought it was his duty to shut that guy up. What he didn't know was that some other representatives of the people were about to try to shut him up.

89

"If this be treason, make the most of it."
Patrick Henry

"I have some good news for you." It was Jim Bennett, speaking to Wellington. They were standing outside Wellington's downtown office. Bennett suggested meeting in person rather than conveying the information over their cell phones because he didn't want the feds picking up the conversation with their monitoring equipment.

"Our friends Debbie Waterstein and Jack Lunn are having lunch in Fort Lauderdale next Saturday."

"That's great. Maybe we can get a twofer."

"That's exactly what I was thinking, but there are some complications."

"Like what?"

"Debbie has become such a big shot that she sometimes has a body guard or two. She's been using them a lot more frequently since the esteemed Senator Garrett met his untimely demise."

"Hmmm. I see what you're getting at. You'll need an assist."

"Yeah, if we want to get them at the same time, we'll need more than one person."

"I hear ya."

"I think we should wait until they exit the restaurant. They'll probably arrive at different times but they'll probably leave together."

"That sounds like a plan. That will also give us time to check out where their limos and bodyguards are stationed. Which restaurant will they be at?"

"SoLita. The name means South of Little Italy. It's an upscale Italian place on Las Olas Boulevard."

"Hmmm. That could complicate things. There's a lot of traffic in that area, especially on Saturday afternoons. There are limited entries and exits. If we try to escape over the bridge it would be easy to trap us. All they would have to do is close the bridge."

"That won't be a problem. The restaurant's on the mainland side of the bridge, close to Federal Highway."

"OK, that makes the escape easier, but still not perfect. After we whack them, the place will be crawling with cops. They could block Federal Highway."

"Yeah, I've thought of that. We could use a couple of stolen cars for the job, then abandon them in a mall parking lot a few blocks away. Maybe we could take in a movie. That way we wouldn't have to try to leave the neighborhood."

"Sounds good. What's playing?"

"Funny, John. I like your sense of humor."

"I think we should use the AA12. I'll load up the mag with Frag 12s. We'll pop the bodyguards first to get them out of the way. If they're standing close enough together we could just shoot a few rounds into the sidewalk between them. The Frag 12s have a 9 foot burst radius. One or two shells might be enough to take all of them out. Then we can focus on Debbie and Jack."

"The voters won't be pleased, John."

"That's OK. They can elect a couple of new hacks to replace them."

"You might want to pump one into the limo window, too, just in case there might be a body guard there. The driver might be carrying a gun, too."

"Yeah, good idea. Let's bring Santos and Tomás in on this. If the two limos are in different locations, we'll need some back-up."

"OK. I'll see if they're available. It'll be a Saturday, so Tomás won't be working. Santos doesn't usually work weekends, either, but I'll check, just to make sure."

"Have them knock out the traffic cameras on the escape route, too. We don't want them to get photos of us. The best time would probably be around 2am on Saturday morning. Traffic will be light and the cops won't have time to replace them by lunchtime. A few well-placed shotgun blasts should do it. But not with the Frag 12s. The shells are too expensive. Have them use regular shells. Tell them not to take out the traffic lights, though. That would cause traffic jams all up and down Las Olas. The cops would have to direct traffic the old fashioned way, one on each corner. We don't need that."

"OK, I'm on it."

90

Saturday morning, around 2am. Santos and Tomás just stole a Toyota with a sun roof. It would be less obvious than a convertible and it would allow them to do what they have to do – shoot out the traffic cameras on the escape route without the need to get out of the car at each intersection.

Santos drove. Tomás sat in the front passenger seat holding a shotgun on his lap. They agreed that Santos would drive because he had trouble fitting his massive shoulders and chest through the sun roof.

The AA12 was in the back seat, loaded with a mag of Frag 12s, in case a random squad car spotted them shooting out the cameras. They didn't want to kill any cops, but they also didn't want to get caught. Certain firearms violations carry a mandatory 5-year minimum sentence, and they figured that blowing out multiple traffic cameras might qualify.

The city purchased most of the traffic cameras with a federal grant. Maybe they wouldn't be replaced, unless the city could get another federal grant. They liked the idea of destroying the cameras. Even though Santos worked for the TSA and was on the front lines of the war on terror, he didn't like it that the federal government was installing cameras everywhere. He knew the cameras didn't do anything to stop terrorists, not the foreign kind, anyway. He figured he was doing a service to the community and to all Americans by taking them out.

Several intersections on the escape route had cameras, usually four per intersection, so Tomás would have to squeeze off a lot of rounds. He wore a thick pad on his right shoulder to absorb the recoil of the shotgun. Without it, his shoulder would likely be black and blue before sunrise.

Las Olas Boulevard would be fairly easy, although they were worried that a squad car might be parked on a side street. Federal Highway would be more dangerous. It was a main highway and at that hour squad cars passed by every few minutes.

They both made excuses to their wives for being away overnight. Tomás told Teresa he was attending an IT conference in Orlando. Santos told Maria he had to work at the Tampa airport, which was too far away to commute. They booked a room at one of the local motels that take cash. After their excursion, they would ditch the car and go there to catch a few hours of sleep.

The job went off without a hitch. The shotgun blasts made a lot of noise at two in the morning, and the people who were on the sidewalks or in their cars at that hour got a brief bit of excitement, but they didn't think to take photos with their cell phones, and no one even considered following them or trying to stop them. They both wore stockings over their heads, just in case. They didn't want to be identified.

The whole adventure was over in a few minutes. They blew out the cameras they needed to blow out, plus a few more for good measure. The police probably wouldn't think the camera caper was tied in to the assassinations until after they had made their escape.

After completing the mission, Tomás sent a one-word text message to Wellington – DONE.

91

"The tree of liberty must be refreshed from time to time with the blood of patriots and tyrants. It is its natural manure."
Thomas Jefferson

"If the representatives of the people betray their constituents, there is then no recourse left but in the exertion of that original right of self-defense which is paramount to all positive forms of government."
Alexander Hamilton

Lunch was scheduled for 1pm. Debbie Waterstein arrived at 12:45pm in a limo with an armed driver and two body guards. But she didn't merely arrive. She made an entrance. She blocked traffic on Las Olas as she got out of the car. The two body guards were large, fit and dressed in dark suits, wearing sun glasses. One of them escorted her inside. The other one stayed outside, and took a position just to the left of the front door. The driver removed the orange cones that had been placed on the street in front of the restaurant and parked in the space that the local police had reserved for her.

It was nearly impossible to find parking on Las Olas Boulevard on a Saturday afternoon. Regular people had to park on a side street or in one of the several parking lots in the neighborhood. Debbie was not a regular person. Power had its privilege.

Jack Lunn arrived a few minutes later with just a driver, who wasn't carrying a weapon, and no body guards. He had to open his own door. He wasn't as high on the food chain as Congresswoman Waterstein. His driver had to find a place to park at one of the municipal parking lots.

When Lunn walked into the restaurant, Debbie was already seated, being served by an entourage of restaurant staff. She got up to greet him, giving him a little air kiss.

"Hi Jack. Glad you could make it. I have a few ideas I want to bounce off you."

"Great. I have an idea I'd like to bounce off you, too."

After some preliminary chit chat they got down to business. Debbie started off.

"Jack, I'm getting really disturbed by these Tea Party types. They disrupted the last election and got some of their people elected. Some of my best friends got kicked out of office. I want to make sure that doesn't happen again."

"Yeah, some of my best friends are gone, too. Those IRS audits we pushed for slowed them down, but didn't stop them. I take it you have an idea that might do the trick?"

"Yes, I do. I plan to sponsor legislation that will shut them up. I'll structure it like a no trespassing bill. It will make it a federal crime to do anything that disrupts the normal business of government. If they demonstrate anywhere around a government building, they'll be arrested for disrupting normal government business. People who hold up a sign with political content on a sidewalk will get arrested if the people driving by slow down to read it. Anyone who makes a statement at a town hall meeting that's disruptive gets arrested. We can word the legislation so vaguely that we'll be able to use it against those Tea Party people practically any time they do anything. We'll be able to have them arrested before they can cause any trouble and the cost of defending themselves constantly will bankrupt them."

"That sounds good to me. The last four or five town hall meetings I went to, someone stood up to complain about my voting record. We could use that law to argue they came to the meeting with the intent to disrupt government business, since those town hall meetings are technically government business."

"Exactly. I think it'll work, but here's the problem, Jack. My staff's too busy to draft the legislation. Could your staff do the drafting? We could co-sponsor it."

"Yeah, I think we could do it. I'll ask Steve to coordinate it when I get back to Washington."

"I have something to bounce off you, too, Debbie."

"Sure, what is it Jack?" The restaurant was noisy and it was difficult to hear what he was saying. She leaned forward to hear better.

"You must have heard about those recent cases where juries let people off for killing government officials."

"Sure. It was all over the news. You couldn't miss it."

Jack looked around to see if anyone was listening. "One guy executed an IRS agent for shutting down his business. Another guy killed an EPA official for shutting down his farm. Some woman wasted two DEA agents for breaking into her house because they mistakenly got the wrong address. Juries set them all free."

"Yes, I remember those cases. The juries found them not guilty because they thought it was justifiable homicide."

"We have to make sure this kind of stuff can't continue to happen. We can't have people killing federal officials and getting let off the hook by some jury and calling it justifiable homicide. If we allow it to continue, everybody will start shooting government officials. There's no telling where it will stop. Maybe they'll start shooting us."

"They already have started shooting us, Jack. They got Tom Garrett. Their note said they plan to get more of us. What can we do to stop them?"

"I plan to sponsor legislation that would classify anyone who kills any government employee as a terrorist. If we do that, the Patriot Act provisions will kick in and they won't be entitled to a jury trial, or any kind of a trial, for that matter. We can lock them up and just forget about them. Or maybe subject them to enhanced interrogation until they have a heart attack."

He snickered as he said it. He liked the idea. It reminded him of recent press reports where several demonstrators who were arrested at a town hall meeting died mysteriously while in custody. Requests for autopsies by the families were refused for national security reasons.

"That sounds like an excellent solution, Jack. I'd like to co-sponsor that bill with you."

"Jack, we have to do something about this secession movement. People are going around collecting signatures on petitions. Some state legislatures are passing resolutions and a few of them have already voted to secede. We have to stop it."

"I agree, but how are we going to do it?"

"I don't know. We could introduce some kind of legislation in the House and the Senate, but I don't know how we could word it so that it would pass. There would be too much opposition."

"How about passing a law that defines treason to include advocating secession or signing a petition to secede or passing a resolution to secede?"

"Yes, that would do it, but again, I don't think we could get enough votes to pass it. The states that want to secede wouldn't support it, and many of the representatives from the other states wouldn't support changing the definition of treason even if they didn't support secession."

"Well, in that case we could ask the president to issue an Executive Order. That way we wouldn't have to go through Congress."

"Jack, that's a brilliant idea. Why didn't I think of it?"

"I'm sure you would have. I'm honored to have beat you to the punch."

"I'll drink to that," Debbie smiled, raised her wine glass and took a sip. "I'll talk to the president when I see him next week."

***

The conversation continued over lunch and dessert. Meanwhile, Wellington's crew scouted out the area and plotted their strategy.

Wellington and Jim Bennett sat at an outdoor café across the street, observing the restaurant. "John, I have a suggestion for amending the plan."

"OK, let's hear it."

"Rather than pump a few Frag 12s into the pavement, let's wait until Debbie gets into the limo, then pump a few rounds into the windows. We can do one round into the back seat, then one into the front seat. That should take out Debbie, the driver and both body guards."

Wellington agreed. "I like it. Let's do it. What about Jack Lunn and his driver?"

"Lunn will probably come out at the same time as Debbie. If he's within range, we can whack him then, either with the AA12 or with a few pistol shots. If his driver gets out of the car with a gun, we can whack him, too. Otherwise, we'll leave the driver alone. I don't like killing civilians if I can help it."

"OK. Sounds good. I don't like wasting civilians, either. I don't mind whacking Debbie's driver, though. I don't think he's a civilian. He looks like Secret Service. Anyone who defends a termite should be treated like a termite." Wellington called in the change in plans to Santos, who was awaiting instructions.

Shortly after 2:30 they emerged from the restaurant together. Jack Lunn's driver was nowhere to be seen, but it was fair to guess that Lunn had called him and that he was on his way. Santos stood around the corner from the restaurant with the AA12, awaiting instructions. Tomás waited in the getaway car. Wellington and Bennett continued to sit at the café across the street, ready to assist if needed.

Wellington picked up his cell phone and called Santos. "Get ready."

Jack and Debbie said their good-byes. Debbie got into the limo on the curb side. One of the Secret Service agents closed her door, walked around the back of the car and got in on the street side. The second Secret Service agent got in the front seat on the passenger side. Jack Lunn continued to stand on the sidewalk, waiting for his driver to arrive.

"Now!"

Santos heard Wellington's command and turned the corner, the AA12 at his side. When he was about 30 feet from the car, he raised it, aimed at the middle of the front windshield and squeezed off the first round. BLAM! The shell hit the window, exploding immediately and sending fragments into the heads and upper torsos of all four passengers.

The blast caused Lunn and the other pedestrians to freeze. All eyes were on Santos as he shifted left and aimed at Lunn. He pointed at Lunn's midsection and squeezed. BLAM! The second round exploded on impact, cutting Lunn in half and sending additional fragments into the car on Debbie's side. Several pedestrians got splattered with his blood and guts, but none of them sustained injuries.

The driver and both Secret Service agents were out of commission, making it safe for Santos to walk around to the street side and pump the third round into Debbie, who was slumped in the seat. It wasn't necessary. She was already dead, killed by the first round. The left side of her head was missing. It would be a closed casket ceremony for all of them.

Santos ran back to the corner, turned right and jumped into the getaway car. Tomás sped off and took the prearranged escape route. Wellington and Bennett were still across the street, sitting at an outside table in the café. Their services weren't needed. As everyone else in the café got up and stared across the street, they stood up and quickly walked toward the lot where their car was parked.

Lunn's driver was a block down the road, on the way to pick up his boss, but couldn't get close to the restaurant. The street was clogged with cars and people, who were running from across the street to see the carnage up close. It was his lucky day. He would be able to attend Lunn's funeral from an upright position.

92

"The duty of a patriot is to protect his country from its government."
Thomas Paine

"It doesn't take a majority to make a rebellion; it takes only a few determined leaders and a sound cause."
H. L. Mencken

"A wise and frugal government ... shall restrain men from injuring one another, shall leave them otherwise free to regulate their own pursuits of industry and improvement, and shall not take from the mouth of labor the bread it has earned. This is the sum of good government."
Thomas Jefferson

After Wellington and Bennett escaped from the scene, they pulled over so that Wellington could send a message to the press and various internet sites.

> Greetings. The Sons of Liberty struck another blow for freedom this afternoon with the killing of Representatives Debbie Waterstein and Jack Lunn.

> Members of Congress who advocate higher taxes and more government regulations need to be exterminated. We are not under taxed or under regulated. Our elected representatives are spending our children's inheritance. Those who advocate class warfare and use the General Welfare clause of the Constitution as an excuse to cram their personal agendas down our throats will be dealt with firmly. Such vermin are gnawing away at the fabric of America. It is up to us and other true representatives of the American people to stop them. We will continue to do so. Let this be a warning to members of Congress. Unless you stop undermining our heritage and return government to its proper function of protecting life, liberty and property and nothing else, you will be targeted, and we will get you.
> SONS OF LIBERTY

The message went viral. Radio and television stations interrupted regularly scheduled programming to report on and discuss the assassinations. Reporters and journalists interviewed members of Congress. Some got defensive, stating that the killers were mentally unbalanced and needed help, always denying that Congress no longer represented the people. Others went on the offensive and advocated more funds for federal law enforcement, more subsidies to local police and more cameras, wiretapping and internet surveillance. Some advocated random searches, confiscation of guns and suspension of the Constitution.

Some politicians tried to minimize the message the Sons of Liberty were trying to spread. One member of Congress said, in a television interview, "I think this is a local thing. If you notice, all the killings took place in Miami or Fort Lauderdale, which are only a few miles apart. It's probably just a small group of people, probably no more than one or two individuals, who are responsible for all this."

"Do you think there will be more killings?"

"It looks that way, unless we can stop them. I plan to introduce a bill in Congress on Monday morning that will provide more funding for local police and will allow the FBI, TSA or other federal agency to commandeer local police forces to look for these people and other groups like them. We'll get the army involved and put a tank on every street corner, if necessary."

When Wellington and Bennett heard the broadcast, they were upset but not surprised.

Bennett turned toward Wellington. "They have a point, you know. We are local. The fact that we're not a national organization is taking the steam out of our message."

"Yeah, I know. If there were more of us, and if we didn't have day jobs, we could take a trip to other parts of the country and whack a few more termites. That would make it look like we're national."

"Yeah, but we can't. We do have day jobs. Besides, we don't have access to information outside of South Florida. We wouldn't be able to find out their schedules or where they plan to have lunch."

"Maybe some copycats will pop up to do the job for us. A lot of people in the rest of the country feel the same way we do. If we can continue to set an example, perhaps people in other parts of the country will pick up the ball and run with it."

"Yeah. Maybe. We can continue to think globally, but we can only act locally."

"Maybe that will be enough."

93

Daniel Frumpton

"It is not honorable to take mere legal advantage, when it happens to be contrary to justice."
Thomas Jefferson

"Through the years, some men have discovered how to satisfy their wants at the expense of others without being accused of theft; they ask their government to do the stealing for them."
W.M. Curtiss

Daniel Frumpton was a real estate tycoon, one of the biggest. He was also one of the most visible. He went out of the way to get his face in front of a camera at every opportunity. He thought of running for president at one time, but decided against it because of all the skeletons in his closet.

He impregnated a few women in his younger days and was quietly and secretly supporting them and their children. If word got out of his extra families, the religious right would be all over it. Neither the Democrats nor Republicans would support him, and an independent run for the presidency would be too expensive. Without the support of the religious right, one of the main groups that would support an independent candidate, he figured he would be wasting his time and money.

Santos checked flight schedules to Fort Lauderdale, Miami and Palm Beach on a daily basis to see when Frumpton would be coming to town. He didn't bother checking the roster for regularly scheduled flights because Frumpton never flew commercially. He always used his private jet. A few hours ago he filed a flight plan from New York to Palm Beach. He would be arriving Thursday afternoon around 4pm.

Santos called Wellington to deliver the news. "John? The next package will arrive around four o'clock on Thursday."

"Thanks for the information. Let me know if you need anything."

"I will." He hung up and contacted Tomás to give him the same information. They would be working as a team.

***

"Jerry, I'm coming down Thursday afternoon. I want you to get the paperwork ready so I can sign it." Daniel Frumpton was in New York, talking to Jerry Goldman, his attorney in Aventura, Florida.

"OK. It will be ready. When would you like to schedule the meeting?"

"How about Friday at 10? That'll give me time to do a few things before the meeting."

"OK. I'll make sure everything is ready to go."

Jerry Goldman was almost finished preparing the paperwork that would transfer the property confiscated by eminent domain to the Frumpton empire. Construction firms had already been retained to build the condos, restaurant and marina Frumpton planned to put on the property once the title had been transferred. After he signed the papers, the families who were being evicted would have 30 days to vacate the premises.

"Did Keith receive his little token yet?" Frumpton was referring to the $20,000 token of his appreciation Goldman gave to Keith Ross, the city manager of Aventura, in exchange for his support for the project. The gift was transferred in the form of cash in an envelope.

"Yes, he received it last week."

"Good. We wouldn't want any last-minute glitches to delay the signing."

"You know, Jerry, I really like this eminent domain stuff. As soon as the property's condemned, the price drops by as much as 50 percent. As soon as the title transfers to me, the value goes up by more than 100 percent. I make a good profit before I even break ground."

"Yes, Mr. Frumpton, it is a very profitable way to do business."

"See if you can find me some more properties in the area that I can acquire this way. Something close to the water."

"Yes, Mr. Frumpton."

Daniel Frumpton didn't suspect that he would not be making any more real estate acquisitions. Many people of retirement age migrate from the north to die in Florida. He would soon be one of them, if Santos and Tomás had anything to say about it.

94

It was Friday morning. Santos was working the afternoon shift at Miami International Airport, so he was free. Tomás had a flexible schedule and took Friday morning off. They waited in a parked car underneath Frumpton's attorney's building, wearing Aventura police uniforms with caps and sun glasses, to obscure their appearance in the event a camera recorded what they were about to do.

Frumpton was due to arrive any minute. They knew about his schedule because Jim Bennett was monitoring Frumpton's phone calls. They pointed the car toward the street so they could see when he arrived. It would be pointed in the right direction for an easy escape. Santos was really looking forward to taking out Frumpton.

"Tomás, I really want to whack Frumpton. Let me do it. It's for my family. Castro confiscated my family's property in Cuba. I want to get back at people who abuse government power to confiscate property. I take it personal."

"OK. I understand. You can do him. But I'm doing the judge."

"Why? Do you have something against judges?"

"Yes, I do. A few years ago one of those bastards revoked my driver's license for not paying a parking ticket. I didn't know it was revoked until I got pulled over for speeding. They never sent me a notice. The cops confiscated my car. I couldn't drive for two weeks, until they could straighten things out. Teresa had to drive me to work and pick me up at night. It was a major hassle."

"OK, you can do the judge. Maybe if we get lucky we can do Jerry Goldman today, too. His office is in the building. If he comes down to greet Frumpton we can get them both."

"Yeah, but I don't think he'll come down to greet him."

"Yeah, I don't, either. Just a thought."

"We can get him later."

"What about the driver? Should we do him, too?"

"I don't know. The Boss wants to minimize the civilian head count, and I do too. The guy probably has a family. Let's wait and see."

About ten minutes later, Frumpton's car entered from the street and parked in a dark corner of the parking garage. Santos and Tomás got out of their car and walked toward Frumpton.

As they got closer, they saw a couple getting out of their car and walking toward the front door. Tomás whispered to Santos, "There are a couple of people walking toward the building. Let's wait until they go inside."

"OK, but we'll have to stall Frumpton."

"Yeah, we can do that. We look like police."

When they got within about ten feet of Frumpton, Santos initiated the conversation. "Good morning Mr. Frumpton. We're here to see that nothing happens to you while you're here in Aventura."

Frumpton looked surprised. So did his driver, who had just opened the door for Frumpton. The driver looked professional, probably ex-military. He was probably packing heat. That could prove to be a problem if they weren't fast enough.

"Do you think I'm in any danger?"

"No, sir, just a precaution."

After the couple entered the building, the mood changed. Santos and Tomás pulled out their guns. Santos did all the talking.

He reached over and opened the car door. "OK, Mr. Frumpton, get in the back seat." Frumpton looked startled. He wasn't used to being commanded to do anything. The driver's right hand made a slow move toward the inside of his coat. Tomás saw it and pointed his gun at the driver's head. "Don't try anything or I'll kill you."

The driver stopped and slowly raised his hands, while maintaining eye contact with Tomás as best he could, given the fact that Tomás was wearing sun glasses. Tomás perceived that the driver was still a threat. He thought about what to do while Frumpton got into the back seat.

"OK, back up, slowly. Take out your gun with two fingers and put it on the trunk of the car. If you try anything stupid, I'll kill you."

The driver did what he said, never losing eye contact. It was something an ex-cop or ex-military would do. He definitely had some training.

After he placed the gun on the trunk of the car, Tomás motioned to the driver's pocket. "Now take out your cell phone and put it on the trunk."

The driver reached into the right pocket of his suit coat, took out the cell phone and placed it on the trunk.

"Now step back."

The driver stepped back. Tomás took the gun and cell phone and put them in his pocket.

"Now open the trunk."

The driver took out his keys and opened the trunk.

"Get in."

"What?"

"You heard me. Get in."

The driver got in. He looked up at Tomás, expecting the worst. Instead of shooting him, Tomás gave him instructions. "We don't like killing civilians, but I will kill you if you don't do exactly as I say. Don't make any noise and don't try to escape for 10 minutes. After that, you are free to go."

As he finished his sentence, he heard two discharges from Santos's gun. Santos had just put two .22 caliber slugs into Frumpton's head with his Ruger Mark 3 Target pistol. It came equipped with a built-in suppressor, so it didn't sound any louder than a good fart.

The driver heard the sounds, too. He nodded his head vigorously to indicate agreement with the terms Tomás had offered. Tomás closed the trunk. He'd donned gloves so he wouldn't leave any prints. He didn't realize what a good deed he'd done. The driver was a veteran. He had a wife and three kids, two girls and a boy. He would be home in time to have dinner with them, although he would have to find a new job. Unfortunately, he wouldn't be able to get a reference from his former employer.

Santos closed the door and turned toward Tomás. "What should we do now? Goldman is upstairs waiting for Frumpton. Should we get him now or should we get him later?"

"Let's get him now."

Santos tucked the Ruger into his belt. They walked through the front door to the elevator. They got off on the third floor and turned left, toward Goldman's office. It was a small office, but large enough to have a receptionist.

The receptionist was blonde, perhaps in her mid-twenties. "May I help you?" She spoke with a slight southern drawl. She looked startled by the appearance of two police officers standing in front of her. The police usually don't come to visit attorney

Goldman. He does most of his work behind the scenes, often in the shadows.

Santos stepped forward. "Yes, we'd like to see Mr. Goldman." He felt good about assassinating Frumpton. He thought people who used the law to steal property needed to be dealt with severely, but he was also nervous. After all, he had just killed someone and was about to execute someone else. Although he had killed before, he never really got used to it, especially when he did it from close range. Shooting someone from a hundred yards away was one thing. Squeezing the trigger on someone who was gazing into your eyes pleading for mercy was something else. Even though Frumpton was a parasite, he was also a human being, a husband and a father.

She got up and escorted them to Goldman's office. "Right this way." She was so startled at seeing two police officers appear in the office that she didn't notice the blood splatters on Santos's shirt.

"Mr. Goldman, there are two police officers here to see you."

Goldman looked up from his desk. They waited for the receptionist to leave, then closed the door. Goldman looked worried. He could sense that something was wrong.

Santos took out the Ruger and pumped two slugs into Goldman's head. His head jerked back after the first round hit and blood spurted onto the paperwork on his desk. He slumped in his chair. They turned around and walked out, closing the door behind them. As they passed the front desk, Tomás turned to the receptionist, "Mr. Goldman doesn't want to be disturbed."

Goldman died instantly, although it didn't matter. They came to deliver a message and they'd delivered it. The Sons of Liberty wouldn't claim responsibility or explain the reason for the hits just yet, though. They wanted to wait until the other two abusers of the eminent domain laws could be dealt with. If things went according to plan, they wouldn't have to wait long.

95

The aftermath of the double killings was predictable. Although killing an attorney was not a big deal, assassinating a New York real estate magnate in Miami was. Especially Frumpton, since he was well-known in both Miami and New York. The manner in which it was done also caught the attention of both the police and the press. It was the top news story of the day.

The FBI placed the Aventura police under a microscope, since it appeared that two of their members were the assassins. The FBI was called in to investigate, since the Aventura police couldn't be trusted to conduct the investigation. There wasn't any apparent motive, which baffled them.

Cameras had caught two people dressed as Aventura police leaving the building at the time of the killing but no one could identify them. They wore sun glasses and caps and their heads were pointed down on the way out the door. There weren't any cameras covering the parking lot, so the police and FBI didn't know what kind of car they drove. Frumpton's driver wasn't very helpful. All he could offer was the same description they already had from the camera.

No one suspected it was the work of the Sons of Liberty. The modus operandi was completely different. They used a .22 caliber pistol instead of a shotgun with Frag 12 rounds. No one contacted the press to claim responsibility.

Santos and Tomás changed their clothes, got cleaned up and went to work. Santos placed the blood splattered shirt into a black plastic bag and tossed it into a garbage bin. They still had two uncompleted homework assignments – Jules Rapaport, the judge who put his stamp of approval on Frumpton's eminent domain case, and Keith Ross, the city manager of Aventura, who supported the confiscations. Their days were numbered.

96

Jules Rapaport

Jules Rapaport was an above-average student, both as an undergraduate and in law school. He earned his law degree at the University of Miami, not an Ivy League school, but it was local, which allowed him to continue living with his parents until age 25, and it was generally considered to be the best law school in Miami. It was also the most expensive, but that didn't concern Jules. His father, a prominent local attorney, paid 100 percent of his tuition.

Jules enjoyed his college and law school days. He didn't have to worry about tuition, paying rent or a part-time job. He could concentrate on his studies. His parents bought him a car for high school graduation so he would have a way to get to school. Whenever he needed clothes, his mother took him shopping, which got to be annoying when he hit his teenage years. He lost his virginity at age 21 to a nice Jewish girl in his sociology class. After law school he worked for his father's law firm for several years, accumulating experience and wealth, which he invested wisely. He got married, started a family and eventually became a judge.

Much of his wealth was the result of shaking down high tech companies. From his undergraduate finance courses, he learned that high tech company stock prices tended to fluctuate wildly, especially when they were in the start-up stage. Whenever a high tech company announced a new product, the stock price would shoot up, as speculators tried to cash in. Whenever the market learned that a high tech company was having a cash flow problem, its stock price would plummet, since cash flow problems often led to bankruptcy. Often, high tech companies would be turning out new products and having cash flow problems at the same time, causing their stock price to jump one week and plummet the next. Jules also learned that trading on insider information sometimes caused stock prices to jump or plummet rapidly.

Jules put the two ideas together and sued high tech companies. He would track their stock prices. Whenever he saw a rapid rise or rapid decline, he would threaten to file a class action lawsuit for insider trading. He didn't bother to look for actual proof of insider trading. There almost never was any, because rapid fluctuations in stock price were part of the normal market process for start-up companies in the high tech industry. The mere fact that the stock price fluctuated was enough to give him the excuse he needed to shake them down.

After threatening to sue, or perhaps shortly after filing suit, he would call their attorney and offer to settle out of court for a few hundred thousand dollars. They would usually pay him what he asked, just to get rid of him, since the alternative could be disastrous for the company. Banks would hesitate to grant loans or refinance existing loans. The stock price would drop. The cost of litigating a class action lawsuit, combined with the bad press, could bankrupt a fledgling company, and both Jules and the opposing counsel knew it.

He never thought of himself as a parasite. In law school, they taught him there was no such thing as a bad lawsuit. If it didn't have merit, some judge or jury would determine that fact and would find the defendant not guilty. Justice would be done. The defendant would have his day in court.

Jules and his family didn't attend synagogue except on the high holy days. He preferred spending Saturdays with his family. He followed a regular pattern. More often than not, he would spend Saturday morning taking his family for a ride on the family boat, a 40-foot cabin cruiser. Not exactly a yacht, but it's all he could afford on a judge's salary, which was supplemented by the income generated from the investment portfolio he accumulated while working for his father's law firm.

Santos and Tomás knew he was a predictable guy. They learned his schedule. They knew he would be visiting his boat between 8 and 9 o'clock on Saturday morning. They were looking forward to meeting him.

97

The definition of a boat is a hole in the water you throw money into. Jules's boat was no exception. Boats cost several thousand dollars a foot and his boat was 40 feet long. The docking fees, insurance and maintenance added up to several thousand dollars a year. It burned 40 gallons of gasoline an hour when cruising. He cruised a few hours practically every Saturday.

Sometimes he took the family around the canals in Fort Lauderdale, which some people call the Venice of America. Once a month or so, he took them to Biscayne Bay for lunch. A couple times a year he took them to the Bahamas, which was only five hours away. Today he wouldn't be taking them anywhere, if Tomás and Santos had their way. They would be saving him a few hundred dollars in gas.

Tomás and Santos arrived at the marina around 7:30. They brought along some fishing gear and pretended to fish on the dock about 50 feet from where Jules's boat was docked, but they didn't have any worms on their hooks or any lures on their lines. They didn't want any fish to interrupt their plans.

They wore gloves, which seemed a little unusual, but nobody paid much attention to them. Their caps and sun glasses looked a lot like the caps and sun glasses on sale at the marina kiosk. They blended in, except for the fact that they looked Hispanic. There weren't many Hispanic club members, although that was changing.

Jules and his family arrived at 8:15 and headed straight for their boat. Tomás and Santos noticed their approach and prepared to activate their plan. They waited until they were all on board. Jules carried an ice cooler and a bag of what appeared to be food. His wife, Leah, carried a black knapsack. Becky, his eight year-old daughter, and Evan, his eleven year-old son, had dark blue backpacks.

After stowing their stuff either below deck or on the main deck, they took their positions. Becky and Evan put on their life jackets and walked to the bow of the boat. They liked to sit at the front when it pulled away from the dock. Leah remained below deck, unpacking the contents of her knapsack. Jules started the three engines and fumbled around with some dials on the panel. Then he walked to the front of the boat to unhook the ropes that secured it to the dock.

As he walked to the stern to unfasten the ropes that secured the back of the boat to the dock, Tomás and Santos jumped into action. They boarded from the back, blocking Jules as he walked toward the ropes. Tomás pulled out the .22 cal. Ruger Mark 3 and pointed it at Jules' midsection. Evan and Becky saw them come on board but couldn't see the gun because Jules's body and the boat were blocking their line of vision.

Jules was startled to see them. He had no idea why they boarded the boat. Maybe a robbery. Maybe a hijacking.

Tomás jammed the pistol into his stomach. "Get below deck. Now!"

Without a word, Jules turned and headed for the stairs to the lower deck. Tomás and Santos followed. When Jules's right foot made contact with the floor of the lower deck, Tomás pointed the gun at the back of his head and fired twice. Jules fell forward, hitting the deck with his face.

Leah heard the noise and turned around to see two men, both holding guns, and her husband, face down with blood oozing from the back of his head. She was too terrified to scream. She just stood there, frozen.

Tomás turned toward her. "Shut up and we won't hurt you."

Santos took out his Sig Sauer P250 and pumped all 18 rounds into the floor. He had it fitted with a suppressor, and it was below deck, so no one in the dock area could hear the shots as they ripped through the floor of the boat. The 9mm rounds made nice holes, but it would take some time before the boat sank.

They turned around, went up the stairs and exited from the rear of the boat. Before setting foot on the dock they unfastened the remaining ropes. When their feet hit the dock, they turned around. Each placed a foot on the back of the boat and shoved it out of the dock space, causing it to go adrift. His wife would be powerless to prevent the boat from sinking, but they wouldn't drown. They all had on their life jackets. But it would make the forensic team's job more difficult.

98

"An oppressed people are authorized whenever they can to rise and break their fetters."
Henry Clay

"For a people who are free, and who mean to remain so, a well-organized and armed militia is their best security."
Thomas Jefferson

Assassinating a judge is a big deal and that's exactly how the media and police treated it. The FBI got called in, and the headquarters in Washington pulled out all the stops to provide resources. No one thought to challenge the FBI's authority, although the killing did not involve interstate commerce and although there was nothing in the Constitution that authorized the federal government to have a police force or conduct any police functions. Everyone just assumed the FBI was operating with Constitutional authority.

Conspiracy theories ran wild, since the hit took place within a few miles and a few days of the assassinations of three members of Congress, a senior official of the Federal Reserve Bank and a real estate magnate and his attorney. These hits were professional, unlike the usual gun related killings, which involved either drug gangs or domestic disputes.

The gun grabbers were calling for the confiscation of guns and the repeal of the Second Amendment. Thousands of people responded by going to gun shops and buying tens of thousands of weapons before they were outlawed.

The problem the police and FBI faced was that they didn't know who did it or why they did it. An examination of the remains of the hollow points and the shell casings might eventually determine that the same weapon was used to kill Daniel Frumpton and Jerry Goldstein, but that would take a while. Tying the three of them together would be more difficult, and would be speculative unless more clues were forthcoming.

The Sons of Liberty were about to give them more clues … but not yet.

99

Keith Ross

Keith Ross didn't fit the mold of the usual Miami-Dade County politician. It was generally conceded that you had to be either Jewish or Cuban to win any elective office. If you weren't in either of those categories, you at least had to have a Hispanic sounding name. He didn't have any of that. Although his mother was half Jewish, his father was Episcopalian, and so was he.

In spite of those defects in his family tree, he managed to become the city manager of Aventura, which was a hop, skip and a jump from the Broward County line. Perhaps the fact that only 21 percent of the Aventura population was Hispanic helped.

He was somewhat concerned about the welfare of his constituents, and whenever anyone complained about something he tried to pacify them and fix the problem. But he was even more concerned about keeping his job. He liked the prestige, the power and visibility that came with running a small suburb, and the extra income opportunities.

One of those income opportunities was the ability to tap real estate developers who needed approval to build in Aventura. A secondary source of income came from approving zoning board variances.

Not all of the income was in the form of cash. Sometimes he received a room full of furniture or a vacation package. He had had so many cruises to the Caribbean that he started refusing free cruise offers two years ago.

He didn't know that the job had health risks … like concentrated doses of lead shot into the brain.

100

Saturday afternoon. Santos and Tomás were having a good day. After taking care of Jules Rapaport, they got some breakfast, took a break, and listened to the radio for news reports of their morning activity. All the news stations were carrying the assassination of Judge Rapaport and they all said pretty much the same thing. The judge was shot and killed. Nobody knew why. There was speculation that it might have been a disgruntled defendant from one of the cases he tried. The boat sank. The wife and kids were able to get off the boat safely.

Jules had a $2 million insurance policy on his life but his family wouldn't be collecting anything. He was 12 days late in his premium payment, which was 2 days beyond the 10-day grace period. The insurance company refused to pay. The family spent $30,000 to sue the insurance company but lost. Justice was done. They had their day in court.

The descriptions of the assailants were conflicting. People at the scene gave different descriptions of the two men seen leaving the boat. Either they wore black tee shirts or white tee shirts. Their caps were either black or blue. Their physical descriptions differed. One of the guys who left the boat was of average size and build. The other was either muscular or fat, depending on who was being interviewed. Santos chuckled when he heard the conflicting descriptions of him. So did Tomás, who accused Santos of being fat. One witness said he thought he saw three men leave the boat.

The police and the courts know how poor eye witness testimony can be. They placed the most trust in his wife's description, since she saw them up close and had some contact with them for the longest period of time. She said they appeared to be Hispanic. One of them was large. She remembered their tee shirts and caps were dark.

Santos and Tomás had one more job to do before they could go home. Keith Ross was scheduled to make an appearance and give a short speech at a public employee picnic to be held at one of the parks in Aventura. They knew where the park was, but they didn't know when he would arrive or when he would give the speech.

It was certain that there would be police present. Police were assigned to the park even when there weren't any official activities scheduled. The police presence that afternoon might be heavier than usual, since a group of about 100 public employees had reserved space. Tomás and Santos decided that whacking him at the park would be a bad idea. However, they needed to be at the park so they could know when he arrived and when he left.

They brought along a bag of sandwiches and soft drinks and decided to camp out at one of the picnic tables about 100 feet from where the public employee picnic would take place. They would just wait, observe and read a book to pass the time. Santos started reading Erne Lewis's *An Act of Self-Defense*. Tomás was halfway through Barry Eisler's *Requiem for an Assassin*. He also took along a copy of Meira Pentermann's *Nine-Tenths*, in case he finished the Eisler book before Keith Ross was ready to leave.

The plan was to follow Ross to his car after he finished his speech, then follow him out of the park and shoot him somewhere between the park and his next destination, wherever it was convenient.

They had changed out of their black tee shirts and dark blue caps and into brightly colored shirts with buttons. Santos wore a white cap. Tomás wore a green, orange and white Miami Dolphins cap. Both wore sun glasses. They looked like they could have been on vacation.

Ross arrived shortly before 12:30 in his own car. No chauffeur. He wasn't high enough on the food chain for that. Besides, he wanted to appear to be a man of the people. Men of the people don't have chauffeurs.

He made the rounds, shaking hands and engaging in small talk with a few of the people. Then he started his speech. Blah, blah, blah. He recited the kinds of things that public employees picnicking with their families wanted to hear. They were doing a good job in tough times. They were appreciated. It was a nice, sunny day in Florida. He kept it short. He knew they really weren't interested in what he had to say. They just wanted to eat their hot dogs and hamburgers and get back to what they were doing before he interrupted them. He was just as anxious to leave as they were to see him leave.

After the speech, he shook a few more hands, chatted a bit and started moving toward his car. Santos and Tomás closed their books, picked up their bags of sandwiches and soft drinks, and started walking toward their stolen car, which was parked about 30 feet from Ross's car.

Santos got behind the wheel. Tomás got in on the passenger side. They waited for Ross to pull out. Then they pulled out and followed him, keeping a reasonable distance behind him.

Ross exited the park, turned right and headed toward Biscayne Boulevard, one of the main streets in Aventura. It would be packed with traffic on a Saturday afternoon.

Santos turned toward Tomás. "Let's get him before he gets to Biscayne Boulevard."

"OK. Let's wait until these two cars pass. Then pull up next to him." Tomás was referring to the two cars coming toward them from about a hundred feet away. The street was a typical suburban street with one lane going in each direction and houses on both sides of the street.

After the second car passed, Santos zipped into the left lane and pulled up alongside Ross. The sudden movement on a quiet suburban street caught Ross's attention. Cars don't just accelerate and pull up next to you on suburban streets. Ross turned his head to the left and saw Tomás pointing a gun at him. He panicked and slammed on the gas pedal, causing his car to accelerate just enough that Tomás's first shot missed him. The .22 caliber hollow point shattered the window behind him, missing his head by a half a foot.

"Shit!" Had Tomás squeezed the trigger an instant sooner he would have been successful. If he had used the AA12 shotgun with the Frag 12 rounds he would have been successful, but they decided not to use that weapon because of the noise.

Ross's car was now well ahead of them, at least five car lengths and gaining distance. It would be difficult to catch up to him. They decided not to try.

Tomás turned to look at Santos and shrugged his shoulders. "Better luck next time."

The fact that they weren't able to kill him didn't really matter. They had more or less accomplished their mission by sending a clear message that people who abuse the eminent domain laws would no longer be safe. They would have to call Wellington to tell him they had failed.

Tomás took out his cell phone and called Wellington while Santos continued driving. They needed to get out of the neighborhood. It would probably be a few minutes before Ross would feel comfortable picking up his cell phone to call the police, but it was best to get out of the neighborhood as soon as possible.

When they got to Biscayne Boulevard they turned north. In a few minutes they would be in Broward County, and presumably safe. If Ross called the police, it would likely be the Aventura police. The Broward County police might not be notified at all, or if they were, it probably wouldn't be until long after Santos and Tomás had blended in with the Saturday traffic in Broward County.

"Hello, John?"

"Hi, Tomás. How ya doin'? Have any good news to report?"

"We weren't able to get him. He got away."

"Ah, that's too bad." From the sound of his voice, he seemed a little disappointed but not mad.

"We were able to squeeze off a shot but he accelerated and we missed."

"So he knows he was being targeted?"

"Oh yeah, he knows, alright."

"Well, that's good. He got the message, although he doesn't know what the message is. I'll send out the announcement so the whole world will know. Good job, guys. You had a good day."

Santos and Tomás were glad it was over. Assassinating people was always a risk. Although the odds were in their favor, there was always a chance that they would get caught, or even killed. Luck had been with them that day. But no one's luck lasts forever.

101

Wellington had to edit his prewritten broadcast announcement. The original version he had prepared explained why Frumpton, Goldman, Rapaport and Ross had been executed. He would have to amend the statement slightly, since Ross was able to get away. Not a big deal. The message would be transmitted, and it would be basically the same message whether Ross were killed or not – that those who abuse the eminent domain laws would be dealt with severely.

One concern he had was how the Boss would take the news. In substance, they had accomplished their mission even though Keith Ross was still alive. The message they wanted to send to those who abuse the eminent domain laws would be received loud and clear regardless of whether the body count were 1 or 100. But the Boss was a perfectionist. If four people were to be executed, then four people should be executed.

Wellington made the edits and sent it out to all the radio and television stations in the Miami area as well as to various websites, both right-wing and left-wing, as well as a few blog spots. He wanted to make sure the message would not be suppressed. In fact, it would go viral, just like the earlier messages had.

Greetings from the Sons of Liberty. We would like to end the speculation surrounding the deaths of Daniel Frumpton, Jerry Goldman, and Jules Rapaport and the attempted killing of Keith Ross. We have determined that they are all termites who are eating away at the structure of American society. They and their ilk must be stopped. We are taking it upon ourselves to stop them. It is the patriotic thing to do.

The one thing they all have in common is their abuse of the eminent domain laws. These laws, which need to be repealed, allow individuals to abuse the Constitution by using the force of government to confiscate private property from the rightful owners and transfer it to people who are little more than thieves.

Daniel Frumpton was the worst abuser. He was the one who initiated the takings. Jerry Goldman was his attorney who handled the transactions. Jules Rapaport was the judge who put the stamp of approval on these thefts. Keith Ross was the local city official who supported their actions when he should have stood in their way. Keith, we are not done with you. Your day will come, at the time and place of our choosing.

Let this be a warning to anyone who uses the eminent domain laws to violate the property rights of the citizenry. We will get you. However, we will offer a reprieve to those who have abused the eminent domain laws in the past three years if they repent and compensate their victims. Those offenders who want to be crossed off our list must make a public apology and must fully and publicly compensate their victims for the full extent of their losses.

SONS OF LIBERTY

***

Nothing changes until there's a body count.

Within 24 hours after Wellington sent out the broadcast message, two Miami area real estate developers went on television to offer a public apology for their past actions and promised to compensate their victims within 30 days. The Dade County Real Estate Board held an emergency meeting and amended its Code of Ethics to list the use of the eminent domain laws as an unethical practice. Violators would be punished by the loss of their real estate license. The measure passed by a unanimous vote. The state legislature in Tallahassee planned to hold a special session to debate whether the eminent domain provision in the Florida Constitution should be repealed and made illegal in spite of the U.S. Supreme Court's ruling approving the practice. John Desir, the president of the Haitian-American Bank, announced that his bank would no longer make loans to finance projects that involved the eminent domain laws. He also announced that he would make a motion at the next meeting of the Florida Bankers Association to list the financing of eminent domain projects as an unethical practice. Keith Ross went into hiding immediately after giving his statement to the police.

102

Sarah walked in the side door, carrying two bags. "John, I just finished picking up the food for the barbecue. I think I bought too much. Why don't you invite Bob and Sveta? They can help us eat it."

Now that Debbie, Frumpton and the others were out of the way it was time to take a short break before focusing on Steinman and his group. Sarah didn't know John and his crew were taking a break. She just thought John wanted to have a barbecue.

"OK, I'll give him a call. If he's like most accounting professors, he probably planned on spending his Sunday reading financial statements just for fun."

He thought about it and decided it probably would be a good idea to invite him. He could use the opportunity to introduce him to the other team members who would also be there. He perceived that Paige wasn't fully committed to the Steinman project and that a little bonding with the other team members might serve to get him in line with the program.

***

Paige's phone rang. He was having lunch with Sveta at Denny's on Collins Avenue in Sunny Isles Beach. Paige liked Denny's because the food was decent and fairly cheap.

"Hi Bob. It's John. How ya doin'? Are debits still on the left?"

"The last time I checked, but I haven't read this morning's newspaper. Maybe someone in Washington has made a new regulation."

"I wouldn't be surprised. If the United Nations published a study stating that Western colonial powers were imposing their oppressive capitalist system on developing countries by insisting that debits be on the left as a condition of getting a World Bank loan, I'm sure someone in Washington would try to make a rule that any company having a government contract must have debits on the right in order to show sensitivity for local cultural values."

Paige was pleased by Wellington's response. It showed that even Commerce Department bureaucrats could have a sense of humor.

"Bob, Sarah and I are having a barbecue on Sunday. Would you and Sveta like to come?"

"Sure. What time?"

"Around 12, give or take. That will give you a chance to get back from church."

"Yeah, right." Wellington was busting Paige's chops. He knew that Paige hadn't gone to church in years. Wellington usually attended church on Sundays because Sarah insisted.

"What should I bring?"

"Sarah already has all the food. Maybe bring some potato salad. That way I'll have an alternative to Sarah's, which is based on her mother's recipe, which I hate."

"OK, John. Always glad to help where I can."

Wellington walked into the next room. He didn't want Sarah to hear what he was about to say. He lowered his voice as he spoke.

"It will also give you a chance to meet the team. They're coming with their families. We've decided to put the Steinman case on the front burner."

Paige froze in his seat. The moment he dreaded had arrived. He tried to maintain his composure and act normally.

"Will your Boss be there? I'd like to meet him. What was his name, again?"

"Very funny, Bob. No, he won't be there. He likes to keep a low profile, if you know what I mean."

"Yeah, I think I understand. He can't go outside until after sundown, right? Otherwise he melts or evaporates or something."

"Something like that. See you then."

After hanging up, Paige turned to Sveta.

"We've been invited to a barbecue at John and Sarah's this Sunday. Can you make it?"

"Ah, sorry Robert. My sister's family is expecting me for lunch. Tell John and Sarah I said hello."

"OK. Will do." He was glad that Sveta wouldn't be able to come. He didn't want her to be in the company of murderers.

One thing he was apprehensive about was meeting the members of the team, since some of them had killed Raul Rodriguez and his girlfriend in cold blood. Anyone who would do that kind of thing was not someone he would feel comfortable having a hamburger with. The fact that they could do it without a second thought sent chills up his spine. He wondered how many other people they had executed, since it probably wasn't their first time.

He also wondered whether he would be able to take them out, if that was what he needed to do to foil the plan. It was the only option he had been able to come up with to save Steinman, but he couldn't figure out if or how he could do it. They were all trained killers. Wellington was being closed-mouth about who his Boss was, and Paige was a neophyte when it came to actual violence. Competing in Taekwondo tournaments was one thing. Trying to kill someone who didn't want to be killed and who could kill you was something else.

He was a fish out of water. Paige wondered whether he would eventually meet the Boss, and under what circumstances.

103

"Silence in the face of evil is itself evil, God will not hold us guiltless. Not to speak is to speak. Not to act is to act."
Dietrich Bonhoeffer

"Totalitarianism must be stopped, whether it comes from the left or the right. It doesn't matter whether the jackboot on your throat is a socialist or a fascist jackboot."
Robert W. McGee

It took Paige a little less than an hour to arrive at the Wellington's house a few blocks from the edge of the Everglades. It was Sunday and traffic was light. It was a pleasant drive, another sunny day in Florida.

He was more than a little curious to meet the other members of the team, but he was apprehensive as well. He liked hanging around patriots, but this group was misguided. They were actually the enemy because they were shredding the Constitution, all in the name of patriotism and national security. Assassinating radio talk show hosts, journalists and professors merely for exercising their right to free speech and free press could not be justified, although a case could be made for executing politicians and others who were trashing the Constitution and taking away the rights of the citizenry.

He suspected the team he was about to meet had been the ones who were exterminating the vermin that had been reported in the press, although Wellington didn't quite admit it. The Boss had cut Paige out of the loop. Paige's view of the team was based mostly on their plan to silence professors and journalists because they decided to exercise their rights of free speech and press in a way that the Boss found offensive.

He continued to think about his options for saving Steinman. The easy way out would be not to save him. Just let them kill him. Choosing that option would not require any effort or action on his part. It would be the safe option. It would allow him to maintain his relative innocence. The problem with that option is that he had ruled it out. Every fiber of his being told him that he must do something.

Another option would be to become a whistle blower. He could tell the authorities. But which authorities? The local police would be one option, but which local police? Each community had its own police force and none of them could be effective against the resources of the CIA, FBI, DHS or any federal agency, for that matter. Besides, he couldn't prove anything and the police couldn't do anything until the act had been committed, which would be too late. They probably wouldn't want to stick their necks out to prevent Steinman's murder anyway. They would be taking a risk by getting involved.

He could contact the CIA or the FBI and tell them that some of their people were about to start a murder spree, but who would he contact? He didn't know how far up the chain of command it went. There was a strong possibility that, at some point, either Wellington's boss or Jim Bennett's boss would find out about it, and at least one of them might be part of the conspiracy. Paige would be dead.

Which brought him to the last option – executing every member of the team himself. One problem with that option was that he didn't know if he could do it. He would have to kill them in cold blood, although he could rationalize that it wasn't really cold blood, but more like a preemptive strike.

Another problem with that option was that he wasn't sure it would be the right thing to do. He remembered the phrase from Ecclesiastes – a time to kill and a time to heal. But the Bible also said "Thou shalt not kill." Those passages were both from the Old Testament. The New Testament said to turn the other cheek. The nuns had taught him that where the Old Testament conflicted with the New Testament, the proper choice would be to follow the New Testament rule. But he didn't want to turn the other cheek. He had to do something.

Retrieving those Biblical passages from his memory banks reminded him of the discussion the nuns had with the class on those points in grade school. One minute they would assert that the Bible was written by God and that it was the only perfect book because it contained no inconsistencies. Then, when one of the students pointed out an inconsistency like the one about the justification for killing, they would reply that where the Old Testament conflicted with the New Testament, we should always choose the New Testament rule, which led to the question, "Why does the New Testament conflict with the Old Testament?"

Their response was that when God looked down on the earth and saw that we were having difficulty keeping the rules He laid out for us in the Old Testament, He decided to lighten up on the rules a little bit and give us a set of rules that were easier to follow. That's why He wrote the New Testament, which led one of the students to ask, "If God is perfect, how could He make such a mistake by giving us a set of rules that were too difficult to follow?" The nuns' reply was, "To question is to blaspheme."

Then there was the question of punishment. Would God punish Paige for killing them? One view, which he learned from taking philosophy courses at Gannon University in Erie, Pennsylvania, is that God really doesn't give a shit. If He did, there wouldn't have been World War I or II, or Vietnam or disease and starvation. He would have intervened to prevent all those things if He really loved His children. The nuns had dismissed that argument by saying that "God works in mysterious ways," which Paige had concluded long ago was not an adequate response. You cannot just assume that the Christian position is the correct one, then try to find a justification for it. You must question everything, even the existence of God, according to Thomas Jefferson.

What if God really does give a shit, in spite of the fact that He doesn't intervene in human affairs? What if He really does punish people for killing other people? Paige couldn't answer that one. He figured it's fair to assume that God wouldn't punish someone for killing in self-defense. Could killing them be considered an act of self defense, or even an act of love, since executing them would prevent further murders of innocent people?

Applying the utilitarian ethical arguments he learned at Gannon University, Paige rationalized that executing them would be the right thing to do if it could prevent more deaths. Antiabortionists have used that argument to justify killing doctors who performed abortions. If killing one doctor who performs abortions could save the lives of hundreds of unborn babies, then it should be – must be – done. Of course, that assumes that abortion is murder. What if abortion isn't murder?

What if liquidating people who espouse socialist claptrap like Steinman results in a net benefit to society? Socialism leads to suffering, poverty, a lower rate of economic growth and the stifling of human flourishing. It prevents individuals from reaching their full potential. The best must be held back so that the self-esteem of the weak and lazy can be salved. If the world would be a better place without socialism, does exterminating socialists constitute a justifiable act? An act of self-defense? If that is the case, then he must not kill the killers. He must allow them to assassinate Steinman because society would benefit as a result. Does it matter that they plan to execute him for the wrong reason – because he opposed U.S. foreign and domestic policy rather than because he is a socialist?

When Paige applied utilitarian ethics to the question of killing the killers, he concluded that doing it would be an ethical act. Their trashing of the Constitution in the name of patriotism and national security was leading us down the road to a totalitarian state where there would be no free speech or free press or privacy. There would be no property rights, since the state could confiscate a person's life savings for any reason, or for no reason. The state was becoming the master while the people were becoming slaves. It is why Dietrich Bonhoeffer, the German theologian and philosopher, participated in the plot to assassinate Hitler, to save humanity. If killing one big Hitler is the right thing to do, then killing a thousand little Hitlers must also be the right thing to do. The fact that Bonhoeffer was executed in the process upon direct orders from Hitler is irrelevant.

Totalitarianism must be stopped, whether it comes from the left or the right. It doesn't matter whether the jackboot on your throat is a socialist or a fascist jackboot. In either case it must be removed. Paige had made his decision. Now he had to find a way to make it happen.

104

As Paige approached the house he could see about a dozen cars parked on the lawn and in the driveway. Some of them belonged to the team. Others belonged to civilians. It looked like a typical country barbecue scene.

He pulled in and parked on the lawn, and quickly took photos of the license plates with his cell phone. He could identify the owners later.

He could hear people talking in the back yard and could smell the meat sizzling on the grill – hot dogs, hamburgers, chicken and beef. He brought along some potato salad to add to the collection of food piled up on one of the tables. He didn't make it himself. He bought it earlier that day at the local Publix in Sunny Isles Beach.

Wellington spotted him as he turned the corner of the house.

"Hi Bob." He walked up and shook Paige's hand. Sarah stood at the food table, fumbling and rearranging some of the items. She saw him, smiled and waved. There were a bunch of children running around, playing catch, swinging on the swing set and splashing around in the small pool.

Wellington reached out for the potato salad. "Let me take this." He grabbed it and walked with Bob to the food table. As they approached the table, he leaned toward Paige's ear and whispered,

"Thanks for bringing this. I really wasn't looking forward to eating Sarah's mother's potato salad."

"It's a nice day for a barbecue, don't you think?" he said as he gave the container to Sarah.

"Yeah. It's perfect."

"Bob, I'd like to introduce you to the other members of the team, but be discreet. Don't talk to them about the job because there are civilians here, too."

"OK, I'll be discreet. Can I look at their wives' cleavage?"

Wellington smiled. "Sure, that will be fine. Just don't be obvious, and try not to drool. There are a couple of nice pairs here today." Apparently, he had already checked them out.

John spotted one of the team members standing off to the side, away from the others. He and his wife were having an animated conversation with another couple. John motioned to them.

"You see the guy standing over there with the green bottle of beer, next to the woman with the nice tits? That's Jim Bennett."

Paige smiled and looked at Wellington. "Jim Bennett? He doesn't look like a Jim Bennett," noting the fact that his features – light brown skin, jet black hair – gave him a Latin look.

"Very observant, you racist pig. Actually, the name on his birth certificate is Jaime Benítez. He anglicized it because he thought it would look better on his resume. His parents are Cuban."

"Let me give you a little background. Jim works for the FBI in Miami. His main job is to keep us informed of FBI activities, since those bastards usually keep us out of the loop. Sometimes we also use him for assignments involving Latin American drug cartels because of his FBI background and training. He's familiar with the cartels because the FBI has him assigned to that area."

They walked over and John started the introductions.

"Hi Jim. I'd like to introduce you to a friend of mine. This is Bob Paige. He's an accounting professor at Saint Frances University."

"Oh, an accounting professor. I didn't know you hung out with guys that high on the food chain. Nice to meet you." He extended his hand, pretending not to know anything about Paige and his background. Actually, Wellington had briefed him thoroughly on Paige a few weeks before.

Paige shook his hand and the introductions continued.

"This is his wife, Ana. They have three kids who are running around here somewhere," gesturing in the direction of the swings and pool.

Ana was holding a plate of food, consisting of rice, beans and barbecued chicken. She was on the short side, a little chubby with short black hair and light brown skin. She was feeding her face when Wellington introduced her. As she put the fork into her mouth she bent forward slightly so that her face was over the plate, which also presented Wellington and Paige with an opportunity to check out her boobs. They were quite nice, a little on the large side, and glistening with sweat. It was a hot day.

"Mucho gusto," she said, as she tried to talk with a mouthful of rice.

Paige chimed in. "What were you talking about? It looked like you were having a lively discussion about something."

"Yes," Jim replied, "We were talking about the differences between Cubans, Argentineans and Colombians. Ana's father is from Argentina and her mother is from Colombia."

Paige remembered a Spanish class he had taken at Seton Hall University years ago. His teacher was from Argentina and she told the class that Argentina was really part of Europe and that Argentinean Spanish was the best. Puerto Ricans, Cubans and

Dominicans didn't speak real Spanish. They got their *r*'s and *l*'s mixed up, when they bothered to pronounce them at all, and often didn't pronounce the last syllable of a word because it only slowed them down.

Jim continued, "Yeah, whenever an Argentinean speaks it sounds like they're giving orders. Jesus was so modest and humble that he was born in Bethlehem instead of Argentina."

Ana felt compelled to defend her heritage and take a shot at Jim's Cuban family background. "Si, but if you tie a Cuban's hands behind his back they won't be able to speak." She was referring to the fact that Cubans were known for using their hands when they speak. Everyone laughed, because they knew it was true.

Wellington turned toward the other couple. "This is Tom and his wife, Jeannie. They live down the street. They moved here from Detroit a few years ago." They looked like a typical white, retired couple from Detroit, in their early to mid-sixties.

Tom reached to shake Paige's hand. "Yeah, we got tired of the snow."

"Nice to meet you."

As they walked away, Wellington whispered into Paige's ear, "He's a civilian." He then led Paige to the next member of the team, who was standing between the swings and the pool. He and his wife were watching the kids play. While walking toward them, Wellington gave Paige a briefing.

"Tomás served in the army in Afghanistan and Iraq. He was mostly a computer guy, but for a few months he was also a sniper. You're sort of responsible for him being on the team, indirectly, since you recruited me and I recruited him. He's a systems analyst for Carnival Cruise Lines, which gives him access to the ports of Miami and Fort Lauderdale and also to information that we sometimes find useful. He's also a firearms specialist. He does free lance work for us sometimes." When they got about five feet away, Wellington started the introductions.

"Hi, Tomás. I'd like you to meet Bob Paige. He's a friend of mine."

They exchanged handshakes. Tomás had had a good morning. Before coming to the barbecue he infected a video of an elderly gentleman whose colostomy bag burst during an aggressive TSA frisk at the Dallas airport and a video, really a tirade, of a New York University professor who was criticizing CIA involvement in Latin America.

"This is Tomás Gutierrez and his wife, Teresa."

"Nice to meet you," Paige said, as he discreetly checked out Teresa, who was gazing into his eyes and smiling. She was small and thin, with long dark brown hair. Her eyes were especially captivating. Her parents had fled Cuba for the United States two years before she was born.

Wellington pointed in the direction of the pool. "That's their son, Julio, over there. He's the one with the red and blue swim trunks," He looked to be about 6 or 7 years old. They chatted for a few minutes, then moved on.

"The last member of the team is Santos Hernandez." Wellington motioned toward the food table. "He's standing over there by the table." As they walked toward him, Wellington continued with the briefing.

"Santos works for the TSA at Miami International Airport. Sometimes we use him to smuggle sensitive items in and out of the country. He also keeps us apprised of security problems at the airport. He was in the Marines and served two tours in Iraq."

Paige noticed Santos's unusual appearance immediately. He didn't have much of a neck. He looked like a lump of muscle with short brown hair wearing shoes.

"Hi Santos. I'd like you to meet Bob Paige. He's a friend of mine."

"Hi. Nice to meet you." Paige grasped Santos' hand, which felt like a small ham hock. Upon meeting him, Paige quickly decided that Santos would be the member of the team he would least like to encounter in a dark alley.

Santos' wife was at the other end of the table. After loading her plate with food, she walked toward them.

"And this is his wife, Maria."

She smiled. "Nice to meet you."

Maria was a white Cuban, the kind whose ancestors probably came from Spain. Her breasts were tastefully displayed, nice little handfuls. She and her parents had escaped from Cuba when she was 17. Their daughter, Rosa, was still at the food table, trying to decide between chicken or a hamburger.

Wellington motioned toward Paige. "Tell Bob your AK-47 story."

"Oh, that?" She smiled. "Why do you like that story so much?" She liked to tell the story, especially to gringos.

She turned toward Paige. "Well, when I was a school girl living in Cuba, they taught us how to disassemble and reassemble an AK-47. They also taught us how to use it. I was trained to shoot gringos if they invade my country, so watch out." She smiled, then added, "Please invade soon. We promise not to shoot you."

Everyone chuckled. As she finished the story, Paige caught her gazing into John's eyes. John was gazing back. It was more than a friendly gaze. Santos noticed it, too. He didn't look happy about it.

Paige surmised that there might be something going on between them. It was plausible. Miami was a horny city. A *Miami New Times* poll found that 73 percent of them lost their virginity by age 18. Sixty-one percent had cheated on a partner. Hispanics were thought to be the most aggressive race in bed by more than a two-to-one margin and were thought to be the most sensual in bed by a more than four-to-one margin. Almost everyone in Miami had had at least one one-night stand. Forty-three percent had had a threesome. Their favorite position was doggie style. The missionary position came in a distant third.

After a few minutes of pleasant conversation it was time to move on. Paige had met each member of the team, except for the Boss. They seemed like a nice bunch of patriotic Americans with good family values. None of their wives knew that their husbands worked for the CIA or that they were plotting to kill journalists, professors and others who dared to speak out against the government. They didn't realize that their adopted country was moving a little closer to tyranny with each passing year, and that they were sleeping with some of the foot soldiers who were leading the country down the path toward totalitarianism, allowing themselves to become impregnated with little foot soldiers for the next generation.

As they continued their walk in the back yard, Paige noticed a strikingly attractive woman with long blonde hair speaking to Sarah. She looked a lot like Ann Coulter, the right-wing political commentator. She was tall and slender. Her long, straight blonde hair extended well below her breasts, which were small and hidden by a loose fitting blouse. Her black pants also were loose fitting, which gave her a modest appearance, or as modest as she could manage, given the fact that she was strikingly attractive and had long legs and long blonde hair. She stood out in the crowd of short, dark Cubans.

Paige motioned in her direction. "Who's the blonde?"

"That's Jennifer Kravath. She's a friend of Sarah's. We met her at our church."

"Can you introduce us?"

"Sure, if you like. But let me warn you. She's a trip."

"What do you mean?"

"You'll see."

John escorted Paige over to meet her.

"Hi Jennifer. Enjoying the party?"

"Yes. Thanks for inviting me."

"You're welcome. It's always nice to have a token gringo or two. This way I don't feel like I'm in Havana."

"Very funny, John. I'm honored to be your token gringo." She looked at Paige, checking him out. "But it looks like I'm not your only token gringo." Paige could feel the sexual tension. Jennifer was hungry, but not for food. Her makeup was perfect, in spite of the hot weather.

It was tough being a single parent. Susan, her 14 year-old daughter, was a pudgy little brat and she was becoming difficult to control. Jennifer was glad to be away from her for a few hours. The party gave her an opportunity to escape.

"Yes, I managed to find another one. I'd like to introduce you to Bob Paige. He's an accounting professor at Saint Frances University."

She extended her hand, while gently thrusting her right hip toward him. "So, you're a teacher. I'm a teacher, too. I teach civics at Martin Luther King Jr. High School."

Her long, slender fingers were soft and sensual, which Paige noticed as soon as he made contact.

"We were talking about illegal immigration," referring to the conversation she was having with Sarah. "I was just saying that if immigrants want to come here, let them come over on the Mayflower like my ancestors did."

Everyone laughed, but from the tone of her voice, Paige couldn't tell if she was kidding or serious. Jennifer was able to trace her family tree back to 1781 in Connecticut. It was possible that her ancestors actually did come over on the Mayflower, although she couldn't find any proof one way or the other.

She brushed her hair aside with her right hand and moved a little closer to Paige. "We need to plant an e-chip in every baby born in America so we can tell who's an American and who isn't. And we need to include a GPS tracking device in it so we can tell where they are. We need to have a federal database to screen employment applications and fine every employer who hires an illegal. Everyone should be required to carry an ID."

"Don't you think that would be a little harsh?" Paige asked, "not to mention a violation of our Constitutional right to privacy? Is it really any of the government's business where we are or who we work for?"

"What? You sound like one of those liberal TV commentators. They should all be tried for treason for giving aid and comfort to the enemy."

Paige felt a sudden desire to egg her on. "Who's the enemy?" The sexual attraction he initially felt for her was fading fast.

"Muslims."

"Don't you mean *fundamentalist* Muslims?"

"They're *all* fundamentalist. If they weren't fundamentalist, they wouldn't be Muslims."

Paige couldn't resist the urge to challenge her. "That's not true. I met some Muslims in Bosnia who drink beer and even wine and whiskey. Some of my best friends are Palestinian Muslims who live in New Jersey."

"You have Muslim friends? What kind of American are you? We should load them all on airplanes and drop them over Saudi

Arabia. I haven't decided yet if we should give them parachutes or just let them go *thump* when they hit the sand."

She continued. "Ferdinand and Isabella had the right idea when they kicked them out of Spain in 1492. America and Europe would be better off without them. If we don't get rid of them soon, they'll breed us out of existence."

Paige responded. "Ferdinand and Isabella also kicked out the Jews in 1492. Would you kick them out, too?"

"No, the Jews are OK. They're part of our Judeo-Christian heritage. Besides, if we kicked out the Jews, where would be get doctors and lawyers? Well, maybe we could kick out the lawyers," she said, only half jokingly.

Her tirade had started to attract attention. A few of the adults started moving in her direction to listen in on the conversation. She had become the main attraction. One man in particular was paying close attention to the conversation, but he was more interested in what Paige had to say. He kept in the background, making sure that there were always two or three people standing between him and Paige. Wellington had made it a point not to introduce Paige to him.

Jennifer continued. "Jesus won't return until Israel is a Jewish state, so we have to support Israel. Once they wise up and kick out the Palestinians, Jesus will be able to return. When Jesus returns we'll have peace for a thousand years and everyone will be Christian."

Paige saw an opening and couldn't resist. "Everyone? What about the Jews?"

"God has a plan for the Jews. The Bible says that only those who accept Jesus as their savior can enter the kingdom of heaven. We'll give them an opportunity to accept Jesus."

"What if they don't take that opportunity?"

"We'll cross that bridge when we come to it."

Maria was listening intently to the conversation. "What do you think of gay marriage?"

Jennifer turned in her direction. "The Bible says homosexuality is an abomination. We should gather up all the homosexuals and stone them, like the Bible says." Turning to Paige, Jennifer asked, in a rather hostile voice, "I suppose you think gay marriage is acceptable."

Paige smiled before answering, knowing she wouldn't approve of his position on the issue. "Actually, I think the government should get out of the marriage business. Marriage should be just another contract between or among consenting adults. The only role for government should be to enforce whatever terms the parties agree to."

"Among?" she asked, in a raised voice. The veins on her neck looked like they would burst. "You mean you're in favor of polygamy?"

"Sure, why not? As long as all the parties agree and no one's rights are violated, what difference does it make? People could have term contracts, too. There's no reason why marriage has to be for life. You could have two-year or five-year contracts, renewable at the option of the parties. It would also drive the divorce lawyers out of business, since there would no longer be a need for divorce. All people would have to do is wait for the contract to expire."

"I can't believe what you just said. Jesus would never approve of that. Marriage should be between one man and one woman. We should make any other kind of marriage a felony."

Paige couldn't resist the opportunity to irk her on. "King David was a polygamist. Wasn't he one of Jesus' relatives?"

"That was different," she was quick to reply. "Times were different then."

"So, you mean the Bible isn't rigid? We should go with the flow and change with the times?"

"No, I didn't say that."

"Then what *did* you say?"

She started to fidget. She couldn't come up with a reply and she didn't want to try. All she wanted to do was leave.

She turned toward Wellington. "Look, I'd like to continue this conversation but I have to go. I have to check on my daughter to make sure no one's impregnating her."

"John, Sarah, thank you for inviting me." She turned and walked toward the front, where her car was parked.

As she walked away, Paige commented to John, "Wow! I bet she's a nasty fuck!"

"I've thought about that myself, but actually she might be quite good. Think of what she might be like if she channeled all that frustration through her pussy."

Paige smiled. "Do you think she has a pussy?"

They both laughed.

105

“'Tis the business of little minds to shrink; but he whose heart is firm, and whose conscience approves his conduct, will pursue his principles unto death.”
Thomas Paine

Now that Paige had met the team, he had a better idea of what he was up against. He thought about his options and how he would terminate them on the drive back to Sunny Isles Beach.

Most of them had had military training. That could be a problem. They would know how to react, not to mention the fact that they would know how to kill him. They had killed before, maybe up close and personal. That certainly was the case for the members of the team who had assassinated Raul Rodriguez and his girlfriend. His best weapon would be the element of surprise. He'd have to kill them before they could switch into defensive mode. If they had time to react, he would be in trouble.

It takes more guts to kill someone when you are looking into their eyes than it does to push a button on a computer thousands of miles away from the target. Computers had made killing much easier. Someone in San Diego could control a drone flying over Afghanistan or Iraq or any other country and dispatch dozens or hundreds of people by pushing a button. No emotion. No fear.

Just like playing a video game, except the enemy consists of living, breathing human beings who probably have loved ones and families, just like the person who's pushing the button.

Paige didn't know if he could do it up close and personal. He'd never executed anyone before. He'd gone hunting a few times but didn't enjoy killing animals. He did it because the other guys in the group did it and they didn't seem to have any qualms about killing living things. Buying hamburger in the meat department was one thing; killing a cow face to face was something else. Terminating a human being who had military training and who could kill you if you didn't kill him first was a whole different ball game, one that Paige didn't want to play.

In his mind, he knew he had to do it. They had to be stopped. But his gut told him it was too dangerous. The easy way out would be to do nothing, but that wasn't an option. It had to be done and he was the only one who could do it.

Wellington would probably be the easiest to kill, at least in theory. He was the least athletic of the bunch. As far as Paige knew, he hadn't had any military training, although, as a CIA person, he probably had some firearms training. The CIA had given Paige firearms training and he was just a professor, a part-time CIA asset. If they gave it to him, surely they would give it to someone like Wellington, who was full-time CIA. He would have to do him fast, before he could pull his weapon, assuming he carried one. He'd have to pick a time and place that would allow him to do it and get away without being seen or identified. Wellington would have no reason to expect an attack, which worked in his favor. He would have the element of surprise.

How to do it was the next question. As part of his training, the CIA had given Paige a Glock 17 and two blades. One was shaped like a T, consisting of a handle that fit neatly into the palm of the hand, with a three-inch, single-edged blade that protruded from the handle at a 90-degree angle. The idea was to punch the victim multiple times in rapid succession, pulling away quickly so the target couldn't grab your hand or take away the weapon. A half dozen successful punches in the right places would cause the victim to bleed out in a matter of minutes.

The other blade looked like brass knuckles and could actually be used as such, but had a spring that could flick out a four-inch blade, if necessary. The design protected the holder from slicing his own hand as he thrusts it into the target because each finger is inserted into one of the four holes in the brass knuckles, which are actually made of stainless steel. The problem with using a traditional knife is that the hand might get sliced as it plunged the blade into someone's body, unless it had a hilt that prevented the hand from sliding during the attack. If O.J. Simpson would have had one, he wouldn't have sliced his hand when stabbing his ex-wife and her boyfriend, or so the story goes.

The advantage of using a knife rather than a gun is silence. Guns make noise. Knives don't. The disadvantage is the mess a knife makes. The person doing the stabbing or slicing has to be very careful not to get any blood on himself and that's difficult to do. The CIA showed Paige how to do that, but it was a skill best learned by practice, and that was something Paige didn't have.

Another problem with using a knife was that you have to get up close and personal. Paige didn't know if he could do that, especially with Santos. Stabbing him would be like stabbing a slab of muscle that had military training and that didn't want to be stabbed. Santos was an especially scary guy, both because of his muscles and the look Paige saw in his eyes when he met him. He had the look of a killer. He looked like he had killed before, and his military background had given him opportunities to practice and hone his skills. The same could be said for Tomás.

Paige had some karate training and knew how to kill with his bare hands, theoretically. He had trained with Sensei Shigeru Kimura, a former all-Japan national champion and world champion in the Shukokai style, in Hackensack, New Jersey, and had studied Tae Kwon Do with Henry Cho in Manhattan and with Masters Brown and Cook in Fayetteville, North Carolina while he was a visiting professor. He even managed to win some medals in karate tournaments, but winning medals was one thing. Killing people with your bare hands was something else.

Paige decided to use his Glock on all of them. He'd just have to find an appropriate time and place, where there wouldn't be witnesses and where the noise wouldn't be a factor.

Although Paige had decided what weapon to use, he still felt uneasy about the decision to kill them. They were all family men. He'd met their wives and children. He'd be creating four widows in the process. Their children would have to grow up without a father.

Wellington caused him the most problems psychologically. He had recruited John. He and Sarah had become friends. He had had dinner with them numerous times. He'd watched their children grow up. He'd have to treat Wellington and the others as targets, not human beings, just as Sensei Kimura had suggested. If he didn't, he would lose, which meant he'd be dead.

106

"Our liberty depends on the freedom of the press, and that cannot be limited without being lost."
Thomas Jefferson

"To preserve the freedom of the human mind then and freedom of the press, every spirit should be ready to devote itself to martyrdom."
Thomas Jefferson

"Have you heard the latest? A lawyer for the TSA agents who were arrested for killing 14 protesters at the San Francisco airport is saying that the National Defense Authorization Act allowed them to do it in the interest of national security." Paige and Sveta were listening to a radio broadcast by Howard Klein, a conservative national radio talk show host, while driving north on Route A1A to Hollywood Beach. They were on their way to a quiet dinner at the Thai restaurant on the beach. Sveta looked at Paige, a shocked look on her face. She reached for the dial and turned up the volume.

Klein continued, "The U.S. Attorney General's office just issued an amicus brief concluding that the agents did not violate the law because they complied with procedures. It argued that the protesters should be classified as enemy combatants because one of them punched a TSA agent after allegedly being assaulted, kicked and stomped on. Ladies and gentlemen, I warned you that this kind of thing would happen if the National Defense Authorization Act was allowed to pass. Now it is the law of the land and my predictions are starting to come true.

"It's time to wake up, America. I told you that this law would allow the military to detain and even assassinate protesters, talk show hosts, journalists, bloggers, or anyone else who holds an anti-government position. Now that there's no longer any distinction between the military and civilian law enforcement, the TSA or any cop on the street can get away with murdering anyone they want for any reason they want, all in the name of national security. They're not going to be prosecuted."

The commentator continued. "I just learned that George Rothstein, the lead attorney for the group representing the families of the murdered protesters, has been arrested for treason. The U.S. Attorney General is alleging that his defense of the protesters is giving aid and comfort to the enemy. The FBI has frozen his bank accounts. The California Bar Association has filed papers to get him disbarred. The judge hearing the case is under pressure to dismiss the protesters' case for being frivolous."

"It's time to stop burying your heads in the sand, America. These acts by the feds constitute nothing less than absolute tyranny. The federal government is out of control and the local and state governments of this country are afraid to do anything about it. Washington is pushing for federal licensing of all firearms, including the firearms used by local police forces. Once they do that, the only people who have guns will be the feds and the people they approve."

"It's our own members of Congress who allowed this to happen. I'm posting the names and telephone numbers of all members of Congress who voted for this legislation on my website. Let them hear from us. It is *they* who are the traitors to this country and to the Constitution. If we don't do ...."

The broadcast went blank. There was nothing but dead air. After about a minute, music started to play. Klein's broadcasts never included music. It was all talk all the time. It appeared that the American Gestapo was at work.

Sveta looked visibly shaken. "Robert, I really don't like what's going on in this country. I thought I had escaped all this when I left Russia. Why doesn't somebody do something about it?"

"I wish I had an answer to that question but I don't. The people in this country are asleep but some of them are starting to wake up."

"Maybe *some* of them are starting to wake up but we need *all* of them to wake up. I don't have anywhere else to go. I have made a life here. I don't want to leave and start all over again." She sounded stressed.

"The problem is that a lot of them support what the government's doing. They believe the only people the government will go after are the bad guys."

"But it's the government who are becoming the bad guys. Don't you understand?"

Paige turned toward her as best he could. He was driving. "You don't have to convince me. I understand, and so do a lot of other people."

"Yes, but not enough other people. I'm scared. The internet connection in my office has started to work much slower than usual. My boss thinks it's because the government's monitoring us. We recently got some government contracts."

"Maybe that's true, or maybe there's another reason, but just to be on the safe side you shouldn't send out any messages that you don't want the government to read. Maybe I'm sounding a little paranoid, but you see what happened to that attorney who's defending the protesters. The feds can do practically anything they want and there's nothing you can do about it. At least not for now."

Paige thought about what Wellington and his group were planning for Steinman and wondered whether they planned to liquidate any more enemies of the state that he didn't know about. He also wondered how many cells like Wellington's were active in other parts of the country and if there were anyone else like Paige who wanted to stop them. He hoped there were others like him, but all he could do for now was think globally and act locally. The interrupted Klein broadcast made him more determined than ever to do whatever was necessary to stop Wellington.

107

Monday afternoon.

"Hi, John? It's Bob."

"Hi Bob. How ya doin'?"

"Fine, thanks. I just got off the phone with Saul Steinman. Their next meeting is scheduled for Tuesday of next week at 7. He wants to finalize plans to have a massive student demonstration to protest the war on terror, and especially the TSA abuses."

Actually, Paige agreed with Steinman on this issue. He felt very strongly that the war on terror was out of control. The TSA warrantless searches and abuses were only the more visible signs that the war had taken a wrong turn. He felt guilty reporting on Steinman. He felt sorry he had taken the assignment but he didn't know how to back out of it.

"Thanks, Bob. That's good to know. I'll get back to you when we figure out how to proceed."

***

After hanging up, Wellington called the Boss and scheduled a meeting to relay the information Paige had just given him. A few hours later they met.

"OK, I think it's time to put this Steinman case to bed. Let's get rid of all of them, not just Steinman. If we whacked just Steinman, one of the others might pick up the torch, although I doubt it. Executing all of them will send a stronger message. Get Paige, too. I don't trust him after hearing that gibberish he was spouting at your barbecue. People like him are destroying the moral fabric of this country."

Wellington was a little surprised at the Boss's decision, but he was in basic agreement with it, although he wasn't happy about the prospect of killing Paige.

"OK. I'll contact the team and work out the details."

"OK. Keep me informed."

"Will do."

After contacting Jim, Tomás and Santos, he called Paige.

"Hi Bob, it's John. I've spoken to the Boss. We need to talk. Can you stop by the office in the next day or so?"

"Sure. How about this afternoon around four?"

"That would be fine. Give me a call when you get to the parking garage."

"OK, will do. See you then."

***

They met at the appointed time and proceeded to the alley.

Wellington spoke first. "I've spoken with the Boss and he's decided to exterminate all of them at their next meeting."

Paige gasped. The moment he dreaded was about to arrive. He didn't know what to say, but he had to say something.

"Ah, OK."

"You sound a little hesitant. Are you sure you're with us on this?" Wellington could detect Paige's hesitation. He perceived that Paige didn't approve of the Boss's decision.

"Yeah, I'm with you. I'm just surprised that he wants to get all of them. I thought he just wanted to kill Steinman."

"Things have changed. He wants to send a bigger message. Anyone who protests about what the government is doing is guilty of aiding and abetting the enemy. That's treason.

"We're going to get together at my place Saturday around four to work out the details. Sarah and the kids will be in Orlando visiting her parents, so we'll have the place to ourselves. Can you make it?"

"Yeah, I'll be there." He didn't know what else to say. It's all he could say.

Wellington continued. "I think we'll proceed along these lines. The professors will start arriving around 7. Let's give them time to get there and settle in. At around 8, you'll make some excuse to go out to your car. That's when we'll come in and do it. You can just get into your car and go home. We'll do the rest."

"OK." Paige didn't know what else to say. He was stunned. The time had come and he wasn't ready for it. Perhaps he never would be.

"OK. See you then."

108

Tomás Gutierrez was at home, sitting in the family room in front of the TV. His seven-year-old son, Julio, was sitting on the floor reading a book. His wife Teresa had just gotten up to go to the kitchen.

His eyes were open. He was looking in the direction of the television, but he wasn't seeing what was on the screen. He was thinking about the phone call he just got from Wellington, telling him that everyone in Steinman's group was to be killed, including Paige and Steinman's wife. The time had come to make a decision. He could either go along with the plan, or he could ask not to be included in this particular hit. He never thought about resigning completely because he believed that assassinating politicians and others who were abusing the Constitution was the right thing to do. He owed it to his family to do something. He couldn't just sit there and let his rights and his son's future melt away.

He briefly thought about killing Wellington, but that wouldn't solve the problem. Not permanently, anyway. Jim and Santos could finish the job without Wellington, and even if he executed all three of them, the Boss would probably replace them with other people he probably wouldn't know. He decided to call Wellington and try to opt out.

He got off the couch and started walking toward the garage. He had to find a place where Teresa and Julio wouldn't be able to hear him.

"Honey, where are you going?" Teresa had just walked into the room with a bowl of potato chips and three glasses of Diet Pepsi.

"I thought I'd go to the garage for a second. There's something I want to check on."

"OK, but hurry back. You don't want your Diet Pepsi to get warm."

"It will only take a minute."

As soon as he entered the garage he turned on the light, closed the door behind him and took out his cell phone.

"Hello, John? This is Tomás. I'd like to opt out of this one."

There was a long pause before Wellington replied. "But you can't do that. You're part of the team."

"Yes, I know. I still want to be part of the team. Just not for this one time."

Wellington exhaled. "Let's not talk about it over the phone. Let's meet somewhere before work tomorrow."

"OK."

Wellington decided to make it as easy as possible for Tomás to meet him. "We can meet some place close to your office. Where do you suggest?"

"There's a 7-11 a few blocks from the Carnival Cruise Lines offices. Do you know where it is?"

"Yeah, I think so. I can find it on the internet."

"OK, let's meet in the parking lot around 8:30."

"OK, I'll see you then."

After they hung up, Tomás went back to the family room and Wellington called the Boss.

Tomás felt somewhat relieved, but also anxious for the matter to be resolved. He tried to enjoy the potato chips, Diet Pepsi and his family, but his mind kept bouncing back to the conversation he had just had with Wellington. He thought about what he would say and how he would present his case.

109

"Hi. It's John. I just got a call from Tomás. He's getting cold feet. He wants out of the Tuesday night event."

The Boss paused for a few seconds before replying. "Well, he can't have out. He's part of the team. Did you explain that to him?"

"We're going to meet tomorrow morning. I'll try to convince him to stay."

"You shouldn't have to *convince* him. You should *order* him to stay."

"Yeah, I know. I'll call you after the meeting."

"You do that."

110

Tomás arrived a few minutes before Wellington. He parked in the corner of the 7-11 parking lot, away from the camera. Wellington pulled in and parked next to Tomás.

Tomás walked toward Wellington as he got out of the car.

"Hi John. Sorry to put you through all this trouble," he said as they shook hands.

"Tomás, you're causing problems for us. You know you can't just pick and choose your assignments."

"But you don't need me on this one. You don't need four people to kill a bunch of unarmed professors. The three of you can do it without me."

"It doesn't work that way. You're part of the team. It would set a bad precedent. Besides, it's a bonding opportunity."

They both smiled as Wellington said it. "Now you sound like some kind of pop psychologist."

"The Boss told me to order you to do it."

"I understand. It's just that I don't think they deserve killing."

"Tomás, what they're doing is undermining what the government is trying to do to stop terrorism. It's treason."

"Maybe the treason law needs to be repealed. I don't think it's treason to speak out against the government."

"Maybe that's true in normal times, but these aren't normal times. We're involved in a war here. The normal rules don't apply."

"I think the Constitution should always apply, especially when things aren't normal. That's when people need protection the most. People shouldn't be punished for what they say or write. If exercising your right of free speech and press gives aid and comfort to the enemy, then so be it."

Wellington was startled by his comment. "I disagree. Look. We could debate this issue all day, but the fact of the matter is, we're going to do it, and you're going to do it with us. That's an order. Are you going to disobey?"

Wellington said it in a tone of voice that was obviously threatening, implying that failure to obey would be treated as insubordination and punished accordingly. He looked him straight in the eyes as he said it, and was waiting for a reply.

Tomás thought about his options. He really didn't have any, at least not at the moment.

"OK. I'll do it."

"Good. I'm glad you came to your senses. I'll expect to see you at the meeting on Saturday."

"I'll be there."

Wellington turned around, got into his car and drove off. As he left, Tomás felt more anxiety than ever. He knew he wasn't going to participate in the executions in spite of his agreement to the contrary, but he didn't know what to do. Failure to obey the order would result in his own death, either by Wellington or one of the other team members. He thought of Teresa and Julio. He couldn't let them kill him, for their sake. He made up his mind. He had to kill them first. It would be an act of self-defense. He would do it on Saturday. He thought about warning Paige, but decided against it. There would be no threat by Tuesday if he terminated them at the meeting on Saturday. If Paige came to the meeting, he could tell him then, after he executed the others in front of him.

He knew that he would have to terminate the Boss, too. Otherwise, the Boss would kill him, or, what is more likely, would send someone to kill him, since the Boss didn't like getting his hands dirty. He wondered what he could do if the Boss didn't show up at the meeting. He decided he would cross that bridge when he came to it.

111

"Hi. It's John."

"What do you have to report?" The Boss was sitting at his desk, having coffee and looking out the window.

"He agreed to stay with the plan, but I don't believe him. I don't think he's going to do it. He's become a liability."

"That's too bad. He was a good soldier. You know what you have to do."

"Yeah, I know. I don't feel good about it, but I agree it has to be done. I'll do it at the meeting on Saturday."

"OK. Call me after you do it. I'll send a clean-up crew to get rid of the evidence. I think you should get rid of Paige then, too. I don't think it's a good idea to wait until Tuesday. He might warn the professors or, worse yet, tell the police or the FBI. That would really complicate our lives."

112

As Wellington drove to work, he wondered whether he should tell Jim and Santos about the decision to kill Tomás and Paige. If he didn't tell them in advance, it might cause a problem at the meeting. They might pull their guns on him when they saw him executing Tomás and Paige, in the mistaken belief that they would be next. He couldn't let that happen. But if he did tell them in advance, that could cause other problems. They both liked Tomás. One or both of them might warn him in advance, in which case Tomás might try to kill him first. Or maybe Jim or Santos would try to kill him. They were good soldiers, but sometimes friendship got in the way of good military decisions, and they were closer to Tomás than they were to him. Either option would involve some risk.

He rolled down his window to get some fresh air. He looked to the left and saw the calm, blue water and sky scrapers. No day was a good day to die in Miami. But someone was going to die on Saturday. He hoped it wouldn't be him.

He made his decision. They were good soldiers. He could trust them to keep the secret, and not to kill him before he could kill Tomás. He would tell them.

A few minutes later he pulled into the parking garage down the street from his office. After he parked, he pulled out his cell phone and called Jim Bennett. He picked up on the fourth ring.

"Hello, Jim? It's John."

"Hi John. Isn't it a little early to be calling? You're a grouchy bastard before your second cup of coffee."

He decided not to respond. "We need to talk. Call Santos and tell him I've scheduled a meeting for 5:30. We can meet at the diner across from your office. But not *in* the diner. In the parking lot."

"It sounds serious. It's not like you to schedule a meeting at a place that's convenient for me. Should I call Tomás, too, or have you already called him?"

"No. Don't call Tomás, and tell Santos not to call him either. The meeting is about Tomás."

Bennett could sense it was something extremely serious, both by the tone in Wellington's voice and by the fact that Tomás was getting cut out of the meeting.

"OK. I'll tell him. See you at 5:30."

***

After they disconnected, Bennett sat at his desk at the FBI office, looking at the diplomas and certificates hanging from the wall. He thought to himself, "Things used to be so simple when I first started out. Everything was always black and white. There were good guys and there were bad guys. There was never any politics involved. Nobody had any psychological problems. You just did your job, and everybody was on the same team. Now everything's different, and it's probably never going to get back to the way it was." He felt sad.

He sighed, picked up his cell phone and pushed a few buttons.

"Hi, Santos? It's Jim."

"Hi Jim. It's not like you to call me, especially so early in the morning. What's up?"

"I just got off the phone with John. He wants to have a meeting tonight at 5:30. It's about Tomás."

"What happened?" He sounded concerned.

"I don't know. He just told me to call you and invite you to the meeting, and not to tell Tomás about it."

"I don't like the sound of this. Something must have gone really wrong."

"Yeah, I'm thinking the same thing. We'll just have to wait until 5:30. We're supposed to meet at the diner across from my office, but not *in* the diner. In the parking lot."

"Wow. That's an unusual place. He always likes to meet in the alley by his office."

"Yeah, I know. It's totally out of context for him."

"OK. I'll see you then. I gotta get back to work."

113

Wellington arrived first, and parked in the corner. It was 5:24 and there were a lot of empty spaces. Santos pulled in a few minutes later. Bennett walked across the street and met them at precisely 5:30.

Wellington spoke first. "Gentlemen, we have a problem." He proceeded to give them the short version of the story. Then he got to the point.

"The Boss said he's become a liability. We have to get rid of him."

They looked at each other, then at Wellington.

Santos spoke first. "But he's not a traitor. He just doesn't agree with us on some points."

Jim chimed in. "Killing traitors is one thing. Killing one of our own just because he *might* disobey an order is something else." He was emphatic about it.

"The Boss said we have to do it. It's a done deal. You guys don't have to do it. I'll do it. I just wanted to let you know, so that when it happens, you won't be surprised. I'm going to do it at the meeting on Saturday. The Boss is going to send a clean-up crew to get rid of the evidence. He told me to do Paige, too. The Boss doesn't trust him."

Jim and Santos both looked at the ground, resigned to the fact that they were about to lose a friend. Wellington noticed, and sensed they may not be fully supportive of the plan.

"Are you guys with me on this? Santos?"

"Yeah, I'm with you."

"Jim?"

"Yeah."

Neither of them was happy about it, but they had to say yes and they knew it.

"OK. That's all I had. See you on Saturday."

Wellington got into his car and left. Jim and Santos stood there in the parking lot for a few minutes, not wanting to leave, but not knowing what to say either. Finally, Santos broke the silence.

"I don't like it."

"I don't either, but what can we do about it? We don't have any options."

"Yeah, I know. But I like Tomás. He's our friend. He's not a traitor. I don't think he should be killed."

"I don't think so either. Do you have any ideas?"

Santos thought for a minute. "We could warn him."

"Yeah. I thought about that, but what would happen if we warned him?"

"He would probably whack John before John could whack him."

"And where would that leave us? What about the Boss?"

Santos shifted back and forth before answering. "He'd have to whack the Boss, too."

"But what if the Boss doesn't come to the meeting?"

Santos became animated. "I don't know. Somebody has to kill the Boss, too."

"Do you want to do it?"

"No, I don't want to kill the Boss."

"Well, I don't want to kill him, either."

"Do we have a choice?"

Bennett thought about it for a moment. "The way I see it, we have three options. We could just do nothing, and let it happen, or we could tell Tomás and let him do it. Or we could do it ourselves. What's your preference?"

"If we don't tell Tomás, it's almost the same as killing him ourselves."

Bennett smirked as he heard what Santos had just said. It was all becoming clear to him what he had to do. "If you had to whack someone, who would you rather whack, Tomás or John?"

"I'd kill John in a heartbeat. I never really liked him. He's a condescending preppie bastard. He thinks he's better than us."

"Yeah, I feel the same way. So it's settled?"

Santos breathed a sigh of relief. "Yeah, it's settled. I want to do it."

"I want to do it, too."

"Then let's do it together. We'll do him at the same time."

"OK. Should we tell Tomás about it first?"

"No. Let's surprise him. If we tell him about it, he'll waste him before we get a chance to do it."

"OK. I can't wait to see the expression on his face."

"Me, either."

"What about the Boss?"

"We can kill him, too."

"What if he doesn't come to the meeting?"

"Then we can hunt him down. We both know where he works and where he lives."

Bennett thought for a moment. "What should we do about Paige?"

“I think we should kill him, too. He’s not that much different from Steinman. Did you hear the crap he was saying at the barbecue?”

“Yeah. He’s not really one of us. He’s one of them. We can do him on Saturday and the other professors on Tuesday. We don’t need John.”

“OK. Sounds like a plan.”

114

"Hi, Bob. It's Saul."

It was Thursday afternoon, two days before the meeting at Wellington's house and five days before Steinman would no longer exist, if Wellington had anything to say about it.

"Hi, Saul. How are you?"

"Fine. I just called to ask you to pick up Sveta before coming over on Tuesday. Rona and Sveta have been talking and Sveta volunteered to help Rona with the food. It will give Rona someone to talk to in the kitchen while the boys are discussing politics."

Paige didn't like what he had just heard.

"Ah, OK. I'll bring her along."

He started to panic. He figured Wellington would probably execute everyone who happened to be at Steinman's, including Rona. The very thought of it made him sick to his stomach. If Sveta were there, they would likely kill her, too. They would have to, since she would be able to recognize Wellington. The die had been cast. He had no choice. He would have to kill them first, no matter what. Or he would have to die trying.

"OK. See you at seven."

"Yeah, see you then."

As soon as he hung up, he started to tremble. He didn't know if he could do it, but he had to. There was no way out.

115

Saturday

John Wellington looked at his watch. It was three o'clock. The meeting was set to begin in one hour. He was visibly nervous. His hands shook as he moved the table into the correct position in the family room. They always shook before a kill. He wanted to position it so he could sit facing the entryway door, which would enable him to see each person as they came into the room.

He felt bad about what he was about to do, but he realized it was the only possible solution. Paige had to go, and he had to go today. Waiting until Tuesday might be too late. He couldn't be trusted. He might alert Steinman and the others if he were allowed to live. Tomás had to go, too. He couldn't be trusted. Allowing a team member to opt out of an assignment would set a bad precedent. He couldn't allow it.

He thought briefly about how Santos and Jim might react when he whacked Paige and Tomás in front of them, at close range. Depending on where they sat, some of their blood might splatter onto one or both of them. He also wondered if they could be trusted to just sit there and let it happen. He didn't think that whacking Paige would be a problem, since they didn't like Paige anyway, but killing Tomás was a different matter. They liked

Tomás. Their families had had picnics and barbecues together. They had been on a number of assignments together since he joined the team a few years ago. They might have second thoughts about letting him kill their friend. He tried to put any unpleasant possibilities out of his mind as he thought about what he had to do.

As he set the chairs in their appropriate places he thought about his first encounters with Paige when he was an MBA student in Paige's financial accounting class. Paige had recruited him, and they had become friends, although he never completely trusted Paige, who seemed too idealistic and principled. He wasn't practical enough to suit Wellington. He believed that Paige didn't seem to realize that it was sometimes necessary to ignore the Constitution in order to do what needed to be done.

He decided he would do it as soon as Paige and Tomás were both in the room. He wouldn't wait. There was no point in waiting. He would be nervous until it was over.

116

Jim picked Santos up at his house a few minutes before three o'clock. Maria, his wife, and Rosa, his nine-year-old daughter, said good-bye to him.

"Bye daddy. I love you."

"I love you, too, sweetie. I'll be back in a few hours."

"Bye honey." Maria was at the door, wearing dark blue shorts that were covered by an apron.

After pulling out of the driveway, Jim broke the silence. "On the way over, I was thinking about how we would do it. If all three of them are there, we'll hit them as soon as we come through the door. If one of them is missing, we'll wait until they're all there."

"What if the Boss doesn't come? John said he might not be able to make it."

"If the Boss isn't there when we arrive, we can ask John if the Boss is coming. If he says yes, we'll wait. Otherwise, we'll just start shooting."

A big grin appeared on Santos's face. "If Tomás is there, he'll shit when we start opening fire."

Bennett pondered the likely scenario. "Yeah. I sort of hope he is there, just to see the expression on his face."

"Me, too. How should we do it? Can I shoot Paige? I really don't like him. He's just like the other professors we're going to get on Tuesday."

Jim paused before answering. He looked out the window and thought about it. "Naw, I think we should do Paige last. He's the least dangerous. He's probably not even carrying. John's probably the most dangerous. We should do him first, then the Boss if the Boss is there. We can let Paige watch, then we can do him together."

Santos approved. "OK. That sounds like a good approach. We've got all the bases covered."

They arrived at 3:52. The only one there was Wellington. Tomás arrived a few minutes later.

117

Earlier on Saturday

Tomás was sitting on the couch, in his living room, watching television with Teresa and Julio. Actually, his eyes were open and he was looking in the direction of the screen, but he was thinking about what he had to do that day. It was Saturday.

He looked at his watch. Three o'clock. Time to go. It would take about an hour to get to Wellington's house on the edge of the Everglades. His gun and two extra mags were already in the car.

"Teresa, I have to go now."

"OK. Have a good time and don't stay out too late." He had told Teresa he was getting together with the boys for a card game and a few beers. As he walked to the car his legs felt a little wobbly. Although he had killed before, he had always killed enemies, people he didn't know, and usually from a distance. Today would be different. He would be terminating friends, up close and personal. He was nervous, but he knew he had to do it. The alternative was unthinkable. He couldn't let them snuff innocent people.

On the drive to Wellington's, he thought about how to do it. He'd wait until Wellington, Santos and Jim were all there. If he was lucky, the Boss would also be there, but if not, he would start without him. Or maybe he would wait until the Boss arrived. He decided that, if the Boss wasn't there when he arrived, he would ask Wellington if the Boss was going to come. If yes, then he would wait. If not, then he would start shooting.

He couldn't decide whether to wait for Paige to arrive. It didn't really matter, since he wasn't going to snuff Paige, although he'd have to explain his actions to Paige after he killed the others.

As he approached Wellington's house, he started to have second thoughts about not snuffing Paige. Although he sensed that Paige was not happy about assassinating professors, if he didn't kill him, he might go to the police and implicate him if he let him live. Or he might go to the Boss if he knew how to contact him. He decided to wait and see Paige's reaction when he executed the others.

He pulled into the driveway, turned left onto the grass, and pointed the car toward the street, just in case he had to make a quick escape. He walked into the entryway, then into the family room, and saw Wellington, Santos and Jim sitting at the table, looking at him. He could sense something was wrong, but he couldn't tell what. He thought that maybe it was just his nerves. Paige wasn't there.

"Is the Boss going to be joining us?"

Wellington leaned forward, and replied, "I don't know. He said he was going to be extremely busy today but might be able to sneak away for a few minutes." As he said it, his right arm dropped below the table. He appeared to be reaching for something.

118

"If it is to be, it is up to me."
Unknown

"Change will not come if we wait for some other person or some other time. We are the ones we've been waiting for. We are the change that we seek."
Barack Hussein Obama

"To survive it is often necessary to fight and to fight you have to dirty yourself."
George Orwell

Saturday. The time had come. Someone was going to die today. The question was who?

It was about an hour's drive from Paige's condo in Sunny Isles Beach to Wellington's place at the edge of the Everglades. Wellington's nearest neighbors were about a half mile down the road. They probably wouldn't hear the shots, and even if they did, they probably wouldn't pay much attention to them. Lots of people went to the everglades for target practice to avoid the fees that ranges charged.

Sarah and the kids were in Orlando, visiting her parents. They wouldn't be back for a few days. The meeting was scheduled for 4pm. Paige planned to arrive around 4:15. That way all four of them would be there, hopefully, and he could start blasting right away, since he didn't know if he could just sit there like nothing was about to happen while waiting for everyone to show up.

He hoped the Boss would also be there, but realized that was unlikely, since the Boss had gone out of his way to be secretive and John refused to reveal the Boss's identity. Paige wondered whether executing all four of them would end the plan or whether the Boss would merely replace them with another team. It probably wouldn't be difficult to recruit a new team, given the fact that so many people thought the same way as the present team members.

Paige couldn't sleep. He got up early and paced back and forth in his living room. His stomach was queasy. He didn't know if he could do it. John had become his friend of sorts. He felt responsible, since he recruited John when he was an MBA student. Then there were Jim, Tomás and Santos. He had met their families. They had a lot in common. They all loved America and what it stood for. They were all patriots. The problem was that their patriotism was misplaced and un-American. Assassinating people who were gnawing away at the Constitution was one thing. Executing people merely because they exercised their rights of free speech and press was something else. What they were doing was destroying freedom in America. Intellectually, he knew he was doing the right thing, but emotionally it was tearing him apart.

Then there was the possibility that he would fail and that they would kill him instead, or that he wouldn't be able to get away with it and that either the feds or the local police would come to get him at some point, at which time they'd either kill him or take him into custody with no possibility of escape. Or maybe the Boss would send someone to get him, if the Boss suspected he was the one who executed the team members.

If he survived Saturday, he could spend the rest of his life in jail, unless he could convince a jury that what he did constituted justifiable homicide and that it was necessary to save freedom in America. Then there was the possibility that he wouldn't even get a chance to have a jury trial. Some laws passed after 9/11 allowed the government to ignore the right to a trial by jury if the person was an alleged terrorist, even if he was an American citizen, all in the name of national security. Having an open jury trial would allow classified information to escape, which would help the enemy, or at least that's what the government could argue. Or they might argue that having a jury trial would give aid and comfort to the enemy, a phrase that had become over-used in recent years. Therefore, a jury trial might not be allowed. All that was necessary to avoid a jury trial would be for the government to argue that there were national security issues involved. It puzzled Paige that more Americans weren't outraged by this government policy, which clearly violated the Constitution.

That was another reason why Paige thought he must succeed. Taking away the right to a jury trial pushed the country one step closer to tyranny. Or maybe the country had already arrived at that destination and the citizenry just hadn't realized it yet.

Paige always liked the phrase, *Live Free or Die*, but he never thought he would actually have to make the choice. No matter what happened today he wouldn't be totally free. Even if he succeeded in his self-imposed mission, he would only be winning a skirmish in a war that could go on for years without any clear resolution in sight. But it was his only option. He had to think globally but act locally.

At 3:15 he strapped on his Glock 17, making sure there was a round in the chamber, which would give him 18 rounds before he had to reload. If he needed more than that, he would be in trouble, but he took along two extra mags, just in case. He grabbed a pair of latex gloves and put them in his pocket. If he had to touch something, he didn't want to leave any prints. His Boy Scout training taught him to be prepared, but his Boy Scout leaders probably had something quite different in mind when they beat that slogan into his young Catholic head.

He became increasingly nervous as he got closer to John's house. He hoped they would all be there. When he was about 200 feet away, he noticed there were only three cars in the driveway, John's, Jim's and Tomás's. Apparently, Santos hadn't arrived yet.

Shit! He thought of his options. He could circle the block and hope that Santos would show up, except that he was out in the country and there really weren't blocks in the city sense of the term. He could keep driving for a few miles, then turn around. Or he could abort the mission, which he knew he couldn't do. Or he could just go in and start blasting whoever was there, then wait for Santos to show up.

He decided to go in and start blasting. His nervousness increased as he pulled into John's driveway. His hands started to shake. He could barely take the keys out of the ignition and put them in his pocket. He took a deep breath. He said a short prayer to his guardian angel to give him the strength to do what he needed to do and to do the job right.

He still prayed to his guardian angel like the nuns taught him, even though he abandoned Catholicism years ago. Although he firmly believed that organized religion was bullshit, he still believed there were other realms of existence and that there were both good and evil spirits. He hoped it would be a good spirit guiding his hand, although he never really thought about the possibility that a guardian angel might help him execute four misguided patriots.

He got out of the car and walked toward the breezeway. The door would be unlocked, so he could just walk in without ringing the door bell or announcing his presence. From there it was a short walk to the family room, where they would be working out the final details.

He walked into the room. All four of them were there, seated at the table. Apparently, one of them had given Santos a ride. He felt relieved, although he was so weak in the knees that he had difficulty walking normally.

As he entered, John looked up and said, “Hi Bob. Come on in. Join the party.”

They all looked nervous. Paige could sense it. Something was wrong.

As Wellington looked Paige in the eyes, he started to rise slowly from his chair. He raised his pistol and aimed it at Paige as Santos, Jim and Tomás looked on. When Tomás saw what was about to happen, he jumped up, whipped out his pistol, aimed it at Wellington and squeezed the trigger four times. The first two shots hit him in the chest, causing him to fly backwards. The third shot, ripped into his left shoulder, causing him to turn slightly to the left. The fourth one grazed his chin as he dropped to the floor.

The sound of the four shots in rapid succession - BLAM! BLAM! BLAM! BLAM! – were loud, made louder by the acoustics in the room, which caused the sound to bounce off the walls.

They served to calm Paige down. His knees were no longer wobbly. He became totally focused and in control of his body. He could hear his own breathing as he inhaled deeply.

As he grabbed for his Glock, Santos rushed him, knocking him to the ground and causing him to drop his gun. Tomás turned toward Jim and shot him twice in the head as he was drawing his gun.

Paige managed to get up and break away from Santos's strong grip. He rushed Paige again, throwing a punch with his right, which Paige managed to partially deflect by stepping to the right and blocking with his left arm.

It was an automatic response, gained from all those years of sparring in Kimura's dojo and Brown's dojahng. He felt Santos's fist glance off his mouth but it didn't hurt. His adrenalin was pumping too fast to feel any pain.

Santos's forward rush with that muscular body caused Paige to partially lose his balance. Tomás tried to draw a bead on Santos but couldn't get a clear shot. They were both moving too fast.

As Santos rushed at him a third time, Paige was able to recover sufficiently to throw a jumping side kick into Santos's solar plexus, causing Santos to fly backwards against the wall.

As he bounced off the wall, he charged Paige a fourth time, but he was off balance. His head was projecting forward, almost parallel with the floor, his feet barely touching the ground. It looked like he was going to tackle Paige rather than punch him.

Paige let loose with a karate punch to his nose, causing the cartilage to snap like a twig and rattling his brain enough to throw off his equilibrium. Santos dropped to the floor, face down.

He was temporarily out of commission, unable to get up, but he was still a threat. If it were an alley fight with a street punk, Paige would have the option of running away, but he didn't have that option now. He knew he had to finish him off. If he let Santos get up, he would be in trouble.

He leapt off the floor and came down on Santos, the heel of his left foot slamming into Santos' third cervical vertebra. He could feel Santos' neck snap. It was over.

Paige let out a sigh of relief. He could taste blood in his mouth. Apparently, the one punch that Santos was able to land had cut his lip.

He was breathing heavily from all the physical activity. As he gulped air, he turned toward Tomás, who was standing about ten feet away, the gun still in his hand, pointed toward the floor.

"I suppose I should thank you for saving my life. What happened just now?"

"Wellington was going to snuff you. He got the order from the Boss. Santos and Jim wanted to whack you, too."

"So why didn't you let them? You're one of them, too, aren't you?"

"I used to be, but I drew the line when they started assassinating journalists and professors. I had to stop them before Tuesday. Exterminating termites like Debbie Waterstein, Senator Tom Garrett and Daniel Frumpton is one thing. Executing people just for criticizing the government is something else. I decided I wasn't going to let that continue to happen."

"Well, I'm glad you decided not to kill professors." Paige smiled as he said it. Tomás reciprocated.

"Where do we go from here? Is the Boss supposed to be at this meeting?"

"I don't know. John said he might be able to stop by for a few minutes, but I wouldn't count on it."

Paige touched his lip, which was starting to swell. "We have to get him, you know. This thing won't be over until he's out of the picture."

"Yeah I know. I think we need to get him today. If we wait, he'll find out about what just happened, and he'll come after us."

"I agree. We'll have to get him in the next few hours." Paige bent over to pick up his Glock.

Tomás thought for a few seconds. "I know where he lives and where he works. He probably won't be in the office today, so we can start with his home."

"Who is the Boss, anyway? I've been trying to pry the information out of John for years, but he always evades my questions."

"His name is Hank Thorndike. He's the southeast regional head of the FBI, but he also has CIA connections. I don't know the specifics. John kept us pretty much in the dark, too, although we have meet him a few times. One time I copied down his license plate number and did a little searching on the internet. He lives in Coconut Grove."

"Let's start there, and hope he's home. If he isn't, I guess we'll have to wait for him."

"Not necessarily. He has a boat at the marina on South Beach. He might be there. It's Saturday."

Paige smiled and looked him directly in the eyes. "I see you've done your homework."

"Sometimes I get curious." He bent over and started picking up his shell casings.

Paige looked around the room, and at the dead bodies on the floor. "We'll have to leave this mess. We don't have time to clean it up."

"Yeah. We need to get out of here."

Paige turned toward the door. "OK. Let's go. You go first. I'll follow you in my car."

"We should probably go in one car. It would make things easier. Let's drop your car off at your place and take mine. I know where the Boss lives."

"OK. Do you know where I live, too?"

"Of course." They both smiled.

As they started to leave, Paige turned around, walked back into the room and put one of the latex gloves on his right hand. He walked up to Wellington's corpse, which was lying face down, grabbed John's right hand, dipped Wellington's index finger in his blood, and scrawled MOSSAD on the floor.

Tomás saw what Paige had done. "Why did you do that?"

"Just think of it as a love letter to Rachel Karshenboym."

"The tree of liberty must be refreshed from time to time with the blood of patriots and tyrants. It is its natural manure."
Thomas Jefferson

119

After dropping off Paige's car at his condo, they engaged in conversation as Tomás drove them to Coconut Grove.

Paige was curious to learn more about his new best buddy. "How did you get involved in this business?"

"John recruited me. He heard about my computer skills and the work I did in Iraq and Afghanistan and he contacted me. He didn't tell me where he got the information, but he knew a lot about me, so it must have been someone I worked with, probably in Afghanistan, because that was my last mission before getting out of the army."

Paige got a smile on his face. "Do you know that I'm the one who recruited John?"

"No, I didn't know that. John was very closed mouthed about that kind of thing."

"As he should be. It's not a good idea to go blabbing about who recruited you or how they did it. The funny thing is that, since John recruited you and I recruited John, I'm sort of responsible for recruiting you, since there's a direct link in the chain between you and me."

"I don't know whether I should thank you or kick you in the balls. If you hadn't recruited John, we wouldn't be in this predicament. Or at least I wouldn't be."

They both laughed. Tomás continued. "How did they recruit you?"

"I can't talk about that, although I can tell you they did it when I was working with the Finance Ministry in Armenia."

"That sounds interesting. You really can't tell me more?"

"I suppose I could. I'm not feeling very loyal to the Company at the moment."

Tomás turned his head to the right to look at Paige. "Well, technically this isn't a Company assignment. It's more of a freelance thing. Some American patriots saw something wrong and decided to do what they could to fix it."

"I hear you. When you can't get rid of the political trash by the electoral process, the people have to do it on an ad hoc basis."

Tomás smiled, exposing his teeth, which looked even whiter because of his brown skin, black hair and black eyes. "Yeah. That's what the Second Amendment's all about. It's not about protecting the rights of hunters. It's about protecting the people from their government. The problem is, where do you draw the line?" Tomás had taken two political science classes in college, which was just enough to pique his interest in the relationship between the people and the government.

Paige had thought about this relationship, too, especially in recent months. "I think it's impossible to draw a bright line to determine who should be killed and who shouldn't, but I think it is possible to establish some general guidelines."

He continued. "I think the people who have earned the honor of being put on the hit list are the ones who have done the most damage to the country, the ones who have engaged in overt acts that result in violations of property rights or Constitutional rights."

Tomás chimed in. "Most members of Congress would fall into that category. They sponsor legislation that violates the

Constitution and property rights. They pass laws that take the property from those who've earned it and give it to those who haven't. They pass laws that violate our right to privacy. The Boss refers to them as termites. They gradually gnaw away at the Constitutional and property rights structure, chipping away at our rights gradually. Nobody seems to notice until the structure starts collapsing. By then it's too late to do much about it."

Paige thought about what Tomás had just said. "That's a good analogy. I think I'm starting to like good old Hank. It's too bad we have to kill him. What about the Frumpton hit? Who thought of that one?"

"Hank did. He thought of most of them. I feel funny calling him Hank. He always wanted us to refer to him as the Boss, or Sir. He didn't want us to get informal with him."

"I can understand that. It's part of the discipline and chain of command thing. I perceive he's a bit of a tight ass, huh?"

"You could say that. I never felt comfortable when he was in the room. But he's not all bad. He understands what has to be done and how to get America back on track. The problem is that he's gone over the edge. He's starting to put people on the hit list who don't belong there."

"Like journalists and professors?"

"Yeah. Some of them are damaging America by spouting collectivist crap, but I don't think that's justification for killing them. Executing people for their views stifles free speech and press, and that's bad for America. Snuffing them would destroy freedom in America faster than letting them continue to spout their gibberish."

"Tell me about his reasoning for the Frumpton hit. I read the press reports, but you know how the press is. They slant things and often leave out the best parts."

"Yeah, I know what you mean, but the press did a pretty good job of reporting on our hits. I think it's because they published the blurbs John sent them after each hit."

Tomás looked at his watch. Six o'clock. They still had a few hours of daylight, which could help or hinder them, depending on how they planned their hit.

He continued. "But getting back to this Frumpton thing, Hank wanted to expand the list to include people who abused the Constitution even if they weren't politicians. Abusers of the eminent domain laws were at the top of his list. Hank had read about some families who had their homes confiscated by the government so that private developers could build on their property. I remember the first time he talked about it at one of our meetings. He got enraged whenever he spoke about it. He wanted Congress and the various state legislatures to repeal the eminent domain laws, since they gave the government the authority to confiscate private property, but he didn't see that as a realistic possibility, so he decided to do the next best thing – execute anyone who used the eminent domain laws to confiscate private property.

"He didn't limit it to just the developers. He thought we should include anyone involved in the chain of confiscation because they were part of the problem. The attorneys for the developers, the judges and local politicians who approved the confiscations were all part of the problem. He figured if he could exterminate enough of them, it would send a message that engaging in eminent domain actions could be harmful to your health. He wanted to create a chilling effect that would alter behavior."

Paige thought about the television and press reports following the Frumpton hit. "I guess he was at least partially successful. I recall reading about some real estate board declaring eminent domain activities to constitute unethical conduct, something that agents and brokers could lose their real estate license for. Some banks announced they would quit financing eminent domain projects."

"Yeah, Hank was really thrilled when he heard those announcements. He offered them as evidence we were making a difference."

"I think he was right. If I were a real estate developer, I'd sure as hell think twice before starting an eminent domain confiscation, especially if it was in Miami. It's too bad we have to liquidate him."

"Yeah, he's made some contributions toward restoring freedom in America, but he's gone over the edge. Besides, if we don't kill him, he's going to kill us."

They had been on the road for what seemed like a long time, driving from Wellington's home near the Everglades to Sunny Isles Beach to drop off Paige's car, then to Coconut Grove. They were within minutes of their destination.

"Hank's house is just a few blocks from here. How do you think we should proceed?"

"Let's do a drive by. I want to see what the neighborhood looks like and how his house is situated. Is he married? Does he have kids living at home?"

"He's divorced. The kids lived with their mother after the divorce, but I think they're all grown and out of the house now."

"So he lives alone?"

"I think so. He never talks about his personal life."

"I don't want to kill any civilians if we can help it."

"I don't either. I think he's usually armed, so we have to be careful. And fast. He'll probably go for his gun as soon as he sees us."

"Then let's make sure he doesn't see us."

120

Paige turned his head toward Tomás. "I think we should approach so the house is on the right side. That way, if he's visible, I can shoot him from the passenger side while you drive. Can you do that?"

"Yeah. He lives on a two-way street. It's set back about 50 feet from the road. Do you think you can hit him from that far away?"

"I don't know. I guess we'll just have to find out."

"Is that a Glock you're carrying?"

"Yeah, it's a Glock 17. It holds 18 rounds if you put one in the chamber. Do you think that will be enough?" He said it half jokingly.

"If it isn't, I think I should find a new partner. What's more likely is that he won't be visible. People in Coconut Grove don't usually hang out in their front yard. They're either inside or on their patio in the back yard."

"Yeah, you're right. I guess he's not going to make it easy for us, is he?"

"No, probably not. He's probably on his guard by now, too, since John hasn't called him. He always wants us to call him as soon as we complete a mission. Since I made it impossible for John to call, he probably guessed that something went wrong."

Paige let out a sigh. "So, we've only been partners for a few hours and already you're making my life complicated. I was going to kill you, by the way."

Tomás looked surprised. He turned his head to look at Paige. "Really? Why?"

"I went there to kill all of you. I couldn't let you assassinate Steinman and everyone else in the room, including my girlfriend. I had to stop you before Tuesday, and today was the only day you would all be together in the same place."

"What made you change your mind?"

"Well, the fact that you had a gun and I didn't had a lot to do with it." They both laughed.

Tomás decided it was his turn to confess. "I was going to kill all of them, too … but not you."

"Not me? Well, thank you for that. Why not me? Didn't you think I was worth a bullet?"

"As I said, I don't think that assassinating professors and journalists is justified. I thought I would execute the others, then check your reaction to see whether you were really one of them. I sensed that you weren't, but I wasn't sure. I planned to kill you if I thought you would squeal on me."

"Well, I think you made the right decision." They both laughed.

"We're almost there. It's right around the corner." Tomás turned onto the street so that Hank's house was on the right side. He slowed down so they could get a closer look.

"It's the yellow house with the two trees."

"There aren't any cars in the driveway. What do you think we should do?"

Tomás thought for a minute before answering. "We could come back later, or we could keep driving around the block until he comes home. Or we could find a way to get in and wait for him inside. The problem is that there's about a one hundred percent chance he has some kind of alarm system, and I don't know how to disarm those things. Jim was the one who always did that."

"What do you think he would be doing right now? You know him better than I do."

"I really don't know. It's Saturday. He might be out with his girlfriend, if he has one. Or he might be out on his boat. Or, in this case, he might be at John's house to see for himself what went wrong. Or maybe if he went to John's house and saw what we did, he might be talking to someone who's higher in the chain of command."

"You think it goes up higher than Hank? John gave me the impression that it didn't go up any higher than his Boss."

"I think it goes up higher. That's just the impression I got from listening to Hank at some of our meetings."

"But Hank's the regional director of the FBI. If it goes up higher, there must be someone in Washington who's pulling his strings."

"Yeah, I thought about that, but I couldn't figure out who it might be."

"Do you think it's someone higher up at the FBI? Or maybe the Justice Department?"

"It could be, but, as I told you, he has some kind of CIA connections, too. It could be someone at the CIA, but it's an off-the-books kind of thing. Nothing official."

"Well, we really don't have to figure out who it is at the moment. What we need to do is find Hank and take him out before he takes us out." Paige thought about the options before he continued. "I don't see many good options. We don't know if he has a girlfriend, so we can't go to his girlfriend's house. We can't break into his house because the alarm would go off. We can't just keep driving around the block until he shows up. He's probably not at the office on a Saturday, especially this late. And we can't go back to John's house even if that's a likely place to find him. That only leaves the marina where he keeps his boat."

"Yeah, that pretty well sums it up. He keeps his boat at one of the marinas in South Beach."

"Let's go. We don't have any time to waste."

121

"Better to die fighting for freedom th[a]n be a prisoner all the days of your life."
Bob Marley

Tomás drove as fast as he could without drawing attention for speeding. It took a little less than an hour to get to the marina at South Beach. Parking was always a problem in South Beach, especially on a Saturday night, but he managed to find a space, probably the last one in South Beach, about a block from the marina.

They got out of the car and started walking. "Do you know which boat is his, and where it's parked?"

"*Docked* is the word. You don't park a boat. I can tell you're a professor. And yes, I know."

Tomás glanced to the left and right to see if anyone was looking in their direction. "I was curious to know more about the Boss. I always felt threatened by him. I thought it might be a good idea to learn what I could."

When they got a few hundred feet from the marina entrance, Tomás stopped, and extended his left arm to stop Paige. "There might be cameras. We need to get some caps." He looked around.

There were several stores across the street that might sell souvenirs, including caps. "Let's cross the street."

As they crossed, he added, "Let's get some glasses, too. They can be sunglasses, if you prefer, but it's getting dark, and we may not be able to see very well with sunglasses. Any kind of glasses that have rims will be fine. If they're prescription, we can knock out the lenses. And don't use a credit card. And be sure to pull the brim down so the cameras can't get a good look at your face. And keep your head down, too."

"It sounds like you've done this before."

"Maybe once or twice."

They entered the first store that looked like it sold souvenirs. It was packed with them, as well as a variety of food and beverages. Tomás spotted the section that sold caps. It was right next to the section that sold sunglasses. He motioned to Paige and they walked over to check out the merchandise. They each selected a cap and sunglasses and proceeded to the cash register. As Paige reached to get his wallet, Tomás stopped him. "This is my treat." He paid and they left.

After walking out the door and before crossing the street, they put on the caps, took the glasses, popped out the lenses and put them on. They threw the lenses into a garbage can on the corner.

They walked through the marina entrance as though they belonged there. Paige moved his hand to the right side of his shirt, which was concealing his Glock. He knew it was there, but wanted to check for reassurance. Tomás did the same to check his Sig Sauer. They took a deep breath. They were both nervous, especially Paige. He had never killed anyone before today, and hadn't had time to recover from the experience, which usually took a few days, if not years, especially for a first kill. He was about to kill again.

After walking for about a minute, they came upon the boat, which was actually a yacht. It was at least 50 feet long, maybe more. The lights were on, but no one was on the deck.

Paige whispered. "You said he had a boat. This is a yacht. Where did he get the money to pay for it on his salary?"

"Actually, it's not his. The FBI confiscated it as part of a drug bust. He checks it out from time to time to see that it hasn't been damaged. Sometimes he takes it out for a spin. It's nice to be the Boss."

As they got closer, they could hear music emanating from below. It was Sade, singing *Smooth Operator*. It seemed appropriate, given the circumstances.

"Like I said, he's probably carrying. And he's a mean son of a bitch. He won't hesitate to use it. We have to be quiet and we have to be fast."

Paige nodded, and they proceeded, slowly, onto the back of the boat. They were both wearing sneakers, which helped, and the boat was sufficiently large that the extra weight from a couple of guys walking on deck didn't disturb the gentle swaying motion caused by the waves. It was dusk, which partially concealed their activity, and most of the other boats were either out or vacant.

As they got to the door by the stairs that went below deck, Tomás motioned for Paige to stop. They drew their guns, and Tomás pushed down on the latch. It wasn't locked. But when he pushed to open the door, it made a creaking sound. As he continued to slowly open the door, the creaking got louder.

All of a sudden, the music stopped. They could hear some shuffling from the interior of the boat, and some whispering.

"What do you mean I have to be quiet?" It was a woman's voice. He was not alone. There was some more shuffling. It sounded like a drawer opening, then closing. All of a sudden, the cabin lights went out.

They stopped dead in their tracks. They knew the time had come to move, and move fast. They had to expect the worst, that he was armed and pointing his gun at the doorway that they would have to go through to get to him.

As they got closer, they could see the outline of two people at the other side of the room. There was just enough light coming through the window from the moon and the marina's lights to make out their silhouettes. They didn't know what to do. The safe thing would be to start blasting away at both of them, but one of them was a woman, probably a civilian. They hesitated.

Tomás recognized Hank. He was on the left. He was holding something in his right hand, probably a gun. He was pointing it right at them.

"Well, gentlemen, it appears we've reached an impasse. If you shoot me, I'll be able to get at least one of you, probably both, so why don't you put down your guns and step into the room. We can have a little talk." The woman looked at him and started whimpering. He grabbed her right arm and held it tightly with his left hand, pulling her closer to him.

"You know that's not going to happen."

"Ah, Tomás? Is that you? And who is your friend? Could it be the infamous Professor Paige?"

Paige felt compelled to say something. "Good guess, Hank. You don't mind if I call you Hank, do you? We've never met."

"Actually, I'd prefer you call me Boss, but I suppose that wouldn't be appropriate in this case, since I'm not your boss." He released the woman's arm. "Turn on the lights, honey. I want to get a better look at these two guys."

She reached over to the wall with her left hand and turned on the lights. Hank Thorndike appeared to be in his early 50s, somewhat overweight, with a bloated face and a pasty white, lumpy complexion. Not exactly a chick magnet. His female companion looked like she was in her early 30s, with blonde hair and a little too much cheap makeup. Maybe she was attracted to him because of the power. After all, he was a big shot FBI guy. Or maybe it was the yacht. It's tough to turn down a guy with a yacht, especially if you're in your thirties with a cheap look about you. Women like her had a short shelf life. She had to take her opportunities where she found them.

"Ah, that's better. Now I can see my two guests more clearly." He reached out with his left hand and grabbed her by her right arm, pulling her closer again. She glanced at him, a frightened look on her face. Then he moved behind her, placing his left arm tightly around her waist while continuing to point his gun at them.

Paige decided to challenge his manhood a bit. "Hiding behind a woman, Hank? That's not like you. Or at least it's not the image of you I had from the conversations I had about you with John." As he said it, Paige moved slightly away from Tomás, creating some distance between them.

"You can stop right there, professor. You two make a nice couple. I wouldn't want you to get too far apart, if you know what I mean."

Tomás tried to focus his aim at Thorndike's head. The Boss noticed what Tomás was trying to do, and put a tighter squeeze on his companion. She turned her head and looked at him again, clearly scared at what he was doing and why he was doing it.

Hank looked directly at Tomás. "You wouldn't kill a civilian, would you? John always told me that he would rather abort a mission than kill a civilian. Do you guys feel the same way?"

Tomás just looked at him, trying to focus his aim on Thorndike's head, which was now partially hidden behind his female companion. All of a sudden, there was an icy silence in the room.

Thorndike broke the ice. "John was supposed to call me after he whacked you two, but he never did, so I got worried. I called him around five, but he didn't answer. So I called Jim and Santos and they didn't answer, either. That's not like them. I figured something was wrong but couldn't go there to see for myself. Too risky. So I decided to proceed with my Saturday night plans with Wanda, here." He squeezed her around the waist as he said it.

She tried to reject his squeeze, but he was holding her too tightly. She was clearly not in a romantic mood any more.

Paige continued to point his Glock in Thorndike's direction, but couldn't get a clear shot. He was doing a good job hiding behind Wanda. "So, what are you going to do with Wanda after this is over, assuming we don't kill you. She's a witness. You can't just let her live." Wanda got a panicked look on her face as she heard what Paige had said. She just realized her prospects for seeing another Miami sunrise were bleak, unless they could kill Thorndike.

Paige continued. "So, Wanda, did you know that Hank here was behind the assassinations of Raul Rodriguez, Debbie Waterstein, Senator Garrett, Daniel Frumpton and those others? You really picked yourself a good one."

She turned to see Thorndike's face, as best she could. He was holding her too tightly to turn more than a few inches. "Is it true? Did you really kill all those people?"

"Don't mind him. He's just trying to upset you. They all needed killing anyway." When she heard him admit that what

Paige said was true, she turned her glance toward Paige. Her eyes were silently screaming, HELP ME.

She could feel his body tightly pressed against her. His right leg pressed against the back of her right leg. Her foot was touching his foot. He wasn't wearing shoes. She was wearing heels. All of a sudden, she raised her right foot and slammed her heel into the top of his foot. He screamed in pain, and bent forward, loosening his grip on her. She broke his grip and bolted to the left, giving Tomás and Paige a clear shot.

They opened up, hitting him six times in the torso. The impact drove him backwards, but he was large and kept standing long enough to pump two shots into Tomás, critically wounding him. Then he turned his gun toward Paige, but before he could squeeze off a round, Paige shot him in the head, causing it to jerk backward. He dropped to the deck.

Paige bent down over Tomás, who was on his back, gurgling blood. "Hang in there, buddy, we're going to get you to a hospital."

"No. It's too late. They're coming to get me." Tomás started talking to someone, but it wasn't Paige. "I don't want to go. I have to get back to Teresa and Julio. No ... Oh, okay ... Wow! ... Wow!" His eyes rolled up. He was gone. Paige felt a chilly breeze for a second or two. Then the temperature in the room returned to normal. It was a hot Miami night.

Wanda was standing over them, just staring, not knowing what else to do. Paige stood up and looked at her. All of a sudden, her look of puzzlement turned to one of fear. He could tell by looking into her eyes that she thought he was going to kill her.

"Don't worry. I'm one of the good guys. I'm not going to hurt you." She looked relieved to hear him say it.

"We have to get out of here. Your prints are probably all over this place. We don't have time to wipe it down. If you don't want a visit from the police and the FBI, we have to get rid of the boat." She just nodded, not knowing what to say.

"Do you know how to start this thing?"

"Yes. He showed me how. Sometimes he lets me steer it."

"Good. Let's take it out to Biscayne Bay."

Paige went up on deck and removed the ropes that kept it tied to the dock. She started the engines. After they pulled out of the marina, Paige set course and cranked it up to 12 knots, which was fairly fast, but not fast enough to attract any attention.

The sun had gone down. It was a beautiful night. There was a three-quarter moon. The neon lights of South Beach were clearly visible. The cool ocean breeze brushed against their faces. Under normal conditions, it would have been a romantic scene.

After they were about a half mile out, Paige picked up their guns and shell casings and tossed them overboard. He dragged their bodies to the deck, weighted them down with some heavy objects he found in the cabin so they would sink, and stabbed them each about 50 times with one of the knives he got from the galley so their body gases would escape as they decomposed. Otherwise, they might float to the surface and be discovered. He didn't want that to happen. It was a trick they taught him while taking a course in Langley. Then he slipped them over the side.

As he dumped Tomás's body overboard, he felt sad that Teresa and Julio would never see him again, and would wonder what happened to him, but he didn't have a choice. He had to get rid of the evidence.

When they reached Biscayne Bay, he dropped anchor and went about preparing the yacht for its final voyage, to the bottom. Wanda had remained silent, watching him.

"Gather up your personal belongings. We're going ashore. Don't leave behind anything that they could use to identify you."

He looked out the starboard side and saw the magnificent Miami skyline, along with the outlines of a few sail boats and several other yachts. It was a good place to park on a Saturday night in Miami.

The yacht came equipped with two jet skis and a dingy. "Feel like taking a ride?" She nodded. He lowered one of the jet skis into the water, then went below deck, where he disengaged the water pumps that cooled the engines, and set the engines on fast idle, which would cause them to heat up quickly. Then he loosened the fuel line. When the engines got hot enough, they would ignite the leaking fuel, causing a fire that would spread quickly, causing the yacht to blow up and sink.

They had to leave. There was no telling how long it would take for the fuel to ignite, but they couldn't stick around to find out. Paige got on the jet ski and started it. Wanda got on behind him, and they took off toward the shore.

About ten minutes later, as they approached the shore, they heard a big explosion behind them. Paige swung the jet ski around to take a look, just in time to see a second, then a third explosion. Then he swung back around and headed toward the shore.

He beached the jet ski on one of the hotel beaches. They got off and started walking toward the hotel. "Act like we belong here. We're going to walk around the side of the hotel, then take separate taxis." She just nodded.

When they got to the street, he gave her instructions. "OK, this is what we're going to do." He pointed to the right. "We're going to walk in this direction and we're going to walk for about five minutes. Then we're going to look for a place where we can get a taxi."

"Why can't we get a taxi from here?" She looked puzzled.

"I parked the jet ski at this hotel. At some point, they're going to wonder whose jet ski it is, and they'll likely be able to trace it back to the yacht. When that happens, they might check taxi records to see who picked up a taxi at this hotel and where they got dropped off. We don't want them to be able to track us, so we're going to take taxis from a different location."

"Oh, OK. Have you done this before?"

"No, I saw it in a movie."

After about five minutes, they came to an upscale restaurant that was attached to a hotel. While they were still on the sidewalk, Paige reached into his pocket and took out the wad of cash he had removed from Thorndike's wallet before tossing him overboard. "Here. Take this and get yourself a taxi. Tell the driver to drop you off someplace, but not at your home. Pick some place that's a five or ten or fifteen minute walk from your house. Or take a second taxi."

She looked at him, knowing it would be for the last time. "OK. So, I guess this is it, huh?"

"Yeah, this is it."

"I don't know what to say. You saved my life tonight."

"Yeah, I suppose I did. But you saved my life, too. If you hadn't stomped on his foot, we'd probably both be dead." She smiled, and looked at the ground, then looked up at him.

He looked into her eyes. "You know you can never tell anyone about this, don't you?"

"Yes, I know."

"Do you think you can keep a secret?"

She smiled. "I usually have a problem keeping secrets, but I guess I'll have to."

He didn't completely believe she would be able to keep her mouth shut, so he wanted to give her a little extra incentive. "You know, you probably committed several felonies tonight."

She looked surprised at his comment. "What do you mean? What did I do?"

"Well, for one, you helped me cover up a crime scene. And you helped me dispose of two bodies. That's three felony counts right there. Then you helped me destroy millions of dollars of government property. And you took a ride on a stolen jet ski that belonged to the government. And the taxi fare I just gave you is stolen property, so you're in receipt of stolen property."

"Do you really think they'd prosecute me? Couldn't I just blame it all on you?"

"Maybe you could. But you helped me dispose of the body of an FBI guy who's pretty high up on the food chain. The feds would give your case top priority, and they'd be looking for someone to blame. They might think you're part of a conspiracy. Even if you prove yourself innocent, you'd have to spend your life savings on an attorney, so even if you win, you'd lose."

He continued. "Then there's the distinct possibility that the people he was working with would want to silence you, just to be on the safe side, in case he might have told you something that could lead back to them."

"But he didn't tell me anything. I didn't know about any of this until you came on the boat."

"Yeah. I know that, and you know that, but do you think they would be willing to take a chance?"

"Well, I guess I'd better keep my mouth shut."

"I was hoping you'd say that."

"Well, I guess I'd better say good-bye, then."

"Yes. Perhaps you should."

"Bye." She turned around and walked toward the restaurant's entrance, where a valet was opening doors for people and putting them into taxis. Paige turned and walked down the street.

122

As Paige walked away he wondered whether it was really over. He thought about how horrible it's going to be when John's wife and kids came home to find their husband/father and the others dead on the floor, but there was nothing he could do to avoid it. He couldn't clean up the mess and he couldn't call the local police so they could clean up the crime scene because all their phone calls were recorded. He didn't want them to record his voice.

He felt bad about it. He and Tomás had made three widows today. He had lost a friend, although Wellington might better be classified as a fair-weather friend, since he had planned to kill Paige. Then there was Tomás, who had been his friend, if only for a few hours.

Was it murder or justifiable homicide? That thought crossed his mind. Will he have to pay for what he has done, either in this life or the next? The question brought to mind a book his brother gave him years ago on the Akashic Record, which discussed how your life flashes in front of you at the moment of death and you see all the things you've done and all the things that have been done to you.

That brought to mind a book he read that was written by a former army assassin who got struck by lightning and was clinically dead for a few minutes before coming back to life. While he was clinically dead, he not only saw his life flash before him but also experienced everything his victims had experienced. He recalled one case discussed in the book where the author put a bullet through the brain of a North Vietnamese army officer with a high powered rifle. When his Akashic Record came to that part of his life, he experienced what it felt like from that officer's perspective. He felt the bullet going into his head and also the grief felt by his relatives when they heard the news that he had been killed.

Would Paige have to experience what John, Jim, Santos and Thorndike had just experienced, plus all the feelings their families had when they learned the news of their deaths? Would his experience with the Akashic Record be the same regardless of whether it was murder or justifiable homicide?

It didn't seem right that the experience would be the same whether what he did was murder or justifiable homicide. He felt he shouldn't be punished for doing the right thing, if, indeed, he did the right thing. Yet if the Akashic Record merely causes you to experience what you did from the perspective of the people you did things to, it seems like the experience would be exactly the same regardless of whether you did a good or bad thing. He wasn't looking forward to learning the answer to that question. He tried not to think about it as he got in the taxi.

123

Sarah called John from Orlando to say hello. He didn't answer his cell phone, which was unusual because he always answered his cell phone, or at least got back to her when she left a message. She got worried but couldn't do much about it because she and the kids were in Orlando, which was a 4 or 5 hour drive from their place in Miami.

The other wives also became worried when their husbands didn't come home for dinner. Maria called Santos but he didn't answer his cell phone, so she called John's house because he told her he would be at John's. No one answered, so she called Sarah on her cell phone. That got Sarah worried.

Teresa called Tomás and Ana called Jim. No one was answering and no one was returning calls. The wives were all starting to get worried.

Ana decided to pay a visit to John's house to see what was going on. She arrived after dark. All the lights were out but there were several cars in the driveway, including her husband's. The crickets were chirping. She decided to go in to see if anyone was there. Perhaps they were watching television in the back room.

She entered through the breezeway and turned on the light.

"Jim? John? Is anybody home?"

She walked into the next room and gasped at what she saw on the floor. John and Jim were lying on the other side of the table, in pools of blood. A small cache of firearms was in the corner of the room.

As she walked toward Jim's body, she started to tremble and sob. She never thought she might be in danger herself. She never thought that the people who killed Jim and the others might still be in the house or might come back. Her eyes were glued on Jim. She bent over to caress his hair. Her shoes were getting stuck in the sticky, congealed pool of blood.

After she gained her composure, she pulled out her cell phone and called 911. She didn't know what else to do. She told the dispatcher what had happened as best she could and gave the address. The police and several ambulances arrived in less than ten minutes. A forensic team arrived a half hour later.

The forensic team took dozens of photos of the crime scene, including the MOSSAD scrawl John had apparently made with his own blood. When the multiple killings were announced on the television and radio, that item was not mentioned. The newspapers didn't mention it, either.

When the crime scene people investigated the scene, they paid close attention to the blood samples splattered around the room. They were able to match all but one to the victims. One drop of blood belonged to someone who was not at the scene, a white male.

DNA technology had advanced to the point where analysts could tell where a person's ancestors had come from. This sample indicated that this person's ancestors had come from Ireland and the Azore Islands. The drop had been found a few feet from Santos Hernandez's body. They checked their databases but whoever it was, wasn't in any of them.

A few days later, the results were in on the ballistics tests conducted on the weapons found at the scene. The police determined that some of the guns found at the scene were used in the Sons of Liberty assassinations. They also found John's computer. The hard drive contained all the messages the Sons of Liberty had sent to the press.

The police considered the Sons of Liberty case to be solved. They closed the case, although they weren't sure if all the members of the group had been killed or if some of them remained at large. Tomás was missing, and so was Thorndike, although they couldn't tie Thorndike directly to the assassinations. Time would tell.

124

"I may not agree with what you say, but I will defend to the death your right to say it."
Voltaire

Steinman put down his coffee cup. "Bob, what do you think of those Sons of Liberty killings?" Paige and Sveta were at his house for dinner. Dishes were clanging in the kitchen, where Sveta was helping Rona put the food on plates. The smells emanating from the kitchen indicated that dinner was ready.

"Yeah, that was something, wasn't it? The killers got killed. I wonder who did it."

Actually, Paige was wondering something entirely different. He more or less approved of what they had done to the politicians, Nelson Fuller, Frumpton and his associates. He firmly believed that those who abuse the Constitution to the extent they did needed to be removed from positions of authority because they violated their fiduciary duty to the people.

He felt really bad about their deaths because they had been assassinating some of the people who were destroying property rights and turning America into a totalitarian state. If he and Tomás hadn't killed them, they could have continued their work.

Although he more or less approved of them assassinating those government officials and the eminent domain abusers, he could not have allowed them to kill Saul, Rona and Sveta. He also couldn't condone the assassination of professors, journalists and others just because they exercised their freedom of speech and press in ways Wellington's group didn't like. They had gone too far. Although they were patriots, they were misguided when it came to free speech and free press.

It reminded him of the Thomas Jefferson quote: "Were it left to me to decide whether we should have a government without newspapers, or newspapers without a government, I should not hesitate a moment to prefer the latter."

Paige looked Steinman in the eyes. "You know, there's speculation that the Sons of Liberty were behind the Raul Rodriguez assassination, too. You remember him? The Cuban radio talk show host?"

"Yes, I remember reading about that. At the time, they were saying it was a group of Cuban patriots who wanted to shut him up because of his position on the Cuban embargo."

Steinman continued. "But back to this Sons of Liberty thing, I find it really scary that it has gotten to the point where people think the only way to settle their political differences is to kill people who disagree with them. That should never happen in a democracy."

"Well, what you say might be true most of the time. We can't go around executing people just because they disagree with us, but sometimes killing can be justified."

"In what case would that be? I can't think of any." Steinman leaned forward to listen to Paige's reply. He raised both eyebrows and looked Paige directly in the eyes. He was so close that Paige could smell his breath, which was a little on the stale side.

Paige explained his position. "If any government can be considered legitimate, it can only be when its functions are limited to the defense of life, liberty and property. Once it goes beyond those basic functions, it starts depriving people of their rights and starts looking more like a tyranny. It starts confiscating one person's property and giving it to other people who have done nothing to earn it. It starts taking away people's rights. When it does that, it starts losing its legitimacy. As it continues to travel down that path, it continues to lose credibility. At some point, the government becomes illegitimate. When that happens, assassinating our elected representatives becomes justifiable homicide, an act of self-defense, because they are no more than a bunch of thieves and petty dictators. When our elected representatives use the force of government to take away our property and liberty rather than protect them, we have a moral duty to our children and grandchildren to stop them by whatever means. Killing them becomes justifiable homicide, an act of self-defense."

125

“If you’re not part of the solution, you’re part of the problem.” Unknown

BREAKING STORY

The following story appeared in the *New York Times Online* edition six days after the Sons of Liberty members were killed in Miami:

> NEW YORK – Senator Chuck Sherman, his body guard and two of his aides were killed this morning while leaving a party fundraiser in midtown. Eye witnesses said they were getting into a limo at about 11:43am when a series of explosions rocked the limo, which was parked at the corner of Madison Avenue and 57th Street. No other injuries were reported. Two assailants were seen getting into a late model black or dark blue sedan heading east.
>
> A few minutes later, members of the media received a message from the New York chapter of the Sons of Liberty claiming responsibility and warning that other executions would be forthcoming. The reasons given for the killings were Senator Sherman’s vote to increase the debt limit, his advocacy to fund a number of projects the group claimed were

unconstitutional, and his instrumental role in the passage of the National ID Card Act, which requires people to carry a biometric tracking device or face arrest and imprisonment.

These killings fall on the heels of the assassinations of U.S. Senators and representatives in Los Angeles and Kansas City and two New York City council members who supported New York City's controversial stop and frisk policy that allows police to stop and frisk individuals without a warrant or probable cause.

"We have it in our power to begin the world over again."
Thomas Paine

NOTE TO THE READER: I enjoyed writing this book. If you enjoyed reading it, please write a review

ACKNOWLEDGMENTS

I would like to thank the following people for their input and support: Teresa Hernandez, who gave me many insights about Cuban culture; Wendy Gelman, who gave me insights about Jewish religion and culture; Thomas B. Sawyer, who pointed me in the right direction when I first started taking courses on novel writing and made helpful suggestions about revising drafts of some of my early chapters; Stephen Mertz and Tammy Barley, who provided professional critiques of later drafts of the manuscript; Steve Cohen and Tom McDonnell, who answered all my questions about firearms, and even gave me answers to questions I didn't think of asking.

Michele McGee, Mary McGee, Joelle Maximilien-Miller, Meira Pentermann, Erne Lewis, Murray Sabrin, Makiko Shinjo, Yaz Hernandez, Maria Taro and Rose Stiffin, who made many helpful suggestions; Roy Migabon, who designed the terrific cover; Alex Brau and Yaz Hernandez, who produced and directed my promotional videos; Cindy Broccolo, Quartney S. Cohen, Ploypailin Kunset and Paola Zuniga, who acted in the videos, and Len Bruce, Tatyana Maranjyan, Evgeny Belov, Gema Martinez, Cindy Broccolo, Mel Shiner and Kris Johnson, who translated or narrated the videos. Finally, I would like to thank my wife, Margaret, who left me alone so I could do what I love to do.

ABOUT THE AUTHOR

Before becoming a novelist, Robert W. McGee was a professor, attorney, CPA and consultant. He has published 58 nonfiction books and has lectured or worked in more than 30 countries. Former clients include The United States Agency for International Development, the World Bank, the African Development Bank and the Central Intelligence Agency. He holds 13 earned doctorates from universities in the United States and four European countries and has won 18 gold and 5 silver medals in Taekwondo National Championship tournaments. He spends most of his time in Fayetteville, North Carolina, Southeast Asia and Europe.

http://RobertWMcGee.com